Cowards, Crooks, and Warriors

J. C. De Ladurantey

COWARDS, CROOKS, AND WARRIORS

iUniverse books may be ordered through booksellers or by contacting:

iUniverse
1663 Liberty Drive
Bloomington, IN 47403
www.iuniverse.com
1-800-Authors (1-800-288-4677)

ISBN: 978-1-4917-6436-7 (sc)
ISBN: 978-1-4917-6435-0 (e)

Library of Congress Control Number: 2015905288

Print information available on the last page.

iUniverse rev. date: 04/23/2015

Every writer must give up something to devote his or her time to constructing a textbook, novel, or even a craft book. With many unfinished manuscripts to my credit, as well as published textbooks, support has come from a number of sources. Sandra "D" is the one and only mainstay in my life. She has let me close the doors and work at all hours, permitting me to get lost in the world of writing.

She was also the one to tell me, "You have so many stories; just tell them." Thanks for letting me tell those stories through the eyes of HH. To our family and friends who were also encouraging and wondered what I was doing—thanks for letting me take some time from our family and friendships to do what had to be done.

While writing has always been my passion, my friend for over 55 years, Mart Shaughnessy was the inspiration to actually make it all happen. While he was an incredible football coach, teacher, father and husband he was also an accomplished author. His encouragement and his own achievements in writing challenged me. I miss him every day.

A special thanks to journalist, editor, and friend Bill Schilt, who provided insightful editing that was so desperately needed.

Lastly, a thank-you to the profession of law enforcement, with a special acknowledgment to those medium and small police departments that serve their communities under the radar screen with their own homegrown officers. Not every police officer experiences harrowing, life and death situations in a career. Many agencies work very hard to keep crime at a low level with depictions of violence and mayhem rare and not up to television or motion picture excitement.

Cities such as Los Angeles, Chicago, New York and other large metropolitan areas generate the news that is fit to print or speak on a daily basis. There is more that goes on than the daily violence that many of our communities face. While he may not be as violent and as engaging as a Jack Ryan, Harry Bosch or Mitch Rapp, Howard Hamilton symbolizes every other officer in a number of police departments throughout the country who daily face the task of protecting and serving their community.

Chapter 1
U-boat

I hate working with informants. They change their minds, can't be trusted, and place your safety in jeopardy. They're all pathological liars, or they play one agency against another. They almost never give you anything of value, and very rarely do they ever give up anyone bigger than they are. We're all told not to use undesirable informants. But to me they're all undesirable. I suppose one's views on informants will vary from cop to cop. I just don't happen to like them.

On the other hand, Donny was much better at cultivating informants and turning the information into great busts. This generally led to multiple arrests, which got him even more kudos than a simple bust would have. And he did it so effortlessly.

I was thinking of all of that when roll call, or briefing, ended. We had the luxury of a briefing room that was well maintained, with up-to-date crime information, video monitors for training, DVDs, posting of wanted suspects, and electronic pin maps telling us the patterns of crime. Every briefing was an immersion in a minitraining program. Orchard Hill Police Department, or OHPD, had the best of everything. All in real time.

"HH!" Sgt. Kip Bennett, the watch commander tonight, bellowed over the breakup of briefing and the side conversations. "Need to see you before you go out."

What the hell did I do now? I wondered.

I put my briefing notes into my leather briefcase. It had been a gift from my kids for my last birthday. I could smell the new leather, and unlike me, it was getting better with age. I walked from my seat in the back row of the room and approached the raised platform, elevated to ensure the watch commander could see everyone and effectively be in command of the briefing. Kip was looking over the electronic deployment worksheet.

"Can I put you on a U-boat tonight? I have a request from Simpkins for him to work with Woford. I know you were expecting to work with Donny tonight, but okay the switch, and I'll make sure you get an early end of watch."

"No problem," I said. "Can I make a call to Clare and let her know to expect me a little early?"

Kip snapped, "Do it!"

He knew I would take a U-boat anytime. I could get an early out or, worst case, at least get off on time, without getting a gun off the street.

A U-boat was generally set aside for officers nearing the end of their training period. When "rookies," "boots," or "probies" graduated from the police academy, they had a one-year probationary period and were assigned to a series of field training officers. After the proby completed training, he or she were generally assigned to the U-boat to hone investigative and report-writing skills, prior to being released from their one-year training, or probationary period.

When there was no one getting off training, I always opted for the U-boat. "U" meant it was just *you* working alone. I didn't care whether I had a partner. Someone, somewhere, nicknamed it U-boat to remind us that we were working alone and to go slow out there, do what the dispatch center and front desk gave us, and stay out of trouble. It didn't hurt that we could work through our "code seven," or lunchtime, and go home early—that is, if the report board was clear. I'd engineer that to happen.

I walked down the wide hallway, which was devoid of photos or anything of significance on the walls. The stark nature of OHPD's hallways were in contrast to every other room in our facility. The message was clear: do not stand around looking at pictures. Get in the field, and leave the administration to us.

As I was thinking that I should call Clare before Kip changed his mind, I heard Donny call my name.

"HH, can I talk to you?" He pulled me into an alcove as if he had some deep secret to confide. "I know you and I were going to work together tonight," Donny said in a rather low tone, "but Wolf and I have a meeting with an informant that may give us some good scoop on a grand-theft auto ring working the north side. I meant to discuss it. But with the shit going on in briefing, there wasn't time. I cleared it with Kip but didn't get a chance to talk with you about it. I owe you for bumping you into a report-writing unit tonight. Can I buy you a cool one at Home Plate at end of watch?"

So that's what this was all about. Donny thought he was dissing me, but he was really doing me a big favor. Spending time with an informant and working till "O dark thirty" in the morning sounded like too much overtime anyway.

"No way, Donny, you don't owe me! I get an early out working the U-boat, and I am going home. I was just going to call Clare and let her know," I said. I wanted to get going to make sure I got all of my gear and paperwork to hit the street by 1600 hours.

The report board had three residential burglaries in the west end. I would plan to complete all three face sheets with the basic information and do all of the narrative toward end of watch to make sure I got off on time—or maybe even early. I made the call on my cell before anybody changed their minds. Clare was excited that she would see me by midnight instead of the typical three in the morning, even if the kids would be asleep.

Especially because the kids would be asleep.

Chapter 2

Composure

It was just after 1900 hours, or seven in the evening, civilian time. I had wrapped up the third investigation—threw some fingerprint powder around the residential burglary or "res burg," to impress the victim, knowing all along I didn't really know the finer points of collecting latent prints. I didn't want to get fingerprint powder all over my clean uniform. Not much had been taken from the home, but we had a policy of printing every burglary.

I had taken reports on three cases—it looked like someone was working the area. I put in a call for one of our Crime Scene Investigation units to take a look at the cases when they could. More than likely, there would be others, with some not reported. *Maybe some juvies*, I thought.

The west end of Orchard Hill is along the beach. Summertime means battling beach traffic, writing parking tickets, and looking for alcohol violations. But summer was just over, and the schools were filled with kids. Our beach patrol was off at 1900, so I thought I would drive down the ramp and cruise the boardwalks for stragglers.

I was patrolling southbound toward the municipal pier when I saw a small group of five or seven, scattered on the sidewalk adjacent to the sand. There were others about a hundred yards away, walking rather fast to their cars.

Something wasn't right. I took my foot off the gas, just to keep it in drive, and slowly moved toward the crowd. My "silent partner" was telling me to be on guard and be alert. And he was usually right.

Three people were moving slowly backward toward the sand. A female adult dressed in beach attire saw me, and waved her arms frantically to get my attention. From about thirty feet away, I saw why—someone was pointing a gun at a teenage girl and two older guys, and the three of them were backing away.

The gunman had his back to me as I put the car in park and slowly opened the door. I crouched behind the open door, grabbed my radio, and whispered into it, "Seventy-five U4, I have a man with a gun at west beach about a hundred yards from the south parking lot. I need a backup; code three."

"Seventy-five U4. Roger. I do not have a unit clear but will find one."

"Great," I muttered.

My eyes never left the subject as he continued to brandish the gun in the direction of the group. I had just cleaned my Glock 21, 45 caliber automatic after qualifying yesterday. *Damn it*, I thought. *I'll have to dump this guy and clean it again.* Funny what you think of at a time like this.

I could see that he was wearing a bathing suit, baseball cap, white T-shirt, and beach shoes. He looked over his shoulder—apparently he heard my car's engine.

"Drop it! Drop the gun!" I shouted in the most commanding voice I could muster.

I didn't faze him. *There's no second-place winner in a gunfight*, I thought, in one of those half seconds you have. It was a voice from my last training class.

My Glock has a strong trigger pull, and I knew I could get off four rounds in less than a second. I was fifteen feet away from the type of confrontation I had trained for.

I had a good body position behind the car door and a solid, firm grip with my right hand, with my left acting like a fulcrum. The muzzle of my weapon was pointed right at his head. I had a good background, as the crowd was on either side of him and there was nothing but empty sand behind him. He turned to face me.

Again, the message flashed in my head—this was what I trained for. It was the perfect scenario. I was thinking that if I gripped weakly and jerked on the trigger like I was pulling on a bell cord, the muzzle would go off target.

That was not going to happen. The car door allowed me to rest my left hand on the open window. I reached down and unsnapped my magazine case to get easy access.

If I need additional ammo, I am in deep shit anyway, I thought.

All he could see was the black-and-white police car, part of my head, and my weapon. But he wouldn't respond to my commands.

"Drop the gun, son!" I shouted again. "Drop the fuckin' gun!"

Where was that damn backup? I didn't even hear any sirens.

Out of the corner of my eye, I could see a yellow flash of a figure run toward me down the walkway from the upper south parking lot. It didn't look like a uniform. Was it this guy's partner? Did he have a gun too? I could be in really deep shit here.

The gunman pointed the weapon at one of the bystanders— but at the same time he was moving toward my position, step by step. It was then it registered: this guy's body language and facial expressions seemed playful but nonthreatening. Was he a retard? If he was, how did he get the gun? I wondered if his gun was a toy. I couldn't tell without taking my eyes completely off the other gunman.

"Face me, down on your knees," I commanded. He did it, and quickly. I could see that he was a big kid, maybe two hundred pounds, but he still exuded a cherubic innocence.

He kept the gun in a clumsy shooting position.

Donny's words echoed in my ears: *"Some folks deserve to be shot."* Did this guy?

It wasn't making any sense. Was it his body language that was off?

I didn't recognize the gun, and I knew my guns … but was it a real gun? *Damn it, where is my backup?*

With the gun still in his hand, he started to walk on his knees, toward me. I could see the other figure getting closer. He was shouting something, but in the confusion I could not really hear him. I was tuning out all outside noise.

Did he have a gun also?

I started to make my move.

Chapter 3

The Move

He was now walking on his knees toward me with a shit-eating grin on his face. *There is a guy with a loaded gun,* I thought, *pointed at me, and he's grinning.*

Was this the way it was supposed to end?

"Not for me," I muttered to myself as I came around from behind the car door.

He was less than ten feet away. I had the position of advantage—I was standing; he was kneeling.

"Some folks deserve to be shot" flashed in my mind again but not this "folk."

Just as the beachgoers and the figure that had been running from the parking lot arrived at our position, I kicked the gun out of his feeble hand and pushed him, face-first, down on the pavement from his kneeling position. It was one swift movement, startling him.

"Put your hands behind your back," I ordered.

He complied. I cuffed him as he lay prone on the ground.

I could hear the distant call of a siren as I knelt over the shape on the asphalt parking lot. By this time a small crowd had gathered, and I couldn't distinguish who the first three beachgoers were, who I would need to identify as the victims in this crime.

Within seconds, the long stretch of pavement running along the beach filled with black-and-whites. The cavalry had arrived—too late, but they had arrived. Sgt. Harvey Stevens approached me. If I could have had anyone out there, it would have been Stevens. He was the senior supervisor and had seen it all. I was confident he would make all right with the world.

I was shaking a little but felt in complete control of my emotions, not realizing I was still kneeling on the subject's back.

I then saw almost the entire shift pull up to the scene. It was AJ Johnson, Bob Gates, Waldo, and, finally, Donny and Wolf.

One of them—I really don't remember who—finally helped me up, took the subject by the arm, and led him to a waiting police car. There seemed to be a lot of commotion, and my head was swirling. I felt like I was going in slow motion as everyone else moved way too fast.

"Slow down, goddamn it. Slow down," I told anyone who would listen.

Now my brain was catching up to my emotions. Where was the gun? Where was the fucking gun? Did I say that out loud or just think it? I wasn't sure. It was then that Sergeant Stevens walked over to me as I stood by my police car, my protection during the ordeal.

He asked, "Is this what he had?" He held up a black .45-caliber handgun.

"God, yes, it was. Thank goodness you found it. I don't know what happened to it after I kicked it out of his hand," I said with a sigh of relief.

"It's a squirt gun," came a voice from the crowd. A man wearing a yellow vest stepped forward, holding a folding chair and a beach bag.

"My name is Willard Roberge, and I'm a chaperone for a group from the Anderson School for the Challenged in Temple City. We had an outing today, and Sammy, here, got separated from our group as we were walking to our van, over there in the parking lot."

I recognized Roberge as the figure running toward me just prior to the take-down. He was a very typical youth director, like a "Mr. Peepers" from the old television show—horn-rimmed glasses, rarely saw the sun, and passive … very passive. I assumed the yellow vest was used to distinguish him from the students and for the kids to identify him. In the heat of the moment, I couldn't see it was one of those vests that identified him as a group leader because I was concentrating on the gun.

"Sammy is one of our … one of our students," he stammered. "I don't know where he got that thing," he added weakly.

That *thing* was a replica of a .45-caliber handgun, but it was a squirt gun. A fucking squirt gun!

I could have killed this kid over a goddamn squirt gun. This mentally challenged kid was still grinning at me from the backseat of a police car. As we're growing up, we're trained to think police officers are the good guys, and those with guns that threaten harm are the bad guys. There is no in between. *Who is the good guy in this scenario?*

And then I wondered, *what do we do now, Sarge? How do we sort this out?* I didn't know, because I was too close to the situation. Was I in trouble? What would we arrest this guy, Sammy, for? Stevens would figure this out. I just wanted to go home.

Chapter 4

It's Over

Sergeant Stevens put the squirt gun in his waistband and started shouting orders. The three beachgoers who were our "victims" stepped forward and started to tell their story. Stevens directed Waldo to take the three off to the side and interview them, one by one. Donny was to talk with the chaperone, Mr. Roberge, and Wolf was to ensure that the rest of the group from the special education school who were in the upper parking lot were all right and under control. Johnson had been tasked with standing next to my car with Sammy.

I'm okay now, I thought. *It's over*. I kept telling myself I'd done the right thing. I knew that. After about fifteen minutes, Harvey approached and told me what I already knew.

"There really is a minor crime here, HH, and so we're going to take an incident report. I doubt anything will come of it. The kid is mentally challenged, and the chaperone is taking full responsibility for his getting separated from the group. We'll book the gun. I'll write this up for the captain to review. I think we have everybody's statements. Understand?"

"I understand," I said, but my mind was in other places, and I think he could tell.

"HH, can I talk to you away from the crowd for a moment? We may have another problem."

I turned my back on the crowd. "What is it?"

"The counselor confided in me that he heard you use the 'F-word' to the boy," Harvey said. "Did you?"

I looked him in the eye. "Yeah, I said it. I said, 'drop the fuckin' gun!' I think I may have said it three times, Sarge."

Harvey looked back at me with his cold blue eyes and said, "Got it."

Harvey Stevens was chiseled out of central casting. He had made sergeant after about six years on OHPD but spent the rest of his career in Patrol. Well, he had a short stint in Detectives, where he teamed up with Valarie, now his wife, but our previous chief had sent him back to Patrol for what turned out to be the rest of his career. He didn't seem to mind, as he was easygoing, a squared-away former marine who let nothing faze him. He was a street cop's dream—as long as you didn't screw up. Because he looked like a recruitment poster, even with a mustache, his quiet and confident military demeanor, coupled with a scar that ran across his left cheek, left no doubt that he was in charge.

I had never thought of myself as a great cop—or, as I preferred to be called, a police officer. I was a good police officer but not a great one. I left that for the Donny's of the world.

But now, all I could think about was what the guys would think. Should I have dumped the kid? I had every right to do that. If it had been a real gun, then I would be lying in the sand. Did I hesitate because of our shooting policy confusion, the talk at briefing today, or my fear of killing someone? There was a clear and imminent threat, yet, I didn't shoot.

The gap of understanding of what I did, and what I should have—or could have—done caused me to hesitate. Maybe my use of the F-word was the difference between shooting him and not shooting. He'd responded to it so I guess using the F-word was the right thing to do.

And for that, Sammy was still alive. But was it composure, keen observation skills, sound tactics, or fear and cowardice that caused me to hesitate and avoid a tragedy? I knew. I knew I was alive, and so was Sammy. But did others know? What would Red Walker and the others say? More to the point, what would they *not* say but just think?

I wanted to go home. I wanted Clare to hold me and tell me I'd done the right thing. As much as I wanted it, however, I had to return to the station and do some paperwork. No matter, I was still going to be home early—or so I thought.

I also wondered what Donny would think. He had purposely avoided me at the scene. Was he distracted with the investigation he had going with Wolf, or was he avoiding me because … because I didn't shoot? I had to know.

Is there a price for being good or making the correct decision? Did I not commit to shoot because I wasn't afraid enough? Had I dumped Sammy, would they have labeled me as evil? I would be just another trigger-happy cop who shot someone before he had all the facts. I would be labeled evil if I shot him, and we found out later it was a squirt gun. Or maybe I was just a coward and couldn't shoot.

I looked around at what was now a very sterile beach. Everybody was leaving. The sand and palm trees, the empty parking spaces, and the litter seemed to dominate the landscape. It was all so much part of the cleanup.

Chapter 5

Home

As much as I enjoyed the street, my real passion was Clare, Marcia, and Geoff. I didn't have to call her to let her know I was coming home early—but I did. I always did. It was my way of telling her that I got another gun off the street, loved my job, and more important, that I loved her and the little guys even more. Funny how you can relate a gun to love, but I guess you can, at least in my case.

It had not always been this way. Clare actually hated my job. She didn't want me to be a cop—or police officer, I should say. She wanted the eight-to-five grocery-store job, home at night, weekends off, holidays together, and no stress. What she got was the graveyard or late-afternoon shift, my sleeping during the day, one weekend off a month, and—until recently—only a few holidays off together. Now, after six years, my seniority was going to get me most holidays off but never New Year's Eve.

And we never talked about the fear. It was just understood. Wear the vest, and you're safe. That's what she always thought, I'm sure.

Clare and I were high school sweethearts, almost. She was a sophomore when I was a senior, but we didn't start dating until the fall of my first semester of college, when she was still in high school. It was always about us as a couple from that time forward. We knew it, and everyone else did too.

I didn't always want to be a police officer. I had a great job in a supermarket, making good money with great benefits. My buddy in school, Danny Sullivan, wanted to be an Orchard Hill policeman from the time he was in high school. We loved our little city of 150,000 people, and we had a tight group that hung out together. A few of the guys talked about what they wanted to do, and Clare was content with me at the market, working my way up to be the third man in charge.

I guess I wasn't too content, though, because when Danny told me he was going to take the written test for OHPD, I told him I would tag along. It was a Saturday morning, the garage was clean, the gardener had done the lawn, and Clare was visiting her mom with Geoff and Marcia. I was bored. I went down to City Hall with Danny and took the test with him. Bottom line: I passed the test, and Danny didn't.

Later, when Clare came home, I casually mentioned my morning experience with Danny.

"What the hell are you thinking, Howard?" She only called me Howard when she was pissed; otherwise, it was Howie. "You know about my cousins, Samantha and Rob," she said with a sigh. "Rob is with LA, and Samantha hates it. He's working vice, he's never home at night and she's drinking herself into hell!"

"Don't worry, dear. I only took the test to keep Danny company. And it was OHPD, not LA. Nothing will come of it." And nothing did come from it, at least not for six months.

I wanted it to be just a job. What I got was a consuming career. And the rest, as they say, is history.

I was thinking about all of that on my ten-minute drive home. Tonight, it seemed like an hour. I wanted a beer, but I wanted to be with Clare even more. Just to talk it all through. I thought I had figured it out. The discussions at briefing clearly had no impact on what I did out there. My instincts and training saved me—and saved Sammy.

Most of us do the right thing. It's expected. Expected by the brass, the public, and most important, by each other. *It's funny,* I thought, *when one of us shoots someone, he's put on paid administrative leave. I didn't shoot but still went through the trauma, and if I needed some time off it would be on my own days off. Shooters are ordered to see the shrink, but not me. If I ask to go because I didn't shoot someone, they'll look at me like I have two heads.*

But it wasn't someone; it was Sammy. He was a real person, with a real name. Most guys who get in a shooting don't know the name of the person they killed. Maybe that's the way it needs to be.

Sergeant Stevens told me to finish the paperwork and go home. By the time I did everything it was almost end-of-watch anyway. With daylight saving time, the night shift went faster because the sun did not go down until almost eight o'clock. It was still well before midnight when I finally pulled into the driveway of our home to see a single light on in the upstairs bedroom. She was waiting up for me.

I was greeted with, "How did you get an early out, Howie? Get another gun off the street?"

"You might say that," I said as I held her for the customary but so-necessary hug.

We sat in the living room and went over everything, step by step. What was amazing to me was that it took over fifteen minutes to describe a five- to seven-second encounter. Everything seemed to move at the speed of thick syrup, pouring out ever so slowly.

We know that police work can be stressful. But that's not the case if you have a Clare around. She simplifies it and adds a dose of reality to it, and her logic is better than any chief of police I have heard.

"Both you and Sammy are alive, Howie. You used good judgment, and you avoided a tragedy. What more could you ask for?" she said calmly. "Isn't that what good cops do?"

I skipped the beer and took a long shower. It was like one of those showers that you look forward to after a long run or a good workout. But the shower hurt. It was like tiny needles hitting my skin, over and over. It was shooting water that was pulsating yet numbing. My skin had never been so tender to the touch. After about twenty minutes, the tension finally evaporated.

I crawled into bed and held her tight. We were like spoons, with her back to me and my naked front along her backside. Without another word, we made quiet and gentle love that resulted in a very sensual climax for both of us. It wasn't because we didn't want to wake the kids. It was the need for tenderness. There is something about post-traumatic sex that is so different from any other form of lovemaking.

"I'm so very proud of you," she whispered.

Is there a price to pay for doing something good? Do we confuse ourselves by wanting to be judged by our intentions, yet we judge others by our interpretation of their actions?

My head was spinning, but who needs a shrink when you have Clare?

Chapter 6

Aftermath

One of the most beneficial things about the job isn't the job; it's the days off in between the workdays. Our family loves going to Newport or just hanging out at home, doing yard work and other chores. But then, the day before I'm due to return to work, there is a craving to get back at it. You feel a need to walk into the station, ready for a new shift, ready to put the uniform on again, see everybody, and act like nothing happened.

Orchard Hill Police Department has a very modern and well-maintained police facility. With three stories, the basement is our locker room for men and women, a briefing/training room, workout room, report-writing computer stations, and a maintenance room. You drive into the compound through an electronic security gate, park your car, and walk right in to the locker room. A very well-thought-out plan. The public counter, records department, the watch commander and sergeant's offices, and Detectives are all on the second floor.

The third floor, where the air seems to be a little thinner, is reserved for the chief and captains, administration offices, and our dispatch center.

On the morning of my first day back to work after the incident with Sammy, I received a call at home from the chief's secretary that he would like to see me a half hour before my scheduled briefing at 1515 hours.

"No problem," I told her. I was always in the station a little early to get caught up on what had been going on during my days off.

In the year that this chief had been with the department, there had been too many changes. Much to the chagrin of our own captains, two of which wanted to be chief, he had come from outside the department to take over. The worst part was that he was from LA. For the old-timers, including the captains, it was a slap in the face.

The last time someone from LA became chief in Orchard Hill was over thirty years ago, when a chief had been sent to prison for I don't know what. Nothing like this had happened, so when the city manager picked this guy instead of one of the captains, many people were visibly upset. I didn't care. Who the chief was didn't affect me one way or the other. I just did my job.

I was so far away from the department brass that I had gone almost an entire year without setting foot on the third floor. I would drive into the parking lot, go to the locker room, get a quick workout, shower, get my leather gear prepared, put my uniform on, make sure I had enough reports in my briefcase, go to briefing, check out a car, and do my job—all on the night (or what we called "PM") shift. I had seen the new chief once, when he came to briefing. I would not be able to make that claim after today.

The chief's secretary, Patty Lanihan and known as Miss Efficiency, was like a Marine Corps drill instructor.

At exactly 1445, she ushered me into the chief's office and announced, "Chief, Officer Howard Hamilton is here to see you."

Like it was my idea, I thought.

The office was vintage 1980, with maple wall paneling, photos of the city, and an expansive view of the parking lot and the mountains. There was a tray with fresh water, two glasses, and an open notebook on the table. The chief walked casually to the end seat, where the notebook was waiting. He directed me to the chair next to his, but my chair was at a forty-five-degree angle, with my back to the door. It made me very uncomfortable.

"I cannot believe I've been here a year, and we've not sat down like this, Howard."

"Neither can I, sir," I said, trying to make him as uneasy as I was.

He took the shot well. "Well, it's my fault. I need to get out of this office more often and come downstairs to see you all more. This isn't police work up here; it's just paper." He looked out the window as he paused, searching for the right words to use on me

18

to make me think he knew the streets. "I wanted to talk with you about your incident the other day and tell you how proud I am for what you did, and most important, what you didn't do."

I could see that he had the report from Sergeant Stevens in front of him—it looked longer than I thought it should be. The incident only took five seconds, but the report was an inch thick.

One of the skills you get early in your career is the ability to read papers upside down as they are in front of somebody else. Sergeant Stevens had done some heavy-duty writing while I was on days off.

"Sergeant Stevens has recommended—and Lieutenant Rikelman has concurred—that you should be nominated for the Award of Merit for the incident the other day. I want you to know I agree with them, and I wanted to be the first to tell you." His eye contact was very penetrating. He was studying me, trying to analyze my reaction to see what I was made of. I knew it.

"Both Sammy and I are alive," I said, as Clare's words rang in my ears. "I think I used good judgment and sound tactics and avoided a tragedy. Isn't that what we're supposed to do, Chief?"

He quickly agreed. "It is, Howard, but it doesn't always work out that way. I don't have to defend this, if you know what I mean, and neither do you."

At first I thought he was taking a shot at me. Then I realized he wasn't. I knew I didn't have to defend what I did, at least to myself. Maybe to the Donny's or Walkers, but not to the Bennett's or me. And for certain I didn't have to defend myself to this man. He knew. He knew!

What he was implying was that there were shootings that were hard to defend. That put us on the defensive rather than the offensive. They were justified but …

The "but" was that we were legally justified in dumping some scumbag. But at what price? There may have been a need to justify it to the community and the media, but not inside. Not to each other. He didn't say it, but he didn't have to.

We both knew he was wrestling with the Red Walker shooting. Neither one of us would bring it up.

This guy isn't so bad, I thought. Better not repeat it in the locker room. Most of the guys were withholding judgment on the new chief. How long was he going to be considered "new" anyway? It'd been almost a year.

We wound down the conversation regarding Sammy, and I figured it was time to move toward the door. He saw I was making a motion and stopped me.

"One more thing, Howard."

I interrupted him with, "Call me HH. Everybody else does." *Oh shit!* I thought. *He is going to bring up the use of the F-word.*

He continued, "I just want to take the opportunity to tell you the captains and I are going to be making some changes around here. I've noticed everybody picks their shift and stays on it for a long time. I don't think that is healthy." He moved some other papers around in front of him. "I see that you've been on PMs for quite a while. Too long, in my estimation. Next shift change, we are going to rotate everyone around. How would you like to go to days and spend more free time with your family?"

"My family enjoys my being on PMs, Chief," I said rather defensively.

"Well, then, they'll really enjoy your being on days." He smiled. "And this has absolutely nothing to do with the incident. Everyone is going to be moved out of his comfort zone." We both rose at the same time. "Thanks for coming in HH," he said with a tone of new familiarity as he emphasized the nickname. "I am sure we will be seeing more of each other. I look forward to meeting your family at the awards ceremony."

You can call me Howard, I thought as I walked out of the third-floor office and headed to more comfortable surroundings. And there was no mention of the use of the F-word.

Chapter 7

The Walker Shooting

And then there was John Walker, or "Red." Tall, slender, with jet-black hair combed straight back. He could have been named "Brylcream" or "Vitalis," but Johnny Walker "Red" fit him, even before the hairstyle change. Everybody walked and talked quietly around him. His serious nature, coupled with his good street work, got him a lot of mileage around OHPD. I thought he was just weird.

I knew that the reference the chief made in our conversation was about the latest Walker shooting.

I have drawn my gun many times in the field but never fired a shot. Red has been on the job two years more than I have and has been in three shootings. They have all come back clean from the Shooting Review Board, so I have heard. No discipline, days off, or anything like that. It's not like I would know about his being disciplined anyway. Unless the union got involved, what goes on in "Admin" stays in Admin. They were all hits, and I think he may have killed somebody, but everyone was quiet about it.

I had been on a string of days off. I tied a few days with comp time and took almost a week with Clare, Marcia, and Geoff. We rented a beach house in Newport and kicked back before school started. When I came back to town, I stopped by the station to make sure I had a clean uniform in my locker for the first day back. I really went in to catch up on the scoop. PDs are notorious for turning those inside rumors into fact. That's when I heard about it.

Red had responded to a call on my beat about a man with a gun. He knew the area and the apartment complex probably better than I did. The way I heard it from Donny was that he parked his black-and-white in a covered stall about a hundred feet from the call. Red walked toward the building, mindful to stay close to a wall, and watched the apartment doors opening and closing from just one side. He was very officer-safety conscious.

He met with the person reporting and learned it was a yelling match between common-laws and other relatives. A gun was seen but not fired.

He walked back toward his black-and-white to broadcast a code four, meaning no assistance needed. It was "just" a domestic violence dispute. As if they were routine.

He was about twenty feet from his vehicle when he heard an engine accelerate down the driveway. The driver came right at him at about twenty-five miles per hour. The parking area was double-wide, and he was on the far side of his intended destination.

Red always had his gun strap undone on a call like this. He quickly drew his weapon. It took him ten minutes to tell the story of what happened, but it was all over in less than three seconds.

Red fired four shots. The suspect took one in the head. Red had reached in the car to turn the wheel so the car would crash into a building. According to eye witnesses, he was a hero, because seven witnesses had followed the suspect into the alley and had been right behind him. Shooting at the driver and turning the wheel as he hung on to the car saved them all from certain death, they said. The common-law was pissed she had lost her meal ticket, but nobody else had a problem with it.

Donny had cornered me in the locker room, just before briefing and away from everybody else.

"I don't like it tactics-wise, Howie. We need to bring it up in briefing, but not with John around." He confided, "I don't want to give these young kids out here an idea that they can fuckin' reach in a car after some asshole! Somebody is going to really get hurt that way." Donny was heated, but then again, he always was.

I was thinking of the book my daughter was reading at home. It was something with the title about being *Wicked* and was the pre-story to what became *The Wizard of Oz*. In Oz, the wizard is wise but human. The good witch represents good, and the bad witch depicts evil.

I'm going to take a look at what evil is supposed to be about, I thought.

"Yeah," I said, "and it's gonna be a Medal of Valor caper … anyway." Then I muttered to no one in particular, "Hero, my ass."

Chapter 8

The Hallway

You're not supposed to talk about a shooting right away. Red was put on administrative leave and sent to the shrink, like everybody who caps a round. Donny and I approached Kip in an alcove outside the briefing room.

I said, "We need to talk about this stuff in briefing, Kip." I nodded to Donny in a manner that indicated we agreed, "I think that we need to discuss tactics in general and, not to cut up Red, but you know these kids we have out there."

I was referring to the new boots we just got out of the academy and some of our shaky second-year "vets."

"He's going to be a hero, Kip," Donny said. "He knew more about what he was doing than all of these other guys put together. We just don't want anybody to get hurt trying that shit."

"Got it," was the stoic reply.

If you could look two guys in the eye at the same time and communicate a message in a few words, Sergeant Bennett did it. Kip was one of those unique people with insights and wisdom beyond any command officer in the department. He was here before nicknames were tagged on to everyone, and out of a respect, he was always "Kip" or Sergeant Bennett. If we were to give him another nickname, it would have been "Switzerland." He was the most neutral person around. Everybody loved him and confided in him, yet there was an element of formal friendship that folded into the personal.

The rumor was that Kip could have been a captain or our chief, but a little thing like a DUI got in the way many years ago. No one knew the exact circumstances, but the bottom line was that he and the chief were both as high as they were going to be in the department. They had both topped out. What a shame.

Chapter 9

The Name Game

What I like most about OHPD comes in twos: (1) we are not LA and (2) the people. And not necessarily in that order.

We pick and choose our crooks. In LA, it's out of control. There are too many crooks. OHPD is selective, because we can be. We border LA on the east and south. Our northern border is an industrial area of the county, and our western line is a natural barrier called the Pacific Ocean. We have four beats and four directions, four high schools, and one private school. I like to think of it like a pie crust. Patrol the edges to keep the inside safe.

Somebody was thinking when he laid out Orchard Hill. Orchard Hill Boulevard is a true east/west main street that eventually runs into Coast Highway and the ocean. South Albion Boulevard runs right down the middle and is heavily traveled by commuters. Good street to write a lot of cites on "non-res" or nonresidents. Easy pickings, but Orchard Hill Boulevard is the real apple orchard. You can easily go through a ticket book once a month. But I hate writing tickets. You take too much shit. Especially from people from LA.

I wasn't always this jaded. And John Wayne was never all that macho. The shrinks call it the "JW syndrome." It used to be called John Wayne syndrome, but with the inclusion of women into our workforce, "Jane" Wayne became as common. Thus, JW.

Somewhere between five and maybe seven years on the job, we become not only more knowledgeable about the job but also invincible and very opinionated. The streets are blue, and we are in charge of them. I can handle any kind of call, and no one from LA is going to tell us how to do our police work. They do it one way, but it's not the only way. We are different; we are OHPD.

When other people are around, it's "Sergeant Bennett," but between us, it's Kip and HH. My parents wanted me to have the initials of a 1950s disc jockey by the name of Hunter Hancock. On the radio, they called him "HH." Howard Hamilton worked just as well, so "HH" it was.

I love Kip like a brother or a father. He has never told me to back off on a situation, only that next time, maybe I could do this, say this, or do that instead. He looks for those teachable moments.

I guess I do have a little of the JW syndrome. It comes around about this time in a guy's career. In six years on the street, you see it all. One of my first felony arrests was for mayhem. A lady cut off her husband's hand with an ax that they kept behind the couch—doesn't everybody keep an ax there?—because he would not turn down the television. In court, she was holding the only hand he had left, and he asked that the charges be dropped. They were. I guess that was justice.

The real gangsters were in LA, but when they ventured over the city limits and past the pie crust to Orchard Hill, they were fair game for OHPD. Even when I got a gun, somehow the charge was dismissed or reduced. I could go on and on about the injustice of our justice system, but I don't care anymore. I go to work, put people in jail, and get all the overtime I want. I never want to work around the brass with all those day-watch maggots that cannot or will not work in the dark.

You can always tell day-watch maggots. Their oxford uniform shoes are Corfam—really, a plastic coating that gives them a perpetual shine. You can never get them to wear Matterhorn six-inch-leather tactical boots or even Magnum lightweight eight-inch side zips. They have not and never will kick a door. They are also the ones in white T-shirts under the uniform shirt. Those on PMs get to wear the black T's or even turtlenecks, with OHPD subtly embroidered on the neck. We work best in the dark.

After my talk with the chief, I knew that there would be a forced rotation for everybody. We all had to take our turns on a different shift. Donny and I agreed that we would go to the union to get this stopped if they tried it. They can't do that shit.

After thinking about it, I guess I really do have the JW. I wear my vest but because we have to, and Clare wants me to wear it.

Orders from the corner pocket, both of them. The one thing I like about OHPD is that we get the best equipment available. Our city has money, and they let us spend it. I get a new vest every five years. A company comes out and measures us for a custom fit. You hardly know it's on, except in the summer, if you are working the east beat. Not much of an ocean breeze on the eastside, but that's where I prefer to work, so I sweat a lot.

I see Jane Wayne in some of the more seasoned females. I don't know who is lesbian and who is not. Nor do I care. The first time I tried to figure it out, I was wrong, so I quit trying. After about a year on the street, they all start looking and dressing alike. They come to work in Levis and untucked T-shirts to hide their off-duty weapons in their waistbands, just like the guys. Most of them keep their hair short. The only thing is, they get to wear one earring in uniform, and the guys do not.

One of the black guys, Marcus Simpson, always wears an earring off duty. One time, he forgot to take it off in the locker room. He showed up at briefing in uniform, with a diamond stud glistening in his left ear lobe. Sergeant Bennett had no mercy on his bro. He didn't insult him but he definitely got the message across. "The manual says one stud but only for females, Simpson. You must have missed that question on the last detectives test. Either that, or you had a sex-change operation and didn't tell us." I love Bennett.

OHPD's females are like everyone else's, I guess. All I care about is that when they show up, they can cover my back, will come if I need help, and will jump into a street fight and shoot the asshole if they need to. One of our best, Pat "Don't Call Me Patricia" Woford, would do all of that and more. She is the poster child for Jane Wayne. She's not really attractive, especially in uniform, but she exudes a commanding presence and has eyes that would freeze a room.

Like most of them, the good ones look you in the eye, as if to say, "Yeah, I'll suck your dick if you want, but I don't think you want it as much as you think you do. And anyway, I want you to have more respect for me than that. If I do you, it's because I want to. That means I got you; you didn't get me. Are we clear on that? I just want you to know I will do what needs to be done and not back off. Are we clear on that?"

We understand each other, most of the time. It's like John Wayne meets Annie Oakley.

The best part about OHPD is the people and their names. Like most PDs, we refer to each other by last name only or by their nickname. Briefing starts with our assignments.

"Hamilton, 75 Robert 4," Kip would say, which meant I was working Beat 4, the east side—my side of the city. Seventy-five referred to my position of seniority on the department, and it changed about once a year. It's very confusing. For some reason, it seems that everyone also has a nickname, and it is played off of famous people.

"HH" wasn't so famous, but everyone went with it anyway. One of my first training officers was Bob Gates, and he picked up the name "Bill" for obvious reasons. Clyde Woodrow picked up the name "Clyde the Glide," not for the basketball player but because he did not walk; he glided so smoothly that he could balance a book on his head. Only Donny Simpkins's friends called him "Marie," after the Osmond's, and our most popular jailer, Jimmy Bowen, got labeled with "the Greek," even though he was black.

Andy Johnson, or "AJ," became "Foyt"; Lance McBride was "Macbeth"; Ralph Waldo picked up "Emerson"—well, you get the idea. Some of the nicknames made you really think about the connection. Hunter McDaniel was dubbed "Tab"; Dale Martino became "Hill."

We violated our own rule about not naming the brass when we labeled Lt. Ib Rikelman as "Norman," after Norman Bates from the movie *Psycho*. Our Norman was a Swede/German with sharp, cutting features and a personality to match.

You got a nickname whether you wanted it or not. That was the game. The challenge was trying to come up with something that tied into somebody famous but stuck on you. They were assigned after you had made probation and been around a year or more. You lost it if you were promoted to supervisor. End-of-probation parties at the Home Plate, or "HP," as we called it, was where the christening took place. Among other things.

The HP was a drinking "hole" for a quick one—it didn't close until two in the morning. Its reputation far exceeded what really happened inside those doors, but the rumors kept the brass and golden boys from showing up. It was fine with us.

Sgt. Kip Bennett saved his harshness for the new black officers, when we got one out of the academy. Being a light-skinned black himself, he seemed to save his sternest demeanor for minority officers. That was just his way of letting them know they were not there for any reason other than they earned it with their performances.

Once an officer completed probation, then Kip became Switzerland, and the officer was accepted. Kip would come up with the nickname, and most of the time, the nickname stuck. He didn't take sides, but he didn't favor you. It was more about trust and proving yourself. I knew it, had tested it, and found it to be the best way to deal with people.

I checked my locker to make sure I had a clean uniform for the next day. The only thing I took out of the station was the tan I got in Newport.

Chapter 10

Officer-Involved Shooting Review

Cops can be brutal. Mostly to each other.

It was the second Wednesday of the month. Payday. Even with direct deposit available to us, some would not sign up and drive in from home to pick up their checks. Generally, it was the single guys on their way to living the good life or those who did not want their wives to see what their overtime check was. For some reason deployment was heavy today, with supervision and brass all over the place.

The 1515 briefing for PM shift was standing room only. Marcus Simpson and the other boots were in the front row. I took my usual chair in the back row, with other uniforms filling in between us. Nobody would dare sit in my or Donny's seat. Detective Valarie Stevens—Val—walked in with several others from the Detective Bureau. "What's going on?"

"We're going to get an update on the annual Red Walker shooting," I commented to those in the back row.

As I spoke, Kip and Lieutenant Rikelman walked into the room from just behind me. Lucky for me, only Kip heard the comment. He clipped my ear with his finger as he walked by. I turned and looked at a stern "Norman Bates," walking like he had a broomstick up his ass, carrying books and an attitude. They were headed to the raised podium and desk area to start the briefing.

It had to be big when both the lieutenant and Kip were working on the same day. Normally, only one of them was on duty at a time. Kip was on his official good behavior today. I loved paydays.

When it was Kip's briefing, he started with, "Here is how we're going to work," and he'd give out the assignments. When the lieutenant handled briefings, it was, "This is the way it is," leaving no doubt who was in charge.

As expected, Rikelman said, "This is the way it is. As soon as we get through the assignments, we're going to go over the shooting of the other night to let you guys know what happened."

Everyone knew who was working with whom, so the assignments were more of a formality and a way for Norman to ease his way in and let people know this was going to be his show.

"Anybody have any questions? Who has the subpoena book?" Rikelman looked around, and I raised it to let him know it had made it to the back row. There were no questions, and he moved his papers around to let everyone know that it was time to review the shooting.

"It's going to be a long night," I muttered to Donny.

To his credit, Rikelman did a good job of summarizing the shooting and keeping it interesting. Donny and I already knew how it went down, but we still had questions. And so did others in the room.

Val was sitting in front of me. She had been around for over fifteen years and still looked pretty good. Her ass had grown a bit, but detective assignments will do that to anyone. She had some Mexican blood in her somewhere, and I think that is what attracted her to Harvey Stevens. As a young officer and one of the first females to work Patrol, Sergeant Stevens liked what he saw and started dating Val, thinking that no one knew.

Police departments are little "Peyton Places" but worse, because we all have guns. Harvey and Val have been married for ten years. I think it works because they're always on opposite shifts. Harvey likes PMs, and Val likes day-watch Detectives. I heard a rumor that Harvey was thinking about pulling the pin and retiring and that he and Val were headed for Colorado. Right now, it was just a rumor.

Val sprang with the first question. "What do we know about the genius who tried to run Walker down? I think I know him from a previous domestic violence case."

Soft enough question, I thought.

Rikelman responded, "You're right, Val. You did arrest him for spousal battery last year. DA didn't file; Mama took him back."

Greg "the Absent-Minded-Squint Professor" Meacham was perched in his second-row seat right behind the probies who were relegated to the first row. Meacham was going to be somebody someday, but he was still a geek. He looked like a college professor who was just a click off. But he was usually right. He always asked the most probing question of the Lieutenant.

"Is there any data regarding the frequency with which officers shoot at moving vehicles and hit them or stop the subject? And how many officers have been hit and injured or killed by cars used as an assault vehicle?"

"Damn," I mumbled to Donny, "my exact question, and the Squint beat me to it."

Rikelman was ready with an answer. "It's a problem, Meacham. It depends on the jurisdiction and the information gathered." Rikelman then proceeded to quote more stats than we needed. Rikelman was a walking encyclopedia and could rattle off statistics like a computer. He finally took a breath.

"That's a bunch of bullshit," Donny said. I was worried he had stepped on it, but Donny saved himself. "Not you, Lieutenant, but I mean, suspects know what is in front of them, and I don't think any asshole is just careless and doesn't know what he's doing when somebody in uniform is right in front of him, and he's driving like a maniac." Donny never had the most tact.

From her third-row seat, Pat "Wolf" Woford stepped in to try to salvage Donny's expletive. "I think that what he's trying to say is that the LA guys are taking a lot of crap in the press about shooting at vehicles, and our policy is pretty clear. We have not had one of these, and LA has them all the time. We're concerned with legitimately shooting someone and getting hung out to dry by the brass."

"I see where you're coming from," Rikelman responded, and he directed his remarks to Wolf, with an "I'll deal with you later, Simpkins" glance to Donny.

"And another thing, Lieutenant," chimed in "Bill" Gates, who had been sitting next to Donny, "where was the suspect hit? Front on or from the side? What was the reaction time? I'm thinking, how much goddamn time do we have to make a decision? What if Red didn't shoot?"

I could tell that Rikelman knew this was not the forum to go into detail. "The OIS team and the DA are still going over all of that," Rikelman said, somewhat flustered. "I do know that there were people behind Walker, following him down the alley. The way the suspect was driving, had Walker not taken the action he did, three people would have been killed."

"That settles it for me," Donny said. "Some folks deserve to be shot! Red is a damn hero."

Oh my God! I thought. *He didn't really say that, did he?* That was not the message that he wanted to get out to the younger boots.

"Let's hit the streets," Sergeant Bennett announced, "and be safe out there!" I was thinking that Kip said that to cover Donny's words, because he knew the lieutenant would get a piece of him.

Now Donny owed three people for keeping him from stepping on it again. And there was no mention of "gun" or "GTA." Not with the lieutenant around.

Chapter 11

First Gun

It was a well-kept secret—or at least I thought it was. Protecting the streets of Orchard Hill was an easy job. Our residents wanted aggressive policing to keep the "assholes"—I mean riff-raff—from LA out of our city. Those messages always came out loud and clear at community meetings. With just over six years on the streets, I knew how to spot the bad guy. I just had to find a reason to stop him, find the gun, and go home.

With over twenty years on the department, Kip was both feared and respected. His gridiron heroics at the local level were legendary, and fifty pounds later, his ebony frame still told us what a linebacker looked like. To him, we were all 175-pound running backs who were not going to get by him.

Sergeant Bennett knew me and those like me. He wanted three things in life: to take guns off the street, locate stolen cars with a live body still in them, and go home safe. Give him what he wanted, and he'd give you what you wanted.

He loved playing games—any game. We would listen for the word. Just one word. Somewhere in his handling of briefing, he would mention it, and we knew. It was like the secret word on the old Groucho Marx television show, *You Bet Your Life*. "Say the secret word and win." If one of the contestants said the word of the day, a duck would come down from the ceiling and Groucho's sidekick, George Fenneman, would say, "And we have a winner!"

"Gun" or "GTA."

The first one to get a gun off the street went home after the paperwork was done. If Kip wanted a "rollin' stolen," it would sound like "GTA," for grand theft auto. But there had to be a body with that stolen car. And it had to be an observation, or "obs," and not from some rinky-dink radio call or a sitting duck with no body inside.

Donny Simpkins and I made eye contact and, through mental telepathy, communicated "Fuck you; I'm gonna get it first." He was better at rollin' stolens, but I had a sixth sense for guns. I could smell them. Not literally, but I knew who was holding.

"Gun," Kip said as he packed up his papers.

I heard it and knew that if I got one in the first two hours of my watch, and it was *my* watch, I could get the reports done and be home in four hours. Working ten-hour days was great, but going home to Clare and the kids was even better.

That was why the guys who knew Kip's rules liked him so much. Get the number, book the body, do the paperwork, don't get a complaint, and you were taken care of. Life wasn't any better. First gun goes home. Like "Ollie, Ollie, oxen free" or "Marco … Polo." First gun goes home, and we have a winner! It's a game.

But not tonight.

Chapter 12

Shift Change and Trick Baby

I try to not let things get to me. I don't pay attention to all of the gossip around the station. I do my job and go home. I like the people I work around and the hype of police work. It is intoxicating. And addicting. And they pay us for it. Pretty damn well, too.

I have always been a pretty private guy at work. I mean, it took me over a year to give my name to the Starbucks girl, just to get a cup of coffee. Can you imagine having to give your name just to get a cup of coffee? Then they have the nerve to write it on the cup for everybody to see! I'm okay with it now, but I do not adjust to new things very well. Change is hard for me.

When the shift changes were posted, however, I was not the only one to have problems with change. There were a lot of pissed-off coppers around OHPD. I knew it was coming because of my conversation with the chief, but I held on to that piece of information, as I didn't want to be viewed as having any inside information about what Admin was going to do.

Donny and the guys were talking about going to the union, doing a lateral transfer to another agency, or at least threatening it. One of the graveyard sergeants who got bumped threatened to retire.

Sergeant Biddle was taking up space on that ugly shift called "graveyard" for a reason. He was working real estate during the day and coming to work at 2230 hours at night. Everyone suspected he was sleeping most of his shift, somewhere on the street. He had a "hole" someplace, but nobody knew where it was. He was making more money than any of us and really didn't need the job. Why was he still around?

The captains were visiting everyone, trying to do damage control. Everyone who didn't want the change was trying to cut deals to trade shifts, complain of a hardship at home, or come up with some other lame excuse.

The biggest complainers were the day-watch maggots, a term of endearment that Sergeant Bennett had assigned to those who started shift at 0630. And eventually, he was going to be one of them. And I was also going to be one of "them."

The policy was that you must do a minimum of three months on a shift other than your first choice. You could bump somebody off his or her shift who had been there more than a year. The boots—Simpson, McDaniel, and AJ "Foyt" Johnson—would stay on their shifts for another month and then get bumped to other shifts and different training officers. Wolf and another guy I really did not know very well, Carter "Jimmy" McCauley, had just completed training and were going to the graveyard shift with Donny. Someone on the third floor had figured this out.

When word finally came down that the changes had already been discussed with the union, we resigned ourselves to the fact that it was a done deal.

The last shift of this deployment period was a Saturday night. When we went end of watch, or EOW, the plan was to take it to Home Plate for a proper burial.

The night started rather strangely. Kip took some comp time and left right after briefing. There would be no "first gun goes home" tonight for me.

Right out of briefing, Jimmy the Greek and McCauley picked up two street hypes on the north side of town, which was the southern border of LA. I responded to his location for a backup. It was still daylight, so traffic was still a bit heavy. They had stopped this guy for a traffic violation and took it from there. They found some heroin and a spoon on the floorboard of the car and wanted a unit to stand by while they completed a more thorough search.

Jimmy the Greek claimed he was black. He had very light skin, freckles, and green eyes. Even though he had been raised by both parents in the nearby community of San Pedro, when he came to OHPD, he told everyone that he was a "trick baby." That had been his name until Admin told us to stop calling him that for fear of a lawsuit. Hell, he told us to call him that; we didn't name him.

I watched McCauley talking to the suspect he had pulled from the car. The Greek started to search the car. I watched the driver, who was handcuffed and sitting on the curb with no place to go. I placed the driver between me and the suspect with McCauley, so I could see everybody. As I was complimenting myself on everyone's tactics, I saw McCauley move his suspect around, have him place his hands on his head, and put him in a cursory search position. *So far, so good*, I thought.

"Spread your legs apart," McCauley ordered in his best academy command voice. It was comical to see it done just the way they teach us in the academy.

"Jimmy" then put his right hand on top of the suspect's hands, which were on his head, and slid his left hand down the suspect's left side. I knew what he was going to do, but before I could stop him, he placed his left hand into the suspect's left front pocket.

As I saw him move to the pocket, I heard McCauley cry out, "Ouch, goddamn it!" He quickly pulled his left hand out of the pocket. Even from my position, I could see the blood.

"You got my shaft, man," the suspect said.

McCauley got the shaft, all right—the hypodermic needle that suspects use to shoot themselves up. This one went right into the palm of his hand.

"Watch my guy, Jimmy! Just watch my guy," I shouted. I went over to the suspect, cuffed him, and then put on a pair of latex gloves I always carry. I carefully pulled the needle and syringe out of the pocket and dropped it into an evidence envelope I had retrieved from my car.

"Just like a fuckin' Boy Scout," I muttered to no one in particular.

The syringe still had heroin residue inside. And now it had McCauley's blood.

It all happened so fast. And now I would be on the subpoena list on this case. Nothin' wrong with a little court time.

"Can you have 50 Robert respond to my location?" I asked the dispatch operator.

We needed a sergeant at the scene as soon as possible. "Also, can you dispatch an ambulance for an officer-involved injury at my location? I am not involved."

The dispatcher knew it was not a request, but I always made it sound like it was. We were supposed to use the ten code system for everything, but I could never get used to it, so I just spoke English. No one seemed to mind.

I could see that the cut was deep.

"You poor motherfucker," I said to McCauley, "Now you have to get a tetanus shot."

"That's not all," the Greek said as he was placing the suspects into the backseat of his cruiser. "Look what I found in the trunk." He walked over to the suspect's car, as the tow truck had pulled up. "Not only are these guys hypes, but"—he paused to raise the trunk lid—"they're into S & M with all of these fuck books, dildoes, ropes, and K-Y jelly and shit."

"McCauley," Jimmy announced for all to hear, "you, my friend, will have to be tested for HIV and AIDs."

The ambulance and Sergeant Stevens rolled up at the same time.

Chapter 13

Rumors

I had forgotten that Lieutenant Rikelman was working tonight. He was quiet during briefing, and let Kip and Harvey run most of it. I had the Sunday and Monday off, so I got stuck working for Rikelman on my last shift on PMs. *What poetic justice*, I thought. He would certainly transform himself into Norman Bates over McCauley's incident.

When Sergeant Stevens and the ambulance rolled up to the scene, I knew it would be only a matter of time before Norman Bates would stick his nose into it. I cleared from the scene and handled three other routine calls in the first part of the shift and kept returning to the station to get an update on McCauley.

The rumor mill is alive and well in OHPD and not too many days go by without someone launching some piece of ill-informed speculation about just anything and calling it the truth.

One of the guys had visited Sea World in San Diego and sat through a lecture on the gossip habits of dolphins. They apparently identify themselves by a unique pattern of whistles and clicks. Scientists proved that when dolphins communicate it's not uncommon for them to use the name of a third dolphin when that third dolphin is not present. They determined from their study that dolphins, therefore, gossip about each other.

We have all been led to believe that these mammals are of a higher order of beings than most. They are the epitome of honor and enlightenment, we are told, comparable to Gandhi, if we believe the scientists.

The term started innocently enough—"The dolphins are loose." Someone would say it, and we would be off and running with speculation. Once the transmission of information or misinformation reaches Mach speed, it's impossible to stop. I was sure that the dolphins were saying that McCauley had AIDS or some other dreaded disease after just three hours into the shift. And I was right.

By 2000 hours, the blowhole of the dolphins was whistling in the Records section. McCauley had "it."

"No he doesn't."

"He has too!"

"He will!"

It was all speculation, and Jimmy was still at the hospital with Jimmy the Greek and Sergeant Stevens. It was getting confusing with two Jimmys working together. McCauley was new, and the Greek had been given his name a long time ago. All of this shift-changing would make things very complicated; particularly for those with nicknames.

I walked into the watch commander's office and saw Norman in a deep conversation with "Foyt"—Andy Johnson. Foyt was working the U-boat tonight, which meant that he was really the gofer for the watch commander. Go for this; go for that. I guess I should have figured that out because I was holding three reports that Foyt should've taken.

Didn't matter to me. I'd engineer this thing to do them all toward end of watch and go home on time to Clare and the kids. Even without Kip's help.

There comes a time when you learn to just go with the flow. I should have been pissed that Foyt had not been monitoring the radio. He should have heard me get those report calls and asked to take them from me. It was his area of the city. But I wasn't upset. Particularly not tonight. Not with Bates around and my wanting to get off on time. And I liked Foyt. Maybe that's why it didn't matter that much.

It wasn't often that I got to work around someone who could have been famous. Foyt was a big football star at St. Christopher's High in the San Fernando Valley. He played linebacker at USC, and everyone said he could have gone to the pros as a strong safety. I guess he didn't think so, because he applied to OHPD and LA, and we scooped him up because we could just process people faster than the big city.

Johnson answered to AJ, Foyt, Johnson, or Andy; it didn't seem to matter. He was in his last month of being a boot, which meant that he would be working the U-boat to sharpen his preliminary investigative skills before getting off probation. That was routine around here.

"HH," Rikelman called as I walked past his desk. The summons was not a request but an order. "Hey, sorry you got dumped on for those report calls the last few hours," he said rather sheepishly. "I had Foyt running some errands. It looked like you were available, so I had dispatch give you those calls. I should have told you. Sorry about that."

I couldn't believe Norman Bates was apologizing to me, but I would be gracious about it.

"Foyt's going to take his code-seven time to work out in the gym. Check the board, and if there is nothing hot, it can wait till he's done lifting," Rikelman said.

"Got it, Lieutenant. No problem. By the way, Lieutenant, McCauley's test for AIDS came back negative. Just thought you might like to know."

I had been sitting on that piece of information for about a half hour, but I could tell the Lieutenant didn't know. The Greek had text messaged me from the hospital. I guess he didn't let Rikelman know.

It is this sort of drivel that makes for prime time and makes it look like I always know what's going on. It pays off. Dolphin gossip is time-sensitive. Accurate information cuts through the bullshit and gossip, and then it just becomes news. The problem is, gossip hangs on whether there is any truth to it or not. McCauley will be talked about as having AIDS, regardless of the test results, and then having AIDS from something other than being poked with a dirty needle. And when the story has run its course, there will be different ones to take its place. When it comes to crime, we want the facts. When it comes to ourselves, we will take the thin reality.

Jesus, I love this place.

Chapter 14

The Broadcast

There were no reports on the board, so I hung around the watch commander's office while Foyt worked out in his attempt to perfect an already great upper body. I wasn't jealous, but his muscle definition made him look like he was sculpted. And it was accented when he was wearing his short-sleeved uniform. His arms filled the sleeves like they were poured concrete, while mine looked like threads hanging from the shirt.

It was around 2230 hours, and I went back on the street for the next few hours. It was slow. The police radio was not chattering like its usual Saturday night self. I still had two reports to do, but I would engineer them for end of watch.

I didn't need the overtime, at least not tonight. Foyt was a newlywed, so he probably needed all the overtime he could get. Tonight would be his turn, if they needed somebody. Not me.

I was in the watch commander's office when I heard it.

"Seven-U1 is in pursuit. What is your location, 7U1?"

I heard Foyt broadcast very calmly, "I'm southbound on Albion, approaching Wilshire. Suspect vehicle is a late model white Chevy, and he is going at least sixty miles per hour. Plate is Sam, Ida, Sam, 925. I see one male. He blew the light mid-phase at Medina, and everyone was looking at me to stop him. Get me some backup."

He's smart, I thought. *Just sit back and let the idiot run, stay on his tail, and wait for the helicopter and backup units.*

"Get an airship on it now," Sergeant Stevens told dispatch.

"Roger," was the response. "I have them on their frequency, and they have a three-minute response."

I jumped in my car and was about a minute away and closing in on his location, but traffic was not cooperating.

"He's slowing down like he's going to turn east on Brownstone!" yelled Foyt, a little more excited now.

I could feel his adrenaline rush through the airwaves. And so could the dispatcher and Stevens. It was like an infectious disease that everyone would catch.

"Hang back till we get there," Stevens ordered, and dispatch repeated, even though on the simulcast, Foyt would hear it.

"Seven-U1, no problem," was the reply.

And then another burst of excitement: "He crashed into the Pep Boys at Albion and Brownstone. The suspect is climbing out of the vehicle!" Foyt shouted into his microphone.

The dispatcher interrupted. "Seven-U1, your plate is a Hollywood stolen, used in a robbery of a pornography store this date, about twenty ago. Armed and dangerous; repeat, armed and dangerous!"

"Roger," was the reply from 7U1.

"Suspect is running east on Brownstone. I need additional units to set up a perimeter. I'm Code Six with the vehicle."

Within forty-five seconds, I was pulling up to the scene as the airship arrived.

Foyt was lying on the ground next to his cruiser and behind the driver's door. His car was perfectly positioned behind the suspect's car, which was halfway into the auto-parts store window. From his vantage point, he had a direct view of the sidewalk that trailed away from the site of the collision and alongside the building.

More than likely, that was the direction of travel the suspect took as he was escaping. The radio mike was still in his left hand, and his Glock was in his right.

And then I saw his vest, draped over the passenger seat. The vest he wasn't wearing.

Chapter 15

The Long Night

Setting up a command post is not science. Find a spot that's away from the key location but is close enough to the action without being in it, with enough room to bring units in; brief them; and get them out and into the perimeter.

Sergeant Stevens knew what he was doing. He found the perfect spot for everybody to report in by radio, get their assignments, and deploy. It was a parking lot just behind the auto-supply business, far enough away from the scene of the shooting but close enough if we were needed to help secure the perimeter. We had this set up well. All corners were covered. We would go door-to-door and tighten the noose and find this bastard. And we needed to do it quickly. Even if it was 2300 hours.

Because I was working by myself tonight, Stevens grabbed me to be his gofer, radio man, and scribe. I could hear the EMT guys arguing with their dispatch center.

"Where are we takin' him?" Their radio dispatcher answered, but I couldn't hear him. Then … "Fuck no. We're not taking him there. They're goddamn butchers! Take him to County Memorial; they know how to handle these things. They do it every day." Somebody was taking charge, and that's what mattered right now.

I went to the command post as Stevens had requested, and we used the trunk hood to map out our plan. Rikelman showed up. When he saw that we were doing what he would have done, he—surprisingly—let us do it. He didn't run all over us and take it away.

"We're going to get this guy, Lieutenant. You can count on it," I told him.

We are the good guys, and that is the bad guy, and we are going to win … again, I thought. And I knew everyone else on the scene felt the same way.

Rikelman was staying Rikelman and not becoming Bates. I was so thankful for that.

Within what seemed like just a few minutes, but was more like a half hour or forty-five minutes, detectives and the brass started showing up. In another hour, it would seem like the world was there.

I called Clare on my cell phone and told her briefly that there had been a shooting but gave no details. I was okay and would not be home for a while. It turned out to be a long while.

OHPD always captures the bad guy—we're known for that all over the region. Much of the reason is the layout of the city, along with the ease of patrolling the main streets and access into and out of our city. When we set up a perimeter, it generally takes only a few minutes and, bingo—we flush them out. We always take the credit, but it was the city engineers who laid out the streets who really deserve the accolades.

Rikelman had left for the hospital. Captain Pearson was at the shooting scene, and Captain Markham was talking to the press.

"Where do we have all of the units now?" Stevens asked me in a rather frustrated tone.

I could tell he was growing weary, and we were only an hour and a half into it. We had set up a four-block corridor and sectored each block with several units. They were going door-to-door, yard-to-yard, and trash can to trash can to tighten the noose.

Word got back from the shooting scene that blood was found in the suspect's car and on the sidewalk trailing away from the collision. He had either been injured in the accident or maybe Foyt had cranked off a round and hit him.

Somebody asked during those first chaotic moments, "Where was Foyt's gun?" I remembered the EMTs removing his Sam Browne belt and handing it to Stevens.

"I gave the belt and his weapon to Detectives," was the reply from Stevens.

We still didn't know if he got off a round. And we wouldn't know for a long while. But that's not what I was thinking about.

Did AJ hesitate to shoot because of my case on the beach? Did he pause just long enough to take a round? How did he get hit if he was behind the car door? Why did he take off the fuckin' vest? We had just been issued a new Second Chance T2 ballistic vest that was the sixth-generation body armor. Why take it off mid-shift? All of those questions were bouncing around in my already cluttered mind.

It was almost 0330 when Rikelman returned to the command post. There was no suspect in custody. More important, there was now no hope, as the lieutenant confirmed what we did not want to know.

"We lost AJ," was all he said.

That was all that he had to say.

Sergeant Stevens was struggling to stay awake. After the news that Foyt had died, he now was almost comatose. Rikelman saw that Harvey was not all there, but in typical fashion, he ignored it and stepped in to get an update on the search in his usual Norman Bates manner.

The word of AJ's death spread like wildfire. Nothing was said on the radio, but it seemed everyone knew. It was like watching a bunch of zombies staring nowhere yet everywhere. Going through the motions of searching for a suspect who was armed and who already had killed one of us was not a healthy environment.

Captain Markham walked over to the command post. "How many LA units do we have committed to the search, and how many other agencies?" he asked to no one in particular.

Because I was keeping records and logs of all information, both Stevens and Rikelman deferred to me. "We have five LA two-man units and four singles from the sheriff and Redondo, Captain, and we have ten of our guys, including detectives."

Markham looked at a rather disheveled Sergeant Stevens. "Well, Harvey, it's been a long night. Don't you think it's time to close up shop and send these guys back to their cities? It looks like we're not going to get this guy tonight. Don't get me wrong; we may not get him tonight or tomorrow morning, but let there be no doubt: we will get him."

Chapter 16

Confrontation

"I don't think we should do that, Captain," Rikelman said in his best Norman Bates tone. Rikelman had a way of responding to a superior officer in a manner that was just short of insubordination.

While he always looked very good in uniform, it was Rikelman's demeanor and stature that came across now. Markham met the challenge with silence. Rikelman saw the opportunity to seize the moment and express his opinion once again. Markham had been listening to the groans of the officers who had traffic-direction duties, as well as listening to the complaints of the press. *What is taking so long? Why is the suspect not in custody?*

Tempers were on edge. With no suspect in custody, the case had failure written all over it—at least for now. With the change of shift schedule to start at the 0630 briefing, fresh resources for deployment would be a problem. I was scheduled on a day off, but others had opted for doing back-to-back shifts for the overtime.

Sergeant Stevens was having difficulty focusing. *What's wrong with him? I wondered?* For once, I was glad to see Rikelman back at the command post. I had heard the grumbling from those on the perimeter—they'd missed him.

The suspect got out of the perimeter, and the consensus was that this was all for nothing—except by those who were making the big decisions.

Lieutenant Rikelman, Sergeant Stevens, and Captain Markham stepped away from the command post for a private meeting. I easily could read the body language. Clearly, Rikelman was in his glory. He was getting a piece of Stevens and communicating to Markham with his best Norman Bates characterization that this command post would not be disbanded, and the search for the shooter would not be abandoned. The three pointed fingers at each other, but

Norman's jaw told me everything I needed to know. He was going to win this battle.

And he did.

He walked proudly back to Sergeant Stevens's command post vehicle as if he had a corn cob stuck up his ass. He told me, "HH, you can broadcast to all of the units still working the perimeter to continue with the search until further notice. We're going to work until at least daybreak or until we catch the bastard."

I could never have been more proud of Norman Bates than at that very moment.

"Got it, Lieutenant!" I said in my best command voice. I reached for the microphone and let everyone know to stay at their positions. I did not hear a groan from anyone. *And better not*, I thought.

With notifications made, we all knew we were in it for the long haul. We had dispatch contact the agencies that still had units assigned to us. The message was clear: let them know in no uncertain terms how much we needed and appreciated their help.

Sunrise was about an hour and a half away. Our bodies were failing, but the adrenaline and bad coffee kept us plodding through the motions.

It was Rikelman who surprisingly started the small talk. "I cannot believe this fuckin' day. Johnson got me out of briefing to ask if he could take care of some personal business. The National Football League Combine had called him about a tryout for the draft coming up. He had to run up to LA for an interview and set a date to be physically tested and perform a bunch of exercises. He was pretty excited."

"You mean the real NFL, Lieutenant?" I said with surprise.

"Yeah, can you believe that? They wanted to get some numbers on him and let some teams look at his stats. You know, how fast he could run the forty, his agility, and what he could bench press. And I don't know what else." He took a deep breath and then said, "He came back very excited and asked if he could hit the weight room during his code seven. I okayed it, and I guess he pumped so much iron that he had trouble getting back into his uniform shirt and opted not to wear the vest. Jesus, Jesus, I wish I had seen him leave the station! Damn it."

"Just something we take for granted, I guess, Lieutenant. I wish I would have seen him too."

And then it dawned on me that I had seen him. I just hadn't paid attention.

Rikelman went on about his visit to the hospital. "Shit, I walked into the emergency room and asked where he was, and they pointed toward a door. Nobody stopped me, so I walked right in to an operating room as they were putting him in some kind of space suit. They said it was to control the internal bleeding. I backed right out of there and didn't know what the hell to do. Somebody said that his family was in the cafeteria, so I sucked it up and introduced myself."

I could tell that Rikelman was having difficulty talking to Stevens and me without choking up. I had never seen him emotional, at least not like this. I would have to reconsider whether he was the first human being I had known who did not have a heart. He had one; it just never showed—at least not until now.

Rikelman continued, "I sat there with the family for what seemed an eternity. His father is an executive at Jet Propulsion Lab in Pasadena, but all he could talk about was the chance for AJ to work out at the NFL Combine. He had been looking forward to that. You could tell the pride he had." He sucked in another breath and then said, "AJ was his only son. He has a younger sister, but she wasn't there. His mother didn't say much, but AJ's wife, Adriana, kept talking about all the time they would get to spend at home together while he was recuperating. They got married right after the academy, so no kids yet but a lot of plans. Mr. Johnson was not too keen on AJ being one of us. He never said it outright, but I could sense it."

I was not going to interrupt him now. Rikelman needed to do this. Like a dump truck, he needed to unload.

"I had to go to the bathroom and excused myself," he continued. "I walked down a hallway and was met by a surgeon coming out of the operating room. 'You with the officer that was shot?' the doc said to me. I asked how AJ was doing, but the doc did not need to tell me; I read it in his eyes. 'We tried,' he said, 'but the bullet did too much damage.' I told him I understood and asked if he could delay notification to the family until I could get our chaplain to help. He agreed."

Rikelman took a few more deep gulps of air, as if he was getting ready to hold his breath underwater, before he continued. "I called dispatch to send Father Mike our way and went back to the family. By this time, they were planning out his recovery—how to take advantage of his time away from the job and saying that he could wait until next year for the Combine. They mentioned how good of a nurse Adriana would be. I was getting sick to my stomach." He held his stomach as if he still had cramps, but I knew he was struggling with his emotions. "I listened to the family make plans for about twenty minutes and then saw Father Mike and the doctor walking our way.

I stood up, and the family turned around. Only two words were necessary—'I'm sorry' was all that was said. They sat there, stunned, for what seemed like forever. Father Mike did his thing, and they prayed. That's when I gave my condolences, told them I had to get back to the scene and that I would keep them posted. So you see why we can't wrap this up. It wouldn't be fair—not to AJ, his wife, or his parents, let alone to us. No, we'll get him. Have no doubt about it—we will get him!"

Chapter 17

The Rising Sun

The best part of working all night is that most of the time, there are not any department brass around. Tonight, however, there were more people with stars and bars on their uniforms than you would see at a costume party.

That's what happens when someone dies in our business. Chiefs and captains are never seen unless there is trouble. And tonight, trouble brought out our department's brass as well as chiefs, captains, and lieutenants from LA and the surrounding cities. It was like a police convention.

The worst part of working all night is the sun. There's a chill that sweeps through the air somewhere between 0400 and about 0445. That little forty-five minute window before 0500 hours warns you that your friend, the night, is about to leave you. It tells you that things will change. I don't know where it comes from, but whether it is winter or summer, there are atmospheric conditions that warn you that something is going to happen.

The light starts to break, and it gushes out one last wind of chill before the sun does away with the night. Everything that the night has hidden is revealed, because light becomes the archenemy for things that happen under the cloak of darkness. It evens the playing field for everything we got away with in the dark. It reveals our blemishes, our wrinkles, and the fading of our colors. If we are not pure in the nighttime, then the sun will correct us. What we can get away with in the dark may stay in the dark but cannot be performed for the sun to see.

And this was a unique sun. It spoke volumes. It numbed our reality; it reminded us of our fatigue; and it confused our sense of reason. It symbolized our failure. Midnight may be the official time that one day transitions into another, but the real change of day is about 0530 hours. We lose our precious darkness and the sun signals us to set aside this night for the new day.

At about 0530, my body, or what was left of it, was spent. I was where Harvey was at 0200. The zombies had taken me over, and I was just going through the motions. Had I been on the perimeter, I would be complaining with the rest of them, but my job here at the command post would not let me get a vote to go home.

And there appeared to be no relief. It was early on a Sunday morning, and the only people on the street were cops, drunks, and newspaper delivery trucks.

Because it was Sunday, we ran a skeleton shift until 1000. That's what quiet bedroom communities do. It was a sun day and a Sunday. The brightness of our solar system on this morning was in direct contrast to the darkness of events that had transpired since last night.

Last night seemed so long ago.

Chapter 18

The Obvious

Whether he is Rikelman or Bates, a person like him never fades, never tires. I could see the wheels turning in his head, as if his forehead was transparent, and the gears were in sync. Sometimes the obvious is right in front of us, but we cannot see it. It becomes our scotoma—our blind spot. We look right at it but cannot see it.

Rikelman was going over the map we had developed, with the area marked off and each house accounted for in the search for a four-block radius. We had a very good perimeter set up. OHPD knew how to do it right. We had trained and trained and had added a few tricks of the trade that made it easy for even the newest of our department.

"So what happened here?" the lieutenant asked.

"What do you mean?" Stevens asked with a yawn.

One should not answer Rikelman or Norman with a question, but this one stumped all of us.

"Who has searched these storage garages that are ten feet from us? Anybody?"

A total of ten one-car garages had been converted to storage sheds for the nearby apartment complex. We had set up our command post in the parking lot adjacent to the sheds and behind the Pep Boys, where the suspect had crashed.

"He could have gone eastbound from Brownstone and doubled back westbound on the next street to throw us off," Rikelman said.

We all looked at each other and agreed. It was Sergeant Stevens who saved his ass, at least temporarily, by advising Rikelman, "I'll get the K-9s to check each one. We've been talking to the manager all night. We can get the keys from him."

"Don't just get the keys, Harvey. Have him go with us to unlock the doors so he can tell us what to expect in each one."

"Got it, Lieutenant."

Sergeant Stevens was already walking away. I knew that he didn't want to stick around for an ass-chewing for missing that little piece of tactical planning.

Stevens approached Sergeant Wickstead, our K-9 sergeant and the LA dog handler. We had two of our dogs standing by and one from LA. It was decided that we would assign two officers to each dog and handler, and each would start at one end of the complex. The apartment manager went with them and opened up each one. We announced ourselves with, "Police. We are conducting an investigation. If anyone is in here, come out now. If you do not come out with your hands up, we will send in a police dog." We repeated it twice and once again in Spanish. That was department policy, not my idea.

Each storage area was small, a little larger than a one-car garage. Some were filled with junk, so it was a painstaking search by the officers and the dogs. The dogs quickly cleared the first eight garages and were working on the ninth and tenth. I heard the manager advise Wickstead, aka "Elton," that the last shed to be searched, the one in the middle of the row, was his paint storage area.

That's when it clicked with me. I had smelled something all night, and it was that damn paint right next to our command post. I couldn't get it out of my head but could not pinpoint what the hell it was. No wonder I had a fuzzy headache. Paint! Lead paint.

Much to both Stevens's and Rikelman's chagrin, the K-9s cleared the last two sheds with negative results. It was quite a let-down for the search teams. While there was concern that the suspect could have been so close to the command post, not finding him meant that the search was probably going to be called off.

And then it hit me!

Years ago, Clare and I had been on a planning committee with the preschool that Geoff and Marcia had attended. We were refurbishing the playground and had been advised that the paint on the swings, jungle gyms, and slides had deteriorated and in the process, the number of particles of lead from the paint had reached a dangerous condition. We were advised that we either had to replace the playground equipment or sandblast and repaint with non-lead-based paint. Furthermore, the hazard increased as chips and dust collected.

I looked at the paint room and saw that it housed old five-gallon cans and what appeared to be relatively new cans as well. I approached Sergeant Wickstead.

"Hey, Elton, if there was a bunch of old lead-based paint in there, would our dogs pick up a human scent, or would the paint camouflage it?"

He looked at me but didn't say anything. I could see him thinking about it.

"If it was old paint, they might not get past the lead odor, HH," he said. "Let's ask the manager." After finding out that the paint was over fifteen years old, the manager advised us that he could not find a place to get rid of it, so he had decided to hang on to it.

"Let's look at that space again," Wickstead and I said to each other almost at the same time.

The large five-gallon paint cans were dusty, but the lead odor was dominant. They were stacked five high and appeared to be at least ten deep. Wickstead and I agreed to move the cans from one end of the garage to the other, just to ensure we had a clear visual of every corner of the shed. I reached for the second stack of cans—and that's when I saw movement.

Then I saw his eyes. Predatory eyes!

Chapter 19

The Punch

"Elton!" I shouted.

Just then, the suspect sprang to his feet. Where was he going? Was this the guy? Where were his hands? Where was his gun? There were too many unanswered questions that I did not have time to figure out. It looked like he was moving toward me or was trying to get by me. He knew who I was by the uniform, and I knew—or thought I knew—who he was.

I didn't have my gun out, as I had been moving paint cans. I knew I was covered by the other officers in the shed, but I was in the line of fire between them and the suspect. Instinct took over. I swung at him with all of my might. One punch landed squarely in the middle of his face, knocked him backward, and sent him sprawling among the paint cans.

"You son of a bitch!" I shouted without thinking. I yelled over and over as I stood over him, holding my hand, which hurt like hell.

I never heard the shouts of "Hamilton! Hamilton!"

I was told later that they pulled me off and yelled for me to stop a number of times, but I never heard them. And I swear I only hit him once. I couldn't believe he was coming after me after killing AJ. I couldn't see his fuckin gun. Maybe he was trying to get the other officers in the garage or trying to escape, as futile as that would be. I didn't know, and to this day I don't care. We had him.

I could not tell if it was red paint or blood all over me and all over him. Either way, my uniform was ruined. A team jumped in to handcuff him, and I moved away—or I was pulled away; I'm not sure. It was all a blur, and to this day, I cannot remember it as it happened.

"I have not seen anyone hit so hard since Joe Frazier and Muhammad Ali," Wickstead said.

"What the fuck do you think you are doing, Hamilton?" Captain Markham barked, "Delivering street justice to this guy?"

When nothing is going on in police work, there is generally a sense of informality that everyone acknowledges and accepts. When there is work to be done, or when the shit hits the fan, we revert to the tried-and-true chain of command and title-calling. Even at this moment of emotional trauma, caused by the death of one of our own, the time had come for the transition to formality.

"No, sir," I said with all of the intestinal fortitude I had left, "I don't know what I was doing." Those spontaneous words would later prove to be my downfall.

There is a warrior in all of us.

Chapter 20

The Cleanup

Just because the suspect is caught does not mean it's over. A number of questions have to be asked and answered by the Shooting Team detectives. With an officer's death, the district attorney's Justice Integrity Division looks over everything.

How did the suspect get to the location where we found him? What was his route of travel from the traffic-collision scene? Did he have an accomplice? Did he throw the gun?

We needed that gun to tie him in to the shooting. What about the robbery he committed earlier? Were there any witnesses, video tape, or other physical evidence that could specifically tie him to that crime? Whose car did he use? From where did he steal it? And were his prints in the car? Did they wrap his hands to test for gunshot residue? Who else could put him in the car, and who else knew that he was hiding in the paint shed?

But these questions were not my problem. Detectives would ultimately arrest and book the suspect for the robbery of the porno store, the shooting of AJ, and initiating a pursuit. I would be listed as a witness officer who'd located the guy after a search of the area. I would have to testify, if there was a trial. I would have to answer questions about such things as why we'd searched the shed, not once but twice; why I'd thought he was the suspect; and why I'd hit him in the mouth.

After the excitement of it all, I knew I could justify my hitting him to a court; I didn't know if I could justify it to those head-hunters in Internal Affairs and the chief. I'm convinced that I can justify my actions to a group of citizens from the community more than some of the dickhead brass we have. Members of the community have much more of an appreciation for the shit we take than our own command officers.

If someone needs to be told he is an "asshole" to calm a situation, John Q. Citizen understands; Captain Markham does not. About a year ago, I admitted to calling somebody a name. I don't remember what I called him, but he said it was "asshole." That word is so much a part of my vocabulary around the station that I very well could have. *Funny,* I thought, *that what I say at the station is so much different from the language I use at home. Why is that?*

I admitted it to Sergeant Bennett, who let the captain know I was very forthcoming. Next thing I knew, I'd received a reprimand, in writing, from the chief. It mattered not to me. After six years on the street, that was my only major complaint. For a street cop it's unheard of. We're bound to upset people in our line of business. Anyway, the world is full of assholes, and he was just one of them.

I knew I was in deeper trouble here. Markham was not going to let up. I just hoped he waited until after the funeral. Even with the suspect in custody, this matter would take months to sort out, maybe even longer.

The robbery in LA had to be investigated by the LA dicks, and a supervisor had to do a pursuit report. The traffic investigation unit had to determine the primary cause of the collision into the Pep Boys auto-parts store. The detectives had the murder of an officer, with a suspect in custody. The Crime Scene Investigation unit had to search for and collect forensic evidence at the scene of the robbery, at the traffic collision site, the stolen car, and the location of arrest in the paint shed. Witnesses had to be located and interviewed. An autopsy had to be witnessed by our Shooting Team detectives, and a ballistics test had to be done on the bullet dug from AJ's chest. The suspect would have to be arraigned in court and a date set for trial.

The suspect was identified as Adrian Junior Palmer. He was of Samoan or Polynesian descent, six foot two, 215 pounds, and twenty-six years of age. But we didn't need his physical description to know who he was.

OHPD knew of Palmer but had never arrested him. He was another local football star who had shoved fame and fortune up his nose. He was a third-team quarterback at UCLA and was slated to be a starter in the future but was found under the influence of cocaine just before a big game.

Just like Stanley Wilson of the Cincinnati Bengals in the 1989 Super Bowl, Palmer could not handle the pressure and searched for the white powder to give him courage. Unlike Stanford alumni Stanley Wilson, however, Palmer could not and did not see the light and ask for help.

The demon of drugs took two casualties: Andrew "Foyt" Johnson and Adrian Palmer. Neither was necessary. While Palmer and AJ played for rival schools, they'd never met on the gridiron of the LA Coliseum or the turf at the Rose Bowl of Pasadena. They were four years and worlds apart in how they lived their lives.

In an ideal world, Palmer could have thrown a pass, and AJ could have intercepted it and run for a touchdown. Both of them would have had their names in the paper—Palmer for making a mistake that may or may not have mattered and AJ for sharing a linebacker's dream. And now, their names would be in the newspaper, but no one would applaud for either school. The score was tied, but there was no tie breaker. Neither person and neither school nor lifestyle had won. Neither life would be fulfilled.

Another name would be added to the list, along with Andrew Johnson and Adrian Palmer. Whether the media decided to print that name—with the outcome still uncertain—was a mystery. Howard Hamilton, police officer. OHPD Form #16, also known in department circles as the "big one-six," or personnel complaint investigation.

Allegation: excessive use of force/brutality.

Chapter 21

The Front Desk

There would be no post-traumatic stress sex at home for the next few days. The days and nights were a blur. Clare had been great. She dropped the kids off at her mom's and just stayed at home while I slept or did yard work with deadened senses. No television or commercial radio, just cable radio that played oldies, jazz, or classical, depending on the mood.

I didn't want to hear what the media was saying. OHPD had not lost an officer in almost a decade. Why had it happened on my watch, to someone I knew? Why wasn't that me on a coroner's slab with a toe tag instead of AJ? I didn't know if I could return to the streets and go back to doing warrior police work. Patrolling the pie crust to ensure the crooks did not get into our beautiful community demanded a price. Now, the ultimate price had been paid.

While Clare didn't like the work I was doing, she was the most supportive partner I could ask for. She knew when not to talk and when I needed to get something off my chest. She listened without criticism or blame and became the best therapist a guy could have. We went through most of the two days, discussing our kids and our plans for the next set of days off and very little regarding the incident.

She did indicate that she'd heard bits and pieces on the news, but she wouldn't go into detail. Thank goodness! I was comforted by the lack of direct conversation, knowing there would be plenty going on at the station upon my return.

Monday afternoon was a time I had set aside to take the kids to the park. Swings and sand, jungle gyms and slides were the order of the day. Simple pleasures always seemed to be the best, and so it was with Marcia and Geoff. We didn't have to spend much to entertain them. They entertained themselves. That was as it should be.

I watched with a father's amazement and pride at Geoff's acrobatics on the jungle gym.

He will definitely be a great athlete, I thought, *and maybe even scholarship material in a sport I like.*

As he hung on the bars, poised to jump into the sand, my cell phone rang. I recognized the number as Donny's.

"Yeah, Donny, what's up?"

"Hey, thought I would give you a heads-up, buddy. Don't know what you did, but they have you working the front desk until further notice."

"Oh, really?" I asked, not expecting a response.

"Yeah, but you know those schedule-makers. They don't know what they're doing. We're short of new guys, so maybe they put you there until the recruits graduate from the academy," Donny said, trying to be convincing.

"Doesn't matter," I lied. "Could use the rest." I knew that it was better than being placed on Admin leave.

The front desk was for the sick, lame, and lazy. While I didn't think I fit any of those categories, I was certain that the chief, Markham, and Rikelman didn't want me on the street under the circumstances. I didn't mind dealing with the public, taking reports, and being the watch commander's gofer but not for the entire scheduling period. I would go crazy. Or get too used to it. I didn't want either.

Chapter 22

Whoops!

The benefits and detriments to working the front desk balanced each other out. Contrary to the Patrol mentality of "no crime will be solved until the overtime," desk assignment meant that I always got off on time—or a little early, if the next watch-desk guy or girl didn't attend briefing. Not getting overtime for a month or so, however, would put a crimp in some of our plans.

Coppers and firefighters live off overtime. That's not a good thing, but we do it anyway. When overtime dries up toward the end of the fiscal year, everybody scurries for off-duty jobs to make up the difference. We then build up our compensatory time off, or "comp time," and usually get another month of vacation as a result. Not too bad. At least for the short term, however, it didn't look like I was going to get either.

I decided to go in to work early for day watch and pump some iron in the weight room. I thought if I could get there by 0500, work out for an hour, shower, and change into my uniform, I could be ready for briefing at 0630. If this was my fate, to be a day-watch maggot surrounded by the brass, I should make the most of it—and look my best doing it. Resignation to my new duties meant perhaps a new mental approach. Would I—could I—make the adjustment?

I pulled into the station parking lot at 0450 and noted that I could easily get my favorite parking space. It was right next to the men's locker room door. I was already in my workout gear, so I placed my toiletries bag in my locker, next to the showers.

The workout room had been recently refurbished by our Peace Officers Association, or POA, and it had all of the modern equipment, including free weights, treadmills, the elliptical, and every isometric machine you could ask for. And at this time of the morning, I would have it all to myself. Or so I thought.

With a back-brace belt and towel in hand, I punched in the four-digit number that gained access to the weight room. The electronic charge activated the lock with a buzzing sound, and I pushed inward, only to realize I had to pull the solid metal door to open it.

The walls had been covered with mirrors, ostensibly to ensure that one would do the exercises in the appropriate fashion and not cheat on the movement of the weights. It was also used to take a look at the progress you made in developing your pectorals, biceps, triceps, and abdominal muscles. I knew I needed a lot of work before I would be measuring my improvements with a mirror.

Something or someone moved in the back corner of the room. With the advantage of the mirrors, I could make out two figures. At first, it looked like someone working out on a mat or slant board. Then I realized what I was seeing—Donny in a T-shirt, with his uniform pants around his ankles, lying on a sit-up board, and Wolf with her head in his lap, giving him a head job. In the weight room!

Donny saw me, but Wolf was otherwise occupied. "Pat!" he shouted as he tapped her shoulder. I surmised they did not hear the electronic buzzer as I entered.

Reflections in the mirrors made it look much more crowded than the three of us alone in the room. I didn't say anything, but I didn't have to.

Wolf exclaimed, "Whoops," got up and wiped her mouth with one hand, and casually excused herself. Donny just sat there with his erection rapidly deflating.

"I didn't think anybody used the room at this hour of the morning," he said.

I remained silent, in my best non-interrogation mode. Sometimes I found that even if you don't Mirandize a suspect but also do not ask anything, they will just babble on and on in the name of spontaneous statements, and you get everything you need. So it was with police officers. Especially with police officers. And so it was with Donny.

I did not need an explanation for Donny and Pat's activities. But Donny was not going to spare me the opportunity.

"We're in love HH, and I know what you're thinking. I'm married, she's a cop, and this is all stupid."

"Well, you hit three of them, but I probably have more. Why her, why here, and are you out of your fucking mind?"

Donny was one of the original good-guy cop warriors. Low-key and assertive in his police work. He never had to resort to the use of force, nor had he ever had to chase anyone. He was a serious but happy guy who would put his life on the line for me or anyone he cherished.

He had his kind of justice, but didn't we all? He just wanted to limit the injustice, and that's why I think he concentrated on recovering stolen cars. They were inanimate objects that he was just returning to their rightful owners. He had more felony arrests, mostly auto-theft-related, and never got a beef from a suspect or citizen. If you looked at him, you would not pick him as a cop. He was dumpy, like the Pillsbury Doughboy. He was out of shape from too many burritos. The last and only time he'd been in shape was at the police academy.

Every police department would love to have someone like him. He got the arrests without fanfare. He could smell those stolen cars a mile away and treated it like a puzzle or a game. I compared him to a Stradivarius violin—a smooth instrument that was limited in number. And there were fewer and fewer of them on the street today.

Our profession had to concentrate on preserving him and letting him stay on the street to perform his magic. We had to find a way to create new artists of the street that emerged to replace the Donny Simpkinses of the world. And not just replace and duplicate but do the job better, wiser, and smarter. The complexity of our world and our communities requires that we not search for and preserve the Stradivarius but replace it with something better.

Had it been Sergeant Stevens or, heaven forbid, Norman Bates who had walked in on Donny and Pat, we would have had to find a replacement for the Stradivarius. I don't think that either Stevens or Rikelman had the deep, dark sense of humor that this situation clearly called for, at least by Donny's and my standards.

Thank goodness it was me. And I pass no judgment on what goes on between two people. Donny is no saint, and I know that. And neither am I. But this was just stupid.

"Amanda and I have not been getting along, and I think you knew that, Howard. I wanted kids, and she didn't. I was getting ready to move out anyway, and this happened. I'm vulnerable—what can I say? Wolf and I had been talking about christening the workout room, and we figured with everything that was going on, no one would be around. Jesus, I'm glad it was you who found us!" Donny pulled up his pants, put his shirt and Sam Browne back on, and we just stared at each other.

And then we laughed like two teenage girls at a slumber party.

Chapter 23

A Day of Days

Today was not a day to look forward to. I went through the motions of a quick workout with the free weights, showered, and was in uniform and ready to go for desk duty by 0615. I checked out my domain at the front desk and, surprisingly, found that the graveyard officer, Charlie "Gabby" Hayes was very well organized. He had not left me a mess to clean up, and no reports were hanging. No half-empty coffee cups or yesterday's newspapers.

"Need a favor, HH," he said quietly. "I have court this morning and need to catch some shut-eye. I'm going to the cot room. Can you wake me about 0800?"

"No problem, Gabby. I'll just write myself a note in case I get busy," I said, scribbling down the reminder.

Gabby was anything but. His nickname should have been "Phantom," because for all practical purposes, he was invisible. He took up space on our roster, and that was about it. I was surprised to find he had court, because I couldn't remember the last arrest he made.

I was sure we would hear something about the funeral for AJ today. It was eerily quiet, but the brass were not in yet. That would happen soon enough. And Donny should have been thankful that most of them don't work out.

I sat through the first ten minutes of briefing and caught Rikelman's eye—he let me leave for my desk assignment. Hopefully, the shooting had quieted down the "Norman" in him.

I had the front desk to myself, and there was no one in the lobby. Our civilian desk help had better hours than we did and were not expected in until about 0800.

I was trying to figure out the daily worksheet when I looked up to see a striking blonde, about six feet tall, walk in to the station. She was mid-twenties and looked like a fashion model. I would

67

have rated her a ten if I saw her in a magazine. She was ten-plus in person. What would she want with OHPD?

"May I help you?" I asked, giving the standard greeting for the desk officer.

"Hi, my name is Melissa Flowers. I understand you're hiring, and I would like to get some information, find out when the written test is, and arrange for a ride-along."

I pointed to the recruitment stand that was in the lobby and then obtained a couple of forms from under the counter and put them in an envelope. "You'll have to talk to the watch commander, Lieutenant Rikelman, to schedule the ride-along. He's tied up right now but should be free in about a half hour." I handed her the envelope, casually inquiring, "How did you hear we were hiring?"

"My father is a deputy chief in LA. I didn't want to go there because of him, but he recommended OHPD, because you guys have such a good reputation." She looked around the lobby with an approving eye. "I was sorry to hear about the loss of one of your officers. I saw the flowers outside the station."

I had not even checked the front of the station when I came in. More than likely, the locals from the community had left them in remembrance of AJ. I made a mental note to check them out and advise the lieutenant.

"That's good to know, coming from somebody in LA, and thanks for thinking about our officer. Not much of a recruitment item, is it?" I mumbled to myself and her at the same time.

There was a quiet but silent affirmation as she sat down to wait for the lieutenant. It was all I could do to keep myself busy. No reflection on Wolf, but Donny had even something more interesting to look forward to if this one made it through background and the academy.

Clare would get a real kick out of all of this when I told her. If I told her. I would at least have a discussion with my "silent partner."

The lieutenant met with the model, and before I knew it, it was 0800. I didn't need the note to remind me, as the only thing on my mind was getting Gabby off to court. It was that slow around the station. It was just another reason why day watch was not for me.

I woke up a very groggy Gabby and sent him on his way across the parking lot to the courthouse in a disheveled uniform. He looked like the *Peanuts* cartoon character Pigpen.

We were very fortunate that the county saw fit to place a courthouse in our civic center. That made it easy to take prisoners for arraignment and attend their trials. No commute or parking hassles like in downtown LA. Another reason Ms. Flowers was smart in picking Orchard Hill PD.

The day was already starting out interestingly.

Chapter 24

Gabby

It was about 0845 hours on my first day at desk duty, and so far there was nothing I had not been able to handle. The U-boat officer would not come in until 1000, but there was nothing on the work board at this point anyway. The administrative staff had started to drift in. Secretaries, detectives, crime analysts, records people, and, sure to follow, the brass. Once again, it was just another reason why I liked the night watch.

I had promised myself that I wouldn't complain about the day shift and working with the maggots, but that didn't mean I had to like it. The last time I worked days was at the end of my probationary period, much like the moment in time that AJ had found himself. He never saw the day shift. No one had come up with this mandatory rotation of shifts until now.

The desk phone rang. Our special order had directed us to answer within three rings, but I got it in one. "Orchard Hill PD front desk. Officer Hamilton. May I help you?" The order had also directed the salutation.

"HH, this is Simpson … Marcus, you know," he stammered. "I'm over at the courthouse and Charlie—Gabby—they just took him out of the officers' waiting room in a stretcher. I think he might have had a heart attack or something. Thought the station ought to know. They said they were taking him to Orchard Hill Memorial." Simpson was talking like he was out of breath but I knew he was in good shape, just nervous and excited. "Hell, the paramedics were even arguing about where to take him. They wanted to take him to some private hospital because that was what their dispatch told them to do. I insisted they go to OH Memorial. They do trauma better there. My cousin—"

"Thanks, Marcus," I said as I made unnecessary notes of what he told me and tried to shut him up. "How did he look, man? He looked like shit this morning, but I thought he was just tired."

"Not sure he's tired anymore, HH. I think he's dead," Marcus said in a very matter-of-fact tone.

I heard the click on the line as it went dead as well.

"Fuck," I said to no one in particular, "we don't need this on the heels of everything else."

I walked in to the watch commander's office and laid the bomb on Rikelman. He gazed at his desk blotter for what seemed a very long time, looked me in the eye, and said in his Norman Bates monotone, "Contact dispatch and make sure they send one of our units to sit with him at the hospital. Get me his personnel package and emergency information sheet with his wife's name, next of kin, and all of that bullshit. Advise the captains and the chief's office. Get us a car ready. We're going for a ride, you and me. First stop is the hospital. Tell Detective Lieutenant Hospian to do some research here to find out who his close friends are in the department, and go sit on his house until we find out his condition. Got it?"

"Got it." I marveled at the calm and determined manner in which he just knew what needed to be done. He just rattled those things off like he had done it a hundred times. *He thrives on this shit*, I thought. Damn, he was good when he needed to be and hell when there was nothing else going on.

I let the captains shared secretary, Vickie, know what was going on, and she took care of the notifications to them and the chief. One of the staff got me Gabby's personnel package, but I knew that Gabby's ex-brother-in-law, Johnny Bresani, worked with Detectives a lot, because he ran our hype car. I went to Detectives squad bay area and clued in Lieutenant Hospian, whose nickname was "the Thespian" because he was so dramatic. He seemed all right with what Rikelman wanted him to do. I assumed he knew that Bresani should not be the one assigned to any of this duty, but I didn't tell him one way or the other.

So this is what day watch was all about.

Simpson came back from the courthouse visibly shaken. He stopped by the desk to give me an update. Rikelman had already gone to his locker to get his Sam Browne belt. He didn't wear his Sam Browne at the watch commanders' desk, but he did keep a handgun on his belt.

I needed to get somebody to relieve me at the front desk so that I could get Rikelman to wherever he needed to be.

"First dead body I've ever seen in a uniform, HH. Pretty scary shit!" Simpson said.

I flashed back to AJ lying in the street with a bullet in his chest. Then it dawned on me that Gabby had worn his uniform to court, rather than a suit.

"He sure looked gone to me, and I don't think the paramedics were too optimistic."

Simpson had just returned from court. With the new shift change I had no idea if he worked last night. We had talked about a nickname for him, and the best that anyone could come up with was his initials, "MS." His parents had already done him enough disservice by naming him after Marcus Allen and O. J. Simpson, so he didn't mind something as simple as his initials. *Pretty easygoing guy*, I thought.

"Marcus, can you hang on until the 1000 desk officer, Sara Hawkins, gets in?" I asked. "I have to go to the hospital with the lieutenant."

"Not a problem. I'm on a day off, and it'd be a good excuse to get next to Hawkins—she's hot!"

"Whatever floats your boat," I joked, knowing the next few hours would not be filled with much humor.

"You need to get somebody to relieve you at the desk, Hamilton," Rikelman said in a manner that was somewhat of an order. "We may be a while on this one."

"Got it covered, Lieutenant. Simpson is handling until Hawkins gets in."

The Lieutenant looked at me as if he was surprised. I think he liked that I was thinking ahead. The hospital was only a few minutes away, but in traffic on a weekday, it became ten minutes.

We drove in silence until we got out of the parking lot. I could see Rikelman's wheels turning as he was thinking about what was ahead of us. "Losing two in just a few days is a first around here," he muttered to the windshield.

I'm never sure he is talking directly to me when he speaks, because he talks to objects and just assumes I know he's talking to me.

"I've been on the job over twenty years, HH, and this is the second and third for me. Before you were hired, about ten years ago, we lost McKinnon in a shootout with a bad guy at a liquor store. Took us years to recover, because everybody thought that our tactics stunk, and we put him in the line of fire unnecessarily. The only dead OHPD guys are the ones who retire. You see the notice of a death and a funeral date for somebody who has milked his pension for a long time, or he retired too soon and the boredom killed him. AJ's and Gabby's deaths will affect us for other reasons, and I don't even know what they are yet."

Rikelman was quite the philosopher. But his last words as we pulled into the parking lot of the hospital hit me hard. "You know, I don't think it matters how they die, Hamilton. Whether you take a bullet, have a heart attack, get in a traffic collision, or get shot by your old lady. When you're dead, you're dead. You're not in the locker room getting dressed, walking down the halls of the station, or going home at end of watch. Your EOW is permanent, no matter how it happens."

Once again, Rikelman was making sense—too much sense.

Chapter 25

The Hospital

The Memorial Hospital staff knew why we were there and ushered us to a private setting off the emergency room. While it was a relatively new hospital, parts of it had been rebuilt after an earthquake a few years ago. It still smelled new and fresh, as if not too many people had died there.

As we were walking by the area where they work on patients, I saw a blue-uniformed pant leg hanging over a gurney. A sheet covered the entire body other than the leg. That told me all I needed to know. His Matterhorn boots were showing.

We got the word formally, and Rikelman wasted no time. He contacted Hospian and told him to make contact with Mrs. Hayes.

"Bring Vivian to the hospital, but don't tell her he's DOA. We'll take care of that here," he advised.

Interestingly, Rikelman seemed to know a lot about Gabby. He knew he had two teenagers, knew his wife's first name and that he had been talking about either retiring or trying to get a detective position. Interestingly, there wouldn't be a detective assignment in his future, and everyone but Hayes knew it.

Gabby was not the most motivated guy on the department. And a warrior cop he was not. His productivity was almost nonexistent. He had moved his family to Canyon Lake for more affordable housing many years ago and drove over seventy-five miles one way to work. Unless it was right in front of him, he would go out of his way to avoid real police work.

My negative thinking had me speculating that if he had been in AJ's position, he would have waved at Palmer as he drove by. He was a smiler and waver, not a go-getter. He was a day-watch maggot in a graveyard-shift position.

Within minutes, Lieutenant Hospian had called back to say they had located Charlie's wife, Vivian.

Apparently, Hospian said, she came to town with Charlie yesterday to stay with her mother, and they were going to have lunch with her after Charlie got out of court. They would then make the drive back to Canyon Lake together. Hospian advised us that he had not told her anything of Charlie's condition. They would bring her to meet us in the emergency room.

As we waited for Charlie's wife to arrive, Rikelman provided an update on funeral plans for AJ.

"It looks like it's going to be Thursday or Friday of this week."

He explained that the captains were thinking about Saturday to accommodate the families, but the chief overruled them. It seems that when he was in LA, they found out the hard way that a Saturday funeral for cops does not work. Policemen are funny that way, and so are politicians. Even in a situation like the death of one of our own, no one is prepared to give up a Saturday, even if it is a workday.

"Funny, huh, HH? We checked on it with a few other agencies that lost guys and sure enough."

I thought about it. I guess it made sense in an odd sort of way. "What about Gabby?" I posed as the electronically activated doors of the emergency room swung open to reveal Lieutenant Hospian, Detective Val Stevens, and Mrs. Hayes.

"We'll soon find out, won't we?" Rikelman muttered quietly.

We both rose to greet the newest widow of the moment for OHPD.

I stood there waiting to do something, anything, with my hands. Val introduced me as "Officer Hamilton." It all happened in a daze, and the next thing I knew, Mrs. Hayes was in Rikelman's arms, sobbing uncontrollably. The lieutenant did not say anything. My first impression was that she somehow already knew, but she did not.

Rikelman pushed her away, holding his arms out but placing his hands on her triceps. "Charlie didn't make it, Vivian. I really am sorry."

"I didn't think he would," she said in a manner that seemed rather composed for the circumstances. "He had been depressed. He had a number of nights with shortness of breath, and I couldn't get him to the doctor. He had not been himself, and I think he was resigned to this. I'm not surprised, Ib. We all knew this day was coming."

This was not the spontaneous eulogy I would have expected from a widow. But then again, how many have I seen? And what is it with the "Ib"?

Rikelman walked with her in the direction of a serenity garden that we had spotted earlier. I took the opportunity to just let them be together. Val and Lieutenant Hospian held back as well. Rikelman knew something that none of us knew, but I couldn't put my finger on it. It appeared that I was the only one thinking about it, as Val and Hospian talked of work-related things.

Was this how it was done? Death notifications by officers were all about just carrying the message. Not comfort and care and holding hands. Or was there more to notifications that made this one and AJ's special? Yes, we knew the people, but was I just numb or so uncaring that I didn't know how to do this well?

It was almost a half hour later when Rikelman and Vivian came back to the waiting area. I heard her ask if she could see him, and they walked to the emergency room section where he was reposed. While it was out of my sight, it was still only feet away. The strange thing was that I did not hear any weeping. There was only silence—a deafening silence.

Rikelman walked out of the sheeted room with the stone-faced look of his Norman Bates character. He shed no tears either. Hospian kept his distance, but Val was sobbing quietly into a Kleenex. We were all trying to handle it like just another radio call. Everyone was showing some emotion but not so much as to totally lose it.

But where was the emotion from Vivian? Is that what happens after years of marriage?

Yes, Gabby was a slug. He also was a father, but I don't know how good of a father he really was. He was a husband, but I don't know how good of a husband he was. What I was hearing, though, was not what I expected. *Perhaps*, I thought, *I expected too much. Is this how Clare would have reacted if that was me?*

Rikelman's words were echoing in my mind. *"It doesn't matter how you die; whether you take a bullet, have a heart attack, get in a traffic collision, or get shot by your old lady. When you are dead, you are dead! You no longer get dressed in the locker room, walk down the halls of the station, or go home at end of watch. It's permanent, no matter how it happens."*

But how others respond and handle the news of someone's demise still baffles me. Hell, my own emotions baffle me.

Rikelman's cell phone broke the subdued mood that had befallen our collective group.

"This is Rikelman," he said in his typical command voice. After he repeated "yes, sir," three times, he ended the call and said to us, "That was Captain Markham back at the station. The chief is on his way here to meet with Vivian. I'm sorry, Mrs. Hayes. They need me back at the station. Steve and Val, can you stay here with her and wait for the chief?"

There was no need to respond. Both nodded as we walked over to Vivian to advise her.

"City personnel and our HR people will be here to assist you, and you know I'm here for you," Rikelman told her. He gave her his cell phone number on the back of his business card.

The ride back to the station proved to be even a bigger eye-opener.

Chapter 26

The Ride Back

We walked out to the parking lot, and Rikelman tried to lighten the mood. He flipped me the car keys.

"Junior man drives, HH. That way, if you get in an accident, it's not the senior guy's fault."

"Makes sense to me, Lieutenant," I responded in a lighthearted, almost cavalier manner.

After a period of somber silence, Rikelman opened up. "You probably figured out that I knew Mrs. Hayes, huh?" he said as the doors closed, and I started the car.

"Kind of looked like that, sir." I was not going to get drawn in to a sense of familiarity and then have him jump on me for letting my guard down.

"Well, Hamilton, when this all plays out, you'll have to make sure you set everybody straight. Rumors around this place fly, so let me tell you the truth, and you keep your ears open. This could get really nasty."

Feeling like I had just been given an order, I acknowledged the newfound trust placed upon me with a casual, "Yes, sir." More than likely, the dolphins were already singing.

"Mrs. Hayes—Vivian—and I were high school sweethearts. We were engaged when she was a senior at St. Elizabeth's and I was in college. Short story was that I went in the marines, and she met Charlie while I was away. They ran off and got married. Funny how we both ended up on the same PD. Recently, Vivian and Charlie were having some problems, and she contacted me. Purely platonic, but we did a lot of talking and a lot of reminiscing. That's all you really need to know, at least for now."

"Who else knows this, sir?" I asked.

"Sergeant Biddle knows, and I've told Markham, but our new chief doesn't know. He will after today. I want everything above board and no rumors, got it?"

"Got it," I responded, in a form that I understood to be another order.

I didn't necessarily like Lieutenant Rikelman, but I really respected his command presence, his forceful demeanor, and his forthright attitude. He was right up front. But now I wondered if his personal life was as orderly.

No one seemed to know much about him off the job. Just who he was for us, on the job. It seemed that he had always been there, as a lieutenant and as a watch commander, for at least the years I had been with the OHPD. He never came to social activities, like a department picnic or Christmas party, and we never knew him to invite anyone over to his house for a get-together barbeque or dinner. Nobody shared Lakers, Clippers, Kings, Dodgers, or Angel's tickets with him, and he didn't carpool. As a matter of fact, no one even knew where he lived.

I made a mental note to look it up in the old master Rolodex that we kept at the front desk for emergency call-ups when I got back to the station. It was bound to tell us something.

As if itching to change the subject, Rikelman commented, "I have to get back to the station. I got a call from Markham that one of our guys, Bresani, didn't show for work today at 1000 briefing. No answer at his house, and no response on his cell. I'll tell you, HH, if it is not one thing, it is another."

I could see him opening up to me as if I was a therapist.

"We spend a lot of time on people issues. I wish we could just go after the bad guys. Catching crooks is easy. If people only knew what we really spend our time doing. This crime shit is the easy part," he said, staring out the window on the short drive back to the station. "This other, this bullshit, gets in the way. Juggling schedules and dealing with our own people's crap. Just let me chase the crook; that's all I ever wanted to do."

"Yes, sir, I responded in my best military voice, as we pulled back in to the station and parked in the watch commander's parking space.

Now I understood why that parking space was right near the back door. When he had to go somewhere or get back to the station, it was all about time and not prestige. But up until now, I hadn't realized that sense of urgency. And I was sure no one else did either.

So this was what went on during the day watch? I was beginning to understand what Kip meant by "day-watch maggots." It was not the people who were the maggots. It was the bullshit. "I would rather chase crooks too," I muttered.

Lieutenant Rikelman disappeared into the abyss that was the station and the third floor. I returned to the front desk to find Simpson still there, clinging to Sara Hawkins like he was her perfume.

"Thanks for sticking around, Marcus, I'll let the lieutenant know so we can see about getting you some overtime," I commented.

"No need for the OT, HH. It was my pleasure." He grinned as he backed away from the small, confining area that we called the front desk.

"HH, you had a phone message. I put it on the clipboard. See you later."

I was not too sure who he was telling, me or Sara. We both acknowledged his departure as if it was our own.

Not much had been done since I left with the lieutenant. I was straightening out the area to put my footprint on it, not realizing that Sara had done the same. It's funny how you need everything just the way you want access to it—notepads, pencils, reports, and even the shotgun we keep under the desk. Without a word, Sara and I drew a line to show where our space was and how we wanted to work. She respected my space and I hers. *This will work,* I thought.

Rikelman returned to the watch commander's office, but I could tell he was not settling in.

"Have Sergeant Biddle come to the station," I overheard him tell Dispatch.

Within two minutes, Biddle was standing tall in front of Rikelman as they both looked through a Thomas Guide map book together. I guess neither one of them liked to use a GPS.

"He lives in Hermosa Beach," I heard Rikelman say.

I knew that Hayes lived in Canyon Lake, so this must be unrelated to the Gabby situation.

Rikelman called me in to the watch commander's office.

"Sergeant Biddle and I are going for a ride to Hermosa Beach, Hamilton. We'll be monitoring the radio, so if you need us or you need report approvals, call in Sergeant Gates from the field to okay them. We may be a while. Lieutenant Hospian in Detectives is also available. He's back from the hospital, but he left Val with Mrs. Hayes."

It was almost like he was giving me the status report and keeping me apprised of his activities. Day watch sure is different.

I'd heard the name Bresani mentioned and figured that they might be going to his house for a surprise visit. Bresani was AWOL—absent without leave. Police officers are not like that, at least not without good reason. For a moment, I thought, *Good grief, is he dead too?* Was he hurt, sick, or just missing in action? And then it came to me—the most obvious of possibilities. With the change of schedule and shift changes, he probably just got his days off mixed up.

"Fuckin' schedule changes," I muttered.

Johnnie "B. Goode," or Bresani, was unique. He was a bit of a loner, like many of us. He was our "hype" expert and ran the hype car, training our young guys about dope. He could smell a needle-using hype like Donny could smell a hot car. He didn't make many arrests, but that was not what he was good for. He knew all the hypes in Orchard Hill and the surrounding communities. His real value was intelligence.

He knew when the good smack was coming to town before it got here. The street told him. When he made an arrest, it was to get a snitch off the street for his own good, or the guy was a big-time dealer. Johnnie B. didn't mess with the little guys and turned most of his information over to the regional Narco Task Force, dubbed LA Deuce.

I looked in the old Rolodex to see if he lived in Hermosa Beach. He did. The address was just one number and sounded like it was right on the water, a place called "The Strand."

I took the opportunity to flip to the R's to check on Rikelman and where he lived. His address was a post office box down the street from the station. That was all that was on file, with a local area code phone number. No next of kin was listed. His first name really was "Ib." *Interesting*, I thought. *Very interesting.*

Chapter 27

Funerals

I saw Captains Markham and Pearson more today than I had seen them in five years on PM shift. There was way too much brass around here for my blood, or anyone else's, I was sure.

The memo had been posted for everyone to see. AJ's funeral was going to be on Friday. Father Mike would officiate; there would be the chief, mayor, and a bunch of dignitaries speaking; a twenty-one-gun salute; bagpipes; and the grieving widow. Probably 90 percent of our department would be there, but there would be more uniformed LA guys, more sheriffs, and more highway patrol than we had in our entire department to pay their respects.

I had gone to a number of funerals for cops. It was expected. "I will go to yours if you come to mine," was the unwritten code.

But the professional police funeral attendee was Johnnie Walker. "Red" went to them all, at least those in California and many times those out of state. All in uniform. He never spoke at them. He merely attended, in uniform, with a black band diagonally placed across his badge, and many times with the chief's or captain's blessing to represent the department.

I guess you could say it was his hobby. And everyone knew it, sanctioned it, and supported his doing it. I just thought it was weird.

Word got out regarding Charlie Hayes's heart attack in court. There were a few calls from some off-duty guys who had been in court but not as many as I would have expected. Speculation was that we would do Gabby's service next week to let some time pass.

Right now, we were all thinking about AJ and his wife and parents. Gabby's funeral was a distant thought. We would just take them one at a time and deal with them. Or at least put on a good show of trying.

But it was not just the funerals that we thought about. The memory of losing two of our own in just a few days was starting to sink in. We were each dealing with it as individuals, and we were dealing with it as a collective department. It was all so surreal.

The rather frigid memo said everything we needed to know about Friday. The time to assemble was two hours before the actual service, to be held at Father Mike's church. The uniform to wear emphasized no short-sleeved shirts, a reference to wearing our uniform hats, and where the burial would be. We were told who the pallbearers were and where the reception would be following the service. Rikelman gave me a heads-up that he'd recommended that I be a pallbearer. I saw my name on the list and thought, *He got his way again.* It even had a reference to a memorial fund set up for the Foyt family. Who thinks of things like that?

All black-and-whites in the procession had to be cleaned and washed. We asked Sparrow Bay PD, our neighbor to the north, to handle our radio calls, so that everyone could attend the service.

The chief was smart in not asking his old agency, LA, to do it. Guys would not go for it. We did not need LA to handle anything for us. After all, we were OHPD. Everybody figured that the chief had experience in planning funerals, because it seemed that in LA, there were at least one or two a year. Hell, they probably had a manual or a written order on how to conduct an officer's services.

Many of us joined OHPD because we didn't want to be in violent communities and a war zone. Here it was, right in our own backyard. Who would have believed it? After all, we were OHPD.

I picked up the watch commander's inside line as it was headed to the fourth ring.

"Officer Hamilton, may I help you?"

"Hamilton," the voice said, "this is Bresani. Is the lieutenant around?"

"He's headed out to your house to find you."

"Oh shit. Let him know I'm at South Bay Emergency Hospital. He can meet me here."

Not wanting to pry, I responded, "Okay, John, take care of yourself."

I contacted Rikelman on the tactical frequency and told him of my conversation with Bresani.

"Got it, thanks, HH." And he abruptly hung up.

It just keeps getting more interesting, I thought.

I was wondering where my uniform hat was. Did I even have one?

Chapter 28

Friday

Our first funeral in over ten years was here before we knew it. If you were in the state and not bedridden and were a member of OHPD, you were expected to be there. And we all were. Word was that "someone" would be making a list and checking it twice to ensure that everyone was there. No one wanted to be on that list.

The union had interceded on the issue of wearing hats. I had found mine, at home, and cleaned it up. Not everyone was that fortunate. There was a run on the uniform shops, but they ran out too. Word came down.

"Wear them if you have them; if not, we understand." I planned on wearing mine.

The black-and-whites were all washed and shined. Everyone had the requisite long-sleeved shirt and tie, the black band placed across the badge, and the thousand-mile stare that said, "Do not talk to me. I am in mourning."

The silence around the station was deafening. No one talked. We just went through the motions and caravanned to the church.

The one thing that differentiated OHPD from others was that many of the guys' spouses wanted to attend with them. We didn't socialize much as a department, but when it came to the death of one of our own, it was obvious that we were family. Clare wanted to attend and sit with me. She rallied other wives to do the same. We were to all sit in a designated portion of the church as a department but with our significant others.

The message was very clear. This could have been any one of us. We knew it, and most important, the wives knew it. They could have been the widow in mourning sitting up there, staring at a coffin covered with wreath after wreath of flowers and banners. It could have been any one of our pictures in uniform staring them in the face.

The speakers were a brother, a neighbor, a former coach, his wife's two sisters, and our chief. Each one described AJ from his or her perspective. The sisters made us laugh out loud when they told the story of how Adriana and AJ met.

They had met at a "happy hour" at Charlie Brown's in the marina. She'd come home all excited and announced to the family, "I've met the man I'm going to marry!" She had said, "And here is the big thing ... he is handsome, in good physical shape, and he has a job ... with benefits!" One had made us laugh, another made us tear up, because cops don't cry, but they all made us proud. We were proud to have known him and honored to have served with him.

The governor arrived a little late, politely apologizing in his brief remarks. To those who cared to listen to a politician at such an occasion, he was okay. He probably would have been bad-mouthed for not being there, so one way or the other, he had to do something. Attending was better than not. He sat looking straight ahead and knew that all eyes were on him.

Father Mike did an incredible job of personalizing AJ and making it feel like everyone in the church knew him. We did. They did. Even for those who could not get in to the church, accommodations were made. Speakers and video screens were strategically placed in the front and sides of the church. We were in an informal formation of uniforms, suits, and those who just wanted to be there. Wherever you were, you could hear and see Father Mike's eloquent reflections, as well as those who gave the eulogies.

If it is possible to hit a home run in a eulogy, Father Mike did it. He talked not of Adriana but to her. He talked to AJ's family and not about them. And he talked to God and not about God.

"Because of your schedules, he knows that you have a hard time getting to the church of your choice on Sundays. He seldom gets a chance to talk to you formally, so that's why he takes times like this, times that are profound and drastic."

I was thinking, *why would he do that if he really cared for us?* Father Mike kept us in such a state of wonder.

"AJ's death is the bottom line of police work. Each of you probably thinks about it twenty times a day. As peacemakers, the community expects a lot of you." Isn't that the truth?

"The community expects you to be more than they are. Better than we are to each other. Your best will never be good enough. Not good enough for the OHPD, not good enough for the community, but your best is good enough for God. You are expected to differentiate between the downtrodden, the weak, the submissive, the controlling, the victim, and the poor, drug-addicted, and just plain bad people … in seconds."

When is he going to make us feel good? I thought. I moved my hat that I had placed between Clare and me and placed it on my right side. I reached for her hand.

"It's long overdue, but today is the day we say thank you! We judge others by the mistakes we think they make, yet we want to be judged by our motives, our intentions."

He then directed his attention to all of us in uniform.

"This senseless tragedy is not what you get paid for. Is it too much to ask that the community and its peacekeepers see themselves as one? There is no division of color here. AJ is black."

I was wondering where he was going with this.

"What color is the grief at OHPD? Let me answer for you. It is colorless. Clear, if you will. Our loss is a human loss. Color only adds to the exciting dimensions."

He sure had a way with words.

"AJ is an art form, a cultural symbol," Father Mike reflected. "He is a sculpture that represents our dominant values. Think of Bartholdi's Statue of Liberty, or Daniel Chester French's seated Abraham Lincoln. They are larger than life. And larger than life takes an enormous commitment of time, energy, and prodigious talent. Heroic or warrior are romantic terms that say 'larger than life-size.'" He had me right where he wanted all of us when he talked about heroes and warriors.

"Being anointed as a hero or warrior sends a message of extraordinary achievement. It is overcoming risk and fears and meeting every challenge. It's a symbol of permanence that is indelible. A sign of maturity, intelligence, and being mentally agile." He paused for effect and to take a breath. He continued, "We want our warriors to be ethical, physically fit, and able to immediately contribute individually, yet be a part of the team. We want them capable of functioning in a complex and ambiguous environment with limited support. We want courage, competency, and creativity from our warriors. That's what AJ was … for all of us. Thank you, AJ, for filling that dash between your date of birth and September 21 of this year." Father Mike turned and paused, looking at the audience and a sea of blue.

"Now, how are we going to fill our dash?"

I couldn't speak or even think after that message. I could only hold Clare's hand and do the thousand-mile stare.

Chapter 29

The Dash

Father Mike's words were embroidered on my brain.

"The dash."

Father Mike was talking about the dates on AJ's tombstone from the beginning to the end. AJ's date of birth was important, but what mattered most was the dash in between 1990 and September 21 of this year. What does that little line mean?

As we were dismissed to line up for the carrying of the casket, I was thinking more about the dash than being one of the pallbearers. I knew Clare was right behind us, but she might as well have been thousands of miles away. I was still trying to piece it together.

If I knew it was the last time I would see someone, how would I be? But you don't know. If I knew it was the last time I'd hear a voice, to spend time and share a day, a black-and-white, a radio call, how would I be? If tomorrow never comes for someone, how do we know, and what would we do? I would never dream it would be me, always someone else. Someone that I didn't know.

I could see now that funerals are not for the person who died. They are for those who had to continue. Could we unwind those relationships and deal with it if we knew it was our time?

It really doesn't matter how much we get paid … about our house or our cars. It sounds like what he was talking about was how we live and love and how we spend our lives. Good grief! My brain was struggling with all of this.

As I gazed out to nowhere in particular and held on to the rail of the casket, I thought, *are there things I would change? Need to change? How much time is left? Is there time to rearrange, slow down, speed up, or be less quick to anger, or appreciate things more, or love more, or better?*

The damn dash was freaking me out! *What am I going to do? What are we going to do?* Had I only known!

Everybody deals with death differently. I watched Red handle shooting someone. I've seen victims' families go berserk and totally lose it. Losing someone I barely knew, literally passing him in the hallway and changing clothes in the locker room, still got to me. I didn't cry about it, but I was feeling like shit.

What were the lessons to be learned here? Obviously, wear your vest was one of them.

Why didn't AJ get a shot off?

Those were questions for windshield conferences, and BS sessions over coffee, or something stronger at Home Plate. Those were things to file away for future reference. You can do the right thing and still get sued, fired, and/or prosecuted today. You never are prepared for the second guessing, headlines, condemnation, or even accusations. It all makes me think that maybe Red was not so bad after all.

Hell, we're not Robocop out here.

Should he have … or would he have … or—oh God, stop that, HH! Way too much urban drama here! It's not my job to overanalyze this thing. That's what the brass does in that rarified air up there. They deal with the legal and administrative issues. I'm going to deal with my buddies, family, and my own reactions.

And that was the tenor of the conversation at Home Plate. With the promise of only "two beers," I told Clare that I needed to debrief with the guys.

Donny, McBride, and Clyde the Glide were going to Catalina tomorrow, and I was working. I was okay with that.

"You aren't pussy-whipped or anything like that, are you, HH?" Donny joked.

"Yes, I am, but that has nothing to do with it, asshole,"

Donny knew the relationship Clare and I had, and he was jealous—I knew it.

"They talk to you yet about your hitting that suspect in the face?" McBride quipped.

"Not yet. Jesus, Mac, we just had the funeral!"

Donny jumped on it. "That doesn't make any difference to them."

J. C. De Ladurantey

"I know," I said, sipping my beer and looking around. "Them" always was reserved for the brass—anything above lieutenant.

"Didn't sleep well last night. How about you guys?" I asked to change the subject. "I'm exhausted, not eating right, according to Clare, and just thinking of that vest hanging over the passenger seat. Jesus!" I muttered with more anxiety than anger as I looked at the bottom of my beer mug.

"Have you cried?" Clyde asked.

"Nope," we all said in unison.

"I hear there's a shrink going to be hanging around the station the next few days," Donny said. "Glad we're going hunting."

I need a head doctor like a hole in my head, I thought—or did I actually say it? *I can handle this. But what is* this? *Was it the shooting, Gabby, Clare, seeing two widows in two days, or Father Mike's message about the dash?*

I raised one finger to the police-groupie, holster-sniffing waitress we all knew but never indulged. "One more round, Sally."

There is a real inconvenience to healing. Then, my cell phone starting ringing ...

Chapter 30

Johnnie B.

The call was from Johnny B. I stepped outside in the back lot of the HP to take the call.

"HH, I need a favor. It looks like I am going to be in the hospital for a few days. Nothing too serious. Can you help me?"

Bresani sounded somewhere between frantic and just totally out of it. *Must be the meds they put him on*, I thought. "Sure, Johnny, what is it?"

"My mom sent me a package of music CDs, and I have them in my locker at the station. Can you go by and bring them to me? She has a sense of humor, so they're wrapped in yellow paper with 'Clinton' written on them. I'm going crazy in here with nothing to do."

"Yeah, I'll just get the master key from the watch commander's desk and get them to you. Is tomorrow okay?"

"Could I get them tonight? I hope it's not too much trouble, but I don't think I can get to sleep, and they may help. Number 110," Johnny said.

I left Home Plate and went by the station. *I better call Clare and explain why I will be late.* She totally understood after our discussion of the day's events.

"If you want to stay at the hospital for a while to visit him, that's okay too," she advised.

That's why I love her. We may have a micro-marriage in that we tell each other everything, but that's what keeps everything so fresh in our relationship. We just share everything about our days.

I quickly drove to the station, got the master key, and hopped down the stairs two at a time. Only supervisors are supposed to use the master key without permission, but nobody was around to challenge me.

Our lockers are where we live away from home. Most of us keep a change of clothes and a few extra uniforms—one to wear every day and one for inspections. It never made much sense having a uniform just for inspections, but it did make sense to look good on inspection day. I often wondered, why not look good every day?

I was thinking of those pieces of trivia when I opened Johnny's locker. I was very surprised at what I found.

His locker was as clean as a whistle. What a surprise. Clare would have loved it—another neat freak. I was glad she never saw mine. It was always a mess. The fact that I knew where every little thing was in my locker made all the sense to me.

Johnny's locker had one uniform, built in shelves, and a shaving kit. Right on top was the CD package marked with the word "Clinton," and hanging from a side hook was a CD player with earphones. It was apparent that he didn't live in his locker.

I put both items into my workout bag, locked things up, and returned the key to the watch commander's desk. No one was the wiser.

Driving to the hospital, I thought of the funeral and how surreal it was. My mind stuck on a young Adriana Johnson, AJ's parents, Father Mike, and of course, Adriana's sisters. My mind then wandered to Gabby, Vivian, and Lieutenant Rikelman. I felt like I was watching a rerun on television or had DVR'd the whole thing to save for future viewing. All of the day just seemed to flash in front of my mind.

Then a funny thing that Rikelman said hit me: "Bresani is Gabby's ex-brother-in-law."

Stay in the now, I told myself as I pulled into the parking lot of South Bay Emergency Hospital. Johnny B. would appreciate that. So would his mother.

I pulled into the parking stalls marked for police vehicles only. "I won't be that long," I told myself, even though I was driving my Explorer.

The parking lot seemed unusually full for ten o'clock at night. The emergency room parking area was cluttered with cars, but visiting hours were over by now.

There must be a full moon, I thought.

I walked through the emergency room entrance because they knew me there. Even out of uniform, I was not a stranger to the nurses and administrative help at this time of night.

"Hey, HH," Donna, the head nurse, called out.

"What's up?" I casually responded as I set my workout bag down near her workstation.

"Where have you been? Did your shift get changed like everyone else's?"

Of course she knew about the shift changes, because we were all in this together, weren't we? Nurses and cops have more in common than cops and firefighters. She knew as much about what was going on at OHPD as anyone who worked there and for good reason.

"Yeah, I am on days for a while. But just a little while. I'll be back. Came to see Bresani. Do you know what room he's in?"

She looked him up on the computer and said, "Room 222. Saw him when he came in. Did not look like the old Johnny B. we know. What a mess. I guess that can happen to anyone if it can happen to a cop."

"It's been a very strange week, Donna," I responded, frustrated.

"It's always strange around here. Look at these people." She pointed to a full house.

People were waiting to get patched up, cleaned up, sobered up, or mended in some fashion. While everyone was in some level of discomfort or pain, mine was of a much different kind.

I looked at what appeared to be familiar faces, even if they were all strangers. I guess some things never change.

I picked up the workout bag and made my farewell. Heading to the elevator, I thought how comfortable I was in an emergency room. None of what I saw or heard bothered me. Nothing.

I stepped out of a very slow elevator to the second floor after waiting for what seemed forever. I went to the nurses' station to let them know I was just dropping something off for Bresani in 222. I knew the nurse at the station by sight, not by his name, and I thought he recognized me too, even though I wasn't in uniform.

Without saying a word, he pointed down the hall and put a finger to his lips as if to say, "Be quiet."

It was a busy floor, even at ten o'clock at night. I saw people who I could have sworn I had seen in the ER, talking to one another in the hallway. It looked like the full moon really was working, as the unkempt dirt bags that favored ERs were right off the street.

I walked into room 222 and was shocked by what I saw.

Chapter 31

Clinton

Bresani was asleep, or so I thought. His face was swollen. One eye appeared shut, and he had bruises on his upper arms.

Jesus Christ, I thought. *What happened to him?* He must have heard me entering the room. I could tell he was not in a deep sleep, just somewhere in that twilight zone between here and there. Thank goodness for legalized modern medicine.

He looked up and seemed to brighten as he saw me. "Hey, HH, good to see you, man." He grumbled, "Good to see anybody familiar, other than the fuckin' lieutenant."

"What the hell happened to you, John?" I must have looked overly concerned because he smiled immediately.

"Oh, it looks worse than it feels. Much worse," Bresani said, as if he had marbles in his mouth.

"I was not going to ask but ..."

"No, no, it's okay. I'll tell you, just like I told Norman. And boy, was he ever Norman today. I went down to the beach early this morning for a run before coming into work and ..." He tried to sit up, so I adjusted the bed switch so it moved instead of him. "The sun was just making light, and I was running down to the pier and back when I saw two guys dressed for the street and not the beach. They acted like I was in their way, and before I knew it, they hit me, got me down, and hit me a few more times. I think I lost consciousness. They took my wallet with cash and credit cards and ran off. That's the short version but all I really remember right now." Bresani moved around in the bed to get more comfortable.

"Wow!" That was all I could muster at that point. "Wow."

"Did you bring my CDs?"

"Yeah, got them right here. Brought your CD player and headphones too, if that was okay," I said rather proudly. He had not asked for the CD player.

"Oh, yeah. The CDs would do no good without a player, but they actually have one right here on the table that's built in to the clock," he said, looking around the room.

"Where do you want them?" I asked, placing them on the moveable stand that served as a lunch tray. "Want me to open them for you?"

He jumped like I had shot him as he reached out to grab the package and headphones. He was a little spaced out from the meds, no doubt. "My mom sent these to me, and I've not listened to them yet. Now would be a good time, as I'll be here for a few days. I'll unwrap them later, after you leave," he said, drooling a bit from the side of his mouth.

"What's with the Clinton thing?" I asked.

"Oh, that. She loved the guy and got some wrapping paper with his name splattered all over it. She lives in No Cal, somewhere up by Redding, and when she sends me stuff, she always wraps it in this. More because she knows I can't stand the guy. That's my mom." He smiled. "Thanks, again," he said with his eyelids drooping. I could tell he wanted to go back to sleep.

"Hey, got to get home to Clare, so take care, and I'll check with you later."

I excused myself, walked past the nurses' station, and made my good-byes to the same nurse I saw coming in. I tiptoed to the elevator with my finger over my lips, mimicking a "shhh." He laughed, almost out loud. The dirt bags were still hanging around.

I took the stairs and walked out to the parking lot to my Explorer. As I approached and used my remote key to unlock, I saw a piece of paper under my windshield wiper. It was a citation for parking in the spot reserved for police cars.

No good deed goes unpunished, I thought.

Chapter 32

Decompression

I called Clare to let her know I was on the way. The short drive home gave me time to decompress a little. It didn't hurt that I'd had a few beers, but I felt as sober as a judge. Whatever that meant.

We had lost AJ and Gabby. Rikelman's words echoed in my head. It didn't matter how they died; they just weren't going to be around. Johnnie B. wasn't dead, but he sure looked like shit. Walker was shooting everything in sight. I didn't shoot when I guess I could have. Were we missing something here? Was OHPD falling apart since our new chief took over?

What could he have done about any of this? I thought. The old joke was that the best chief was the last one and the next one. We were very good at making a hero of the last guy, except that he almost went to prison. We knew this guy wouldn't last more than five years, so the next one had to be our best bet.

As I turned on to my street, the only thing I thought about was Clare, Geoff, and Marcia. I had missed Geoff's soccer game, but maybe they had expected that. Were they all getting used to my missing events in their lives? I hoped not. I was sure Clare had something good planned for my next stretch of days off. I only had one more day, and then those four big days off were looking better and better.

I pushed the button to open the garage door and slowly eased into the spot to the left of Clare's car. Sitting there in the garage, I waited for what seemed a long time before the headlights automatically went off, and I was sitting in pitch black in my own garage.

Somewhere in the back of my mind was a recollection that Clare had told me to replace the burned-out light bulb in the garage door opener. I think it was last week, and I had not had two minutes to even do that.

I sat in the dark, thinking about all that had happened. My thousand-mile stare was back, and thoughts were like a ping-pong ball in a windstorm, bouncing around from one thing to another and not settling on any one in particular.

I have no idea how long I was there, but I was startled by bright lights flashing.

"Are you going to sleep in your car or come on in?" Clare joked as she flicked the garage light on and off like a strobe with one hand and held a glass of red wine in the other.

"I think I'll come in," I said, trying to laugh. Leave it to Clare to put a spin on that ping-pong ball.

Clare was her usual intuitive self. The kids were fast asleep, and another glass of red wine was sitting on the kitchen counter. She had been waiting for me.

There was no "How was your day?" or "Tell me about it," or even a recap of Geoff's soccer game. There was no "let me tell you about my day," or neighborhood gossip. There was a new flower centerpiece on the kitchen table, and the house was immaculate, as usual.

"I hope you had dinner, but if not, I can warm up some lasagna that the kids and I had … and make you a salad."

"Sounds good," I said with more enthusiasm than I had. I could tell that she was going to wait until I said something about what I wanted to talk about. Damn, she was good.

"How was Geoff's soccer game?" I posed the question with as serious a query as I could muster.

"He's getting better, but quite frankly, I don't think that's his sport," she confided, looking around to ensure that Geoff had not come down from his room. "We're not all good at everything we try to do, so I guess we just keep searching until we find out what we're good at. He'll find it," she said confidently.

"Yeah, we all do," I said, without much energy behind it. "Where did you get those beautiful flowers? I know our hydrangeas don't look that good."

"Suzie O. called and said she had more than she could handle from her garden and asked if I wanted some. Before I could even think about it, she showed up on the doorstep with a bouquet. All I did was trim them a little and put them in water."

"I love them." And I meant it. "And I love you." We touched our delicate wineglasses together in a toast, just as the microwave sounded that the lasagna was ready.

Chapter 33

What's New?

I had one more day of work and then four days off. Maybe I could talk to the lieutenant and see about adding some comp time on the end of those days and take a week off. Day watch was no match for me right now.

I went to the station early to get a light workout. As I went to the weight room, I was hoping I wouldn't find Simpkins and Wolf going at it again, but then I remembered that Donny was in Catalina with McBride and Clyde the Glide.

There was not much going on in the station. It was eerily quiet. I had a clean uniform in my locker, so I wore workout gear to work that day. I took a look at the board and saw that I was slated for desk duty again. I guess with all that was going on, the chief had not resolved my use of force case yet.

I went through the motions of a workout but my heart was not in it. Halfway through my routine, Rikelman stuck his head in the gym door.

"Hey, HH, if you promise to not get into trouble, can I put you on a U-boat today? I have some deployment problems. Cannot meet minimums, and I have a light duty I can assign to the desk."

"Sure, as long as I can get Shop 885."

"You got it. Just tell Williamson in the kit room I said it was yours."

Williamson was the civilian services officer in charge of the shotguns, car keys, flare boxes, laptops, and everything else that mattered logistically. You needed to stay on his good side, or he would mess with you—things like giving you a dog of a car, an uncharged laptop, or even a dirty shotgun. People in charge of logistics are king around here.

Shop 885 was the new black-and-white we'd just received. It needed to be driven tenderly to break it in to about five thousand miles before turning it loose on Patrol. The U-boat usually got the new cars to break in.

Shop 885 was a Dodge Charger with built-in technology to die for. There was a place for everything, from reports to GPS, and the new Power Crunch computers that tied in to every database imaginable. There was a built-in video camera, and the trunk was huge and full of items like a handheld test kit to identify drugs, explosives, and gunshot residue, with actual results while you waited. It was like having your own chemist.

It was technology originally designed for the military but with a law-enforcement version made just for us. It was tagged with the name ZPAK. Most of the technology we had been using was able to only test one item; explosives or drugs. It's not as good as the Crime Lab equipment, but it does give a presumptive test, which is enough to arrest.

What I liked most about the Charger was the leg room and the light bar. You could customize how you wanted the strobes to work with red, blue, and white lights. Too many switches to choose from, but I really liked it. I could slide right in to the driver's side without worrying about bumping my head. The car just projected a firm enforcement image. Whether it would hold up for 130,000 miles or not was the question.

OHPD had always been on the cutting edge, but this chief knew what he was doing with technology. He was slowly endearing himself, at least to me. I wondered what he had coming next. Rumor was, "they" were looking at on-the-body video systems to record all of our activities. Sounded like fun stuff to me, but I also knew that our union would want to have a say in it.

Does the fun stuff ever end? It did today.

I showered and got dressed in plenty of time for briefing. I walked by the kit room where Williamson was getting ready for the day shift. He caught my eye with a "I know you get 885" look. We communicate sometimes without saying a word.

I went by the desk to make sure my space was not being invaded by anyone. The watch commander's phone was ringing, but I didn't think it was my job to answer it. Rikelman was not around, and I didn't see any supervisors from the prior shift. It stopped ringing. And then it started ringing again.

"Can there be a sense of urgency to a ringing phone?" I said out loud. "All right already, I'll answer it!" I went through the "OHPD. Watch commander's office. Officer Hamilton. May I—" and I was interrupted.

"HH, so glad to get you!" It was Donny.

"What's up, big guy? How's Catalina?" I thought he'd called the watch commander to weasel another day off.

"Listen up, goddamn it, and do not interrupt me, you hear?" There was a moment of silence and then he said, "There's been an accident over here. I was putting a rifle in the gun rack on our rented jeep, and the damn thing went off. I think I hit the trigger with the stem of the rack. I thought Clyde had emptied the chamber, honest to God. It fuckin' took Clyde's head almost off. Sheriffs are here doing an investigation. You got to get Rikelman and the captain in on this. I am so fuckin' sorry, HH. So fuckin' sorry!" He started crying and babbling on about the same thing again.

"Is he dead?"

"Fuck yes, he's dead! Half of his head is gone. It was a 223, for Christ sake!" he shouted into the phone, referring to the caliber of the weapon. "You got to get the lieutenant for me!"

Chapter 34

Air Ship and U-Boat

I put Donny on hold and dialed the in-house intercom. "Lieutenant Rikelman, can you come to the watch commander's office? Code two and a half." I thought that might get his attention.

It did. He walked in carrying his briefing binder. He must have been preparing for roll call in the records unit, as it was just out of sight of the W/C's office.

"I got Simpkins on hold for you, Lieutenant. He's still in Catalina, and—"

"Tell him he cannot get another day off," he interrupted. "I need every swinging dick to be here at work, damn it."

"I don't think that that's what he is interested in, Lieutenant. There's been a shooting over there and—"

Rikelman picked up the phone before I could finish with the information.

"Rikelman!" he shouted into the mouth piece. And then he was quiet. "Okay … Okay … Okay … Let me put you on hold, Donny." He turned to me and said, "Get me Captain Markham and the chief on the phone and the sheriff's AERO Bureau. We need an airship. Call Hospian for a team of detectives to stand by, and I'll get back with him. Get me Clyde's home info and next of kin. Get Father Mike on standby, and let me know when you have done all of that. Understand?"

"Yes, sir."

He went back to Donny and asked him some simple questions. Not anything to do with the "accident" but what time of day it happened, where he was, who he had talked to, if he'd said anything to the sheriffs he should not have said, and where Clyde and McBride were now.

I love to see Rikelman in action. He wastes no time and knows exactly the information he needs and nothing more.

I contacted Captain Markham and the chief and put them both on hold for Rikelman. Markham was at home, and the chief was at a chamber of commerce breakfast meeting already. I let them know I was working on an airship.

The sheriff's AERO Bureau was expecting our call. I don't know how or why they knew, but they asked if we needed two ships or if one four-seater would be enough. I started counting heads and asked if they had a six-seater.

"Nope, but we're working on it."

"Then we'll take two. One for the chief and captain and maybe the lieutenant, and one for our detectives."

"Our detectives are handling the investigation over there," was the reply.

"We know, but the chief would like our guys to take a look at it before the scene goes away."

"Got it," said the nameless person on the other line. I had no idea to whom I was talking but I figured he was more important than me.

"I see by our records that you have a helipad landing on your roof. We'll get in touch with your dispatch when we're a few minutes out. Shouldn't take long."

How do they know we have a helipad? I wondered.

Not long after that, I heard the chopper overhead of the station.

The OHPD union had negotiated a minimum staffing level that we dubbed "MSL." It was really a cash cow for anyone who wanted overtime, but it was done in the name of officer safety.

MSL meant that "they" had to field a certain minimum number of patrol units on each shift. If there was not a minimum of seven units and a U-boat report car, according to the memorandum of understanding in our contract, technically, they had to go to a pre-prepared list and call people until they found someone willing to work on an overtime basis, at time and a half. I usually did two extra shifts a month but not much more, as I valued my time off more than the OT.

That didn't mean that there were not "sluts" out there who would work at the drop of a hat or the ring of a phone. There were always guys or girls going through a divorce, buying a boat or vacation home in Montana, or lusting after a new Porsche.

MSL was used today because Bresani was still in the hospital, and the lieutenant had given away the store to let Simpkins, McBride, and Clyde the Glide go to Catalina. I didn't know who they called in, nor did I care, but somebody was cashing in on Clyde's death. Jesus, what a world.

I looked at the report log that listed crime reports to be taken and saw there were only two. I could get my coffee and make sure that 885 was stocked up, gassed, and ready to go.

The airships had lifted off from the roof, and I figured that the lieutenant and captain and maybe even the chief were headed to Catalina with the detective team right behind them. It made sense when I went through the watch commander's office and saw Sergeant Biddle at the lieutenant's desk.

Kip had escaped getting transferred to days for now, so I was stuck with Biddle.

"Got the reports off the board, Sarge. Got you covered," I muttered. He didn't even look up.

I loaded Shop 885 with my briefcase and put my workout bag on the front floorboard. I didn't want to leave it around the station. Things had a tendency to disappear—in a police station, for crying out loud!

I pulled the backseat out, more out of habit than anything else, checking for contraband that might have been hidden there by a suspect. The Charger had not been used for Patrol as of yet, but I still went through the trunk. I took out the very lightweight ZPAK that I might get a chance to experiment with.

I made sure the test card was in for a suspected drug substance, rather than explosives or gunshot residue. I figured I might come across drugs more than the other items. I placed it next to my briefcase on the passenger side, jotted down the mileage, and was ready to get out of the station.

Thank goodness I had the U-boat.

Chapter 35

Traffic and Bowling Alone

The radio was dead quiet. Not much activity other than our motors writing tickets to the early-morning commuters. Orchard Hill was a drive-through community for those who lived in the wealthy northwest part of the "Hills" overlooking the Pacific Ocean.

We were a pass through from Los Angeles to the Bay Area and the Bay Area to LA. From 0600 to about 0930, traffic was a nightmare, and everyone was late to work or wherever they were going. Speed was not a factor, but trying to beat red lights or driving with your head up your ass—or HUA, as we coded it— caused rear-enders and hot tempers. No one wanted their beautiful car even bumped, let alone totaled.

Our residents were laid back and law abiding. The people from the Hill were complainers and tried to throw their weight around with "I know your Chief or Councilman So-and-So."

"Sign here, ma'am. I'll tell him you said hello," was my standard reply.

I got my first cup of coffee at my favorite spot, Peet's. Even though it was founded by some Cal Berkley graduate, and I had gone to USC, they didn't ask for my first name. Hell, I was in uniform, had a name tag, and, to my knowledge, was the only OHPD that went there. Everyone else went to Starbucks. I think it was because Starbucks gave uniforms free refills, just so they would hang around longer.

With six Starbucks in the city, the chief had received complaints from someone about the number of uniforms having coffee together. He put out a policy that there were to be no more than two uniforms at one time at any one coffee spot, and that included supervisors. The underlying message and tone of the policy was "And you will pay for your coffee."

The bitching started with "So this, from our community policing chief?"

That's why I went to Peet's. Avoid the crowd.

I put my coffee in its holder, backed out, and was leaving the parking lot when I saw some kids that looked like they were peeking into parked cars. I stopped abruptly, and my briefcase and the ZPAK went flying to the floorboard and onto my workout bag.

I pulled out of the traffic lane, continuing to watch the kids as I went around to the passenger side. I was placing everything back on the front seat when I noticed that the ZPAK light indicator was red. *Must be low on batteries*, I figured, making a mental note to check it out when I went EOW.

I saw that the kids were just looking for their friends and were probably just a little rambunctious. Kids will be kids, I guess.

The coffee stayed hot while I took care of the first two report calls. Somebody had broken into a car in a gated underground garage at one of the "secure" condos a few blocks from the station. Not hard to figure it could have been one of the kids that lived there already and wanted a car stereo. I recommended to the owner that he might want to consider a car alarm, but I think that fell on deaf ears. I threw some powder around and found a few prints at the point of entry. Something to work on later, I mused.

The next call was all the way up to our northern border. We joked that it was our "ghetto" because it was right at the edge of the exclusive Hills. They were Orchard Hill's wealthiest community with houses in the one-million range, but the Hills were three-plus million and counting.

The call was listed on the board as an illegally parked vehicle. I don't know why Dispatch gave it to me, but it was a slow day, so I thought, *what the hell*.

I pulled up to the address listed and was met by a lady still in her housecoat, standing in her driveway. I could see a car parked across her driveway entry and noted it was an older model Honda Prelude.

"Could be stolen," I muttered to myself. I entered the plate number into my in-car computer and, without waiting for the result, got out to meet the complainant.

We exchanged morning greetings, and I tried to convey that I could see the problem and why she'd called. She insisted on telling me anyway.

"Have you asked any of your neighbors if it's one of their cars, ma'am?"

"No, I figured you would do that. Look at it. Do you think it belongs in this neighborhood, Officer?" she said with a tone that bordered on snobbery.

I didn't answer her question but returned to my computer screen to see the registration information. It wasn't stolen but had a few traffic warrants for unpaid parking citations in the Santa Cruz area. It was registered to an A. Agopanian in that city.

"What are the names of your neighbors on either side?" I asked.

"On that side, I think its Godfrey, but I don't know the names of those people. They're Armenian."

"Could it be Agopanian?" I asked.

"I don't know, but I guess it could be."

I went to the door of her neighbor's house and was met by a stunningly beautiful middle-aged lady, who introduced herself as Violet Agopanian. She explained that her daughter got in from UC Santa Cruz the night before and must have parked in the next-door neighbor's driveway by mistake. The streetlight was out, so she did not know it was a driveway.

Ms. Agopanian came out and introduced herself to the lady who had called. She apologized and said she would have her daughter move the car immediately.

"Aren't you going to write the car a ticket, Officer?"

"No, ma'am, I think the matter has been handled to satisfaction. What is your name, ma'am? I need it for my report."

"Madison. Julie Madison."

I entered her name into my computerized log, along with the disposition of how I handled the call.

I thought back to a book I had read for school called *Bowling Alone* by Robert Putnam. The focus of the book was that our community bonds have steadily weakened. Do we really know our neighbors less well than our parents knew theirs? How do people stay connected with friends and neighbors? Do people have neighborhood get-togethers, barbecues, or poker games anymore?

Once we bowled in leagues. Now we go bowling alone.

Chapter 36

In-N-Out

The day was moving rather slowly. I finished the two investigations on the U-boat board and checked in with the front desk. "Nothing else right now" was the report from Sara. More important, there was no news about what was going on in Catalina.

Today, Clare had planned a dinner picnic at Dana Beach with the kids and our new Labrador puppy, Bentley, after Geoff's soccer game. We laughingly called him Bentley because that would be the closest we would come to owning one. We had "our" spot at the jetty, where we could see the boats, paddle boarders, and even the kayaker crews as they made their way against a backdrop of seawall and seagulls. It was a summer favorite.

Engineering to get off on time was the most critical challenge of the day. Well, in addition to getting the update on Catalina.

I reflected on my last call. Was the lady evil or racist? I didn't think either. If we have neither evil nor good, are we just neutral? Are we just Switzerland, as my friends like to refer to me and Kip? We label evil, treat it with disdain, and yet recognize that we'll never eliminate it. Traces of it will always be there. It's in our culture, next door, or even in our families.

I waited in line at the In-N-Out drive-through on Temple Avenue for my standard triple-triple with cheese, wrapped in lettuce, protein-style. It was a block from the station, but I still preferred to eat in my patrol car. Clare had packed a small cooler with ice packs and three bottles of water for the shift, as she did every workday.

As I paid for my lunch and drove to the next window to pick up the food, I still thought about good and bad. "If we managed not to do evil," I almost said to the young girl handing me a lap cover, "or remain uncorrupted, have we just not been tested? Maybe our price has not been met."

My train of thought was broken by the radio.

"Seventy-five-U1, 75U1, phone the watch commander via landline."

I acknowledged with a quick "Roger that" to the dispatcher.

Using my cell phone, I phoned Sergeant Biddle on the watch commander's line.

"HH, we're backed up with calls, so I need you to handle a welfare check on Kensington. You know those older Victorian homes in the 400 block? It's 417."

"Yes, sir."

"There's a lady there by the name of Virginia Karsdon. Hasn't been seen for a while, and the neighbors are concerned. Drop by and check it out, and get back to me. It's kind of important. That's all you need to know right now."

"Any word from Catalina and the lieutenant?"

"Yeah, when you finish up, come by the station, and I'll fill you in."

I loved the Victorian homes on Kensington. Clare and I coveted them in our dating years. We fantasized about living on Kensington, even back then. We had done enough research to know that the Victorian homes on Kensington Road were a Queen Anne Victorian style, adapted during the 1840s and made popular in the later 1800s. We walked through a few of the homes whenever one would go on the real estate market, but because of their unique style, they always sold fast or were passed down from generation to generation.

I was about seven minutes away, so I thought about my last "welfare check" and remembered it was a couple of kids left alone while their parents went to the movies. The parents had turned off their cell phones in the movie, and the kids wanted them to come home. They received no response, so they called 9-1-1. Made sense to me.

I thought back to the contemplation of evil again. Seeing evil in our community and in the context of leaving kids at home while you go to the movies is challenging and difficult at the same time. Nobody means anything to happen, do they?

I parked one house south of 417, shut off my engine, and just studied the street for a moment. It was just like I remembered it. The street was silent in its own way. It was like a scene out of San Francisco.

There were no leaf blowers or lawn mowers in the background, yet every yard was neatly manicured, with shaped bushes, lawns that looked like carpet, rock and border formations to accent a geometric pattern, and mailboxes to match the Victorian image. What a postcard! *When did they work on them?* I pondered.

The homes were freshly painted, or at least it seemed that way. They were like dollhouses that grandmother and granddaughter would play with. It was a painted lady on the outside, and I was sure that they were all "dressed" on the inside. Slate-tiled roofs, rooted in the English style, front-facing gables with cantilever porches, columns and bay windows that must have been time-consuming to clean, all sparkled in the afternoon sun. They were gingerbreaded, with every amenity in place, at least from the exterior.

And then there was 417. It was obvious it had not been well maintained. While it was not dirty or unkempt, it didn't have the same allure as the neighbors' homes. It just looked a little run down compared to the rest of the neighborhood.

There was a clear pathway to the porch area from the sidewalk. A wrought-iron archway covered with a morning glory vine that had seen better days bridged the white picket fence on each side of the gate.

I started to open the unlatched wooden gate when a voice said, "Officer?"

I turned around to see a man of sixty or so, dressed in casual but clean clothes. I just knew he lived on Kensington. He just "fit." After six-plus years in police work, I knew who fit in a neighborhood and who didn't.

"Ginny lives here. We've not seen her in a while and were concerned."

I asked if he was the one who'd called, and he nodded his head. "I know Sergeant Biddle, so I called him on his cell. Hope that's okay."

"Of course it is, Mr. ..."

"Bauman. Tom Bauman."

Of course Biddle knows him, I thought. *He's in real estate and would have his claws on all of the high-end homes in Orchard Hill.*

"Okay, Mr. Bauman, why don't you wait here, and I'll see what I can find out."

Chapter 37

Almost Home

Because most of the people on Kensington had a few bucks, to say the least, I figured that "Ginny" was probably on a world cruise or something like that. Bauman had indicated that she wasn't seen much and was something of a recluse. I noticed a shopping cart on the side of the house that was from one of the local markets. It looked like she would possibly walk to the store and use the cart to bring items home. Not a theft, like the signs at the markets say, just a "borrow."

I took my time walking up to the porch area, being cautious not to disturb anything. *Just my training coming through*, I thought. The porch covered the entire front of the house and had a matching second-story balcony structure.

The windows were double paned, and the front door exuded a solid strength that said, "Bet you can't kick this door in." I didn't have to, as the door opened to my touch.

I pushed the door open with my left hand and kept my right hand on the butt of my gun. *No reason*, I thought, *just training*. "Hello? Anybody home?" I inquired in a loud voice. I couldn't see inside yet, so I pushed the door slowly. I noticed the intricate design pattern of the door-hinge plates and made a mental note to let Clare know about them. She was into decorative excess and Victorian hinge plates were certainly in that category.

I didn't get a response after several shout-outs, so I stepped back and radioed for a backup to "assist with the search of a house with an open door." I received a quick response from the dispatcher that everyone was tied up with something and no one was available. I guess that was why Sergeant Biddle gave the call to me. *So much for minimum staffing*, I thought.

I asked Mr. Bauman to stand by the door as I went in and told him to keep his cell phone handy if I needed any assistance.

I opened the door as far as it would go, and a whoosh of musty air came rushing out, pushing its way to fresh air. What I saw as my eyes adjusted to the lighting was nothing short of astonishing.

I called out again. My voice was absorbed by the stacks of newspapers, large dark-green trash bags and balls of rope or twine that were all strategically placed in the entry and what I guessed was a living room. *We have ourselves a bit of a hoarder,* I thought.

I glanced at some of the papers and noted that they were at least ten years old. The *LA Times, Wall Street Journal,* and the local paper, the *Daily Wind,* were stacked throughout the floor in neat piles. I could see a pathway was established, with mini-corridors made between the stacks.

In one direction, the path led to a kitchen, and in another direction, I could see a hallway that led to a staircase. All of the hallways were lined with wainscoting. The ceilings were tin Dado treatments. When Clare and I had looked at the last house that had been on the market, she had researched every element that we would consider if we ever won the lottery. This is the style of home we would seek out.

"I'll clear the kitchen first," I said to my fictitious partner, "and then take the hallway and stairs."

Bauman shouted into the house, "Everything okay, Officer?"

I acknowledged that it was but that I was going to continue looking. *This is not a crime scene, just a welfare check,* I told myself. I didn't see any need to take any more precautions than I normally would. I would still rely on my training. Thus far, only the hinge plates on the door were something Clare would get excited about.

My corridor led me to the kitchen area. It was spacious, with no food on the counter or drawers opened. That was a good sign. The kitchen appliances were customized for the period, as I saw the subtle but distinctive logo "Heartland" that signified a bit of opulence.

I opened the refrigerator, careful not to disturb anything, and noted cheese that had gone bad and some outdated milk cartons, one half-and-half and a 2 percent. *Just like home,* I thought. The cabinetry was meant to evoke those gracious Victorian-era homes, to include a "farmer's sink" with a ceramic front.

Nothing else was out of the ordinary, but after looking again, I saw four more quarts of half-and-half, four jars of pickles, five ketchup bottles, and three jars of mustard.

I continued backward, careful to only retrace my own steps and work my way to the hall and stairwell area. There were three more rooms on the first level, all with ornate wood carvings that spoke Victorian era with straight lines, long ago placed strategically throughout the room. The heavy beveled glass displayed flowers of all kinds added to fruit, birds, and branches. Fireplaces were in the form of gas-powered pot-bellied stoves, but I could not smell any leaking gas lines that would indicate foul play.

The distressed oak wood planks were so natural as to almost blend in to the wainscoting and heavy wallpaper.

The insulated silence came from the massive size of the home and all of the treasures compiled by its occupant. Nothing else made a sound, peep, or even a creak, except for my walking motions.

I cleared the first floor rather quickly, just looking for any signs of life as opposed to searching for a suspect. I didn't look in closets, under beds or the stacks of quilts, or the garden leaf bags full of who knows what.

Just for drill, and so Bauman could hear me, I continued to call out, "Hello! Anyone home? Mrs. Karsdon? Ginny?" I knew no one was home, but it was time to be thorough. And have a witness to it as well.

I looked at my watch and thought, *hey, this could be my end-of-watcher.* I didn't officially get my code seven, but no cop worth his salt goes hungry. Thank goodness for In-N-Out. If people only knew what and how most cops think.

Chapter 38

A Third Story

As I climbed the winding stairs to the second level, I continued to meet the presence of the house and its intricacies. The decorative themes had not changed. The furnishings and attention to detail continued.

I thought back on what I knew about hoarders. Not much. I knew that it was about clutter and accumulating a lot of things that the person thought were important, but no one else did. It was one of those obsessive-compulsive disorders. I knew that hoarders placed their belongings strategically so that the normal living areas could not be used for their intended purpose.

I assumed it was a sickness of some kind and that people accumulated items that they valued by buying or stealing them or maybe just picking up items that had been discarded.

All I knew about the family name was that somebody owned a local car dealership in town named Karsdon's Chrysler-Dodge. Maybe Ginny was related to them, but I wasn't sure how. Maybe Mr. Bauman knew the story, but he was two flights away now. Maybe Biddle knew. There were a lot of maybes going through my head.

I reached the second-story landing and called out again. The sun came through the beveled windows, revealing a prism of colors like a kaleidoscope. I didn't need my flashlight, but it was now my security blanket.

I could see that there were four rooms on this level, and, after looking at three bedrooms, I found a sewing room with an old Singer sewing machine, complete with a built-in light that was still on and pedals to move the sewing needle. That was just another thing to mention to Clare. Maybe when Ginny got home, I could ask if we could come over and look at the architecture. For

Clare, it would be like going through an old department store and conducting an inventory.

I looked down the hallway and saw another set of stairs leading up to a third story. It wasn't as ornately carved as the first stair set, but it still shouted Queen Anne. I figured that maybe Ginny kept her most prized possessions on the third floor, keeping her treasures away from anyone who may tread on the first or second floor. If she was a hoarder, she probably wanted to stay in control of her possessions or whatever she valued most.

Hell, I thought, *I have a bunch of items in my garage that Clare wants me to throw out. Old wrenches and screwdrivers, a box of washers and screws that I might need one day. Maybe I'm a hoarder too.*

I called out again as I rounded the banister to continue my search. The answer came back in the form of a deafening silence.

I figured I had eliminated the porch area, first floor, and the rather expansive second floor. It sure would have been nice to have some kind of backup from other blue suits, but time was not on my side. *Oh well,* I thought, *only have the small third floor and maybe the backyard and detached garage to go.*

What was I looking for? I wasn't sure, but I felt I needed a sense of completion to the search. I owed it to the neighbors, or at least to Mr. Bauman. Or even Ginny.

The house was solid and structurally sound. There was nothing to interfere with anyone calling out, either human or animal. It was as quiet as the proverbial church mouse. Nothing was moving but me.

Sweat was rolling down my back, as it was getting stuffy. I never saw an open window on any level, and I didn't think the house had air-conditioning. All of this caused the heat to rise to the top level. It was becoming stifling under my Kevlar vest.

As I walked along the small corridor, I thought I could smell something burning or something that had been burning. It was paraffin or a candle of some kind. I wasn't sure what it was, only that it was not a phantom smell. It was real.

Up ahead was the last room to be searched. It looked to be shaped by the outside gable with a slanted roofline. The door was partially closed. I inched my way along the wainscoting, being careful not to have my gun belt scratch it. Or worse, have the wainscoting scratch my leather.

Maybe it was like a loft? I thought. Then I slowly pushed the door open with my flashlight hand and placed the other hand on my gun butt. The door creaked like the sound effects in that old radio show my parents used to talk about, *Inner Sanctum*.

Probably hasn't been opened in years, I thought. I was wrong.

Chapter 39

Candles

She was face down on a bed that took up most of the room. Her face was into a pillow like she was diving in a vat of marshmallows. Her long, silver-gray hair was tied in a ponytail down to the small of her back. I guessed that she was a large woman compared to Clare. Maybe she was five foot eight or ten and well over 160 pounds.

Other than her hair covering a portion of her body, she was totally nude. But it didn't stop there. I could see the postmortem lividity and figured she had been dead for at least six to eight hours. In the position she was in, lividity was so noticeable that it was clear she more than likely died right here. Strangely, there was very little blood.

The musty odor was rapidly becoming a mix of still, heavy air and death. The small amount of blood from the wounds had clotted. Interestingly, there was no large pool of blood near any of her wounds. Maybe she had died and was then slit open.

By my academy training and some briefing discussions with homicide dicks, I had a limited understanding of the signs of death. She was in full rigor mortis. The stiffening of her body, from her head to her legs, would have taken about six to eight hours. I knew that it developed in the face and jaws and gradually extended downward to the neck, chest, arms, abdomen, and finally to the legs and feet.

What really got my attention were the candles and where they were placed. On each leg, on the back of the thigh, there was a slit wound with a candle placed strategically inside the wound. The colors of the candles looked odd. At one time, they had been lit. On the back of each arm, the slits were repeated, and small candles placed in the triceps. There was a long, thin purple candle projecting from her rectum. I could tell that the wax had melted down into her anal body cavity. There were blue candles, brown, green, and orange.

Her back was clean of any candles or wax, but there were several slices that appeared to open a wound in a unique and methodical pattern. I was puzzled. I could find no significant accumulation of major bleeding. I opted not to check her pupils or do anything else to see if there were any vital signs, such as a pulse or respiration.

I looked around the room to see if I could find a stash of candles, a knife, matches, or anything that the killer could have used. *Better save something for the detectives to do*, I thought. *Nothing is going to go anywhere, not now.*

It looked like an altar or something from a horror movie. But this was real. Who would have done this? Was she already dead when the slits were made? What was the significance of the candles? The paraffin had covered much of the wound areas, so it was hard to tell if she'd bled out. She may have been suffocated by the pillow and then the suspect, or suspects, did what they did. Her neck was turned in an awkward fashion, so maybe she was also strangled. I wasn't sure of anything at this point.

"I'm sorry, Ginny." That was all I could muster. "So fuckin' sorry."

I don't have a gallows police humor when I am by myself. I've joked with the guys at different death scenes, and the more tragic the better, it seemed. I remembered Donny surveying the maggot hordes on an undiscovered suicide, and out of the blue, he barked, only as Donny could do, "I'm dying for Chinese right now!"

We all laugh at callous comments, but the average Joe will never appreciate our humor. Then again, they're not the ones who will have to make the notification to the next of kin or help the coroner lift a lifeless, stiff body onto a gurney.

I found myself trying to carry on a conversation with Ginny. I thought about the candles arranged on her body like it was a side altar in an old church. Here I was, talking to her and smiling about it, or maybe I was praying. There are some things that are too terrible to laugh about. The humor will hopefully come later.

At the HP. Everything else, the dicks and the coroner would have to sort out.

I made sure that all of my notes were in order. The key to these types of cases is the importance of notifications and the key times—like my getting the call, arrival to the scene, and when I called the detectives. Weather conditions and outside temperature, traffic flow, and the list of initial witnesses are all vital pieces of information. It's needed to refute alibis, show the detailed nature of the investigation, and to establish the environmental conditions that exist from the time we know about the incident. It can never be recreated, so documenting everything is key.

As I walked down the stairs, I called Sergeant Biddle on his cell phone. "Better get the homicide dicks rolling here, Sarge. I have a DB. Looks like a homicide to me," I said, knowing it sounded stupid.

"Is it Ginny?" Biddle asked.

"Probably, but not sure what she looks like. No pictures of her in the house."

"Caucasian, late sixties, long gray hair down to her ass."

"Sounds like her."

"Oh Jesus!" Biddle muttered.

Chapter 40

The Wait

I was coming to grips with the fact that this was the most gruesome crime scene of my short career. Everything else paled in comparison. I had seen people who had died of natural causes or had been decapitated in a traffic collision. This was my "helter-skelter," my "skid-row slasher," my "night-stalker."

I tried to take it all in. My first thoughts were, *do not screw up this crime scene! You can never go back and reconstruct what someone has destroyed.* I didn't want the detectives to blame me for not controlling the crime scene. Not this one.

I received a confirmation from Biddle that detectives were notified and on the way. That could mean twenty minutes or two hours. I looked at my watch. It was almost three o'clock. Where had the day gone?

I knew we were shorthanded today, and there were some detectives still over in Catalina. I didn't know how they selected who would get this one. All of that was a mystery to me. I never could figure out the system for who was on call, whose case it was, or who was just helping. All I really cared about was getting off on time and getting to Geoff's soccer game and then to Dana Beach.

I went to my car and retrieved the crime-scene tape and a few evidence markers. I was not about to start identifying anything or touching anything. I put plastic gloves on and noticed Mr. Bauman approaching me from my blind side.

"She's dead, isn't she?"

"There is a dead body in there, but I don't know who it is, sir. Can you describe her?"

He gave the exact description that Biddle had given. "Ginny was a cut from the past. A bit of a hippie type. Her brother is David Karsdon of Karsdon Kars on Albion Boulevard. They've been around here for over twenty years in the car business." He paused for what seemed like a very long time.

Oh, that Karsdon Kars, I thought. *This is big!*

"I think he bought her the house and gave her living expenses. He's a nice guy, but we don't see much of him. Not much of her, really. Place has been a bit rundown by our standards. The homeowners group was getting up the nerve to confront her on the way she kept the place up. Or didn't."

He would have talked more but I was moving around, trying to make sure that the entire property was taped off and no one would make a mistake and step someplace they shouldn't.

"I'll be waiting on detectives for a few minutes, Mr. Bauman. They'll want a statement from you and anyone else that can shed light on the circumstances."

"Circumstances? I mean, she's dead, but natural causes, right?"

"Don't know yet," I responded as I could see others from the neighborhood now starting to gather. "Just taking a precaution here." *Where the hell are the detectives? I have a soccer game to get to.*

I contacted the Detectives front desk again and was told there would be a "slight delay" in the detectives getting to my location.

"What do you think their ETA will be?" I tried to ask politely.

Janet, the Detectives secretary with the always crusty attitude, said, "They'll be there when they get there, HH. It's almost end of watch for them too."

"Who do I get for this one?" I asked.

"You get who you get," Janet bit back. "But it's going to be Oakes and our new detective trainee, Walker."

"Walker? Red Walker?" I did not see that coming. "These day-watch maggots are killing me! When can I get back to PMs?" Another soccer game missed; it was all I could think about.

Chapter 41

Biddle

You need a scorecard to keep track of things going on around here, I thought. Walker to detectives? Right after a shooting? Who in his right mind would have done something like that? *Never mind*, I thought. I had more important things to think about.

With no one to relieve me, I was stuck at the homicide scene while detectives took their sweet time getting here. Then I'd have to stick around until their work was done, protecting their backsides—and miss another of Geoff's soccer games and our trip to the beach. I didn't know who would be more upset, Clare or Geoff.

I was standing in front of the old Victorian home, looking at the parapet and gables, when Sergeant Biddle drove up in our new Tahoe SUV for supervisors. It was all tricked out with a portable command post setup with video capability. I think you could even sleep in it if you had to. Biddle would probably figure out a way to do that as well.

I had known Biddle since I came to Orchard Hill PD, because he had over twenty years on before I started. He was the consummate old-timer in every way. He never missed a code seven, never got wet, and went home on time. I never saw his name in the subpoena book and for sure never saw him in court. He was mildly overweight, but it looked good on him. His slicked-back black hair, streaked with gray and perfectly cut every day, gave him movie-star looks for someone in his fifties. At over six foot three, he commanded respect without throwing himself around. After a while, I figured out that all he had was a commanding voice that people paid attention to, but he had no follow-through or attention to detail. Just a voice.

Most of us ignored him, did what we wanted to do, and let him know what we did. He would always say, "Great job, guys. Keep it up," even if it wasn't according to the book. It was the path of least resistance; for him and us.

Rumor had it that he was getting ready to retire, because his side job—real estate—was becoming his primary job. Guys had bought and sold houses with him, invested in apartment buildings, and even built custom homes on land he had sold them. At least that's what I heard in the locker room. It was kept quiet because he was a supervisor, and it was not smart to be in business with someone who made money from your transactions and could tell you what to do as well. I just never jumped in to all of that. Seemed like a conflict waiting to happen.

Biddle walked up to me like he had just dismounted from a horse. He looked at the house and then at me. "This is Ginny's place, all right. Can you walk me up to the body, so I don't mess with any evidence, HH?"

Without answering, I stepped in front of him, taking the first three stairs to the porch. I reached back and handed him a pair of rubber gloves, just as he was pulling out a pair from his pocket.

"As you probably know, she was a bit of a packrat, so be careful where you step, Sarge. Just follow me." I traced my previous steps, except for the detour to the kitchen, and finally came to the third-floor landing. "Be ready for a bit of a gruesome scene, Sarge. It's not pretty."

We both put our hands in our uniformed pants pockets, and he followed me into the final bedroom.

Biddle looked at the body, candles, and dried blood, took in the room, and backed out to the hallway. It all happened very quickly but with no real sense of urgency.

"That's Ginny," he said very matter-of-factly. He turned and walked down the stairs in an immediate and fastidious manner, yet with no sense of rush or "I've got to get out of here" mentality.

What was that all about? I wondered.

We reconvened at the front of the house, each of us taking in a bit more fresh air than we would normally do. After what seemed to be a lot of dead air between us, Biddle broke the silence.

"Ginny was a bit weird, to say the least. Did anybody say anything to you? Have you talked with anyone yet?"

"I was going to leave it to the dicks, but I do have the info on the reporting person, and did talk with him for a few minutes. I have a list of all license plates within the block but have not checked the garage here."

"Good, they'll need that and more. Do you know anything about the Karsdon's?" Biddle prodded.

"No, not really. Just that they owned the Chrysler-Dodge-Plymouth—I mean Chrysler-Dodge—dealership on the auto mall row. Seems funny not using all three. When did they stop making Plymouths, Sarge?"

"It's a long story, HH, but they stopped making Plymouths for good in 2000–2001. The name Plymouth came from the pilgrims at Plymouth Rock because Mr. Chrysler used the back end of the *Mayflower* ship as his first logo. Weird how that happens, huh?"

"Yeah, I guess so," I said, thinking that it was interesting information but wondering how he knew it.

"What did you know about Ginny?" I asked, trying to buy time until the detectives showed up.

"I knew her husband, Jack Brick, way back, when they were together. He left her for somebody even uglier and with no money. Go figure. She never changed her name during their marriage, either thinking it would not last or she liked the Karsdon tag. But she's a throwback to the '60s, and the family just tolerated her and her trust fund."

"What's the connection to the dealership?"

"That's her brother, David. He and his wife, DeDee, built up the dealership from scratch here in Orchard Hill. David's father started with Chrysler-Plymouth in Chicago. David learned the business end from him and came out here in the late 1960s. His father was the car dealer to the Mob in Chicago. In the 1940s and '50s the heavy-duty crooks needed cars, but the banks wouldn't give them loans, and they didn't want to pay cash." He looked tired and walked back to his black-and-white to take a seat. "Old man Karsdon saw a business opportunity and went to the banks and cut a deal with them. He would put up his name and credit if they would finance the loans. He went back to the Mob guys and said he would keep them in cars. He tricked out the cars, gave 'em the best deal he could, and only made 1 percent on the loan."

He reached for his notebook, apparently looking for something he could not find. "The Mob guys loved it," he continued. "David's father made money, and the Mob never missed a payment. So there's honor among thieves, as they say."

"How did David benefit?" I asked, now that I was sucked in to the story.

"David was working in the office as an apprentice, trying to learn the business. He said nothing, heard everything and kept his mouth shut."

"So, what's the connection here? With you. Other than knowing Jack Brick?"

"You know those new patrol cars we started to get in? The Dodge Chargers? We're getting thirty of them, and the chief put me in charge of coordinating the change-out. They are great cars and handle fantastic. We're always after comfort, performance, and rear-end crash safety. I think we got all of that with the Chargers. And only two thousand dollars more than the Crown Vic boats or the Caprice."

"Okay, but I still—"

"We get them from Karsdon."

Holy shit! I thought. *Holy shit!*

Chapter 42

The Dicks

I was trying to sort this new information when a plainclothes unit pulled up in front of the house. Detective Oakes and Walker got out and popped the trunk as they talked among themselves. I waved but knew they saw me.

Sherman Oakes had been in homicide since I came on the job. "The Silver Fox," as he was called due to his premature gray hair, was the epitome of a homicide dick—gently overweight; custom white short-sleeved shirts, no matter what the temperature; always a blue tie to match his eyes; a custom-made holster for his Glock that he would never use; and carrying a notebook the size of Montana. Evidence envelopes stuck out of his suit jacket pocket, and as soon as he was through here, there was no doubt that he would find his way to Home Plate.

His parents did have a sense of humor, naming him after the city of Sherman Oaks, which was just a suburb of LA. Why he didn't go to LA, I'll never know. For sure, I wouldn't ask him. He'd bite my head off. Yes, I did have a little fear of him.

Walker had two years on me, but with his shootings and penchant for catching bad guys, he too was up there on the list for "top cop." But now he had reverted to being a "boot" to Oakes. *His nose is so far up Oakes's ass that Oakes could use it for toilet paper*, I thought, laughing to myself. Oakes approached me, with his cigar-breath leading the way.

"What do we have, HH?"

With Biddle standing in the background, I wondered why he was approaching me and not the Sarge.

"We have a DB in the third-story bedroom, sir. She's a bit of a packrat so it's all pretty messy."

"Do not, do not 'sir' me, HH. I'm the same as you, okay? Let's get that straight!"

"Yes, sir … I mean, okay." *What a fool,* I thought. *What a fuckin' fool I am out here.*

I filled him in on what I had done, the witness list, the homicide log, and list of cars. I pointed out Mr. Bauman and the fact that I had cleared the other rooms in the house. "I guess you'll not need me then, huh?" I said, hoping to sound convincing.

"Of course we do, HH. Stick around; I may have more work for you to do."

"But I have a soccer—"

I tried to tell him but he walked away, with Walker right beside him.

I got on my cell and called Clare to break the news.

"Their game was canceled. Brett Simmons, the coach's mother, died today," Clare said. "So stay as long as you need to. The beach can wait. I'll take care of things here. You take care of things there."

Death seemed to be everywhere.

The job of a uniform at a homicide scene is not very exciting. Detectives put all of the information together, but they use the blue suits to do the leg work. The operative term is "gofer." Go for this, go for that, and just go for.

I started to knock on doors. No one knew Ginny very well, but they knew her to say hi to or wave from a distance. *They probably go bowling alone too*, I thought.

Oakes had much more for me to do than just hold the tape or keep his log. Did they all share a gardener? Or a housekeeper? Did anyone have any day-to-day contact with her? Did she get visitors? Had I or Biddle notified the coroner?

Of course we hadn't called the meat wagon, I explained. Department policy is that only the detectives can make that call. It had more to do with the fact they didn't want to wait around while the dicks did their investigation. They just wanted to come in, pick up the body, and move on to the next one.

As the result of too much time being wasted, the Coroner's Office had asked the chief to change the policy to have the detectives call them when they were ready. Made sense to me, but the guys were pissed. It just seemed like it took their authority away. The union was always bitching about anything the new chief was doing. *Who cares?* I thought. *Really!*

Oakes asked me to find out all of that and more.

What the hell did he have Walker for if I was doing all of that? But I would never say that aloud to anyone.

I turned over the list of license plates within a one-block radius. He wanted to go another block on each side. I put together the list of neighbors, with addresses and phone numbers. He wanted daytime phone numbers as well. I obtained the name of Ginny's former gardener, according to Mr. Bauman, but Oakes wanted everybody's gardener. It was obvious that Ginny did not have a housekeeper, but Oakes wanted the neighbors' housekeepers. At least for all of those with Victorian homes.

"And oh, by the way, if they have someone who works on their homes that specializes in Victorians, then get that information as well. While you're at it, find out if these houses are Jacobethan or if they are really Queen Anne Victorian."

How the hell does he know, and why does it matter? I thought.

Whatever information I collected, I gave to him as soon as I got it. That was a mistake. It never seemed complete, so he would send me back for more details. After one or two lessons, I figured it out. *Do not bug me until you have IPS,* or "important police shit."

Bauman was probably going to be my source, as he seemed to be the busybody on Kensington Road. He was full of information.

"Lately, Ginny didn't have a gardener; she did it all herself. Once in a while she would have somebody do the heavy lifting, but I don't know where she got them. I don't think it was any of the regulars around here." He seemed sure of himself, but it would not hurt to verify his information with someone else.

I asked if the homes were Jacobethan or Queen Anne. He looked surprised that I knew the difference.

"These are legitimate Queen Anne. They were built sometime between 1870 and 1910. The Jacobethans were earlier versions of

Victorian homes and were constructed from 1830 to 1870. You can tell, because we have more sophisticated gables and larger porches."

You could also tell that he was impressed that I knew my architecture. Or at least the Oakes version of it. Now that was IPS.

Chapter 43

Home at Last

I finished my part of the crime-scene duties by about seven o'clock. Not bad—four hours of overtime that I could take as "comp time" later. At time and a half, it was almost a full day off. Can't beat that! I dropped by the station to go end of watch, get out of my sweaty uniform—that uniform had death smells all over it, so it was headed to the cleaners—and sign off.

I drove on to my street and pulled up to the driveway. It wasn't Kensington Road. It was home. I walked into the house and was met with a glass of red wine, a smile, and a hug from all three. *It doesn't get any better than this*, I thought.

The kids' homework was done, and Geoff and Marcia were playing a computer game called Dragon Vale. I'd never heard of it and was not sure I wanted to. Had I been gone too long to not know what my kids were doing?

"Sorry to hear about your coach's mom," I said to Geoff. "Too bad about the game being canceled."

"Yeah," he said not even looking up, "but she was old. In her sixties or something like that." We all agreed, even with a twinge of sadness.

"When is the service?" I inquired.

"Not sure yet. It just happened, and they have to sort out all of that," Clare chimed in. "We'll probably go, don't you think?"

"Unless I have to work."

"I don't like this day-shift stuff, Howard. It gets in the way of our lives."

"I know, Muff. I know." Muff or Muffin was our term of endearment for each other. "Dear" was the term we used when things got a bit heated. "Just another month or so and I'll put in a request to go back to PMs. There's too much crap on days. Not real police work."

Not real police work? I thought. Losing three officers, responding to a homicide, and seeing the gruesome results of a sick, pathetic psychopath—what was real police work, anyway?

As Clare was warming up whatever was left from the kids' dinner, I stared into my wineglass and thought about my time on days.

Being on PMs was all I'd ever wanted. It gave me the morning to get the kids off to school with Clare. We would go to Peet's for coffee and share a pumpkin scone. We would come home and work on the house, and I would make motions to start getting mentally and physically ready for work. If the kids were out of school, like in the summer or during holidays, we would always plan something at the beach, a park, or just go shopping at the mall. That was our life, and I loved it.

PM shift made me feel like a warrior, even if I never got into a fight or shot someone. I was engaged in assertive police work—stopping suspicious people, settling disputes, and catching at least one bad guy every day or two. I had a mind-set that I had predetermined responses to a person's movements, where his hands and eyes were at all times. It was always a part of the game. Think about every contact as a possible confrontation. Plan for the worst and react before he could, and you go home every night without your uniform being torn up, using your gun, or even having to threaten its use.

There is a certain mental readiness when you're on the street that nighttime only enhances. I don't like to do things for the first time. I have a plan for every move and a counter plan if that doesn't work. It's not about wanting to be in a fight or anything close to that. It is more about always being prepared to face any challenge and refusing to quit or, more important, winning. Never losing and always winning.

Clare and I religiously work out. Sometimes we do it together and sometimes separately. She has a schedule, and so do I. It includes running, swimming, and yoga. It includes eating right, getting enough rest, and taking vacations together as a family.

I think that's where I get my attitude. The right attitude. Police work is not for everyone, and you don't have to be a charger or go to work each day like you're fighting a war. That, to me, is not the warrior's mentality. Clare and I have increased our tolerance for stress together. We maximize conditioning, but we're not fanatics. It's not how much weight you can lift but how you operate under long periods of stress. We push each other in a positive way. I know what she is doing, and for the most part, she knows what I am doing.

Those of us who make it through are the ones with a survival mind-set and a positive attitude. That's why our language is always positive. The glass is always half full. I save any negatives for the station. Clare does it more for me than for her, because I'm the one faced with the real world.

Every day before work, I do what has become my routine. It can happen before or after a workout, on the way to work, but never when I get inside the station. I learned the trick very young in life. During the 1984 Olympics held in Los Angeles, I saw an interview with Dwight Stones, an Olympic high-jumper who won the gold medal, not for jumping the highest but jumping the same height as the Russian, yet having fewer misses. That was the difference between a gold and silver medal—fewer misses.

A reporter asked him what he does just before he jumps. He commented on the fact that his head bobbed up and down before he started his run to the bar. Stones said, "I'm watching myself take the seven steps to the bar and going over the bar and landing in the pit. I do that three times, and then I just follow my visual footsteps and go over the bar, because I have already done it three times."

The reporter asked him the obvious: "Have you ever seen yourself hit the bar?"

Stones' response was simple: "Why would I ever want to see myself fail? I've hit the bar, but I have never seen myself hit the bar, because I only see success."

I rehearse while almost in a trance. And I do it every day before I get to work. I will have a successful day and not go home in a body bag or banged up. Hell, I don't even want to tear my uniform. I will do whatever it takes to see myself successful. Every day. I play to win every day, but I am not in a war. I just want to go home. Does all of that make me a warrior? Was Dwight Stones a warrior? I don't think so.

And anyway, what is Dragon Vale, and will I have to learn that now?

Chapter 44

The Day before a Day Off

There is always some excitement about returning to work after being off. I always feel refreshed coming back and a bit tired on that last day. Maybe today would be easy and not filled with soap-opera drama like it has been. But then, that is the anomaly of police work. You never know what to expect.

I got my workout in and found the cleanest uniform I had. I just hoped that Norman would not have a formal inspection planned for today. I passed by the watch commander's office and noted that I had a few messages in my box. The board on the wall showed I was working the U-boat again with Shop 885. *So far, so good*, I thought. This could be an easy shift.

When I got back to the station last night, Sergeant Biddle had told me the ugly details about the shooting in Catalina. It was pretty much the same information that Donny had told me over the phone.

According to Biddle, they had finished shooting at one location and were moving to another. They had unloaded the weapons, or thought they had, and Donny was putting Clyde's long rifle back on to the overhead rack in their rented jeep. He apparently misaligned the trigger mechanism and slid the weapon forward on the rack. The trigger assembly was pushed on to the protruding bracket of the rack, hit the trigger, and sent a round right into Clyde the Glide's head. Clyde obviously had not unloaded his rifle prior to giving it to Donny to mount.

The investigation had concluded it was an unfortunate accident.

We all knew Clyde, but as much as you think you know someone, there is always something you don't know. I found out that Clyde had been in the Jesuit seminary, studying to be a Catholic priest. He had quit just before final vows and felt he had a calling to police work instead. He lived with his wife and kids in San Pedro and just seemed to be a regular guy. Now, he was another casualty of the OHPD death list.

And we had not even had a chance to bury Gabby.

With no Kip at the helm today, there would not be an early out, even if I took a gun off the street. I took my time putting books and report documents into my briefcase and sat through a boring roll call by the lieutenant. He was wiped out and let everyone know it. Not that any of us were normal, but he had been on the front lines with all of these deaths. We were just casual observers, compared to what he had experienced.

I strolled to Shop 885 in the parking lot and set up my office in the front seat. I opened my briefcase against the passenger door, turned on the computer and radios and checked the overheads to make sure they were working. I did the customary search of the backseat for contraband, knowing there would not be anything, as the vehicle had only been used for report writing and not for transporting prisoners. It was just what I did every day.

All of the lights were in order, turn signals worked, and most important, the cup holder was where it should be. I had moved the new narco detection device to the front seat on a just-in-case basis. I would rather have it at the ready than rummage through the trunk at an inopportune time. *All in the name of officer safety*, I thought.

First stop was Peet's. I backed in to a parking stall so I could see the front entrance, made sure my belt radio volume was up so I could hear the radio calls, got my usual medium coffee and scone, and returned to the patrol car. My thoughts strayed to whether I should stand by the front fender or just sit in the car. I looked around the parking lot to see people coming and going to the various shops in the small center and decided to sit in the car and familiarize myself with operation of the narco detection device.

The ZPAK, as it was called, came from the military and could detect narcotics, explosives, or gunshot residue. It was a preliminary screening device that gave probable cause to pursue a further investigation. A card is placed in a side slot that presents a visual signal, indicating the presence of the test substance. For

Patrol purposes, the most common item to test for would be narcotics, so I stuck the test card for drugs in the side slot. *Looks pretty uncomplicated to me*, I thought.

It looked like the sampling area was large enough that it would optimize even the smallest sample test. I guess the bottom line was that it needed to be ruggedized, accurate, and inexpensive, or cops would destroy it. It looked to be all of that.

I saw that the actual chemistry happens inside the device and that a positive test would be reflected by a red light. A negative test would show as a green light. *Strange*, I thought. *Shouldn't it be just the opposite? Shouldn't it be red for negative and green for positive?* Then I remembered the first time I looked at the ZPAK. It had fallen onto the floorboard and my workout bag from the front seat a few days ago. The red light had come on, and I assumed that it had not been charged properly.

Was there something wrong with the device, or had my bag come in contact with something?

Chapter 45

The Messages

I made a mental note to stop by the narco dicks to see what they knew about this ZPAK and if I had one that was inoperable or BO.

I finished my coffee and looked at the messages I had picked up from the front desk. There was one from a Mel and one from a Mrs. M., both with numbers I did not recognize. I used my personal cell phone to call Mrs. M. It was the lady with the illegally parked car problem from what seemed a million years ago. Mrs. Madison, I remembered. She called to apologize for her actions on that day and did not want me to remember her as a bigot or, worse yet, a bad neighbor. I assured her that I understood, but she kept on insisting that I stop by so she could further explain herself. I assured her I would.

I asked if she had called and left a message as "Mel," but she had not. So on to the next call. After six rings, I was greeted with a very abrupt voice-mail message: "This is Mel. I'll call you back if you leave a number." It was an unfamiliar female voice.

I decided I didn't know a "Mel," and went to punch off, when call waiting showed the number calling back. I answered, "HH, here."

"Who is this?" asked a female voice.

"Who is *this?*" I countered.

"Why are you calling me?" the voice asked coyly.

"This is Officer Hamilton of the Orchard Hill PD, returning a call."

"Oh, now it makes sense. This is Melissa Flowers, but I left the message days ago."

"I'm sorry," I responded, "but I've been on some days off and just saw the message this morning. What can I do for you?"

"I don't know if you remember me, but I visited your department a few weeks ago and told you I had applied for OHPD. Do you remember?"

"Yes, I do." I tried to sound casual, knowing I was talking to one of the most attractive women I had seen in a long time.

"I passed the first part of the test and have an oral board test coming up in a few weeks."

"That's great," I said, trying not to seem too interested.

"I was wondering if we could meet for coffee, and you could give me some pointers on taking the oral test, you know?"

There was a long silence as I thought about her request. A notice had circulated that we were testing, and the chief was looking for volunteers to be on the oral board for entry-level applicants. I could not remember if I'd raised my hand in briefing or not.

"Sure," I finally blurted out, without really thinking of all of the ramifications. "I could do that."

"Great!" she said. "Can we do it next week? I need some time to get my thoughts together so you can have something to critique."

"Okay, let's meet at Peet's on Albion in Orchard Hill. How about next Monday at 10:00 a.m.?" I said, while sitting in the very parking lot where we would meet.

"Sounds good. See you then, and thanks, Officer Hamilton."

"Call me HH."

I pressed disconnect on my cell phone and sat there for just a moment. Was that the right thing to do? What did I know about oral board preparation? I had been lucky when I applied for OHPD. It was a time when they really needed people, so I could have said about anything and they would have hired me.

Kip was right. This day watch was full of maggots. Things that had nothing to do with warrior police work but just got in the way. Every day; every damn day.

I called the front desk to see if there were any reports hanging to be assigned.

"Not right now," answered Sara, our Services Officer that Simpson had the hots for.

"Good," I said and then advised her and Dispatch that I would be with the narcotics detectives but available for calls.

I needed a quick lesson on the ZPAK. I must have missed the training sessions at briefings while I was off, because the device' didn't seem to respond right, or I had my head up my ass. "Probably both," I muttered.

As I drove to the station, I kept checking the radio, as it was extremely silent. Either nothing was happening today, or my radio didn't work. *I think it just may be one of those days.*

My mind drifted to the conversation with Ms. Flowers. I knew I could get my hands on some oral board material from our HR department but—and it was a big but—was this the right thing to do?

"Of course it is," I rationalized. "What could hurt by coaching a possible candidate for our department? It couldn't hurt anything and may even be a benefit."

After that bit of logical thinking, I realized that I was on a day off next Monday. I didn't recall that Clare had anything planned. It was going to be just a good catch-up day around the house.

I could just take a break and leave the house for an hour. I would let Clare know that I had been asked by a potential candidate for the department to help with preparation for the test. I wouldn't be gone for more than an hour. What could it hurt?

Would I let her know that candidate was a girl—and that she was a ten on a ten scale? Maybe. Then again, maybe not …

Chapter 46

Narco Dicks and Surprises

They had tried to recruit me into Narcotics more than a few times. I knew just enough about the job that I didn't want it. At least not right now. There were some things I liked about the assignment but too many things I did not.

First, there was plenty of overtime. That was the best part. Narco dicks made a lot of money from overtime, just because of the nature of the job. The downside of that was they worked odd hours and for nights and days at a time.

They could work twenty-four hours straight. Most cases developed where you could not pull off a stake-out or undercover operation and just say, "Shift is over. I'm going home." It just didn't work that way. Clare would never understand. She might like the overtime but not the time away from home.

The worst part was, for some reason, you had to look like a dirt bag. Long hair, maybe a beard or at least a constant five-day growth, and clothes that looked and smelled like you got them from the Salvation Army. Some of those guys even looked like they had not bathed in a week. Not my cup of tea.

I walked in to the Narcotics office carrying the ZPAK and the instruction booklet. The office was really just a big square room with squad tables, desks and chairs, a couple of interview rooms, and an office for the lieutenant in charge, Lieutenant Cartwright.

As I remembered, eight detectives and two sergeants worked both Vice and Narcotics for OHPD. There was not much vice to enforce in Orchard Hill, but the narcotics and other activities they were assigned kept them very busy. I recalled that they worked with "LA Deuce," the regional narcotics task force for the entire south side of LA County, but other than that, I didn't know much about their activities.

I saw Sgt. Sam Barber and recognized him because he was still clean-cut, having just been assigned to the unit. There were two office doors behind Barber's desk, and both were closed. I could hear voices but had no idea who it was.

"Is this a good time, Sarge?" I asked Barber.

"What do you have, HH? We are a bit busy right now."

"I'm having some trouble figuring out how this ZPAK works. Are you familiar with it?"

"Yeah, we found those at a narco conference and talked the boss into getting them for our department. We used asset forfeiture money to buy them, so they didn't come out of the city's budget. What's the problem?" Barber queried.

"That's cool," I said, "but if I, get a positive reading, shouldn't the green light come on after I insert the card or does the red light mean a positive? The manual is confusing because the red light keeps coming on."

"What do you mean?" Barber said. "You should only get a positive reading with a red light, not a green one."

"Well, I had it on the front seat and had to stop fast, and it fell to the floor onto my gym bag, and when I went to pick it up, the red light came on."

"Had there been narcotics on the front floorboard of your patrol car?"

"No," I responded. "It's one of the new Chargers, and it hasn't been used for Patrol yet. I'm working a U-boat. To my knowledge, nobody else has used the car accept for report taking."

"That's a bit strange. Have you used your gym bag to transport any drugs from any arrests that you've made?" Barber was trying to ask questions as innocently as possible.

"No," I responded quickly.

"Go get your bag, HH, and we'll see what's goin' on."

I left the ZPAK with Sergeant Barber and returned to Shop 885 in the parking lot. I noticed several extra cars in the lot but didn't take much notice, as I now was more interested in our little experiment.

I retrieved the gym bag and noticed that I still had a smelly T-shirt and shorts, along with my running shoes with stinky socks stuffed inside. *Probably should take those clothes home and wash them once in a while*, I thought.

I returned to the Narcotics office with the gym bag and set it on Barber's desk. Barber wasn't there, and I didn't see the ZPAK where I had left it.

I was looking around for the ZPAK when Barber came out of one of the back office doors. He was holding the ZPAK.

"It works just fine, HH. I just got through testing it. Is it okay to let me see your gym bag?" he asked as innocently as he had before.

"Sure, that's why I brought it up here."

Barber took the gym bag and asked, "What's in here, HH?"

"Just my workout shirt, running shorts, socks, and shoes. Why?"

"No reason."

Barber brought up the ZPAK to come in contact with the gym bag and activated the test button. In about five seconds, the red light came on.

"See? That's what happened, and I couldn't figure it out. Red means a negative reading, right? The green is a positive, right?"

"No," Barber said rather sternly. "Red is positive. Let's take out your gym clothes and test them separately." After testing each piece, Barber looked straight into my eyes with an accusatory glare. "They test positive as well."

"What the fu—?"

I didn't finish my statement because I looked behind Barber and saw Lieutenant Rikelman and a man and woman I didn't recognize as OHPD.

They had come from behind one of the closed doors. Rikelman was in his civilian clothes but no tie. The other two were dressed in street clothes that signaled undercover narcotics, most likely from the regional task force.

Silence filled the room.

Chapter 47

Not Me

I took a deep breath but decided not to say anything. Barber broke through the frost that had enveloped the room.

"When was the last time you washed your workout clothes, HH?"

Before I could respond, Lieutenant Rikelman jumped in. "Whoa, whoa, whoa, Barber. Where the fuck are you going with this line of questioning? Do you know what that sounds like?"

I kept my silence.

"Let's start over with this, shall we?" Rikelman said, taking the lead, as Barber realized he had been outflanked. Rikelman summarized what had transpired since I had walked in the door to make my innocent inquiry. He received affirmation from Barber on the facts, and I nodded but remained silent. The man and woman had yet to say anything.

Rikelman looked directly at Barber in the way that only Rikelman or Norman Bates could. "Are you interviewing Officer Hamilton, or interrogating him, or what?" Rikelman looked at me with a look that said, "Keep your fucking mouth shut and let me handle this."

"I was just asking a simple question, Lieutenant," Barber said.

There was silence again. After what seemed an interminable amount of time, Rikelman turned to the man and woman—I assumed they were undercover officers—and queried, "Is this the person you saw at South Bay Emergency Hospital entering the hospital and going to room 222, where Officer Bresani was being treated?"

In unison, both answered in the affirmative.

"And is that the bag he was carrying when you saw him enter the hospital and go to Bresani's room?"

The answer was the same.

"And did he leave the hospital still carrying the bag?"

Yes, again.

I am in some deep shit here, I thought. *Really deep shit! And I don't know why.*

Clare always said that sometimes, silence can be your friend. I was not sure that was the case right now. Barber and the two undercover detectives were staring at me; Rikelman was not. He was staring off into space.

"Do I need a rep here? Do I need Meecham?" I asked, just before my mouth started to dry out.

Meecham was OHPD's resident squint. He was a ten-year street cop who was smart as a whip and just geeky enough not to look like a typical cop. Everyone knew he was going to law school and as soon as he passed the bar, he would leave the department and defend cops accused of wrongdoing.

Right now, he was getting his wings as a defense representative for officers accused of misconduct. If someone filed a "one six," or formal complaint, you contacted the Orchard Hill Peace Officers Association, or OHPOA, and they would arrange for Meecham to be there to protect your rights. Peace officers had a unique Bill of Rights that made sure that they received a fair investigation and didn't get trampled on by the public, their supervisor, or the brass.

All of that was going through my head as Barber glared at me.

Rikelman broke the silence. Somebody needed to. "Whoa, hold on here, Barber. You don't know this officer like I do. I just need five minutes with him, and we can straighten this out."

"Fine with me, Lieutenant," Barber said as he moved his chair away from his desk. "Be my guest. You seem to know what's going on here."

Rikelman looked at me, and his head motioned to follow him to one of the back interview rooms. "Give me five minutes, maybe ten," he said.

I followed him to the room he had just left with the under-covers or UC's. He opened the door and asked me to sit down and take a breath.

I sat down and then asked the question that was swirling in my windstorm of a head. "Am I in trouble here, Lieutenant? What the fuck is happening?"

Chapter 48

Are You Kidding Me?

I took another breath as Rikelman stared at me with those Norman Bates eyes I had always feared. They penetrated into my soul as I tried to match his look with my own. He won again. There was deafening silence.

"Do you know who's in the room across the hall from us right now?" Rikelman finally asked.

"I have no idea, Lieutenant."

"Are you sure?"

"Of course I'm sure! How the hell should I know who's in an interview room in Narcotics? I came in here to get some training on a piece of new equipment. That damn ZPAK! And now this?"

He paused and then nodded. "Never mind. Okay. I believe you. So you have no idea what's going on here?"

"No, but you could tell me." I started to gain some semblance of confidence.

"I am not going to tell you much. Just that the people in the next room are Lieutenant Cartwright, head of Narcotics, and Johnny Bresani. Does that mean anything to you?"

"Bresani?" I asked incredulously.

"Yes. That's all I am going to say right now, but let me assure you that you do not need a rep. You just need to tell me the story of how you got to visit Bresani while he was in the hospital. Got it?"

"Okay. That's easy."

I explained everything, ending with Bresani's having called from the hospital to ask me to pick up some CDs from his locker. I said I got the master key from the watch commander's desk, as nobody was around. "Am I in trouble for that? Is it about the master key?"

Rikelman shook his head. "No. Go on."

I told him about the CDs being wrapped in paper stamped "Clinton" and that I'd put the CDs in my gym bag, returned the master key, and taken the CDs to Bresani in the hospital. "That is it, Lieutenant. That's all I did."

"Stay right here. Do not move. Stay put, understand?" Rikelman walked out of the room before I could respond.

For now, I was not going anywhere—although I didn't know if it was because I wanted to get to the bottom of this or because they would not let me leave.

What was Bresani's role in this? I wondered if it was some kind of narco investigation, or if the chief would walk through that door and ask for my badge and gun. I counted 175 perforations in each of the acoustical tiles that lined the walls of the interview room.

Finally, Rikelman and Barber came into the room. I hoped somebody had some answers. And they did.

"We'll try to fill in what we know, HH," Rikelman said. "First, I want you to know I just had a quick meeting with Barber, Cartwright, and the chief, and they are completely in agreement with how we are going to deal with you."

"Deal with me? What do you mean 'deal with me'?"

Rikelman glared at me in exasperation. "You got caught up in something big, HH. Only you didn't know it. I'm convinced that you had nothing to do with any of it. We know that now. We're going to treat you like a witness, a very cooperative witness."

"*What* do you know now? Geez, is anybody going to tell me what the hell is going on here?"

"You deserve to know, but you are ordered—yes, ordered—not to repeat anything you hear. Understand?"

I nodded in agreement.

"So here is the short version …" Rikelman stood up and started his lecture. "Bresani did not get robbed on the beach. He was beaten up by two Columbian drug dealers that he was working for." I started to say something but he held up his hand and continued. "Bresani had shaved a kilo of coke that he received from these guys, mixed it down, and then tried to sell it back to them for his cost.

He has been dealing for about a year and knew everything that was going on regarding the drug trade in the South Bay. That's how he made his arrests. The regional task force got wind of it from his competition and snitched him off to a UC. We've been tailing him for about six months, but we also wanted to move up the food chain to see where it was all coming from. We knew Bresani was not going anywhere. He had it too good."

The dust was starting to settle in my windstorm of a brain at this point. I could see where this was headed. Or at least I thought so.

"Johnny is not the smartest knife in the drawer. He started to get a little cocky with his sources. He even kept a kilo in his locker at the station here. That's where you came in."

I nodded like I understood and I guess I did, for now.

"Johnny almost ate it on the beach," Rikelman said, "as these guys were serious about fucking him up. They just got interrupted by some witnesses. We tapped his phone at the hospital and knew he called the station but didn't know he talked to you until we listened in. You did what you did, and we knew that you were delivering his stash to the hospital. We were waiting for you and saw you arrive, carrying the gym bag. You're lucky no one stopped you who didn't know what you were carrying."

No shit! I thought.

"The task force team followed you to Bresani's room, saw the drop, and saw you leave. We made sure you got the citation on your personal car, just to tie in any loose ends if you denied you were at the hospital."

Son of a *gun*, I thought. *Those were the dirt bags I saw in the ER and in the hallway as I left the hospital room.* They were creeping me out, and they were narcs. And they were doing surveillance on me—a suspected drug-dealing cop!

Chapter 49

Worse

It was all starting to sink in. Barber took over for Rikelman. "When you brought the ZPAK in to see if it was working right, I knew you were okay. Well, I was almost sure. Nobody in his right mind would place himself in jeopardy or be so stupid as to walk in here with the story that you did. Just for the record, however, red is a positive for a controlled substance, and green is a negative."

I was still not certain that Barber totally believed I was innocent. I could see it in his eyes. Rikelman had the upper hand, however, so I felt like I had a friend in the room.

"One more little piece of information that you should probably know, HH," Rikelman added.

I said nothing, not being sure I was allowed to talk at this point.

"You knew that Bresani was Gabby's ex-brother-in-law, didn't you?" Rikelman asked.

"Yeah, but I don't know all of the details. We didn't socialize off the job," I responded.

"We know that too," Rikelman said rather smartly. "Well, Bresani was married to Gabby's little sister Belinda. Gabby ... let's call him by his name, Charles, just to respect his memory"—we all agreed that nicknames were for the living—"Charles introduced them after he came on the department and met Bresani. The marriage lasted about three years, no kids but a lot of turmoil. Charles sided with his sister, of course, but no one knew the details about the divorce except Belinda, Vivian, and Charles."

Rikelman took a deep breath. I could tell that this was taking a lot out of him. He had been through too much with the Anderson case and "Clyde the Glide" McBride. "Bresani and Belinda were divorced over a year ago. Belinda started to confide in Charles about Bresani's abusive behavior. He had already moved Vivian out to Canyon Lake in anticipation of his retirement. He didn't want to be around the department and specifically did not want to be around Bresani. He worked shifts around him, so they wouldn't run into each other."

Makes sense to me, I thought. It was like a dysfunctional family. Working with your ex-brother-in-law on the same department was pretty weird.

Rikelman continued, "The commute was killing Charles physically, and he started staying with Vivian's mother or at Belinda's apartment and would go home on his days off. It was not working out well. Then, Belinda laid the bomb on Charles that Bresani was dealing dope."

"Holy shit!" I said out loud involuntarily.

"Yeah, HH, all of this took a toll on Charles's heart."

"Bresani killed Charles! He fucking killed him!" I said.

Everybody in the room seemed to agree.

Rikelman had always been one for drama, but this series of events didn't need any more.

But there was more.

"Here is where it gets interesting, HH," Barber said. "On the day of his death, Charles had made an appointment with Lieutenant Cartwright to go to the regional task force. Cartwright thought it was to arrange a loan for Charles to work there. It was really set up to spill the beans on Bresani. Belinda had pushed Charles to do something. That was why Vivian came in to town. Not just to pick him up from her mother's. They were going to have lunch after his court in the morning and go to the task force. Charles was under a lot of pressure."

It was my turn to stand up. I was the only uniform in the room, yet I had started out as the accused. "What now?" I asked.

"This is ours to handle, HH," Rikelman said. "We're moving forward with prosecution as soon as we wrap up the investigation. Bresani has a coke habit he has to kick, but he can do that behind bars. You get to go out there and handle your radio calls. Thanks for being so patient with us, but we needed to put all of the pieces of the puzzle together."

I walked out of the interview room feeling an overwhelming burden had been lifted from my shoulders. I looked back at Rikelman, Barber, and a very quiet Lieutenant Cartwright and nodded. Not much more could be said, and I think we all knew it.

I reached for my workout bag.

"Hold it, HH. That's evidence," Barber said in his official tone. "We'll need to keep it for a while. Send it to the lab and have it tested. You can have the stinky clothes, but the bag is ours."

"Can I at least have a bag to carry them out of here?" I asked.

"Sure. And take the ZPAK with you as well. It works." Barber smiled when he said that. We all did.

Chapter 50

What Now?

There was sweat running down the back of my bulletproof vest. I took what seemed like the longest walk ever taken from the second floor through the station to where I'd parked my car. It was not hot inside or outside, but I was exhausted.

I wondered if I should have asked for a rep and if I was going to still be in trouble for being stupid. Christ, Bresani was going to prison, and I'd delivered him the goods that would put him there.

I was seeing the world of police work in an entirely different light—daylight! I'd been so comfortable working the PM shift and putting real bad guys in jail. I was over two weeks on this shift and had not made one arrest. *What the hell is wrong with this picture?*

I looked at the uniformed faces I passed in the hallway on my way to the patrol car. I knew these guys and girls. Or did I? Who was going to die next? Who was going to be fired or go to prison? Who was going to be the next captain or chief?

I needed another cup of coffee before I did anything. I walked to the front desk, and it was business as usual. I grabbed my list of report calls from Sara, advised Dispatch I was back in service, and realized it was already 1400 hours. I had been in Narcotics for over three hours.

Sara commented as she handed me two calls, "Boy it's been a real slow day, HH. Absolutely nothing going on. I have to keep hitting my handheld to make sure it's still working'. How is your day?"

"Kind of slow on the streets, Sara, kind of slow."

I made my way to the parking lot and Shop 885. I put the ZPAK in my briefcase and rolled my window down just in time to hear, "HH, got a minute?"

What now? I thought.

I always hated those words because it was usually when I didn't want to be bothered, and it never took a minute. I looked up to see the chief. He looked like he had just finished a run. He was sweaty and a little out of breath but looked just like he stepped out of a magazine anyway.

"I hope they were not too hard on you in there. Everything is going to be okay. Keep doing the job the way you do it. We will handle this garbage."

"Thanks, Chief. This day shift is an eye-opener."

"Stick around; it only gets better," he said, walking away wiping sweat from his brow.

I wondered whether it was a coincidence or planned that I kept running into the chief.

Chapter 51

Dinner

"Can you get a babysitter tonight so we can go out to dinner?" I asked Clare through the hands-free Bluetooth connection in Shop 885. "I'll try to be home on time."

Clare knew there was something going on but did not pry, prod, or inquire.

"How about Steak & Bake, the place where the baked potatoes are the size of footballs, with that chicken giblet gravy, cheese sauce, all-you-can-eat Caesar salad, the cheese bread, and decadent onion rings, and oh yes, the steak?" I gave her the menu but she knew it by heart as well as I did.

The S & B, as we called it, had been our restaurant since high school. We had gone to her senior prom dinner there and every other special occasion. It was just a good excuse to load up on carbs and comfort food that broke through our regular lifestyle of healthy eating.

I had my one-weekend-a-month off coming this Friday and did not have to go back into the abyss until Tuesday. I was yearning for yard work, "honey do's," and family. Not necessarily in that order, but manual labor sounded very good right now.

"Just to be safe, I'll make reservations for seven o'clock and see if Mom can come over for a few hours," Clare quietly responded.

"Should be home by five. Love you."

I pulled out of the station parking lot and headed west to the ocean and my next call. Two malicious-mischief reports later, I still had forty-five minutes before end of watch. I was close to Mrs. Madison's house, so decided to stop by and get that issue off my plate.

I put myself "out for investigation," or code six at her address, just to make sure I did not get another call before EOW. I wanted to make sure I got off on time.

I parked one house west of her location, because it looked like her gardener had pulled his van and trailer full of gardening equipment across her driveway.

How poetic, I thought, remembering my first visit to her home and how her unknown neighbor had invaded her space.

I walked past the gardener's van and noticed the placard on the door.

Kensington English Gardens, specializing in Victorian restoration and English serenity gardens. Bernard "Bonzo" Kensington, proprietor.
There was a local phone number and artwork, like a Monet painting, on the panel. *Very meticulous*, I thought. Clare would like this. I took a quick picture of the van with my cell, complete with the placard and phone number.

I found my way to the front door of the Madison house and rang the bell. Mrs. Madison didn't look much different from the morning when I'd seen her a few weeks back. It was late in the afternoon, and I could swear she was wearing the same thing I saw her in the first time we met.

She was rather matronly but gentle and typically matured for a woman in her sixties. Nature had been kind to her, but she was not doing anything to preserve her youth like some women do. She had been working in the backyard with the gardener—obvious from her gloves and long-sleeved shirt, and a hat to protect her from the sun. She had light perspiration above her upper lip. She clearly loved what she did.

"Here," she said, motioning to me. "Come sit on the back patio." Without asking, she poured two glasses of ice water and beckoned me to sit.

I looked at her expansive backyard with walking pathways and tiered levels. It went to the top of a hill with a riding path for horses that separated it from an even more expansive wilderness.

"My husband and I are passionate about our gardens."

"I can tell," I said as I absorbed the massive display of seemingly every kind of plant imaginable. Clare would do anything to see this. *Maybe I could take some photos on my cell phone and show them to her at dinner tonight*, I thought. Better ask first.

"We're going to tear out much of what you see here and turn it into a complete English garden. But that's not what I wanted to talk to you about." She again motioned for me to sit. "The last time you were here, Officer Hamilton, I was not very hospitable. I want to apologize for any impression I may have given you about my neighbors and our relationship."

"You don't owe me an apology, Mrs. Madison. I have neighbors too," I responded lightly.

"No, I do. I am not a bigoted person. I was in the Peace Corps years ago and served in some rough countries all over the world. I know about living in poverty, and I know about living with different … people."

She seemed to be choosing her words carefully now.

As she spoke, I saw a figure about halfway up the slope of her yard and kept my eye on what I thought could be an intruder.

She saw me looking and said, "Oh, that's Bonzo, my new gardener. He's an expert in English garden landscaping and is going to help us redo the entire yard."

I relaxed and smiled. She could tell I had my antennae up, and my attention had been drawn away from our conversation.

"How did you find him?" I asked, hoping she would keep talking about her yard instead of our previous incident.

"You know those homes on Kensington Road, down the hill?"

I nodded.

"Well, Bonzo does all of those homes on the street and has for years. I think his father even did the original landscaping and some of the home restoration. He may have even been related to the people who originally named the street, because that's his last name as well. Or it is for business purposes anyway."

I looked up the slope again and saw Bonzo methodically pulling plants out of the ground, working the soil, studying the plants and looking at his handiwork. He was bundled up in black pants, heavy boots, long-sleeved khaki shirt over a sweatshirt, and heavy garden gloves. He wore a wide-brimmed straw hat to protect his face from the sun, so there was not much of him to see.

"I have been on his list, waiting for an opening in his schedule. He called last week, and we jumped right on it."

I asked if I could take some photos of her backyard to show Clare, and she beamed with pride as she posed, waving her arm to show it off. I took a few pictures with her in the foreground and thanked her for the ice water.

We walked to the front of the house, and as we were saying our good-byes, she said, "We are having the Agopanians and their daughter over for a backyard barbeque this weekend. Thought you would like to know. You and your wife are invited, of course."

"I'll check with her, but I think we have plans this weekend," I said, trying to avoid eye contact.

I think we both knew it was a bad idea, and we let the matter drop.

Chapter 52

Steak, Bake, and Bread

I told Clare that we had a lot of catching up to do but that it could wait until our dinner. She made reservations for seven o'clock.

I was home by five. It was hard being a day-watch maggot. It was Friday night, and I was going to dinner with my wife while uniforms were hitting the street, looking for the bad guys.

"What's wrong with this picture?" I muttered to myself while I took a quick shower.

When I saw how beautiful Clare was, all decked out in a new outfit that she had no doubt selected for this evening, I thought, *Nothing is wrong, absolutely nothing!*

Her earrings glistened like they were radiant diamonds, but I knew better. I had yet to give her real diamonds. She wore a white pants suit with a small silver necklace with a "C" etched with fake diamonds. Her hair was curled like she'd just come from the beauty shop, and her nail color—fingers and toes—was a deep red, almost black, that made her look like she just stepped out of a magazine.

She beamed at me. "The necklace and earrings are from Anthropology, pantsuit from the Nordstrom Rack, hair by Connie, and nails by Clare. All for just over a hundred dollars. Do you like?"

"Do I like?" I echoed as I handed her a glass of white wine. "Wow. Is that really you? That little housewife in the bathrobe I left this morning?"

"It's Steak & Bake time, and I am not talking just about the restaurant, so let's get started, honey."

"How about if we just get a room?" I suggested.

"You're not getting off that cheap. It's a package deal. I starved myself all day."

"Sounds good; let's do it," I said sheepishly.

We kissed the kids, thanked her mom, and were out of the house by six thirty. It was 1830 at work, but six thirty at home. I was thinking about what had happened that day as we strapped ourselves into the car and backed out of the driveway.

She saw the look in my eye and said, "Hey, knock it off, Howard. Leave the station at the station. At least for tonight. We have a lot of family stuff to catch up on and a full weekend to unwind, okay?"

How does she know what I was thinking? I thought. "It's a deal, but I do have a fun thing to share that is just too good not to discuss. Not really work-related, but ..."

"Maybe Howard. Maybe."

As we walked into the darkened restaurant, the smell was unmistakable. It was a mix of the cheese bread, mesquite barbeque, and a crackling fireplace. The ambiance extended to the waiting area—red velvet wallpaper, erotic paintings of semi nudes on the walls, just as it was when we'd come here for senior prom. The paintings almost went unnoticeable because they blended so well with the heavy wood décor that spoke of a time past.

Our table was ready, and we sat with our backs to the wall, looking out at the other patrons. Clare looked more elegant than she had in a while. *Or is it the wine?* I thought for just a moment. We turned sideways toward each other and engaged in talk of family and weekend plans. It all sounded so good that I almost forgot what my day had been.

As we moved to the red wine, the chef brought out the salad cart and prepared a mix of romaine lettuce with their special seasoning, anchovies, and dressing. Another waiter came by with a basket of cheese bread wrapped in aluminum foil. It was too hot for us to open, so the waiter pried the foil with tongs and placed the golden-brown crusted jewels across the small bread plate on our left. We both stared at the still sizzling cheese sauce that was melting into the crevices and along the crust. What better time to bring it all up.

"I may have found us a new gardener today," I said. I hoped to tie everything into our house plans.

"Really?"

"Yes," I said as I cut the cheese bread into bite-sized pieces. "It all happened on a call I had."

"Tell me about it."

"You know those homes on Kensington Road, the Victorian homes that we just love?" She nodded and smiled.

"Well, I found the guy who does all of the landscaping for them. He's doing a new English garden design on a house I went to. I have his van photo on my phone, Clare. Want to see?"

"Not right now, Howard. Let's just enjoy the dinner."

"I think I'll spend some time this weekend playing with design ideas to take our yard to that next level. Seeing this yard today really motivated me. What do you think of doing everything in English garden-type plants?"

"I think it's great, Howard, but I have something else to talk to you about."

"What's up?" I asked.

"The kids and I have discussed it, and we kind of like you working days and being home at night. It seems like we're more of a family with you at the dinner table and having periodic weekends off, rather than our being quiet in the morning, and you creeping in at all hours." As she finished speaking, she immediately took a big bite of salad as she waited for my reply.

I took a bite of cheese bread and gulped too much red wine. I finally got everything down my throat as my mind was trying to grasp the enormity of her statement. "You mean you had a family meeting without me to discuss this?" I asked incredulously.

"Well, we just discussed it," she said defensively. "I don't think you could call it a meeting. Just a ... a ..."

"Oh, just a discussion, huh? Was it put to a vote or anything like that?"

"No, no, nothing like that. Geoff actually brought it up. He said that even though you might miss a few of his games, just like you do now, that being home at night was like having a regular dad."

"A 'regular dad'? What the hell is a 'regular dad'? I am a regular dad." I didn't mean to be so loud, but my voice carried past our little cubicle, as I saw a few heads turn in our direction.

Clare took a long sip of wine. "He didn't mean it like that, Howard. He just would like to see more of you at this stage in his life."

I thought about it and decided to come at this from a different perspective. It was apparent that what I was trying to do was not going to be fruitful. "Clare, the work on day watch is so different. I am having a tough time adjusting to it right now."

"What do you mean, different?" she asked after another sip of the grape.

"Let me tell you about today," I said. "You know about what I did on the PM shift, but today was just a typical example of the bullshit on days." I then told her the story about Bresani, Gabby Hayes, Sergeant Barber, Lieutenant Cartwright, and Rikelman. "I thought I was in deep trouble today, Clare. I thought I could get suspended or lose my job. Rikelman was the only person on my side." I finished my salad, went for the cheese bread, and washed it down with more wine.

"Norman Bates came to your defense? Really?" She laughed so hard, I thought she would tear up. Her hand went under the table and rubbed my thigh. We both laughed at her comment.

"Yes, dear, Norman Bates saved my ass!"

The wine had done its job.

Chapter 53

Pots and Perennials

The main course came, but we turned down more wine, knowing that there was more at home. The cheese bread soaked up the wine, as did the steak, onion rings, and baked potatoes with all of the fixings. We would both head to the gym this weekend to work it off, if the sex did not get rid of the calories. Both would seal the deal.

My first priority for the weekend was to get smart about English gardens. I checked some websites and found an expert out of the University of Vermont, Department of Plant and Soil Science. I didn't know they even had such a major.

English gardens are not just for the English countryside. They can thrive anywhere and add charm and tranquility to any garden. Done right, they evoke a natural feeling because they look like you have not planted them; they just grow and create their own beauty.

According to my research, there are three keys. Select three or four main colors to create continuity. Then, group flowers together, creating balance and harmony within the bed by using the shaping of the leaves, blooms, and plant texture. Create some curved borders at least three feet wide so that as you wind through the garden, your eyes get surprised by the next turn.

A third ingredient that seemed important was the garden accessories. Things like entry gates, trellises with vines, benches, a fountain, or even statues. I thought one comment said it all: "Your tools, even the water cans, should be antique, not Home Depot."

The last recommendation was to make sure you picked potted plants that were the same color. They could be different sizes and shapes but the color keeps a foundation for the plantings. The newer English gardens were using bold colors, even if it was not the traditional look.

The usual trimming tips were included, and a long list of plants was recommended, none of which we had. Roses, both climbing and free-standing, delphiniums, foxglove, clematis, and all of the varied perennials had to be added to the mix.

The most critical element of all, I thought, was the money. The expense was for the initial outlay. The list of accessories could be endless. I guess that's why you work with experts who know how to do the job right. And maintenance, maintenance, maintenance. It all sounded like a lot of work and a lot of money.

Well, there was overtime.

The weekend was moving way too fast. The list of things to do seemed endless. There was Geoff's soccer game on Saturday morning, gymnastics class for Marcia in the afternoon, grocery shopping at my old store (where I worked before the PD), and maybe church on Saturday night so we could sleep in on Sunday.

On Sunday I found myself puttering around the yard, trying to visualize an English garden. Our property was about a quarter of the size of the Madison's yard. I figured they had about an acre, including the slope. We had no slope, just a plain grape stake and cinderblock fence. Now, I was thinking we needed new fences.

Last night had been a dream evening with Clare. After the discussion of staying on the day watch, being a decent dad, and going through the Bresani escapade, we settled into a very romantic evening.

After ten years of marriage, she was still stroking my thigh under the table at our getaway dinners. The anticipation of making love when we got home was almost more than we could stand. It could have happened right there, had we had one more glass of wine.

I pulled out my phone to look at the photos I took at the Madison home. I could see what the professor from the University of Vermont was saying about the plants and pots. Maybe I needed to drive by the Kensington homes, because they seemed to be more in line with my yard design plans. The Madison yard was too much for me to grasp, just out of sheer size.

I was thumbing through my photos and accidently hit my calendar icon. I looked at Monday and saw an appointment for ten o'clock. I opened it and saw three letters in caps: "MEL."

Oh shit, I thought. Melissa Flowers. At Peet's.

Her number was in my phone, so I could call her and cancel, but my first thought was, *why should I? It's just an innocent meeting to talk about her oral board. Or is it? Yes, it is, dammit,* I said to my inner self. It was.

I'll just keep the appointment, brush up on my oral board tips, and get on with my day. So as not to alarm Clare, I'd just say I was tutoring a prospective applicant for OHPD and leave it at that.

It's been said that there are lies and damn lies. I don't know who said it, but leaving out critical information is not a lie. It's just not the entire truth. There are always incentives to underreport information. Providing only partial information is not cheating. The media does it all the time. If I worked it right, I would not lie. I would just leave out critical information that would unnecessarily complicate our lives. Unnecessarily.

Chapter 54

Monday

It all went very easy. Too easy. Just a casual, "I'll be back. Meeting somebody for coffee to talk about the job."

And off I went.

I arrived at Peet's about five minutes early. I picked a table that was visible from the street and opted not to get a coffee until she arrived. I had obtained some information on taking an oral exam and how to prepare. Maybe I could just give it to her and be on my way.

She arrived right on the dot at ten o'clock. We said our hellos and got our coffees and returned to the table. She was dressed in Levis and a sweatshirt with running shoes and no makeup. It did not matter, as she still looked radiant.

"No uniform today, Officer Hamilton?"

"No, I'm on a day off. And call me Howard, or HH."

"Oh, I'm sorry. I didn't want to bother you on a day off. I know how important they are to you and your family."

"Not a problem. This shouldn't take too long, and I could use the break from yard work."

I handed her a packet of the information I had collected. I explained to her the process. There would be a Human Resources specialist, a member of the community, and one member of OHPD, either an officer or detective.

"Oral boards are no different from you and me," I lectured. "They are just people who want to hear you talk and try to figure out a little about you and how you make decisions."

She listened very attentively, looking right at me, or through me, I felt.

"Your key is preparation. You need to know about our department and about our city. There's information on all of that in the packet. You also need to know about the job, but that should not be too difficult, because you come from a police family."

"That can be good and bad, I guess. What do you think?" She queried.

"I agree, so I would talk to your dad about that. I think the fact that you want to distance yourself from LA is good."

She was taking notes as fast as I was talking.

"You should try to do another ride-along just before your board," I suggested, remembering that I had set her up with Rikelman for a ride-along. That seemed so long ago. "Be prepared to talk about yourself, your employment history, current events, and why you picked OHPD. Know your strengths and weaknesses. Dress in a conservative suit and stick to the classic combinations."

"I have a date in a few weeks to get another ride-along in."

"I know you'll make a good first impression when you go in there, but remember to greet each person on the board with a strong handshake and a 'nice to meet you' greeting. Don't sit down until they tell you. Oh, and if you can, ask the proctor the names of the board members, and pay attention when they introduce themselves. Generally, the proctor will introduce you to the chairperson, whoever that is, but the others may introduce themselves."

"Wow, you really do know this stuff, Howard."

"Not really. It's all just common sense. Now, while you're in there, keep eye contact with each board member and not just the one who asks the question. If you don't know something, don't try to BS them. Just tell them you don't know, but you will get the right information if placed in that situation. You're not expected to know all of our policies and procedures."

"That's good to know." She continued writing.

"Just be yourself and you'll be fine, Mel."

"Yeah, right! I have screwed up interviews before."

"With any other PDs?"

"No, just some dead-end jobs that I didn't want anyway."

"Okay, at the end, they will ask you if you have anything else to add. Take that opportunity to tell them again why you want the job, why you're the most qualified, and all of that crap. Just take a few minutes to summarize everything and then stand up, shake their hands, and leave as confidently as you came in. And don't take the wrong door out and walk into a closet!"

We both laughed and finished our coffees.

"I think that you'll do well, and that there will be many more oral boards in your future on OHPD, Mel. You're ready. One last time now—do your homework, dress the part, make a good first impression, be yourself, and don't BS them."

"I guess that goes for a lot of things, doesn't it?" she said as she gave me a very firm handshake.

"I guess it does. I guess it does," I said.

We parted company, and I watched her walk to her car on the far side of the parking lot. No hug or other eye contact. I was home free, and all of the worries of what could have happened had been for nothing. I passed the first test and was relieved.

At least for now. At least for now.

Chapter 55

Three Days

For a weekend, I got a lot done. I was consumed with the kids' activities, reflected back on the great dinner on Friday night, and was basking in the afterglow of some great lovemaking with Clare. We looked at the photos of the Madison backyard and the gardener's van with the logo of what I thought was a Monet painting. Clare was motivated.

The remaining time had been spent in looking at my yard and deciding whether or not an English garden was indeed feasible.

With three days off, it was easy to get back into the family mode. The meeting with Mel had merely been a minor distraction. I didn't give much thought to OHPD. Not until my phone rang, and I looked at a number I did not recognize.

"This is Howard," I answered rather tentatively.

"HH, Walker here. When are you due back at the shop?"

"Red, what's up? I didn't recognize your number. Coming in tomorrow. Why?"

"Well, here I am, a detective trainee, and Oakes went on vacation. The nerve of the guy. In all fairness, it had been planned, but they've not teamed me up with anybody. I have some leads to work on with the homicide on Kensington and could use some help. I'm up to my ass here."

"Can you get me loaned to Detectives?" I asked, thinking I knew the answer to that question.

Walker was quick, "I don't think so, but you can try to stay on the U-boat and just do some snooping for me. I'm spending a lot of time getting my victim's profile worked up and dealing with the crime lab on shit. Nothing else is getting done."

"Can we meet tomorrow? In the morning?" Walker pleaded.

"Sure. I don't know who the watch commander is going to be because Rikelman is on a special assignment, but I'll work on it.

Do you have a list of witnesses who need to be interviewed? Stuff like that?"

"Yeah. Do you have a tape recorder?" Walker asked. The conversation was going back and forth in staccato fashion now.

"I do. Department-issued, too," I replied.

"Bring it," was Walker's order. "I've not had a chance to even interview the original RP. What's his name? Bauman or something like that."

"I can do that," I flicked right back. "I think I even have his number in my notebook. At least get an initial one out of the way, and if you need anything else, you can go back when Oakes gets back from vacation."

It will also give me a good excuse to go back by Kensington and take some photos of the yards, I thought rather selfishly. "I'll meet you right after briefing. How about Peet's on Albion?" I thought I would probably be there anyway.

The soccer games, gymnastics, great dinners, and the English garden were in the past. The workweek had begun. In earnest.

Chapter 56

Coffee

As usual, I went in a little early to pump some iron and shower at the station. It was easier than waking everybody at zero-dark-thirty in the morning at the house. I had a clean uniform to start the week and a fresh change of civilian clothes to keep in my locker. Being a creature of habit, that was my little ritual when I had more than a few days off—prepare for the unknown.

Getting in the station early also permitted me time to polish my leather and make sure I had fresh ammo. And I could catch up on the crime happenings and rumors that occurred while I was off. Mostly, it was for the rumors. It was always good to see if the dolphins were running.

The dolphins were loose regarding Bresani. Everybody thought they knew. I played dumb and just let everybody fill me in regarding what they'd heard. Some of it was true, and some was just embellishment to fill in the holes. All in all, it was pretty much on target. Bresani had been dealing dope, kept some at the station, was beaten up by his competition, and was rolling over on them in exchange for a lighter sentence. The lighter sentence part I did not know about.

No one mentioned the Gabby Hayes connection, and I didn't say anything. Nobody knew about my delivering the dope to his hospital room or that I had been interviewed by Rikelman and the task force. I hoped I could keep it that way.

Sergeant Biddle was still the watch commander while Lieutenant Rikelman was on a special assignment. No one knew, but everybody figured it was the Bresani matter. Biddle was not the great communicator and so briefing was short and sweet. No training, no crime updates, and no rumors.

I advised him that I was meeting "detectives" at the Kensington homicide scene to provide some uniformed visibility for an hour or so. He was fine with that. I figured he would be good with anything to further the Karsdon investigation.

There were two calls on the report board, and I took them both. Mondays are notoriously busy, with business owners returning to their shops and discovering they've been broken into, or a car dealership experiencing burglaries from their auto fleet, or a school being vandalized over the weekend. *Just your typical day in the neighborhood*, I thought. And it was.

Walker was waiting for me at the coffee spot. With me in uniform and him in a shirt, tie, and sports jacket to hide his weapon and cuffs, everybody figured him for a detective, I guessed.

We sat at the same table where I'd sat with Mel. *Weird, just weird*, I thought.

We talked about family and what we'd done over the weekend. Walker did not seem that interested in talking about the homicide, at least not right away.

Finally, he blurted out, "Have you ever killed anybody, HH?"

"No."

"I am having some … some problems. Head problems." He pointed to his forehead and looked around to see if anyone was listening. "And nobody to talk to. I'm driving my wife crazy, and I don't care what you say—I refuse to see that damn shrink of ours, because all he says is, 'You did a great job, John, a great job. You took a bad guy off the street!' Shit, I know that, HH, but it was permanent. Fuckin' permanent. You know it, HH. This is a game-out here. I don't care if we see these guys again. The two I killed will never be seen again. Never!"

I tried to get to the crux of the problem and not belabor the issue. "Hey, Red, I'm no shrink, but we can talk. I always wondered if you took any of your 'incidents' seriously. You seemed to be holding up pretty well. At least that was how it looked to all of us."

"Really? You couldn't tell?"

"No, we just figured you had it handled."

"Handled, hell. After this last one, I was a basket case. My wife, Kelly, thinks I have a death wish and would prefer to be taken out by a shooter than to do the shooting."

"To be honest, that has been discussed."

"I sit in my room for hours and just replay them over and over again. It's like a video I keep seeing. And it always ends the same. I win; they lose."

"That's the way it's supposed to be, John. We *are* supposed to win. That's what warriors do. Win!"

"Then why don't I feel good about it? Andy Johnson didn't win," he countered.

"Sometimes things happen for a reason, John. They just happen for a reason."

He stared at me without saying a word. "You know, HH, that is the stupidest thing I have heard, and it makes way too much sense. What are you, a fuckin' psychologist or something?"

"No, John, just married a long time."

We both laughed like little kids, and everybody looked at us. Or it seemed that way. We finished our coffee, promising to meet again just for laughs. As we walked to our cars I said, "Do you really need help on the Karsdon case?"

"Hell yes, I do. That really is why I called, you know. Let me know what Bauman has to say. I've interviewed some of the neighbors but no one knows much. Or at least they're not talking right now."

"Any suspects?"

"Not yet. Find me one."

"When is Oakes back?"

"Two more fuckin' weeks. Can you believe that?"

"Let's wrap it up before he gets back then," I joked.

"You're on, buddy. You are on."

Walker walked back to his unmarked detective car with an energy I had not seen in him before. It must have been the coffee.

I handled the report calls within the hour. I took the basic information and had the victim sign off on my laptop. Electronic signatures had been quite the new revelation as we entered the digital age, but I was still not comfortable with it.

I maneuvered my Charger toward Kensington Road. It was Monday, not a street-sweeping day. Those were reserved for Wednesdays, with trash days on Tuesdays. The city was well known for its planned execution of public services in addition to its overall strategies for traffic calming and park utilization. Each resident received three trash cans, except for the residents of Kensington Road. One trash can was for refuse, one for recycled items, and one for green waste.

The Kensington Road people received dispensation from use of the green-waste trash can because they had petitioned the City Council that "their gardener" would dispose of all greenery and that it was built in to their gardening fee. They did not want to pay for it twice. Because of the clout they had with the council, it passed unanimously.

I thought I would see what cars were on the street and compare it to the notes I had taken on the day of the Karsdon homicide.

As I approached the entrance to the Kensington Road community of homes, I was struck by the fact that this homicide was still being referred to as the "Karsdon homicide." Normally we nicknamed them without using the victim's name. I made a mental note to talk to Walker about it.

Our department was no different from many others. Gallows humor has helped us keep our sanity over the years. I have heard cases discussed at some of our in-service training with other agencies. It seems that OHPD gives nicknames to our officers, but other agencies give nicknames to their more egregious cases. Some of the names are funny, some are stupid, and some are just gross. "Hag in the Bag" referred to a case in LA where a woman's body was found in a trash bag. "Bitch in the Box" was a case in San Francisco where they found a hooker's body in a refrigerator box. "Dunce in a Dump" was a body we found in a trash can of an old dope dealer who had overdosed on his own bad drug.

I drove up and down the street several times, jotting down license plates and vehicle descriptions. I noticed the Kensington gardener van and the attached trailer parked on the street. I could not see the gardener in the front yard of any of the homes on the street. It was that time of year. When early October arrived it would mean colors would be changing throughout the city, but more so on Kensington Road.

Maybe Bonzo is in the backyard of one of the properties, I thought. I took a few photos of the lineup of cars on each side with my cell phone. Another just-in-case move.

I pulled up to Mr. Bauman's house and saw that he was sitting on the porch, reading a newspaper. He was decked out in a short-sleeved white shirt and bright blue tie. Bauman sitting there like he was waiting for me was *convenient*, I thought, *very convenient*. Too convenient, was more like it.

Chapter 57

"Mr. Wilson"

I found a vacant parking space a few houses away from the Bauman residence. I jotted down the license plate numbers and vehicle descriptions. I wanted to make sure that the number matched the car and that I was not dealing with cold plates on a hot car. Having the make and model would at least ensure I was dealing with cars that belonged in the area. I would check out the registered owners later.

I could see Mr. Bauman peering over his newspaper as I pulled to the curb. Black-and-white patrol cars have a way of getting attention whether you are just driving down the street or parked. Everybody likes to watch. It's black-and-white fever.

I unbuckled the seatbelt and casually got out of the car. I think he could tell we were destined to talk, as he put the newspaper down and gave me a wave.

"Hello, Mr. Bauman," I called out—the greeting was the way Dennis the Menace greeted his neighbor, Mr. Wilson, on the television show. He was dressed for work, but I was not sure if he had a job or was retired. *Something else to discover*, I thought.

Mr. Bauman looked like someone who had either earned his place in the sun or inherited his position. I would bet that he earned it, but I was destined to make that determination before leaving.

Even from the Bauman porch, I could tell that the interior of his home was Victorian in every way.

"Doing well, Officer Hamilton. Doing well. How goes the investigation on Ginny?"

"Coming along, coming along," I said, mirroring his double greeting. "That's why I'm here to talk to you, if I could."

"Certainly. I was wondering when that would happen. Are you handling the investigation?" He seemed to know that detectives should have contacted him long ago.

"Oh, no. Just trying to help out wherever I can. Detective Walker will be by in a few days. He asked me to stop to see you, just to let you know we were not asleep at the wheel."

"I see."

"How long had you known Mrs. Karsdon?" I thought I could gently nudge him to start a conversation.

"Thirty-plus years. I knew her and her husband. We were all friends in the neighborhood, you know. All of us. Thirty-plus years."

"That's a long time, Mr. Bauman, a long time." I hoped the less I said, the more he would say.

"Yes, it is. Yes, it is."

I looked at him to continue, and I was not disappointed.

"Since her husband left, she had become something of a recluse. Everybody felt sorry for her. She was handy at anything. Had a workshop in her garage, could do electrical, minor carpentry, and gardening. Ginny was very self-sufficient, very self-sufficient."

"What can you tell me about her ex?" I asked, making reference to Sergeant Biddle's buddy, Jack Brick.

"Jack was an okay guy. Pretty low-key. Pretty low-key."

"Where is he now?" I thought he was probably dead or living across town.

"He moved to Florida—Pompano Beach. Haven't seen him in over ten years. Ten years."

"I guess that eliminates him," I said, smiling. "Exes always are the first suspects, you know."

"Not that he would try to slip into town unnoticed and do the dirty deed, Officer Hamilton. But he had no reason. If she was alive, he would keep getting her money. If she died, he'd get nothing. That was the deal."

"Do you have contact information on him?"

"I do, I do."

"If you don't mind, I'll fill in Detective Walker on our conversation and have him come by to take a formal statement."

"That would be good, good, Officer Hamilton." He paused for what seemed a senior moment and asked, "Who else have you talked to?"

"I'm not sure who they have talked to. Any ideas?" The line was thrown out there like a true fisherman.

"I was an engineer, Officer Hamilton. An engineer. Not working now, but my mind is still sharp. There could be a few people who know what happened. Or maybe just bits and pieces. I'm sure you know how to build a case, so I won't insult your intelligence, but Ginny was an interesting lady with some real quirks."

"We're looking at all of that right now," I said.

"Walk her property, and you'll see some things that may help you out. Now, I want to assure you that I don't know who did it, but I think the answer is there somewhere."

Our eyes met, and he communicated very effectively that he thought this was a very solvable case. Very solvable.

I took Bauman's recommendation literally. Somehow, I felt like we would need to talk with him again. "We" being the operative word, as I felt more a part of this investigation than any call I had ever been on. It was becoming a part of me like no other.

I decided to walk the neighborhood. I went from home to home, and patterns of landscape as well as architectural design became imbedded in my mind. I was looking at the same things, yet each was different. There were various grain forms of gravel walkways, yet they wound around the sides of the homes differently, each with its own pattern. Multiple sets of wrought-iron furniture graced each of the grounds, yet none was the same.

And there were the sculptures, statues, angelic figures, stone-carved bodices with cherubs, and mystical ladies. Was I in London or Liverpool, Downton Village or Manchester? It was hard to tell.

I took mental video streams of each yard as I passed by the gates, pathways, and drives. If I turned my back on the streets and the distractions of cars that were parked or passing by, I had visions of being elsewhere. And for various moments, I was transformed to another time.

I came to the Karsdon home and gazed at the entrance. I walked through the entrance gate and to the porch. The path to the porch was lined with iron crescents depicting various phases of the moon. The gravel walkways were splotched with a mix of baby tears and oxalis as they wound around to the detached garage behind the house.

The Karsdon house was different, but I could not put my finger on what that difference was. Yes, it was in an advanced state of disrepair compared to the other Queen Anne residences. That was to be expected. Ginny had lived alone, and the house had sat for almost two weeks. I looked at my notes. The homicide was on September 22 and today, was the sixth of October. Exactly two weeks.

The house was still sealed with the telltale red crime-scene tape placed strategically on each door and doorjamb. I assumed that Walker had not had the opportunity to do another walk-through of the house since the body was removed. We needed to do that—and soon.

Eventually, the property would be turned over to the family. I was now certain that the house contained the information we needed to solve this case. Would we see things on our next visit that we had not seen on the day we discovered the body?

Very possible, I thought. *Very possible. And Mr. Bauman thought so too, didn't he?*

Chapter 58

Hook Up

As I finished the otherwise uneventful day shift, I made a mental note to contact Red. I knew that it was my obligation to get in touch with him. It was his case, and he should know about anything I found out.

I returned to the station, unloaded my black-and-white, and went straight to the report-writing room to finish up meaningless crime reports that would go nowhere. It was close enough to end of watch that I knew I would be home on time again. Other than the Karsdon homicide and our multiple deaths, everything seemed trivial.

I was wandering the hallways on the way back from getting a Snickers bar from the vending machine when I saw Walker and Rikelman come out of an interview room.

They seemed an odd pair—Norman Bates and Red. They both saw me at the same time and simultaneously stated, "Just the guy we wanted to talk to."

I looked around to see who they were looking at. "Who? Me?"

"Yeah, you." They mirrored again. We all smiled at the exchange.

"Got a minute, HH?" Lieutenant Rikelman queried.

"Yes, sir. For you, I do." We had not talked since my encounter with him on the Bresani matter.

We went back into the interview room. Rikelman sat in the cold metal chair reserved for suspects and directed me to sit in the only other chair in the room. Walker stood. Something was up. Something was definitely up.

"Detective Walker has been telling me about the assistance you've been providing him in that Karsdon homicide."

"Yes, sir."

"Does the case interest you, Hamilton?"

"Yes, sir, it does. Very much."

"Oakes is on an extended vacation up in bum-fuck Wyoming somewhere, and we're not sure when he gets back. Walker, Lieutenant Hospian and I met to discuss what we could do to help out on this case. He"—he pointed to Walker—"seemed to think you knew about the case and that if Patrol could spare you, you guys could hook up, on a temporary loan at least, until Oakes gets back."

"When would it start, sir?"

"ASAP. Tomorrow, hopefully," Rikelman responded in a rapid-fire fashion. "Do you have something else planned that would delay it?"

"No, sir, it's just that I would have to talk it over with Clare."

"Jesus, HH, do you tell her everything you do here? That could be a problem," Rikelman responded.

"Yes, I do … well, most things." My mind wandered a bit after that question, but I caught myself just in time. "Well, shift assignments, but not the nuts and bolts of what we do, sir."

"I understand, HH. I'll let you sit with Walker here to talk about hooking up tomorrow. Just keep me posted on any overtime, because I think it still may come out of my budget and not the detectives'. I'll deal with Hospian on it. Any other questions, Hamilton, or are we done here?" he said in his typical staccato rhythm. He will always be a little different.

"We are done, sir. We are done."

For some unknown reason I was talking like Mr. Bauman. Repeating my phrases twice. Now I was thinking that way as well.

Chapter 59

Update

I still had thirty minutes left of my shift. Dispatch showed me out to the station on reports.

"I have one report to finish up, Red. Can I meet with you in about fifteen in your office?"

"Done," he replied.

I hurried through the report and told Biddle I would be upstairs in the dicks' bureau.

All I knew about "dicks" was that the term came from the comic strip character, Dick Tracy. Police slang was different from agency to agency, but that one stuck with just about everybody. It was like we had created an urban dictionary or something. Some things captured our humor, though some of it was too colorful to print. It seems that in addition to our codes for the statutes we have our own language, but the various PDs I have been to all refer to it as the "dicks' bureau."

I found Red in an office. Another one of the chief's changes was that he took detectives at the working level out of individual offices. It was his opinion that there was better communication between everyone if they worked in an open squad bay with tables. Only the supervisors had private offices. I think it was another one of his LA things. Red found a vacant room so he would not be disturbed, and that's where I found him.

"How's it going?" I asked.

Red looked up from his black binder with dividers, photographs, and paperwork. "Some days, a black-and-white was much easier, HH."

"I see that. Hey, I was out to Kensington today and talked with Mr. Bauman. Have you had a chance to talk with him?" I knew the answer already.

"Does it look it?" Red said, rather exasperatedly. "Sorry. Didn't mean to jump on you, but I am drowning here. No Oakes, and everybody else here is working on his own thing. You'll be a lifesaver. When do you start?

"Will tomorrow be soon enough?"

"No, but it will have to do." Almost as an afterthought, Red said, "I've been thinking ... how about you call Bauman and arrange an interview with him for tomorrow. Ask him who else we should interview and set up those things before you go home today. I can use the help, HH. Shit, as it is, I'll be here till nine tonight anyway."

I agreed to take care of what he wanted. *I can do that on my cell on the way to Geoff's last soccer game*, I thought. Another good job of engineering.

What I failed to realize was that it also might be my last little bit of engineering.

Chapter 60

First Day—The Murder Book

I had gone home and broken the news to Clare. Her only response was a smile. Then she thought about it. "You'll need some nice dress shirts, a few ties, and some new slacks, so let's go shopping this weekend. I'm excited."

"I guess I can get along this week, because detectives work a four-ten plan. Red said we are usually off on either Fridays or Mondays, but with this case there may be a bunch of OT."

I came in at 0600 and got a good workout, showered and was in the detective squad bay by 0715. It felt strange not putting on my Kevlar vest. It was like I was half naked. Detectives did a lot of shuffling paper, going to court, or interviewing witnesses. That did not require a vest. You just had to know when you needed one and were obligated to have one at the ready when it was needed.

I looked around the room. I was not alone. Maybe half of the detectives were at their tables, going over papers, working on computers, or on the phone. Coffee was made, and somebody brought in a box of fresh donuts, coffee cake, and muffins that were begging to be chosen.

I wandered around the squad bay but did not see Walker. I knew most of the detectives, some by sight only. In almost seven years, I had not been up to the second floor more than a dozen times. There had been no need, so I really had no idea what went on.

I walked to the office where I had last seen Walker. He was sitting there just as I had left him last night. I noticed that he had a clean shirt and new tie but I smirked. "Did you sleep here, Red?"

"Just about. Sit down. Let's lay out a game plan for the week."

We discussed the case for about an hour. He went over the autopsy report, the list of potential witnesses, and what had come in from the sheriff's crime lab.

"The trace evidence is backlogged, but the prints were taken by our CSI guys and nothing really came up. Her prints were all over the place, and some of the people she had working on the place periodically were in all the right places but nothing out of the ordinary."

"What did they say was the cause of death?" I asked, thinking I knew the answer.

"According to the autopsy, her windpipe was damaged, and she may have been choked or strangled. She also suffered a heart attack, maybe from the strangulation. She was dead before the suspect made an altar of her and slit her. That's why there was not as much blood. Not sure where she was killed, because she was moved to the bedroom on the upper floor and placed on the bed. The postmortem lividity confirmed that. Sherman attended the autopsy and has asked for more of a workup on some other things they found. He didn't indicate what it was before he went on his annual 'killing Bambi' trip."

"Killing Bambi?"

"Yeah, he goes deer hunting every year at this time and just walked away from this one. Has a cabin in Wyoming somewhere and takes a few of the guys with him. Every October. Leaves me with the case and putting together my first Murder Book."

"What's a Murder Book?" I asked, hoping I didn't sound too stupid.

Walker pulled out a thick black binder from his stack of papers. It had over twenty dividers, the case number, and "Karsdon" on the spine.

I could see that Walker was a bit stressed. "Let me get a cup of coffee, and I'll look this over," I said.

Walker took a deep breath and as he walked out of the office said, "Give me about an hour, and I'll be ready to go. Review the book, make some calls, and set up some interviews based upon what you find in there."

"Got it," I responded trying to be somewhat flippant.

I took the Murder Book and found my way to the coffee. Somebody had made fresh coffee but there were no cups. Then I realized that each detective had his own personalized cup. I went to the shelf to find a paper cup. I felt like a stranger in a crowd. No one really acknowledged I was there. Everyone seemed to be focused on what they were doing, and there was not a lot of idle chatter. I found an open squad table that looked like it might have been Oakes's. I took the hour to familiarize myself with the book.

It's an efficient way to keep things organized, I thought. Some things just cannot be transferred to a computer, and it appeared that this was the case with homicides.

From my academy training, I knew that homicide investigations hinge on the accuracy and completeness of the written reports and case documentation. Memories blur with time. With attorneys looking for ways to get their clients off by any means necessary, the days of stuffing things into an envelope or your suit pocket were in the past.

I could see that the dividers broke the paperwork down into official reports, informal reports, and more formal progress reports. There were forms for witness information, transcribed interviews, press releases, and evidence. The various crime and evidence reports, autopsy documents, photographs, and even crime scene surveys with measurements and sketches were cataloged. Phone numbers scratched on a notebook page were sheathed and saved.

I worked backward from end to beginning and found the most important item in the front. It was a chronological log listing of everything that Walker and Oakes had done thus far. And I mean everything—dates, times, who they talked to, and a brief summary of what was found. They even logged when they called someone and got no answer.

I went back to the photos. The first set of photos took us down Kensington Road as we approached the house. The street sign and house numbers were evident. The next series was the grounds, the gardens, and approach to the porch area, followed by a photo of the front door and the entrance down the hallway. The packrat conditions were depicted in living color, along with the kitchen, refrigerator contents, and every room on the first floor.

The camera then led to the stairwell to the second floor. We walked up the stairs and went room to room until we came to the last room, where I found Ginny.

What could have been termed gruesome or even sickening was really just evidence now. Various colored candles protruding from wounds I had observed firsthand. The candle in her rectum, her head turned in an awkward manner, perhaps signifying strangulation. The photos were now just documentation. I would need to study them to make sure I did not miss something important. Right now, everything was important, and we had to go in a hundred directions before we focused on one or two items.

I looked at the last page of the photographs and noted a computer chip. It was labeled with the case number and the victim's name. The notation indicated it was a video of the crime scene. It was also date stamped with "September 22" and the year.

Ah, technology, I thought. Maybe we should book this into evidence and not keep it in the book.

I stared at the photos one last time and then thought, *where are the photos I took with my cell phone of the cars parked in the neighborhood?* I had e-mailed them to Walker, but where were they?

Chapter 61

Stupid

It was 0930 by the time Walker came up for air.

"Get the idea, HH?" he asked, referring to the Murder Book.

"Uh-huh," I said, and we then discussed the plan for the day. I suggested that we try to contact Bauman, do a sit-down interview, and maybe develop a list of all of the frequent workers on Kensington. I indicated I would like to see his profile of our victim.

"Hey, now you get the idea. I see why Rikelman wanted to put you on the case. Better watch out, or you will never see night shift again."

We were interrupted by a greeting, "Welcome to Detectives, Hamilton." It was Lieutenant Hospian.

"Thanks, Lieutenant … I think."

"I'll give you a few days, and, then let's talk a bit. Let Walker show you around, and then I'll tell you how it's really done."

"Sounds good, sir."

Hospian was dressed to the nines in an expensive suit, a shocking-red tie, and shoes that looked Italian. I could tell his dress shirt was custom-made, complete with cuff links and monogram.

What an egomaniac, I thought. I looked to Walker, and he seemed to have read my mind. We chuckled in agreement as Hospian walked away, totally oblivious.

"Word is that he has less than a year to go for retirement. He and Biddle are starting a full-time real estate office in the city. Can you believe it? In this economy? I'm not sure he gives a rat's ass about this case," Walker commented.

"Oh, yes, he does, Red. If he and Biddle are partners, then he does give a shit."

I told him about the conversation I'd had with Biddle regarding our victim, Ginny.

"Shit," Walker replied. "He'll probably track this case just to get the listing from the attorneys who will settle the estate. Isn't that a conflict of interest?"

"Could be, could be," I muttered.

Walker changed the subject abruptly. "Any questions about the book?"

"As a matter of fact, yes; I have one question. Where are the photos of the parked cars in the neighborhood that I took and e-mailed to you?"

"I deleted them, you stupid shithead."

"Deleted them? Why?"

"You took them with your personal cell phone, right?"

"Yeah, so?"

"Do you have anything on your cell phone that you would like to see in the newspapers?"

"No."

"Well, Mr. Goody Two-shoes, if we put your photos in the book, then a sharp defense attorney will want to subpoena the source of the pictures, which would be your personal cell phone. That's why we use department-issued phones. If we take a picture with them, they would serve a *subpoena deuces tecum* on the department's phone to get the records of everything we used in the investigation. Do you want your cell phone records to be brought into court when we catch this guy? Every call to your wife or any business dealing?"

"I see your point. Sorry about that. Thanks for catching it."

At first I didn't think too much about it, other than it being a good investigative note to self. Then I thought about it a little more. Mel's phone number was in there.

Stupid is as stupid does, I thought.

Walker and I finally made our way back to Kensington Road. On the way I filled him in on the last discussion I had with Bauman and that I would let him take the lead on the interview.

"It depends, HH. If you have a good rapport with him, I can just fill in the blanks. Did you tape record his interview?"

I nodded.

"Did you get his permission?"

"Did I have to?"

"It wouldn't hurt. We will this time around. You never know what you miss that you pick up later. And I think Bauman may know something. But he may not even know he knows."

Trying to dodge all of my errors that Walker seemed so skilled at identifying, I changed the subject.

"By the way, the dicks' coffee sucks! How do you drink that shit?"

"I don't. And don't try to change them. I'm not sure they've ever washed that pot completely. Did you see the buildup of crud on that sucker?"

"I did. By the way I have to tell you, Clare and I love those homes on Kensington. I've been looking at some of the plants, and I may steal some of their landscaping ideas."

"Great. Just don't dig any up while we're there."

As we pulled on to Kensington, I saw that Ginny's trash barrels were at the curb.

"Make a note that Tuesday is trash day, HH," Walker said. "You never know what becomes important."

"Okay, but who put out our victim's trash?"

I could see the white van with the metal trailer parked in front of Bauman's home. It was hard to tell where the gardener was, as he was in the backyards for most of his time here. Then I answered my own question. "I think the gardener may have put them out."

"That reminds me, HH—we need to get a list of the different service people who frequent this street. I would bet it's the same for every one of the houses here."

Walker and I were thinking alike. "I'm a half step ahead of you. I got some of that info last night from Bauman, and he was going to get us the rest today." An idea popped into my head. "Red, two things. Before we meet with Bauman, let's walk up and down the street. Take a look at the houses, their approach, their furniture and landscaping. Let's look at what's the same and what's different."

Walker maneuvered the plain detectives' car, an old Crown Victoria with too many miles, into a parking space.

I turned to him as we sat looking down the street. "I don't know why, but it's important if you consider that some days it is the same and some days it changes. Ask yourself what is different among all of them or what is different from them and our victim's home. Like you say, we don't know what's important right now, so everything is."

"Go on."

"Well, somebody put the trash cans out to the curb right? But it wasn't our victim. We should probably look through them before they get picked up. Do we need a search warrant, or is there no expectation of privacy?"

"What? Are you studying for a test or something, HH?"

"No, just some stupid thing I remembered from the academy. Do you remember—?"

Walker interrupted me and for good reason. The trash trucks were coming on Ginny's side of the street. We had to act fast.

"We call this an exigent circumstance, HH," he said as he turned the car off and got out to open the trunk. As he did, I saw something that I had never seen before, particularly in a plain detective's car.

There was a large pine box with a stenciled label of "OHPD Homicide Kit #1" on its lid.

"What's in the box?" I asked.

"Right now, rubber gloves," he answered as he opened it and handed me a pair. "Put these on. Sometimes you can't wait for CSI."

We hurried to the Karsdon trash cans, easily marked with their address. After quickly getting the gloves on, we pulled the trash barrels from the street to the side of Ginny's house.

Chapter 62

The Kit

I was feeling like a boot all over again. This was all new to me. It was after ten o'clock in the morning, and I had not even used the police radio or written a ticket.

"Tell me about the kit, Red."

We walked back to the car, and he opened the top to show everything that was neatly placed inside. There was a collapsible shovel, rope, coveralls, gloves of all kinds, heavy-duty lights, mirrors, evidence envelopes, plastic bags, and tool boxes with workshop items.

"Get the little shovel and some envelopes," Red directed me, "and maybe a plastic bag or two. We're going Dumpster diving." He smiled.

I stood in the street where Ginny's trash cans had been to make sure we kept the space in front of the house to ourselves. Walker backed the car into that spot with the trunk lid up. We went back to the trash cans on the side of the house; I had shovel in hand. I carefully opened the top of the waste cans and saw that they were about half full.

We dumped the contents of the recycle bin, carefully sorting through for anything of evidentiary value. Interestingly, there was not much inside—that should have been no surprise. Ginny, hoarder that she was, kept everything, including cardboard, bottles, and cans.

The refuse bin was another story. Rotted food, half-eaten yogurt packs, carcasses of several Cornish game hens, egg shells, what looked to be unused cleaning rags, and other junk, including a crumpled pair of gloves with ground dirt that was visible to the naked eye.

"See anything, HH?" Walker queried as he completed taking photos of the trash we had laid out.

"Not really."

"Well, put anything that is not food or obvious junk in an envelope or bag for now."

I picked up the rather decorative cleaning rags and placed them in a plastic bag. The gloves I put in an envelope. They looked like typical gardening gloves but what the hell. Better safe than sorry.

Being the junior detective in this operation it was clear who was going to put things back into their respective containers. And so I did.

Mr. Bauman was in his usual spot on the porch in his short-sleeved shirt and blue tie, reading the morning paper. He looked amused as we approached him with gun belts showing as we discarded our plastic gloves in a nearby trash container.

"How are you fellas doing this good morning?" He greeted us like we were old friends, and I guess after today, we would be.

"We're doing well this morning, Mr. Bauman. Do you remember Detective Walker?"

"I do, I do. Come sit, sit. Coffee?"

"Sure. Can't be as bad as what I had this morning at the station," I quipped. Walker quietly declined his offer.

"Here's the list of all of the workers around here, Officer Hamilton. Just like you asked. Just like you asked. Their names, phone numbers, what they do, and the days they are around here. Thought that might help too."

"Maybe it will, Mr. Bauman, maybe it will." *Damn, I thought, he had me repeating myself now.*

I poured cream into my coffee, and Red stepped in to take the lead in the conversation.

"Mr. Bauman, do you mind if we tape record our interview today? We have a lot to sort out, and it gets hard to remember everything or write everything down."

"No problem, fellas. I figure everything I say is on the record anyway."

Walker quietly hit the on button of the briefcase tape recorder he'd brought from the car.

"Fancy," Bauman commented.

Walker opened with, "How long have you known Ginny?"

After about ten minutes of background information, we determined that his relationship with Ginny had been friendly but distant, with no familiarity of any kind. He reiterated that he had known Ginny's husband, Jack Brick, better than he had known Ginny and that to his knowledge, Brick still lived in Florida. He gave us Brick's contact information.

Walker upped the ante a bit with his next question. "Tell us what you know about Ginny's activities or outside interests, Mr. Bauman."

He took a deep breath. "What do you want to know?"

"Everything you know, Mr. Bauman, everything," I blurted out.

He poured himself another cup of coffee. No cream, no sugar. He looked at both of us, pulled his chair closer, and started his story.

It seemed that Ginny had helped her brother David get the car business going in the early years. She had moved here with him from Chicago after their father passed away. The business grew slowly at first and then took off.

"I only heard that they had a falling out. That was about ten years ago. Do not know what it was about, but the only connection to the car dealership now is her name. Karsdon. Karsdon."

I could see Walker making a note to interview the brother. We both knew where to find him. I made a mental note to reinforce the connection between Mr. Karsdon and OHPD. I was unsure how much he knew. Then I remembered that I had briefly discussed it earlier in the day.

"There was one thing that started happening about ten years ago, maybe eight years; I'm not sure," Bauman continued. "She got into one of those mind-bender groups. You know, one of those groups that try to convert you, but they really want control over you. I would call it brainwashing."

Walker perked up. "What do you mean? A cult?"

"Don't know if you would call it a cult, maybe you would, but she used to be churchgoing. That stopped. She started telling people that religion was wrong and that what you always thought was right was actually very wrong. She just was not the same. It was like she was being reprogrammed." He stared off into a distant spot as he gathered his thoughts. "I don't like to say disparaging things about the dead, officers, but she was getting weird, really weird. She would be gone for a week here and there and return even more intense about her beliefs. It was like she was going through some indoctrination or something. Probably was. Probably was."

He took a sip of his coffee. I thought he was getting this information off his chest more than he was being interviewed regarding a homicide.

"My wife, Beth, and Ginny had been friends for forever, a long time. About eight years ago, Beth decided to have nothing more to do with her. Ginny was challenging our Christian faith, and we just didn't take that lightly. She was a Christian—Catholic, I think—but that was up until about ten years ago."

Walker took a deep breath and asked, "Do you mind if we talk to Beth?"

"I don't mind a bit, son, but she's been dead for over five years now."

Way to go, Walker. Way to go.

Chapter 63

More Details

Bauman developed a more reflective mood than he'd had at the beginning of the interview. There was no doubt that asking about his wife's relationship with Ginny brought back some painful memories. Death has a way of freezing time and stopping the energy that might be behind a story. In this case, it signified the end of an interview. It was a very informative one at that.

Walker tried to work his way out of the hole he had dug. "Who else should we talk to, Mr. Bauman?"

He thought for a while and then responded, "Well, if I were you, I'd talk to Herb the plumber. He's on the list I gave you. He and Ginny were good friends. These homes are old and have a lot of plumbing problems. Herb knows them all. He does." He thought for a minute longer before offering, "I'm not sure what David, the brother, can do for you. He's a bit standoffish, but he may know something. I know he oversees her trust accounts and had more control over her spending than she did."

The trash trucks had returned to Kensington for their second pickup. Due to the noise generated by the trash pickup mechanism, Mr. Bauman paused until the truck had cleared the front of his house before he spoke again. "I would also talk to Bonzo, our gardener. That's his van and trailer over there." He pointed to the opposite side of the street. "His name is Bernard, but we all call him Bonzo. His family goes back over one hundred years of gardening on this street. I don't know why, but the street was named after one of his relatives, or he lets us all believe that."

"I see his van but never see him," I chimed in. "Why is that? Does he spend all of his time in the backyard?"

Mr. Bauman smiled. "He is a master at the English gardens that we all have. We pay him a pretty penny for his services, but look at what he produces." Bauman waved his hands as if to show us again the magnificence of Kensington Road. It was not necessary. "Bonzo has a unique system. He does backyards one week and front yards the next week. Then he changes it around, doing just the opposite. It's all about the growth patterns and his search for what he calls "serenity."

Walker rolled his eyes at the serenity comment, "What the hell is serenity, Mr. Bauman?"

That question got a laugh out of him. "My good man, you don't know what 'serenity' is?" Mr. Bauman seemed to perk up and sat with his back directly against the wrought-iron chair. "Serenity is what we all have as a goal, Detective Walker. It's that feeling of calm, a relaxing time, or perhaps even just a moment where all is right with the world. It is the absence of stress or anxiety."

From the look on his face, I could tell that Walker was thinking this was getting a little weird.

Then Bauman added, "Listen—hear it?"

"Hear what?" Walker and I both said at the same time. And then we heard it.

It was a musical sound. Off in the distance but clearly, someone was playing an instrument.

"I was hoping you would be here to hear it. That is serenity being attained—for all of us here on Kensington Road."

"Where is it coming from?" I asked.

"We never know which yard it's coming from, at least most of the time. But we all know that it's Bonzo. He's spreading the news that there is serenity on Kensington Road because his plants are in alignment and his gardens are perfected. One home at a time."

We continued to listen for at least a minute.

"When he gets finished with a yard and finds serenity in his accomplishment, he reaches down into his boot and pulls out a wooden flute that his grandfather made back in the 1920s. He plays a song for about three minutes, and it is surreal. Hours later, he will move to another yard and if he obtains serenity—only if he does—we hear it again."

"Does he reach serenity in every yard?" I asked.

"Oh, no. It varies from house to house. We all listen for it and hope that someone, somewhere in our neighborhood arrives at Bonzo' s serenity."

Chapter 64

Regroup

The beauty that was Kensington Road was taking on a different feel now. Walker and I walked in silence to the car. The sounds of the flute music had stopped. As we sat in the Crown Vic looking down the street, we could see that Mr. Bauman had returned to his newspaper.

We both watched as the gardener emerged from between the houses and walked slowly to his van. He was clad in his khaki long-sleeved shirt, with a sweatshirt as an undergarment, and black pants over sweat pants. He obtained a rake from the trailer and returned to a backyard. There were no leaf blowers on Kensington Road.

"What next?" I posed to Red.

"Well, I think we have a list of people to track down. How about we go back to the station. Let me work some more on her profile, you call the brother and get an interview for this afternoon. Can you handle the brother by yourself?"

"At least the first interview, yes. It seems the more we go back to people, the more they talk. I can do that if you also set up interviews for tomorrow with the workers that Bauman gave us."

"What about seven?" I asked, referring to lunch. Code seven in Patrol was based on who was available to handle your calls while you ate. I didn't know how it worked in Detectives.

"Are you an In-N-Out fan?" Red asked.

"You bet."

"That takes care of today, anyway."

We drove through the takeout area, ordering the same thing—a three-by-three with cheese, animal protein style, complete with fries and a vanilla shake. While we were waiting in line, I made some notes. I decided to broach the subject that was on my mind.

"What do you think about the mind-bender comment Bauman made?"

"Yeah, I've been thinking about that," Red answered.

"I think we should do a walk-through of the house again. Can you get the Coroner's Office to release it?"

"I'll work on that this afternoon. Maybe try to do that tomorrow."

"Back to the mind-bender comment, Red. Do you know anybody who knows anything about that stuff?"

"No, do you?"

"I do, but it could be a problem."

"Why?"

"He goes to my church. But there is one minor issue. He's LAPD."

"Oh shit," Red said. "Oh shit."

We both laughed about it, knowing that Hospian would have a fit asking them for help.

"Do we have to tell him?" I asked.

Chapter 65

Day One

The afternoon activities for day one proved to be very fruitful. I was able to get an audience with Mr. David Karsdon, Ginny's brother and owner of Karsdon Chrysler-Dodge. He was eager to help, but I could tell that he had given up on his sister a long time ago.

"She got into transcendental meditation about ten years back," he told me. "As executor for our family trust, I just paid all her bills and only touched base with her when I spotted an unusual transaction."

I asked what he knew of her transcendental meditation activities over the years.

"Not much. I think they just wanted her money. I didn't think it was a religion as much as it was a movement and a method for her to achieve some kind of inner peace or mental relaxation. But then I think it went past that, to a point where she was talking about religion and other things. We were all becoming stupid or ignorant, and she was the only one to 'get it'—whatever 'it' was. She lost me, and we cut off communication."

"Did she give them a lot of money?"

"Not through the family trust," he responded.

"How about drugs? Was she doing any kind of drugs, to your knowledge?"

"Not that I know of, but I haven't seen her in years, even though we both live in Orchard Hill. Strange, huh? But Jack, her ex-husband, might know."

He continued to describe her activities over the past few years.

"She changed what she ate, lost a lot of weight, and trimmed down a bit. Her sleeping habits changed, and, as I am sure you have seen, she became a hoarder."

"Yes, we saw that. How do you know all of that if you hadn't seen her?"

"This is a small town, Officer Hamilton. Even with 150,000, we know one another and people talk. I had heard that her personality changed and she lacked any real emotion. Even her neighbors could not connect with her anymore."

"To your knowledge, did she have any friends, male or female?"

"She used to. But I couldn't tell you who they were. She was into that house. Always fixing something. Always working in the garden. That damn garden of hers was her lifeblood. I have bills and bills for gardening and other house repairs."

"Could I get a copy of those, Mr. Karsdon?" I asked.

He knew where I was going with that question. "I'll have my secretary prepare copies," he assured me.

"Just a few more questions, Mr. Karsdon," I said as I saw him glance at his watch. "To your knowledge, did your sister have any enemies?"

"No, not to my knowledge."

"Any idea who would want to kill her or benefit from her death?"

The question hung in the air just a little too long.

With some hesitation, he responded, "No, but let me think about it. I've posed that question to myself on more than one occasion, but I'm not sure I can answer it."

I had one last question. "Do you think she left transcendental meditation and got involved in something more sinister?"

"I do, Officer Hamilton. I do."

Mr. Karsdon agreed that if I had any follow-up questions, he would make himself available, either in person or by phone. He then presented me with perhaps the biggest dilemma I had been faced with, even though it was day one. "Officer Hamilton, can I ask you a question?" He paused as if he really didn't want to ask. "Am I a suspect?"

"We haven't eliminated anyone as a suspect yet, Mr. Karsdon," I said honestly. "It's too soon in the investigation." I felt that it was my turn to put someone on the defensive at this point. "You handled the family trust, Mr. Karsdon. Was Ginny's will in that trust?"

"Yes."

"And are you the beneficiary of her inheritance, or is someone else?"

"I am the executor of the estate, but I can tell you, Officer Hamilton, I do not need her money. I have plenty of my own, and I take umbrage with that inference."

"I was not inferring anything, Mr. Karsdon. But if I could ask again, are you the beneficiary of her inheritance?"

"I honestly can't tell you. Not because I don't want to but because I don't know. But I will find out and let you know."

"That's why we have not eliminated you as a suspect yet, sir. The answer to that question may help us. I hope you understand." As I rose to leave, I gathered my notes and turned off the briefcase tape recorder. *Damn,* I thought, *I did it again. I forgot to get his permission to record our conversation.* "Mr. Karsdon, I owe you an apology, sir."

"You do?"

"Yes, I should have gotten your permission to record our conversation."

"I just assumed you were recording it, Officer Hamilton. Isn't that what you guys do, even if you don't get permission?"

"No," I countered defensively. "That's not what we do."

"Okay, but did you record it?"

"I did."

"See?" He paused for the optimum moment as he saw me to the door before saying, "And no warrant is necessary with us. Not ever, Officer Hamilton; not ever."

Chapter 66

Colors

I phoned Walker on my way back to the station. I gave him an update and asked if we had interviews for tomorrow.

"We do, but come on in because I want to go over some things. How was Karsdon?"

"Interesting, Red, very interesting."

I hung up and pointed the Crown Vic in the direction of the station. I realized that I had not checked in with Clare all day. I usually had touched base at least three times by now.

I got her voice mail as I pulled into the station parking lot. I parked in a vacant Detectives slot and looked at the black-and-white fleet lined up for the evening shift. Three more new Dodge Chargers. They still had the paper insert in the license plate from Karsdon Kars and a phone number. I wondered when detectives were going to dump the old Crown Vics and move into the twenty-first century with a new Karsdon Kar.

I found Red in that same office.

"What's the matter, Red? Don't you like to work in the squad bay tables?" I teased.

"Too many looky-loos. Those ghouls just want to look at photos of dead people. I don't have time for that."

I filled him in on the Karsdon interview. "We may have to go back again," I said, beating him to the punch, "but he said that whatever we need, a warrant won't be necessary."

"That's good to know."

"He also asked if he was a suspect."

"He did, did he? What did you tell him?"

"I told him that we haven't eliminated anyone yet, that it's too early in the investigation."

"Cool." He cleared his throat and pointed to an array of pictures of Ginny as I had found her—on the bed, complete with candles, head twisted, and minor blood seepage. "Take a look at these photos," he said. "What do you see?"

"I see what I saw when I found her," I said, describing the scene again.

"Now look at this picture." He showed me the five candles lined up on a clean sheet of paper, with a ruler showing the measurement of the length for comparison purposes and our case number written on the paper. "This was taken by our CSI people after the coroner removed the candles from her wounds and ass."

"I see a brown candle, a blue one, green, orange, and violet. That's what was in her at the time I found her, just like I said. So?"

"Well, you really do have observation skills, HH. You are a fucking genius. But here is my question. What do you *not* see?"

I was not sure where he was going with this. I studied the photos of the candles again.

"Let me give you a hint. What colors of candles do you have at home?"

"White, red, maybe pink …" And then it hit me. "There were no white candles, no red ones, or even black candles."

"You're damn right, HH. There are no red or white candles. No black candles either. Why? I'll tell you why. After listening to Bauman, I think we're dealing with some kind of ritualistic cult. Some kind of religious, fanatical idiot who fancies himself some kind of high priest. The use of these candles has something to do with all of this."

"So what now?" I asked.

"What now? We need your guy from LAPD, your voodoo guy."

"He's not a voodoo guy, Red. He is just a guy with expertise in the occult and ritualistic movements."

"That's what we need. Can you get him?"

"We probably have to go through a bunch of hoops here to make it happen, but I think it's worth it." I called Clare to get his phone number. I wasn't sure where he worked in LAPD, but Clare knew his wife through church. "I'll make you a deal, Red," I said as I waited for Clare to answer the phone.

"What's that?" Red said cautiously.

"I'll take care of this end"—I pointed to the phone—"and contact him about his availability, if you handle Hospian. Deal?"

Red came back with his standard one-word exclamation: "Fuck!"

Clare finally answered, and I tried to make my request sound as innocuous as possible. "Hey, can you get me Rex Holcomb's phone number? It's in the church directory, but I think it's under his wife's name."

"I'm not at home right now, Howard. Is it important? And you have not called me all day! What's going on?" Clare retorted.

"Been tied up, but when do you think you'll be home?"

"In a few minutes. Is it important?"

"Kind of. Better yet, if you get his wife—what's her name?— maybe she could call him and pass on the message to call me on my cell."

"Her name is Bonnie, and that sounds like a good way to go. Will talk to you soon, I hope." She hung up rather abruptly.

Walker came back into the office. "Here's the deal, HH. They're not against it, but they don't want to turn this case over to LAPD. I told him we only need this guy, whatever his name is, for a few hours. Once we find out where this so-called expert in the occult works in LAPD, Hospian will have the chief call his boss. Maybe they know each other—who knows? Did you get hold of him?"

"Not yet." I explained the problem in getting his number. "He'll call me on my cell after Clare contacts his wife."

I was hoping that there were not too many hoops to go through. After all, it was all police work. And more important, it was VIPS—very important police shit. Who could argue with that?

Chapter 67

Rex

"How are things in that quiet little burg of yours, HH?" Rex Holcomb asked. It hadn't taken long for him to call after Clare had called his wife.

I never knew too much of what he did for work, but I knew he knew something about religious groups. He was an ecumenical minister at St. Elizabeth's and probably could have been a priest in another world. He had four kids. I wondered when he worked, because he was always around the church, doing something.

We did the quick family catch-up and then got down to business.

"I understand you may have some expertise in splinter religious groups, mind-benders, or the occult," I said.

"I've been told that, yes."

"We think we may have a homicide that fits that bill, but we're not sure."

"Are you working homicide, HH? Thought you were in Patrol."

"I was, but I'm on loan for this one. Can I give you some background on what we have?"

"Sure."

I went over the case, with Walker coaching me on some of the finer details. After I finished with the overview, Holcomb responded, "I may have to look at the crime scene. Is it still intact?"

I assured him it was.

"How's your new chief, HH?" he said rather tentatively. "We hear you guys aren't too crazy about him."

"Well, it's an adjustment right now, but I like him."

"Any time you want to give him back, we'll take him. We have a real clown here right now."

Trying to get back to the business at hand, I asked, "Should we have our chief call yours?"

"No, have him call my captain. Better yet, have him call our deputy chief in charge of investigations. I think they're friends or old radio car partners. Just tell him you'd like me to look at your case. No more than a day. Could be good PR. The deputy chief's name is Flowers. He should know the number."

"As soon as we get the go-ahead, I'll contact you, and we'll set it up. If you hear first, give me a call. When can you do it?"

"How about tomorrow?" Holcomb said.

"We have some interviews lined up for tomorrow."

"Then let's do it Friday," he said.

I covered the mouthpiece of the phone and whispered to Walker, "He wants to do it tomorrow or Friday."

Walker shoved a piece of paper in front of me. He had just received the funeral notice for Gabby. It was Thursday, at 1000 hours, tomorrow. I had not even thought about it until now. *I really had my head up my ass on that*, I thought. The notice was the same for Andy Foyt Johnson's, with only minor modifications.

I looked at it stoically. *Funeral services for … will be held at … Wear Class-A uniforms … procession of officers … immediately following the services … a reception is planned for …*

It was then that I realized that if we shoved everything over to Friday it would be on our day off. Detectives are on a strict four-ten schedule, with half of us off on Fridays and half off on Mondays, and it rotates every other week.

"Let's do it Friday, if we get the go-ahead," I said, with Walker nodding in agreement. "Friday will work for us on this end."

"Sounds good. Will keep in touch. If not, we'll see you and your family at 9:00 a.m. Mass on Sunday, right, HH?"

"Right," I replied. But neither Red nor I were thinking about church.

"I'll get the okay for the OT," Walker said with a grin.

No solving of the crime before there is overtime! Isn't that what the T-shirt says?

And Deputy Chief Flowers from LAPD! Wasn't that Mel's dad? Things were getting weird—or weirder!

Chapter 68

Juggling

Walker had been setting up interviews for Thursday. He had contacted Herb the plumber, Bonzo the gardener, and Philippe the electrician. He arranged for Herb and Bonzo to drop by the station to discuss the Karsdon case, and Philippe would be interviewed about two in the afternoon.

Gabby's funeral had become an interruption of our case. There had been some discussion of whether or not it was a real "on-duty" death or just a heart attack. The chief intervened and said that Officer Charles "Gabby" Hayes's death was considered as on duty. He was in court, in uniform, and unless proven differently, heart attacks were presumed to be duty-related. Once again, the chief was on the side of the troops, but the Peace Officers Association was still not happy with him.

My thoughts were a little different than the mainstream. Even different from Walker's. "If they only knew," I mused. "If they only knew."

As far as I could tell, the dolphins were not talking about any connection between Bresani and Gabby. Only a handful of people knew the story, and no one was talking. Yet.

I contacted Clare to see if she was available to go to the funeral tomorrow.

"Of course," she replied. "Anything else going on?"

"I'll fill you in when I get home."

My biggest decision was whether I was going to wear my uniform or go in a suit. After all, I was working detectives and had to get back to work in the afternoon.

Red was able to reschedule two of the interviews, Philippe and Herb, for Thursday afternoon. Bonzo was unavailable until the weekend or Monday. Scheduling everything was becoming a nightmare. We were going to walk the crime scene with Holcomb on Friday, so that was out.

"HH, how about we just set the Kensington interview for Saturday afternoon about one o'clock? Shouldn't take us long. That way we can have Monday off."

"I think that'll work. I'll just let Clare know that I'll be gone a few hours. No big deal."

As we were putting our paperwork together, the phone rang. It was Lieutenant Hospian on his cell. "We got the okay to use that detective from LAPD," he told Walker. "What's his name?"

I could hear Hospian's comment as he spoke in a very loud voice. "Holcomb," I whispered to Walker. "Rex Holcomb."

Walker repeated it to Hospian.

"And no problem on the OT request. The chief wants this case cleared."

Walker placed the receiver back on the hook and muttered one word: "Ka-ching."

I had developed a bit of a pattern with Clare since I had been on day shift. Within an hour of being home, I would run through my day, and she would do the same. It got us on the same page every day. Tonight would be no different.

I had not told her the details of Ginny's death, only that she didn't need to know. She was more fascinated with the Kensington homes and what I had learned about the architecture, gardening, and the history of the street.

We talked about Mr. Bauman and his knowledge of the street and the preparations for Gabby's funeral. We also talked about my bonding with Red.

"Can you step away from the investigation for one day, or has the funeral been an inconvenience?"

How did she know that? I thought as I looked directly into her inquisitive eyes. "I think we've got that worked out, but you may not like it."

"Oh."

I let the silence sit there for just a second too long; I could tell. In a very matter-of-fact way, I said, "We moved a few interviews from tomorrow to Friday. Then—"

"Friday?" she interrupted. "But I thought that was your new day off with the weekend?"

"Well, it was, but the funeral screwed things up."

"Oh, so Gabby's death *is* an inconvenience?"

"Clare, we've got to stay on this case. It's important." I figured I would drop the next bomb on her and get it over with. "I have to go in on Saturday, too, for just a few hours."

"So not only are you working on a day off, but you have to go in on a Saturday too?"

"Once we get control of this case, it'll smooth over, and I'll be back to Patrol, Clare. Ease up."

"Ease up? *Ease up?*"

I did not want to have her upset over my new schedule, so I lightened the moment with, "Hey, there is a saving grace here."

"And that is …?"

"It's all on overtime." I tried to smile when I said it.

"Well, in that case, you can work the whole weekend!"

We hugged, and I felt a little relief—but just a little. Maybe it *was* all about the money.

Chapter 69

Gabby's Day

Charlie Hayes was one of those individuals who deserved his other nickname, "the Phantom." He had gone through an entire career without making a ripple. Many at OHPD didn't even know him, Vivian, or that he was the ex-brother-in-law of Johnny Bresani. It was very possible that the captains and lieutenants didn't know him, and he had been here for over twenty years.

I mean, they knew who he was, but they may not have known him as a person, as an individual. He was an employee with a locker, a body to assign to a shift and attend briefing. He was someone to schedule for a vacation and issue subpoenas to and someone to pass over for a field-training officer or detective trainee. He received benefits, including sick time, family leave, and deferred compensation. He was a personnel folder with an assigned serial number. He was someone else to cover for workers' compensation and schedule for medical examinations.

But not today. Today was his day and his day only. Charlie Hayes was a loving husband, as far as we knew, and a son, a parent, a neighbor, and an uncle. He was more than the picture in uniform on the altar of Father Mike's church today.

Oh, yes, the picture. He was decked out in his Class-A uniform with a tie in front of a powder-blue background, with just enough room for a partial glimpse of an American flag over his right shoulder. He was smiling, but it was the same smile he would show a traffic violator after a citation.

"Just sign the damn thing so I can get back to doing nothing" was the look he gave us all.

The picture had been the chief's idea. Once again, he had come up with something that they did in LA. The guys were not happy about it. Particularly Charlie.

The chief had a professional photographer come in and take a photo of each employee in his or her uniform, but he also wanted to schedule a group shot of everyone in uniform or business attire. Because it was by appointment only, over a week's period of time for the individual shots, everyone could schedule it on duty. The department would pay for the first one, but you could order more if your ego persisted. And for the majority of us, it did.

Everyone except Charlie. He was on vacation and wanted overtime or to schedule it when he came in again from his home in Canyon Lake, a two-hour drive on a good day. Sergeant Bennett found a way to tie it in to a subpoena. Charlie would get his OT that way.

Then, the day of the department photograph was also a day off for him. He went to our Association and filed a grievance that went all the way up to the chief. I never did know how it was resolved, but he was there, standing tall for the big day. The group photo was taken.

Who would have thought that the guy who had complained the most about having his picture taken in uniform would be one of the first recipients of its ultimate benefit? His wife had confided in Lieutenant Rikelman that they had no photos of him in uniform until the department took them.

Maybe that's why the chief wanted to have the photos taken after all, I thought.

Father Mike was his usual eloquent self. He didn't go back to the dash as an example, because someone must have told him that Gabby did nothing to fill that space. He did talk about Gabby's wife and kids and what a great family guy he was. He also was able to find some funny stories from members of his parish who'd had run-ins with Charlie. It was all just another good funeral, if there is such a thing.

I sat in the middle of the church, in uniform, holding Clare's hand throughout the service. In my mind, I was thinking of taking her home, changing clothes, and rehearsing the questions I was going to ask Herb the plumber and Philippe the electrician in just a few hours.

I looked around the church but could not find Walker. Was he here?

I had noticed that the memo said that the burial was private, for family only. That was fine with everyone, I was sure. A procession was led out of the church by a bagpiper and a color guard. There was no twenty-one-gun salute. It just didn't seem right, under the circumstances.

Clare and I made our way to the front area of the church as they loaded Charlie into the hearse that would take Vivian and her family to the cemetery. I caught her eye, and we connected for just that split second of understanding. I didn't see Rikelman near her, but I knew he was not far away.

Walker appeared out of nowhere. "I'll see you in about an hour, HH."

I had planned to introduce him to Clare, but when I turned to her and back to him, he was gone.

"Oh, well, another time," I told her.

I took her home, changed into a shirt and tie, and told her I would be home for dinner.

"What time?"

"When we finish."

We shared a quick glance of acknowledgement and left it at that.

Chapter 70

The Plumber

I was at the station by one forty-five, fifteen minutes before our first interview. Walker had already reserved the room, set up the video and audio equipment, and made sure the front desk knew we were expecting a witness.

Herb the plumber did not disappoint us. He was on time, clean, and presented himself as an astute but not-so-articulate businessman. Plumbers charge for their services like some doctors. Just looking at something will cost the customer. Diagnosis and repair are all extra. And that was Herb.

Herbert D. Midcrest had been in the business for fifteen years. After a three-year stint in the navy, where he learned his trade, he found himself back in the LA area and decided to set up shop in a relatively affluent area, the South Bay. He was not married, attended a secular church, and had one felony, driving under the influence arrest in the late nineties, but nothing since.

I am not that good at interviews. I haven't done enough of them to know all the ins and outs of how to set the table and walk an interviewee down the path. I had a feeling, based upon Walker's style of police work, that he didn't have the gift of gab or know how to get the most out of an interview. Our first team effort would be a high learning curve. I hoped that Midcrest was not the suspect in this homicide, or he would play us more than we would play him.

We got past what we assumed were the majority of his background details rather quickly. He was a certified plumber and proud of that. He had studied the plumbing issues on the majority of Kensington Road homes. He researched their plans, knew where the pipes led, and knew how to correct any problems that came his way. The Kensington Road people used him a lot and, in his own words, "Took good care of me, and I took good care of them."

I decided to get to the point of our meeting. "Tell us about your relationship with Mrs. Karsdon."

"Ginny?" I knew we were in trouble when he queried the very first question.

"Yes, Ginny. Mrs. Karsdon."

"Mrs. Brick? Ginny?"

"I think she changed her name back to Karsdon after her divorce," I said.

"Oh!" he said, a bit surprised. "She's been my customer for over fifteen years, she has."

"Was it always a casual relationship? Nothing personal between you two?"

"No, nothing like that. I mean, we would have coffee after my work at the house, and we just talked about life and the world as it was."

"Did you ever *linger*"—I made air-quotes with my fingers— "after you completed your work and had your coffee?"

Apparently, it was not pointed enough.

"What do you mean?" he asked.

"Well, did anything ever happen of a sexual nature?"

There was a pregnant pause, during which I was not sure if he was going to lie or if he was thinking I was full of shit. "No, like I said, nothing like that."

We worked our way through their history together and found he was brought in to Kensington by Philippe the electrician. They had been on several new construction jobs together and hit it off in terms of being able to work together. That was over fifteen years ago.

"We socialize a bit, Philippe and me—you know, a few beers— but he has a wife, and I don't."

Walker spoke up for the first time. "How often were you at Ginny's house?"

"Oh, every few months. Those traps and septic tanks are getting real old. We had talked about going to higher-pressure toilets and replacing some of that old copper piping. I guess that's not going to happen now, is it?"

I noticed he was fidgeting a bit, but I was not sure why he would get nervous. He was wearing a long sleeved shirt, and if I turned the heat up a bit, maybe I could get him to roll up his sleeves. I could see tattoos on his wrists that looked like chain bracelets. He had some obscure lettering on his forearms that I couldn't quite make out.

I excused myself momentarily and returned after turning up the room temperature. Walker was talking to him about how much time he spent with Ginny and how much he knew of her business and family.

"Can I get you a drink, Mr. Midcrest? Coffee, water, or a soda?" I offered.

"I'll have a Coke, if you have one."

I made my way to the vending machine, purchased a Coke, and brought it back into the interview room. "Do you want anything to eat?"

"No," he said as he rolled his sleeves up to reveal a series of tattoos up both arms. The heat had done the trick.

"Are you religious, Mr. Midcrest?" I asked as I pointed to various items of body art on his arms.

"I am."

"What kind of music do you listen to?" I was hoping that Walker was picking up my line of questioning.

"Why do you ask?"

"Oh, I just thought I saw a tattoo of an old album cover of one of my favorite groups on your arm."

"I like heavy metal, if that's what you mean."

"I thought so," I responded.

Walker figured out where I was going and interjected, "Do you mind if we take some photos of your arms, Mr. Midcrest?"

"Why? Am I under arrest or something?"

"Oh, no, I just think that they are so unique, well ..." Walker had backed himself into a corner.

"What my partner means, Mr. Midcrest, is that these are identifying marks that we have never seen before. If our investigation leads us to determine that you had anything to do with Ginny's death, we want to know as much about you as possible." I paused to see if he was getting nervous. "Right now, you're not under arrest. You are free to go at any time, but we need as much information as you may have. You can help us or not; it's up to you." I looked him directly in the eye. "Do we understand each other?"

"We do."

We took our photos.

The remainder of the interview did not reveal anything that was fruitful. He had been in the house many times, so we might find his prints. He had been on all floors, the basement, and garage.

Since our encounter in the interview, he was being more cautious. He trod lightly in trying to convince us he didn't know of her wealth. But I still was not satisfied.

We were butting up to our next interview and wanted some time in between to ensure that he and Philippe did not meet or exchange any pertinent information regarding the case. We also needed to compare notes on our observations.

We were done with Herbert Midcrest, for now. But just for now.

Chapter 71

Philippe

Walker and I spent ten minutes reviewing what we learned from Midcrest. We were both certain that he knew more than he was telling us. Our goal was to not let him think he was a suspect, only that he had not been eliminated. We didn't want him to "lawyer up" and shut us out from getting the information we needed.

We made sure that he left the building by another door and didn't see Philippe in the waiting room. The problem would be how to ensure that no one talked to Bonzo.

Philippe Montoya was almost a carbon copy of Herb. He had the requisite long-sleeved shirts to cover the tattoos and a misdemeanor criminal record that we already knew about. He was married but had no other family. He had been servicing the Kensington homes for a few more years than Midcrest, having been brought in by Bonzo Kensington. Walker and I both found that unique and more than a coincidence.

"Tell us about your relationship with Ginny," Walker said as an opener.

Right away, Philippe went on the defensive. "Before I answer any of your questions, I need to know if you think I did this … this to her. Do you?"

I gave him the same pitch I'd given Midcrest. "We have not eliminated anybody right now, Mr. Montoya. Nobody. Can I call you Philippe?" I smiled, just to let him know this was not an interrogation.

"Who have you talked to so far? You talked to Herb or Bernard?"

Walker decided to take the low road. "Listen, Mr. Montoya, we're investigating a death here. A homicide. We ask the questions here, not you. My partner was nice enough to tell you that we have not eliminated anyone as a suspect, but right now, you are just a witness. If we change that, we'll let you know. Got it?"

There was silence in the room until I finally decided to break it. "Philippe, let's just talk for a while and see where this goes, okay? I think that after today, we can answer a lot of questions."

He nodded in agreement but turned to face me full front and place Walker in his peripheral sight. I figured it was the good cop/bad cop thing and also was more of a "fuck you" to Walker than a message that he was just going to talk to me.

Philippe had done work at the Karsdon car dealership and was referred to Ginny from David Karsdon over twelve years ago. He prided himself on being a master craftsman and knew others who were good at their trade as well. At first, he laughed with Ginny that she didn't need a plumber, because plumbing was just like electrical, he told her, only with water instead of electricity.

That was, until he tore into a few of the walls in her home and others on Kensington. That's when he knew he was over his head and needed someone who knew what he was doing with pipes. He had worked with Midcrest on other jobs in the area and liked his work. He called him to find out if he knew his way around copper and galvanized pipes and brought him into the Kensington row of homes.

Philippe was more talkative than Midcrest, but we didn't learn too much more. While he warmed up to Walker a little, he was still very openly directing his comments to me.

I again had turned up the heat in the room at our last break and now offered him a water or soda. He declined. He did not roll up his shirt sleeves, so as we were winding up the interview, I decided to make my move. I could see that he was tatted on his hands and wrists.

"I am fascinated with those tattoos you have, Philippe." I saw he had letters across his knuckles—F, A, F, D, F. "Were you in a gang at one time?"

"No, it's just a family thing."

"Can we see the rest of your art work?" I asked, referring to his forearms and biceps.

"I would prefer not."

I thought about it for about ten seconds and looked at Walker. "It's okay by me if you don't want to show them to us. How about you, partner?" I asked Red.

"You got something to hide, Mr. Montoya?"

"No, sir," he said, staring directly into Walker's face. "I do not. I just feel that it's some kind of invasion to my privacy; that's all."

"I get that," I returned.

"Me too. Maybe another time," Walker said, to my own surprise as well as Philippe's.

We went down another road of questioning that went absolutely nowhere. After over two hours with Montoya, it was time to wrap it up and go home for dinner with Clare and the kids.

We all agreed that if Philippe heard anything, he would call either Walker or me. We exchanged business cards and walked him downstairs to the lobby and to his truck. Our goal was to part on friendly terms and leave it open to interviewing him once again. After we obtained more information.

"You have been very helpful with this case, Mr. Montoya. We want to make sure we stay in touch. Feel free to call us if you think of anything. Perhaps we'll contact you in a week or so, after we learn more and touch base again. Is that okay?"

I was looking for some hesitation, but I saw no look that said, "Why would you want to talk with me again?" He seemed to think that he had told us something important, but even he didn't know what it was.

Leave him guessing, I thought. *Just leave him guessing.*

I wondered if we were screwing this up or doing it right. But I wasn't going to let Walker think I had lost my self-confidence, or worse, lost confidence in him. Should we have advised Herb and Philippe of their Miranda rights?

At my last in-service training, they mentioned that unless you focus on a specific suspect, you can keep your line of questioning more like an interview. That means that if we are just asking questions to seek information and the information is provided voluntarily, then we are just interviewing. Had we done an interview, or had we done an interrogation?

My view was that we were not focusing on any one person. We were just gathering information at this point. Walker agreed.

This was a homicide that had major repercussions in the community, and we were the blind leading the blind. Both of us agreed on that point, but we sure as hell were not going to let anyone—whether it was Herb, Philippe, or Bonzo, or even Hospian—know that we were uncertain on how to handle this. That was between Red and me.

Overall, I thought we handled the first two interviews well. Walker and I had different interview personalities. He was more of the "just the facts," Joe Friday type, and I was a bit more personal and folksy. I listened to what they had to say, while Walker watched and examined their body language. He watched the interviewees' hand movements, gestures, facial expressions, and movements. I was listening for speech patterns—their rhythm, breathing, and pauses.

We both worked to assure the other that we were on solid ground and had obtained enough information for the day. After all, we had really only worked a half day, after spending time at Gabby's funeral in the morning.

I looked up at the clock. "Jesus, Red, it's six o'clock!"

"Yeah, so what?"

I looked at my cell phone. I had turned it off during our interviews. There were three calls from Clare, but only one text message: *What time can we expect you?*

I texted back: *Just finished up. Be there in 20.* "Got to run, Red. What time tomorrow?"

"We told Holcomb to come to the station at nine, don't you remember?"

"Oh, yeah. Nine, it is. We can go over the photos and then go to the crime scene. Has that been cleared by the Coroner's Office?"

"Done."

Chapter 72

Impressed

I have known Rex Holcomb for almost as long as I have been with OHPD. For about two years, though, I didn't know what he did for a living because he was the guy at our church who did the readings before the priest read the gospel. He gave out communion as an ecumenical minister and greeted people with our pastor after Mass.

Geoff once mentioned that he'd met one of the four Holcomb kids at a church function, and they'd talked about their parents. Geoff brought the information home, and I found it uniquely interesting enough to approach Rex one Sunday. Since then, we had socialized a little and become friendly but not best friends. In one of our conversations, I found out that he was an avid weight lifter and an expert on various off-beat religious factions, which included the occult and Satanism.

At last night's dinner table, I mentioned to the family that I was meeting with Mr. Holcomb the next day. That was after I apologized to Clare for not checking my text messages and having my cell ringer off. There was a casual acceptance, but I could tell that while she may have liked my getting a day shift for a while, we had to work out some things regarding our communicating during my workday.

Rex Holcomb was right on time. We met in the lobby of our police building, and he was dressed in business casual, no tie. He had his LAPD identification clipped on his jacket pocket and looked like he had just come from a workout, freshly shaved, damp hair, but very presentable.

I introduced him to Red, and we walked up the stairs to Detectives. He seemed impressed with our facility.

"This place is so clean! Nice photos on the walls; everything is organized; and it sure is quiet," he offered.

"We like it," Red said, leading him into our office.

We got right down to business. Red gave him an overview of what to expect at the crime scene, some background on our victim, the interviews we'd conducted thus far, and the fact that we were meeting with Bonzo Kensington tomorrow.

Red broke out the photo book he'd put together to go with the Murder Book. He walked Holcomb through the picture story and explained about our victim's tendency to hoard, but it was self-evident. He then took him into the murder scene, with Ginny lying on her stomach and the candles protruding from her body.

Holcomb said nothing. He looked at each photograph, studied certain ones more intently, but did not ask any questions. He took no notes. "Do you have any DMV or booking photos of the people you're interviewing or have interviewed?" Holcomb asked.

"We do," I said, showing him Midcrest, Montoya, and Kensington. "I'm still waiting on Bauman's photo from the Soundex system, but it should be here eventually."

Red spoke up. "Here's a photo I'd like you to look at." He showed Rex a picture on his computer screen that he had transferred from his cell phone from yesterday's interview. "These are tats from Montoya, the electrician. Both he and Midcrest wore long-sleeved shirts. Montoya let us photo his hand tats. We didn't see his arms, only up to his wrists. He had F, A, F, D, F on his knuckles. Mean anything to you?"

"Possibly," Holcomb replied. "Can we go to the crime scene?"

We gave Holcomb a quick tour of the department. As we walked down the stairs to the parking lot, he looked at the report-writing rooms and the supervisor's and watch commander's offices. We showed off our black-and-white fleet of new Dodge Chargers, complete with all of the laptops, GPS, and trunk equipment. He was impressed—until we went to our car.

"I see you got stuck with the old Crown Vic."

In defense, I responded, "Our cars are on order and should be here any week now. Patrol comes first here."

He just nodded. I didn't want to offend him by laughing at what his agency's reputation was about their cars and equipment. It was common knowledge that they were not up to speed on their equipment or cars. They drove their cars until they could not. The stories abounded of LAPD being in pursuit but their patrol cars died or just burned up right at the scene of the pursuit. That would not happen at OHPD.

We talked about family as Walker drove us to Kensington. Red didn't add anything to the conversation between Holcomb and me. It was only then that I realized that I didn't know anything about his kids or much about his wife, Bonnie. *I'll have to fix that,* I thought.

We approached the Kensington address from the south; I'd always approached it from the north. Now, I saw the street from a different perspective. The color scheme of the homes seemed changed; it looked like a different street.

We pulled up on the opposite side of the street from Ginny's home. I had always parked on the same side of the street as her house, just a few houses away.

I made it a point to advise Dispatch that we were code six—out for investigation—at the address. We didn't want the neighbors thinking that they had burglars or even realtors at the residence. Dispatch could field any inquiries and assure any caller that it was just the OHPD doing a follow-up. We joked that the Crown Vic would tell most people that. I did it anyway. Just a force of habit.

Walker went to the trunk and obtained new evidence seals, a pen knife, and the instamatic camera. He pulled out the thin rubber gloves and distributed a pair to each of us.

"Good thought," Holcomb said as he looked up and down the street at the homes, their yards, and the cars parked on the street. "Beautiful," he said. "Beautiful. Queen Anne?"

"Yes," I said. "Great homes."

We walked through the gate and up the steps, carefully checking if anything had been disturbed. I made a mental note that someone was keeping up the outside, as the small grass areas had been mowed, plants had been carefully trimmed, and there was evidence of raking of leaves. I saw Rex looking at the various tin crescent moons that marked the pathway to the porch.

Walker initialed and dated the evidence seal on the door well, broke the seal with a pen knife, and used a key we had obtained to gain entry. He opened the door slowly. When it was completely open, I took one step inside. I was very surprised at what I found.

Chapter 73

In

The three of us stepped into the foyer. Walker closed the door. I don't know why I was surprised, but I was. The interior of the house was exactly the way I had found it on September 22. Exactly.

Papers were still stacked up, with pathways still in place for ingress and egress to other rooms. The only change I could tell was that the kitchen smelled worse than it had on the day I discovered Ginny. Once the house was released as a crime scene, someone would put all of that food out of its misery.

We took our time on the first floor, as Holcomb seemed to be looking for specific items in the cupboards and closets. He didn't say anything, just looked and moved slowly from point to point and room to room. He spent an inordinate amount of time in the living room. He went through her CD and DVD collections and looked at what was in her CD player, her library, and books and magazines. He opened a few books and put them back.

He studied the artwork on the walls, the contents of the drawers of every hutch or dresser. He opened more cupboards than we had at the initial crime scene but still did not say much. He went through her wine collection, as minimal as it was. I could tell that Walker was a bit unnerved by Holcomb's attention to detail but he didn't say anything to prompt any kind of response.

After about an hour downstairs, we moved up to the second floor. I showed him how I approached each room, in what order, and reiterated the fact that everything was the same as I'd found it on the day of the discovery.

The three of us approached the room where Ginny was found. Although there was the mess that the coroner and paramedics had made, the crime scene itself, for the most part, was still relatively intact.

There were gauze wrappers on the floor. Small amounts of blood had seeped through to the mattress and dried. We had obtained the sheets from the Coroner's Office and booked them into evidence, hoping for some DNA or other trace evidence, such as hair or fibers.

The three of us stared at the bed for a very long time. I was reflecting on Ginny's body and the protrusion of the candles from her wounds. I'm sure that Walker was as well.

Holcomb only had the vividness of the photos he'd seen at the station. No one said anything, and I could tell that Walker was getting antsy. I had figured out some of his quirks, and they were not so different from mine. One of the main differences between us, I decided, was that I had more patience. We both let go of the urge to ask Holcomb any questions at this point.

After going through the drawers in the room where the body was discovered, he moved to the attached bathroom. He examined the medicine cabinet's contents and located her makeup drawer, examining the contents without saying anything.

"Is there a garage?" Holcomb asked. We led the way to the detached garage. Walker's keys fit the lock, and we turned on the light.

A vintage Jaguar was gathering dust in a space that could accommodate perhaps three cars. There was a workbench, garden tools, and candles. Lots of candles in all colors.

I realized that I had never been in the garage. Had Walker or Oakes? There were no photos of it in the Murder Book. I wondered if this could have been the original crime scene.

I could also see that there were small cherub statues—wooden and cement figurines; paint cans, spray cans, and broken fountains. It was as cluttered as the house.

Holcomb finally spoke something that made sense. "Okay, you guys have time for lunch? We need to go someplace where we can talk."

We shed our latex gloves, resealed the house and garage with evidence tags and today's date, and taped off the entrance to the porch.

Walker quickly punched a speed-dial number on his cell. "Darrin, this is John Walker. Can we get your booth in the back for a private meeting in about ten minutes?" There was a pause on the line. In less than ten seconds, Walker responded into his phone, "Thanks—see you in a few." Red was proud of himself. "I have a friend who has a little Irish pub called Dublin's. I figured it was Friday, so you mackerel-snappers probably want some fish and chips. Darrin has the best in the area. He's just a few miles outside of Orchard Hill in the county. Good place to go for food and privacy."

Rex and I looked at Walker and laughed.

"Hey, you idiot," I said jokingly, "we can have meat on Fridays now. Where have you been for the past thirty years?"

"I don't keep up with that stuff," Red responded rather defensively, "but you'll still get the best fish in town at Dublin's."

We pulled into the parking lot of a little strip mall. It was not in the greatest part of town, but there seemed to be a number of cars parked, including a sheriff's patrol car and another Crown Vic.

Law enforcement was notorious for sticking out like a sore thumb in public areas. That's the case when we think no one knows who we are. How obvious is a Crown Vic, guys in suit jackets with a bulge on the right side, or somebody with a short-sleeved white shirt and tie when the rest of the world is on casual Friday?

Darrin escorted us to the rear of the restaurant, and we walked past the three county sheriffs, two in uniform and one in plain clothes. We gave each other a casual nod of acknowledgment.

We had the best spot in the place, a very cozy booth that was almost as good as a private room.

"Nice job," Rex said to Walker after we were seated and handed menus. "I think we all know what we're having, right?"

We laughed about it, ordering three fish and chips and Arnold Palmers all around. Cops are very predictable.

As we took our collective breaths regarding what we had experienced in the morning, Holcomb stirred things up a bit.

"Now that we've walked the scene, here are the rules—they're the department's rules, not mine, but I abide by them."

Red and I nodded and waited for Holcomb to continue.

"This meeting never took place," he said. "You don't know me, from a professional perspective, and for all practical purposes, I never saw the crime scene, met with you, or discussed the case. Got it?"

Walker and I looked at each other, a little puzzled.

"There's a reason for all of this. My department does not want me on any crime scene logs, follow-up reports, or subpoena list as a witness. Are we clear on this?" Holcomb stared at us, and we nodded in agreement. "I'll be your fly on the wall, and you can call me at any time. That's how this works. And here is why."

Holcomb told us the details of his training in the study of religious cults, the occult, and Satanism. When he was studying to become an ecumenical minister for St. Elizabeth's Church, he met a Jesuit priest from a secluded retreat house in the San Gabriel Mountains. After the priest found out what Holcomb did in his law enforcement career, he talked about offshoots of the Catholic Church, the danger of certain cults, and their propensity for crime and violence in the name of religion.

"I was able to convince the department to let me work with this priest, study the various factions of these off-beat religions, and get some understanding of how they think, just for the purpose of using the information to provide motive and background. I worked extensively on the Night Stalker case and Richard Ramirez back in 1985 and studied the Charles Manson murders in the late sixties. I've made trips to the Graduate Theological Union in Berkeley and to Europe. I use my own money and have developed some knowledge of what to look for."

I nodded again, and Walker did the same.

Holcomb continued, "I'm retiring next year but will be available for investigations like yours. I can only put in 960 hours a year, so don't drain me of all of my hours on the next case. Are we all on the same page?"

Once again, Walker and I nodded our heads in agreement.

233

Chapter 74

Lesson One

"Okay, here is how it works," Holcomb said. "No notes; just listen. After we're through, I'll give you some homework to do. But feel free to ask questions as we go. I'm not going to make you experts, but by the time you get through this case, you'll know quite a bit." He settled back into the booth. "I've studied many of the visible mind-bending cults that are out there. They're not just after converts. They want their followers' minds with absolute control. They want to modify people's behavior and get their money."

Walker and I were both riveted to every word Holcomb said. We were locked in. Our Palmer drinks had arrived, but we didn't even realize it.

"I've studied—I mean, *studied*—Hare Krishna, founded by Lord Chaitanya, and the Christian factions like the Unification Church of Sun Myung Moon, the Children of God group that started right here in Huntington Beach. I've also looked at the Way International and the teachings of another church called the Local Church, developed by an individual who calls himself Witness Lee."

Our food arrived, delivered by the owner, Darrin. That broke the spell we were under. Walker asked for their special secret sauce, which turned out to be a pomegranate Italian balsamic vinegar, barrel-aged eighteen years but manufactured in Los Alamitos, thirty minutes south on the freeway. I made a mental note to tell Clare about it.

After Darrin redirected his attention to the other customers, we started in on the incredible fish and chips. We all agreed that the church should reinstate the no-meat-on-Fridays rule just so we would have an excuse to have Darrin's fish again.

As we slowly worked our way through the food, Holcomb continued his lecture.

"I've studied the various factions of the Satanic Church, including the many spinoffs, I can tell you that the real Satanic Church, headquartered in San Francisco, does not like all of these spinoff satanic groups that are out there. It gives them a bad name—can you believe that?"

"Unbelievable!" I said.

"That leads me to my assessment." While he had not lost us yet, Rex Holcomb now had our undivided attention. "Your case is a typical satanic cult case. By that I mean it was done by some spinoff group of the Satanic Church. That's satanic"—he used his sticky fingers to make quote marks—with a small "s". There are hundreds of those all over the country. They're not affiliated with the big church. They just use some of their teachings."

We finished our food and asked for another round of Arnold Palmers. As we were licking our fingers of the pomegranate balsamic vinegar, Holcomb said, "Many of the people involved in these types of movements don't hold regular jobs. They need money. That's a part of their system. Sometimes they develop a contract with their converts to pay them or give up their possessions and part of their income. It is a tithing thing. Similar to the way many real churches do today, like us Catholics, or the Mormons, or the big Christian churches."

I thought it all made sense but didn't want to interrupt.

"They ask for donations of any kind or sell nonsense literature. Many of these groups assign quotas to their people and call it 'litnessing.' There is a central fund, and a percentage is always sent to the parent church. When all else fails, they beg. It's a multimillion-dollar operation, and most of them are tax-free. Pretty good scam, huh? Not that much different from what we do in the Catholic Church, really."

I shook my head in amazement.

"The bottom line is that these fringe fundamentalist groups are sub-Christian cults. Just because you use a biblical vocabulary and quote scripture and talk about some form of a god does not make you a church. They all point at each other and say they are the only true religion and don't acknowledge that any of the other organizations are legitimate."

Holcomb sat back in his seat. We looked over and saw that the sheriffs had left the restaurant. We had the back end of the place almost to ourselves.

Holcomb had done most of the talking, so we let him finish his lunch in peace. He looked up with a final lick of his fingers. "Ready to discuss your case?"

We were.

There comes a time when a case starts to make sense, even if you don't know who the suspect is. I was moving things around in my mind, trying to line things up. Holcomb was helping that along.

"As I mentioned, you have a satanic ritual but by some people who only think they know what they're doing. Your victim is involved with it, but I am not sure how. If she had money, which may be the connection."

I thought about Holcomb's admonition not to take notes. "Can I just jot some things down while you talk?"

"As long as it relates to your case and not to me," Holcomb said.

"Okay," I agreed. Walker did not seem to feel the need to take notes. He just listened.

"Your victim had a preoccupation with the moon. Specifically, crescent moons. The walkway to the porch had metal crescent moons turned in the wrong direction, giving off the symbol of sacrifices."

I put a big question mark by the notes on crescent moons. I would do my own research on this part.

"The homicide took place on September 22. That's significant, because it's the Satanic Church's fall holiday. What was your victim's birthday?"

Walker had the rapid-fire response: "September 22."

"That's the date that their sexual activity is in its peak. Their birthdays are the days when they rededicate themselves to the cause. Do you have any sign of intercourse or other sexual activity?"

Walker spoke up. "My partner, Sherman, attended the autopsy, and he's on an extended vacation, so I don't know what the coroner did in regards to that."

I responded, "I've gone over the autopsy report, and there's no mention of sexual activity." I made another note to contact the Coroner's Office to discuss this in more detail.

"Let's move on," Holcomb said, looking at his watch.

"Do you have to be somewhere, Rex?" I said.

"I do. In just about an hour."

"What else do you have?" Walker posed.

"Well, your victim was studying Satanism. I found her Bible, and it was marked at all of the right locations—the passages by Isaiah, Corinthians, the book of Revelation, the Gospels of John and Matthew; all of those have references to Satan and Lucifer, the Prince of Darkness."

I could not write fast enough.

"Your victim also had Satan's journal in her library. It's called the *Book of Shadows*. She subscribed to their national magazine, *Continental Association of Satan's Hope*, or *CASH*. You could have mistaken it for a financial magazine very easily." He sat back and took another breath.

We were all exhausted. Just listening and thinking about this was emotionally draining.

"I saved the best parts until last," Holcomb said with a grin. "Well, almost the last thing. I still have to give you your homework."

Chapter 75

Candles

I looked at my watch; it was already three o'clock. We had arrived at Dublin's at about twelve thirty and had taken up Darrin's best booth for over two and a half hours. *He hasn't asked us to vacate for other customers, so Walker must have some pull here*, I thought. ·

Holcomb continued. "The biggest tip-off I saw that this is one of those weird spinoff groups were the candles—those in your victim and those in the garage."

I made a note to make sure we went back and picked up those candles and booked them into evidence.

"I was surprised that we didn't see any black candles. They're the all-purpose satanic ritual tools. They're used against enemies as well as for protection. They're also used to break up negative thoughts. It's their power color."

I made a note to look for black candles.

"The colors of the candles used in your case are significant. The blue ones were positive affirmations regarding spirituality, healing, and meditation. It brings harmony and serenity to the scene. I saw a lot of blue candles in the garage. The brown candles are a sign of uncertainty or indecision. There is something going on there, and you need to take a look at it."

Finally, I had to ask Rex to stop for a moment. "This is important, Rex. Can I tape this part? I'd rather listen than write."

Rex paused for a moment and then said, "Just to take notes from the tape and then erase it. I don't want to get a subpoena. I would be in deep shit with my department."

I broke out the digital recorder from my briefcase, and Holcomb continued.

"The green candles are about good luck. Just like here at Dublin's and the shamrocks all around. It symbolizes affection, not sex or lust. It also has a dark side for jealousy, greed, and suspicion or resentment. Interestingly, the orange colors are used to stimulate sex and energy, like the sun. It's about sexual attraction and lust, much like the red. I don't know if you noticed, but there were no red or black candles."

"I noticed," I responded, and Walker nodded his head in agreement.

"Red is more about lust, passion, and anger, bloodshed, or revenge. I didn't see any. The violet or purple is used to remove curses, to heal, and to influence those in power." Holcomb stopped abruptly. "I gotta go."

Walker stood up first, as I was stuck against the wall. "Thanks so much for your help, Rex. I guess HH has your number in case we have any more questions."

"He does," Holcomb said, "but here's my card with my phone numbers at the office."

"You mentioned homework?" I queried.

"Oh, yes. I want you to get some books to read up on this. Bottom line is that if we were to rank this on a ten scale of your suspect being just a religious nut or a Satanist, I would say you are dealing with a six or seven. Definitely not big time. Maybe, like I said, a 'satanist' with a small "s." He mentioned five books by different authors. My recorder was still on but I jotted the titles down anyway. "There's no sense my being the only one who knows all of this shit," he said with a smile. All three of us looked at the bill that was carefully placed on the table by a pretty, but way too young, waitress.

"You're the one's making the OT, HH. That's the least you can do," Rex joked, looking at the check.

I was embarrassed that I just didn't grab it, rather than being suckered into picking it up.

"You get the next one," I responded in defense. "And there will be a next one."

Chapter 76

Tomorrow

Red and I drove back to the station in silence. We both had a lot of thinking to do about this case and what we had screwed up. Rather than go in to the office, we sat in the parking lot.

"Can we talk about this for just a minute?" I asked.

"God, yes, let's. Did I say God?"

We laughed.

"When are the coroner's guys going to release the house to us?" I asked.

"They have."

"Okay, well, I think that's good because we have to go over the house with a fine-tooth comb with CSI again but not until after we do some reading. And," I cautioned, "Let's not bog down the lieutenant with any of this, not just yet. We need to act like we have our stuff together."

Walker posed the question I was going to ask him. "What about tomorrow? Our interview with Kensington?"

"I think we postpone it. Let's reschedule for some time next week. I think I'll go to the library instead. I'm going to do some Internet surfing tonight. Want to meet me sometime tomorrow?" I offered.

I was thinking that with soccer season over and the holidays coming that I could take the kids to the library and kill the proverbial two birds with one stone.

Red reacted quickly. "I'll call Kensington and reschedule. You go to the library and call me if I should come down to meet you. I have some things to do tomorrow any way. Will that work?"

"It works for me," I responded. I wondered if it worked for Bonzo.

I looked at the black-and-whites stacked diagonally along the wall, face out. It was change of shift. But for the fate of this new assignment, I would be ending my day of work and putting my uniform and my day into my locker, not to open it again until the next time.

Until this case was resolved, I was going to take it home with me. Literally and figuratively.

It was starting to envelop me. I could not stop thinking about Ginny, Mr. Bauman, Karsdon, Midcrest, Montoya, or Kensington. I saw the inside of the house differently now. Hell, I saw the entire street differently. I mentally leafed through the photos and the Murder Book.

Jesus, I thought, *we don't even have any real suspects*. We still were gathering information. Collecting what we thought were bags of junk. Making a list of witnesses or persons of interest.

I couldn't leave any of it alone. Holcomb had started it all, but I could feel him passing the baton like we were in a relay race. He had started things off, but it was ours to anchor and take to the finish line. I knew that now. It was my turn—our turn. I felt like it would or could consume me with its tentacles and then wrap me in cellophane. Only visible to me. That is, until I got home, and Clare could tell what was going on. She always could. And it had only been a week. Was this what my weekends would be like?

I took my time walking upstairs to Detectives after leaving Walker in the parking lot. I had my briefcase with me but needed some supplies before going to the library tomorrow. I picked up a new legal tablet and hunted for new batteries for my digital recorder.

It was a joke around the station that after the first of October, you couldn't find a battery, because everybody stashed them for their kids' toys in preparation for the holidays. Minor thefts of city property, I suppose. After the first of the month, you had to go to a supervisor to get batteries, because they just seemed to disappear.

I obtained three triple-A batteries from Sergeant Biddle and took a few pens and pencils from the file cabinet in Patrol. All with his blessing. The only catch was that I had to give him an update on Ginny's case.

I told him that it was coming along, and we were doing a bunch of interviews. I promised that if I needed to get his help, I'd call. I hoped he understood, but I could tell he would have liked more information. "Wouldn't we all?" I mumbled to myself, "wouldn't we all?"

I was home by a little after four o'clock. I was glad that I didn't have a city car to bring home. The extra car would have been in the way because I'd have to home-garage it—I couldn't park it on the street or in the driveway. That meant one of our other cars would be in the driveway or on the street. It was all much easier without a take-home car.

I found Clare in the backyard, gardening. We exchanged hugs, even with her garden gloves on.

"Have you talked with that guy who does English gardens yet, Howard?" she asked.

"Well, that's a long story. Bottom line is, not yet." *Maybe never,* I thought. "Hey, any plans for tomorrow morning?"

"No," she responded, "I thought you had to work."

"I just have to go to the library. Thought you and the kids would be interested."

"Library?"

"Yes, have to do some research," I said.

"Let's check with the kids at dinner," she replied.

"What's for dinner?"

"Fish and chips," she answered. "Okay?"

Chapter 77

Fish and Chips

With next to no energy, I opened my desktop computer and Google'd a few key phrases—mind-benders, Satanism, and use of candles in rituals and spells. Everything that Holcomb said was right there. The descriptions of the various religious groups, the quoting of various scriptures, and the Satanic Church liturgy were all online. There were pages and pages of detail regarding the use of color, with distinctions for rituals. It was as if Holcomb had written it, not just read it.

I made notes of the names of key authorities on the subject and their writings. Locating books with the titles of *Christ versus Religion,* or *Jesus Christ Is not God,* or *The Beautiful Side of Evil* could cause any librarian to look at me like I had two heads or none at all.

I printed out some reference material and placed it in my briefcase, or thought I did. I'd find out later it was not like leaving it in my locker.

Clare had prepared a small salad to go with the fish and chips, along with a glass of Pinot Gris. Geoff and Marcia were a little fussy but dinner was uneventful.

"What did you do for lunch, HH?" Clare asked.

"We met with Rex Holcomb at a place in the county, Dublin's. Heard of it?"

"Yes, Maggie's been talking about it. Great fish and chips." She dragged the food reference out slowly, and we all laughed.

Geoff stopped laughing long enough to interject, "Whose is the best, Dad? Mom's or Dublin's?"

"Well …" I paused just a little too long to be comfortable. "Here is the deal." I could feel the three pair of eyes drilling into my brain. "Here's the deal," I said again, more for effect than to just

243

repeat myself. "Both Mom's and Dublin's are good, because I think they fix them almost the same way, but ... the difference is not in the fish and chips. The difference is in the pomegranate balsamic vinegar they served with it. It made all the difference in the world. If we got that special sauce, Mom's would win, hands down." I was pretty proud of myself. My look at Clare seemed to ask, "How was that for an answer?"

Smiles all around.

"Can I change the subject for just a minute?" After getting a grudging agreement, I asked, "Who's up for a trip to the library tomorrow morning?"

It was unanimous.

I explained to Clare that my mission at the library was more than for Geoff and Marcia; I had my own motives for going.

After the fish-and-chips dinner, and everyone getting a good laugh at my expense, Marcia broke out her Dragon Vale game, Geoff went to his room to do whatever young boys do, and Clare brought out a book to read. It was *Wicked*, the book Marcia had just finished and raved about.

"So you're reading kids' books?" I joked.

"Well, the title intrigued me, and I wanted to make sure that Marsh was not reading something she shouldn't," was Clare's rather defensive reply. "I've just found the story captivating, and I think we may go see the play. As a family. Interested?"

"Anything to do as a family interests me. Maybe you can tell me about it sometime. As you can tell, I don't have any time to read for enjoyment. At least not right now."

I opened my laptop and started researching the books that Rex recommended. I wanted to have my list in place for tomorrow's library visit. The house phone rang, and Clare answered. It was Red.

"Hey, HH, sorry to bother you at home, but I wanted to go over some things for next week, if you don't mind?"

"No, I was just online, checking out those books that Holcomb recommended."

"Well, I canceled our interview with Kensington and rescheduled it for late in the afternoon on Wednesday. He was fine with that."

"Okay."

"I think we need to go over to the Kensington house on Monday and scoop up some of the evidence based on what Holcomb told us."

"Okay, but aren't we off on Monday?"

"Yeah, but I don't think that stuff should just sit there, HH. If I had my druthers. I'd go right now. I did go over and put seals on all windows to make sure we can tell if anyone is tampering with it, including the garage."

Jesus, I thought, *we are fucking this case up by the numbers! That should have been done long ago.*

"It shouldn't take too long, but I've already lined up two CSI guys to help us," Red said.

"What time Monday? I'm going to the library tomorrow to get those books. Why not wait until Tuesday if you've sealed everything up?"

Walker paused for a moment. "Earlier the better. How about seven?"

"Okay, but why not Tuesday?"

"Haven't you heard?" Red asked. "Clyde's funeral is on Tuesday, ten o'clock."

"Holy shit." I had forgotten all about Clyde and Donny. My head had been in this case, and the entire series of events was lost to me for days. "Do you have the particulars?"

"His funeral is at their church near where he lives in Rancho San Pedro. It's not that far, but it won't be like Johnson's or even Gabby's. I doubt that we'll have many people, so we do need to be there."

Rikelman's words rang in my ears: "*It doesn't matter how they die. When they are gone, they're gone.*"

Oh yes, it does matter, I thought. *It does matter.*

Chapter 78

Books

"Do you mind if I read with the light on for a while?" Clare politely asked.

"Do you mind if I snore?" I joked. "Of course not," I added as she kissed me good night and jumped back to *Wicked*.

It didn't take me long to fade. So this is what a day off was like for a detective?

I haven't had a dream for a long time that I could remember, not for a very long time. But last night, I dreamed heavily and woke up at five-thirty in the morning with a vivid recollection of every moment …

I was walking through Ginny's house and seeing things differently after Holcomb's crime-scene analysis. How could he have seen things that we didn't see? It was there, but we didn't know what to look for. He did. I saw the colored candles, sticking out like a sore thumb. I saw her DVD collection, her books and magazines. I saw the moons lined up in the gardens. What looked like normal décor or landscaping took on a completely different hue—it was luminescent, saying, "Collect me, for I am evidence."

Later, I retrieved the *Daily Wind* newspaper from the driveway as our sophisticated coffeemaker, a jura capressa, warmed up to make my favorite latte. My favorite time of my day off was relaxing before everyone got up to start their day.

It's no use trying to sleep when your body clock is geared to one time and one time only. I was surprised that it hadn't taken me very long to adjust to the day-shift schedule. I went to the sports page to catch up on local teams. What caught my eye was a full-page ad for Karsdon Kars—"Your family-owned and local car dealership." It reminded me that I needed to go by the dealership and pick up the records that Mr. Karsdon had promised me regarding the family trust payments for Ginny's living expenses.

I'll go on my way back from the library, I thought—and then thought again, *No, you will not! Today is Saturday, and it can wait until Monday!* If Clare only knew what was going on in my head.

We arrived at the library just as they were opening the doors at ten. The kids and Clare scattered to their respective areas of interest, with Geoff headed to the adventure section, Marcia to the fantasy series, and Clare to the books-on-CD section. I had no idea where to go, or where to look. *When in doubt, go to the reference desk*, I mused.

I broke out my list of titles provided by Holcomb and approached the rather plain-looking, middle-aged man wearing a sweater vest and bifocals. *Right out of central casting*, I thought.

I showed him a list of the books.

He paused for too long as he read my list. "We keep *these* kinds of books downstairs, in our basement," he said rather stiffly.

"Can I go down there?" I asked.

He shook his head. "Not without an escort."

I had to weigh whether or not to tell him that I was a police officer conducting an investigation. I opted not to tell him. It would get too complicated.

He locked his desk drawer, made a phone call to let someone know he was going "downstairs," and said, "Follow me."

The library was near the civic center and had been recently renovated. It was an older building but modernized to accommodate technology. The addition of DVDs, CDs, and various other items were to ensure that libraries wouldn't go the way of the dinosaur or telephone booths and render themselves obsolete.

I followed my new friend downstairs and could smell the must that permeates old books. Mr. Researcher went to his computer, pulled up some numbers, wrote them on my list, and once again ordered, "Follow me."

We walked to the rear stacks that were cantilevered to the right, as if the weight of the books was more than the shelves could handle. It looked like no one had been back here for decades. He pointed out two rows.

"That's what we have in this subject matter. If you don't find what you are after, I can order from another library. I'll wait by the card catalog for you. Try not to linger, as I have other patrons upstairs."

"Yes, sir," I said, as if I was talking to Lieutenant Rikelman. I quickly found four of the books but couldn't locate the final one on my list. I walked back to the card catalog, where I rendezvoused with my new friend.

"Here are a few others you might be interested in regarding your topic," he said, handing me a list of numbers and titles. I returned to the stacks and found the recommended books, wondering if Holcomb had read these.

"Can I check out these six books, and can you order the one I couldn't locate?"

"Six is your maximum, so when the other one comes in, you must return at least one. It should only take a few days."

Even libraries have their rules. And I thought the police department was rule-driven.

Chapter 79

Weekends

I enjoy my job because it really is not a job. It has become a lifestyle. Shift work, dealing with people's worst, and periodically solving something is always part of the "fun" of police work. But to me I was doing everything I could to ensure it was not my life. My family was my life.

Some people go to work and come home to rest so they can go back and give it their all. I'm not like that. Or I try not to be. For the last six years I have been going to work on my way to living my life. First with just Clare, then Geoff, and then along came Marcia. My days off are what I live for. At least thus far. It may seem like a contradiction, but it is not.

We left the library with our stash, a collection of books and CDs and a DVD for tonight to watch as a family.

This is what days off are for, I thought. I honestly believed that this last Friday and Monday would prove to be anomalies.

We decided to go to the four thirty Saturday afternoon mass at St. Elizabeth's so we could sleep in on Sunday and have brunch at home. We arrived at the church a few minutes early and saw that the lecturer was none other than Rex Holcomb. He was sitting on the altar, reading from his missal in preparation for his readings.

He didn't see me or other members of the family, as he was fastidiously reviewing the scripture. He looked up, over our heads, to see that the priest wanted to start the Mass. He introduced the priest and then the scripture readings and advised the membership to turn off their cell phones and pagers.

I wonder if he ever turns his off? Do these people know what he does and what his expertise is? I doubt it.

After Mass, we slowly made our way out the side door. The priest and Rex were greeting parishioners and wishing them well.

I made the overture. "Hi, Rex. Nice readings. You've met Clare and the kids, haven't you?"

"Yes, good to see you guys again. Don't see you often at the Saturday services."

"Well, we change it around every once in a while," Clare said. Then there was silence.

He looked over our shoulders to the next couple exiting the church and greeted them. We moved on to the car.

Strange, I mused to myself. *Did he not recognize me or did he purposely not want to chat about the homicide? Could he shut all of that out and concentrate on just church and the congregation? No, he knew who I was. But this was church and nothing more. After all, isn't that why we have days off or weekends away from work?*

I never minded working Sundays. I would go in about two in the afternoon and get ready for the night shift. On the day shift, I just made sure I engineered to get off on time because Sunday dinners were the high point of our evening.

Clare went grocery shopping and the kids attended to homework in preparation for next week. I looked at the yard and stack of books I had checked out at the library. The books were calling to me. The yard work could wait; after all, we were going to be digging things up to transition to an English garden sometime soon.

I read the Sunday paper but nothing interested me. I grabbed the books, selected one at random, and took it to the patio. My plan was not to read from cover to cover but to check each book's content so that if I needed a reference, I'd know where to look.

I picked *Mind Benders* by a guy named Jack Sparks. It examined cults but only covered six or seven. It was a "them against us" type of writing that addressed the dangers as well as the history of many of the more popular cults in the United States. He divided them into Eastern and Western cultures, and I found his assessment as would be expected of a Christian from Berkeley. I copied his bibliography on our home copy machine, as he'd referenced many books.

The next book blew my mind. It was in outline form, but the title said it all: *How to Deal with Satanism.*

Holcomb thought our case was more aligned with people who *studied* Satanism than with those who practiced it, including our victim. I noted that there was quite a history of Satanism, with the story of Lucifer as well as specific citations from the Bible that referenced the worship of evil. I wondered what version of the Bible the author, Marilyn Hickey, was citing. That was a good question to ask Rex. I made a note to that effect.

Hickey went through the various rituals, signs of Satan and the doctrine adopted by the Satanic Church. The chapter I found most interesting was "How and Why Some Get Involved with Satanism." I also was consumed by her explanation of the devices utilized as tools or symbols. No doubt, Holcomb had read this as well.

The other books also had good information but were more philosophical about evil and the creation of hell.

There was too much to think about, so when Clare returned home with a trunk full of groceries, I jumped up to help bring them in. I casually remarked to her that I might have to go in for a few hours on Monday.

"Oh, really?"

"Yeah, no big thing, but Red and I have some catching up to do." Then I added, "And one more thing. Clyde's funeral is Tuesday."

Chapter 80

A Day Off

Clare looked at me like I had two heads. "Do you realize what's going on here?"

I thought I knew but found out I didn't.

"What is going on in our beautiful city of Orchard Hill?" she asked. "We have lost three acquaintances over the past few weeks. Doesn't it bother you that the funerals we're going to are at the 'cop shop'—our own Orchard Hill PD?"

"Of course it bothers me. How can it not? I work with these guys," I said sincerely. "But I try not to bring it all home."

"So you've compartmentalized it to only affect you on your workdays? Can you really do that, Howard?"

I was not sure I had explained myself to her or my own satisfaction. "I am trying to deal with it as best I can Clare, but I didn't want you to have to carry my burdens. Particularly not here in our home."

"Your burdens are mine," she said rather pointedly. "Actually, they are the entire family. You wander around here in a daze and think we don't know what's going on, but we do. We *all* do."

"I have a lot on my mind right now, Clare," I said defensively, "and I thought I could just hang it up in my locker at the station, but I can't. I kind of need these days off to unwind or walk away from things for a while. Let's just enjoy it. All of us."

I could tell we were going to revisit this again, but Clare knows when to change the subject or walk away. She chose to walk away today, and I was comfortable with that.

For as long as I can remember, I have bought Clare a living plant as a gift for every occasion. We celebrated her birthday and our anniversary only a month ago, but it seemed like years since we'd had that long weekend together. I had found a fancy five-gallon pot with deep-blue hydrangeas. I'd bought two for an outrageous price but the pots were included, so it was a good deal. It was now time to put them in the ground, adding them to our garden. I wasn't exactly certain where to place them or how much fertilizer to use, but then I thought that after the interview with the gardener next Wednesday, perhaps I could get some advice from him.

But we had to get by Tuesday and the funeral first.

I wondered how Donny was doing. I had not even thought of him in this last week, and he was one of my best work buddies. Good grief, what was happening to me? To OHPD?

We had an hour before dinner, so I went back to the "office"—a shared room where Clare and I had put two small desks—and called Donny. After six rings, I was ready to disconnect before it went to voicemail when I heard a groggy "Hello."

"Donny, HH here. Are you okay?"

"Yeah, I'm okay," he responded, though his voice was feeble. He was not okay.

"Hey, Clyde's funeral is Tuesday. Will you be good to go?"

"I don't think so," he murmured.

I didn't know what to say, so I asked, "Where are you?"

"I'm at home."

"Donny … have you been drinking?"

"Of course I've been drinking!" he shouted. "Wouldn't you? My life is shit. My wife has left, and I killed Clyde. Jesus, wouldn't you be drinking? What the fuck is going on, HH? Is the world going to shit?"

"Yes, it is, Donny, but it has nothing to do with you."

He laughed his ass off at that line. "You are so right, my friend. It is going to shit. I didn't fuck it up, but I may have made a contribution."

We both shared the laugh that he needed so desperately. He was clearly miserable.

I apologized for not staying in touch, but this was not about me; it was about Donny and how miserable he was. I asked, "Have you gone to church, or seen Father Mike, or gone to a shrink at least?"

"No, but that all sounds like good things to do, right after I get laid. Or should I do that first?" He laughed again.

I could tell he was going to be all right, but he did need some time to sort things out. "Donny," I said seriously, "I think you need to call or go see Father Mike and discuss with him whether you should go on Tuesday. If you asked me for advice, I would say to stay home and be with your pain. Don't drink yourself into oblivion. If you went to the church in Pedro, it might be too much for you. We can go to the gravesite together later and talk it out. That's my two cents." I was really thinking that Clare would have given him this advice.

Donny paused, I figured, to gather his thoughts and clear his head. "Your two cents makes sense, HH."

Thanks. Listen, I'll be okay. I just need to get through all of this shit."

I was on a roll now. "I would also call Kip and get some time off. I think he's smart enough to figure it out already. Maybe by Friday of next week we can get together and bounce some things around."

We hung up with the promise to check in with each other after Tuesday. But I wasn't done. I knew Donny, and while I didn't think he would do anything stupid, I knew he was a mess, and I didn't want to take any chances.

I called Father Mike and filled him in. While he was not surprised, he knew he had his work cut out for him. If anyone could handle Donny, other than me, it would be Mike.

Chapter 81

Back Again

Walker and I agreed to meet early Monday morning on Kensington Road. I wisely showed up in jeans and a collared shirt, rather than a suit and tie. We might have to get dirty this time.

I was the first to arrive, even after stopping for a coffee, but it was only a few minutes before Walker and the CSI guys—well, one guy and one girl—showed up. Joanie was one of our former dispatchers who had taken enough forensic courses to qualify as a crime scene investigator. She was still on probation but knew her way around crime scenes. We were lucky to get her supervisor as well, Beanie Reis.

Walker had the Crown Vic with the homicide kit in the trunk and jumped in to pick out evidence tags and envelopes. He put a few other items in his pocket that I didn't see and then laid the crime scene diagram on the trunk hood. He identified each room that we would search as well as the garage and exterior premises. We would work as a team and go methodically, room to room. CSI had already printed the interior but had not printed the garage area, as they had not gained access last time. That was good to know, as both Walker and I had assumed they had.

There was so much to keep track of in this case, and with Oakes gone, we needed to fill in the blanks as best we could.

Walker dug deep into the homicide kit and came up with two paper-thin pairs of coveralls. He handed me one, and he got into the other. We gloved up, and he handed me a white face mask, saying, "Just in case."

I put it in a pocket and followed him and the two CSIs to the gate.

"Before we cut the seals on the door," Walker instructed, "I think we should walk around the property. We should photograph everything before we pick it up and put a ruler near it for size and perspective. Let's get the metal crescent moons that are lining the walkway first. We'll leave the fountains." He laughed, and we all laughed with him.

I noticed that the dirt between the plants had been freshly tilled. Had Kensington already been here? His van wasn't parked on the street.

"Let's leave the garage until last," I suggested. "That way, we'll know what we saw in the house and inventory the garage for comparison."

Walker agreed.

"Did you notice that someone has been doing the yard work?" I asked.

"I did," said Walker. We worked the yard in clockwise fashion, starting at six o'clock and moving to twelve. We called out specific items observed and Walker would acknowledge that he added the item to a hand sketch that would be later transposed to a diagram. We still didn't know what we were looking for on the outside. The pickings were slim as we returned to the six o'clock position.

It was time to enter 417 Kensington Road for the third time.

We entered the front door, just as I had done on September 22. The hallway that led to the parlor had not been touched. We decided to look at the kitchen first. Things were getting ripe. The smell coming from the refrigerator might be a good reason to use the face masks that Walker had given us. We didn't locate any candles or other cult-related items in the kitchen.

We moved to the library and parlor. I had the list of books to look for and was surprised to find them neatly filed on the shelves. I found a King James version of the Bible with the various readings earmarked with little Post-its.

In addition to the material I remembered seeing, I found two others. One was a magazine, *The Black Flame,* and the other was a book titled *Lucifer Rising.* I also found the book Rex had observed, *The Book of Shadows.* All went into an evidence envelope.

I located the *Continental Association of Satan's Hope,* or *CASH,* magazine that Holcomb had seen. Both items referenced their founder and high priest Anton LaCrioux and his sister Zeena, a high priestess. There was another reference to the current president of the Satanic Church, a Mr. Peter Gilmartin. *Interesting,* I thought. *Sounds like just regular people.*

I flipped through the pages, trying to remind myself we would have ample time later to analyze what we were collecting, but I found it irresistible.

It was apparent that Ginny had been dabbling in her newfound religion. With no one giving her much attention in her family, or for that matter on Kensington Road, she was undoubtedly searching for someone to care about her or at least pay her some attention.

I saw a calendar on her desk. It was marked with key dates. Four months—March, June, September, and December—had earmarked the twenty-second. Halloween was asterisked, as well as other dates. All of the markings were like various codes written in the margins. Halloween was coming up. I wondered what happened on Kensington Road on Halloween.

We finished the first floor. It was like a Christmas in reverse. Instead of bringing in bags of gifts, we were coming in with empty bags and leaving with full ones. We were bearing gifts of crescent moons, books and magazines, CDs, and DVDs. All were marked for the most gruesome homicide I had ever seen in my brief career.

I located a series of DVDs from a production house called the Full Moon Collection. The outside covers chronicled satanic worship, with an emphasis on sadism and violence. The CDs reflected heavy-metal performers with some of the strangest names I had never heard. Another new experience.

The search of the second floor revealed a few items but nothing more substantial than what we'd found on the original search.

We decided to take the same tact in the garage as we had in the house, using the grid system. That would keep us all together so we could discuss things as we went along, and it would give us four passes over the same areas.

We took our time, photographing as we went. We each had sketches of the garage and marked where we located each item, photographed it, and then put it into an evidence envelope and then into the bag.

We made sure that each person who located each potential piece of evidence was identified. This case, assuming we captured someone, could go on for years in court. Remembering what we were doing today meant having good records.

Our CSI people were the best. Each piece of evidence would be transported to OHPD and booked in our sub-basement evidence room. It would be moved only when we had to take it to court.

We didn't know what we were looking for, except for the candles. Everything else had become a question mark. We eventually searched the workbench and storage cabinets. Neatly stacked in their respective individual packages were various colors of candles. There were six packs each of blue, brown, green, gray, orange, red, purple, yellow, and white. We looked around the rest of the garage. Where were the black candles? I did remember that there were no black candles embedded in Ginny's body, but Rex was adamant that somewhere we would find black candles.

I noticed there were some garden tools that looked new—trowels, rakes, sledge hammers, shovels, and clippers.

"All of my garden tools are much older than what we have here," I mentioned to Walker.

"I see it too, HH. What do you make of it?"

"Could she have replaced old tools all at once? If she used Kensington, why would she need these new tools?" Another question without an answer. Wednesday's interview with Kensington might sort all of that out. *Or confuse us some more*, I thought.

By eleven o'clock, it felt like we had already put in a full day. I was tired and vaguely remembered that I had one more errand to do, but I couldn't think of what it was. And then it hit me. Go by the Karsdon dealership and pick up the bank records for Ginny's trust account.

Just another line for the chronological log, I thought. I finally remembered what else I had to do on my day off—fill out an overtime slip. "Oh well, no big deal." Ka-ching!

Chapter 82

Cleanup

Investigations of any kind are never like they're portrayed on television, which never seem to show the dirty work. We collected enough evidence at the Kensington house for a small storage room or to fill a U-Haul. Between the Crown Vic and the CSI van, we were able to get everything back to the station, transport it to the evidence preparation room, and conduct an inventory. We tagged and bagged and ensured that the master division report number was affixed to each item. We sequenced each item and asked that certain items be dusted for prints. We were not expecting much, as we collectively agreed that the killer or killers wore gloves.

The day was slipping away. Again.

We resealed the residence and agreed to contact the Coroner's Office before we released the house back to the family. This case would not be thrown out by having our crime scene contaminated by anyone.

I needed a shower. I thought about showering at the station but decided to take care of it at home. It was after three in the afternoon, and I still had not been by Karsdon Kars to pick up the accounting information. For insurance, I had been periodically texting Clare to keep her posted on my status.

I called Karsdon's Kars just before leaving the station to make sure the information was there. I was told that David Karsdon was out of town, but an envelope with my name on it was on his desk. I advised them I would be by in about twenty minutes.

I went down to the locker room to make sure I had a clean uniform for Clyde's funeral tomorrow. I wanted to go in uniform because he worked nothing but Patrol, as did I. I felt it was to honor his memory more than anything else. I would take it home with me and go directly to the funeral from home rather than go by the station. Clare and I could just drive and have some alone time on the way.

I picked up the package at the car dealership, looked at the new car showroom for a minute and thought, *If we buy thirty patrol cars or more from these guys at those prices, that's a lot of money. Add to that whatever number of detective cars and that amounts to well over a million dollars.*

The envelope was thicker than I had anticipated. As soon as I got to my car, I looked at its contents. There was a brief letter from Mr. Karsdon. The envelope held five years of bank records of the Karsdon family trust, established in 1966.

"This will take some real analysis to figure out what we have, but we should probably hold off until we get deeper into the case," I muttered to myself. I was not going to go through it now or even tonight. This was something that Walker and I would do together.

My brain was getting fried, and it was only Monday.

Chapter 83

Funeral Three

If you take the surface streets, Rancho San Pedro is about a thirty-minute drive from our home in Orchard Hill. Maybe you can get there faster on the freeway, but using the streets is my preferred method of travel. Freeways are unpredictable and boring. I know the streets, and they make me feel more comfortable. Law enforcement always feels it owns the streets. The Chippies may feel they own the freeways but they're so impersonal. Yes, I do mean both the Chippies and the freeways.

Clare and I got the kids off to school, enjoyed a light breakfast, and dressed with time to spare. I checked in with Walker to let him know I would meet him at the Rancho San Pedro Presbyterian Church about thirty minutes before the services were to begin. We would both be in uniform.

I was pleasantly surprised at the turnout for an off-duty death. I was also relieved not to see Donny in the crowd. I did see McBride and offered him my condolences. He was with his family, walking into the church with Clyde's family. After a quick introduction to the newest OHPD widow, the conversation was brief.

Father Mike was escorting the Woodrow family as others just mingled about. He nodded to me with the unspoken communication that he had talked to Donny. I was relieved.

There were close to one hundred uniforms from various agencies, the majority being OHPD, LAPD, and the Sheriff's Department. I commented to Clare that even though this was considered an off-duty death, Clyde still had many friends in the cop community.

Protestant services are different from the traditional Catholic events. I was surprised to see Father Mike and wondered absently if he would be in trouble for attending a non-Catholic church event. It turned out that he would have a role in this service as well, so I guess that God doesn't care which religion we are or how we mingle.

Our OHPD family has been exposed to a variety of services, with the emphasis on life, death, and what we do in between. Clyde's was uniquely different and came from an unusual perspective.

Unbeknownst to many of us, Clyde Woodrow, or "Clyde the Glide," had been in the Jesuit seminary, studying to be a Catholic priest. Just short of his vows, he left the priesthood, disappeared for a year, and then joined the Marine Corps, serving four years and leaving with the rank of staff sergeant. At some point in his life, he showed up on OHPD's doorstep to apply for a job. This was all contained in the program handed out at the church entrance.

It was standing room only inside the small church, but someone had made sure that the uniforms were up front. The chief and his command staff were there but in civilian clothes.

From where Clare, Walker, and I were sitting, we could see four large photographs surrounded by flower arrangements from a variety of sources. There was a photograph of Clyde in casual clothes with his family, one in Marine Corps dress blues, the OHPD uniform picture that our chief had encouraged everyone to do, and a photograph of a young Clyde Woodrow in a cassock, worn by those who are in seminary training. It was a full life in four poignant photographs.

Nothing was said about how he died, only that he loved guns and that we lost him too soon. I was thankful again that Donny was not here to listen to the story of Clyde. No one really knew the real "Glide"; each of us only knew a part of him. And no one had referred to him as "Clyde the Glide," but those of us "in the know" knew.

After introductions and songs that immortalized Clyde, we were introduced to his pastor. There was no discussion of why he had left the Catholic Church, only that he had been a loyal member of the Presbyterian Church for a long time. We heard the story of how he and his wife, Yvonne, had met. She was a waitress at the International House of Pancakes, or IHOP, and Clyde was a pancake fanatic. Either in or out of uniform, he would make his way to the IHOP where she worked, almost on a daily basis. There was marriage, two daughters, and the requisite boat and vacation home in the mountains.

Father Mike was his usual self and shared experiences and discussions with Clyde over his tenure in the seminary. He then talked to the assembled audience as if he were Clyde himself. "Don't grieve for me," he begged, "for I am free. Yes, I have tasks undone but I cannot stay another day." As a collective group, we fell silent. "I no longer laugh, love, cry, work, or play," he said. "I have lived a full life and savored it all. Perhaps it was brief, but I had much love and many friendships and good times. God saw me getting tired, so he asked me to go with him." He paused for effect and ended his short tribute by saying, "I guess I was really better than most, because we always say he only takes the best."

He then reached into the hearts of everyone in the church, in a way that only Father Mike can, and said in closing, "If I only knew it would be the last time I would see you, I would have tucked you in more tightly or hugged and kissed you one more time. I would have taken more pictures. I would have shared more days with you and given you that extra minute. I would not have assumed you knew I loved you but would have said it again, each and every day. I would have said I am sorry, forgive me, and thank you, or I'd have reminded you it will be okay."

He paused a final time and then said, "Because if tomorrow never comes, there will be no regrets today. We only get to be here a little while. Some for a very long time, others much less." He looked out to the assembled and said, "Let's do the best that we can. Clyde would be proud. How many of us could say our best was as magnificent as his?"

There was no mention of the dash.

This was Clare's and my third funeral in just a few weeks. Many people go through their lives attending only one or two funerals. We had yet to lose any family. Would there be more from OHPD? My homicide case was yet another death I had experienced. Up close and personal.

The drive back home on the freeway was short—and in silence once again. I didn't want to just drop off Clare and leave. We kissed and hugged a little bit longer than normal. We had to.

I went into the house and put on a suit and tie. It was just another routine workday for a detective trainee. I was just on loan and destined to return to Patrol—who knew when?

I hung my uniform on a hanger and placed it in my car so I could return it to my locker at the station. I decided to keep the black band on the badge and place it on my badge holder affixed to my belt.

Chapter 84

Half Day

Walker and I agreed to meet in the office at about one-thirty to go over the evidence and discuss the status of the case. I was getting a little concerned. Were we spinning our wheels here? Why were there no real leads, and why was no one in custody? Those were the only answers that Lieutenant Hospian or the chief cared about. We had an update meeting scheduled with Hospian on Thursday afternoon. I was hoping we would have something good to tell him. Coming to work at one-thirty was like working a half day.

I arrived at the station and parked in my usual spot. I looked over at the mechanics' garage area and saw the garage staff and Sergeant Biddle supervising the unloading of three plain Dodge Chargers from a transportation semi-truck and trailer, with the logo on the side: "Karsdon's Kars."

"Here they come," I said to no one in particular. "The million-dollar deal, in progress."

I marched right up to the second floor like it was a habit. Hell, I'd rarely gone to the second floor over the past six years. *Maybe when Oakes gets back, I can just go back to the streets on PM shift*, I thought, *and forget about these day-watch maggots.*

Walker had left me a note that he was down in the evidence basement. I took the stairs and found that the CSI team and Walker had just completed packaging and marking all of the items we had collected and had completed the evidence report with the master list—by item and where it was stored in the Homicide section. All items had been bar-coded, entered into the system, and placed on shelves that were marked and coincided with the bar-code tags.

We were lucky to have such dedicated people, but I always had thought of Joanie as a dispatcher, so it was hard to think of her as a CSI trainee, working with Beanie Reis, our lead crime scene supervisor. She didn't like to be called Joanie because of her last name, Maroney. She preferred Joan, but OHPD had tagged her with "Bony Maroney," after a 1950s song of the same name and the fact that she was as skinny as a rail.

Walker and I both thanked Joanie and Beanie for their tireless efforts and went upstairs to the office once again.

"That was a big job they did, Red. They opted to not go to the funeral and got everything done. When this is over, we should write them an 'atta boy' and an 'atta girl,'" I said as we ascended the stairs.

Without missing a beat, Walker commented, "Joanie went to the funeral. She sat in the back and left early." He gave me a long, hard stare. It communicated nothing and everything.

I paused for just one step. "You have to be kidding."

"Nope. You don't know shit when you work PMs. Have you noticed that she has put on a little weight?"

Does he mean she's pregnant—with Clyde's baby?

By the time we got to the office, I pushed that conversation from my mind. We had a homicide to solve.

We found a vacant interview room and worked on bringing the Murder Book up-to-date. I worked on the chronological log, listing the activities we had been involved in over the last few days that related to the case.

I made it a point to identify the books I checked out of the library as well as obtaining the financial records of the Karsdon trust. I also entered information regarding going back into the residence, making reference to the evidence report. I knew all of this information would be critical to the case once we got someone in custody, but only Red and I knew the work that went into creating this monster.

Red was sifting through the photos of the crime scene, looking for something. Anything. I told him that I had obtained the financial records from the car dealership and showed him the three inches of paper.

"How about we go over that tomorrow afternoon? Don't forget we have that guy Bozo, or Bongo, or something tomorrow morning at ten."

I had almost forgotten about that. Yes, we had another potential witness or maybe even a person of interest to talk to, and more important—to me, at least—I needed some gardening advice.

"That's right," I said. "Maybe he can give us some leads. By the way, his name is Bonzo—Bonzo Kensington, the gardener."

Chapter 85

Not Knowing

For once, we were able to wrap things up on time. I arrived home by five o'clock and finally enjoyed my time with the kids. Clare had prepared a great dinner once again. I was settling in to some form of normalcy. It was scary.

I glanced through one of the books I had checked out but really didn't have my heart in it. I needed a break. Dealing with this case, the funerals, and deaths was starting to take a toll. Clare knew it but chose to distance herself right now. Perhaps that would change once the kids went to bed, and we had some alone time.

We fell asleep in each other's arms, knowing more intimacy than that would have to wait until later. It was still very satisfying to hold her and be held. I never could have imagined that feeling before Clare.

I wanted to get to the station early in the morning and get a good workout. Clare and I had missed each other as well as our couple's yoga class, so hitting the weights was becoming critical to my mental and physical health.

I arrived at the station at six, pulled into my favorite parking space, and pulled my gym bag from the rear seat. I was walking toward the back door when I saw the chief get out of his car.

He smiled. "Officer Hamilton, how are you?"

"Doing okay, I guess, Chief, but how are you? You're in early today." It was amazing to see him at times other than eight to five. "You've had quite a baptism of fire since you arrived, sir."

"I have, HH. Say, how is that homicide coming along? I'm getting a briefing tomorrow, but I know you and Walker have been working hard on it. I see all of the overtime slips, you know."

"You just have to stay on the trail, Chief. I'm sure you know that," I responded.

"I do. I was in charge of Detectives for years. Can I give you some sage advice?" he asked.

"I think I could use some right now, Chief."

"Well, just between you and me, one of the things I learned early on is to realize it's all right to *not* know. Don't identify someone early on and try to prove your case. It's much more interesting when you work not knowing than to have someone in your sights who might be wrong." He took a breath and exhaled slowly. "You can have approximate answers and possible beliefs about who the suspect is and different degrees of certainty about different things. Do you get what I am saying?"

"I do—I think, sir."

"I am never absolutely sure of anything," he added. "I have made many mistakes on cases when I thought I knew. Then I realized that I didn't know. That's all right with me. I go on to something else, because I don't have to know the answer of who did it—not yet."

I nodded my understanding but didn't speak, as he seemed to want to say more.

"Not knowing who did it right now shouldn't frighten you. Let the evidence lead you to the suspect and not the other way around. And do you know why, HH?" he asked with a smile.

"Why?"

"Because there is pure pleasure in finding things out."

I thought about that statement, and I would for days to come.

"How do you like our new cars?" he said, waving his arm to show off the Dodge Chargers.

"They are great, Chief. Just great." I wondered if he knew what I knew about Karsdon's Kars.

He will tomorrow, I mused. *He will tomorrow.*

Clare had bought me three new dress shirts and a few new ties from Jos. A. Bank. It seemed like they always had a sale. I liked them all. They were interchangeable with my slacks and sports jackets, and while I was not looking like a GQ model, they worked.

I brought one in to wear today. Still, I could not wait to go back to Patrol and just worry about uniforms being cleaned.

Throughout my workout, I thought about the advice I had received from the chief. Not worrying about who the suspect was right now was hard to take. But it was necessary to do this case right. I decided not to tell Walker about my conversation. I didn't want him to think I had a direct line to the chief. We were the grunts, and he was the general. Grunts don't talk to the general.

Walker was knee-deep in his paperwork when I went upstairs at zero seven thirty.

"I called the lab on a few items they have, HH. They said they may have some preliminary information by later today. Not on any of the stuff we picked up yesterday but some of the items that we booked on the day of the homicide. They're backed up, as usual. They had the nerve to tell me that ours was not the only homicide in the county! Go figure," he said with a grin.

I had not seen Walker so relaxed and in control. In Patrol, he was a loner and quiet, but he also seemed to be a person in turmoil. Today, he was joking around like nothing was bothering him.

"You sound like a happy camper today," I told him.

"More than you know, HH. It's a very good day, and we're going to get this bastard, eventually. I just feel it."

I tried to put what the chief had told me in my own words. "I know, Red, but I think we should be cautious and not jump on one person or set our sights too high. I think I would be content with letting the evidence lead us to this guy. I think we can gather all of this information and just get pleasure in discovering who we are dealing with."

"This will be a good week for that," Walker responded. "I just feel it."

We went over the evidence report we had written the day before, with the help of Joanie in CSI. There were a lot of unanswered questions that we hoped Kensington could fill in. It was still on our list to interview David Karsdon and canvas the neighborhood for other potential witnesses. I was hopeful that Mr.

Bauman was having luck with identifying neighbors who might know something.

We made our to-do list for the week, and before I knew it, it was nearly ten o'clock.

It was time for Bonzo.

Chapter 86

Time for Bonzo

The phone rang. I was hoping that it wasn't Kensington canceling. It was an inside line that told me that perhaps he was downstairs in the lobby. He was.

"Send him up with a hall pass," I joked to the front desk.

We issue visitor passes for anyone who goes beyond the lobby area of the station. All employees have to wear their ID cards if not in uniform. If a person doesn't have an ID card or visitor's badge, that person is fair game to challenge. This was another policy introduced by the new chief. I thought it was a bit much, because unlike LAPD, we knew everybody in our agency. We knew who was a stranger, a victim, or a witness, and we surely knew who the suspects were. *A bit over the top*, I thought, *but then again, we are in a post-9/11 world.*

Bonzo Kensington was right on time. He was dressed in his work clothes and boots, the same as I had seen him at the Madison residence—black shirt and pants with black sweats underneath. I assumed it was because of all of the heavy brush he worked in on a daily basis.

We exchanged greetings, and he made no mention of having seen me at the Madison home nearly a month ago. He was hatless, and I saw that his black hair was kept short. He had very smooth light-mahogany skin for someone with a career of working in the sun. He had a bit of a farmer's tan that wearing a hat all day will give, but other than that he was a reasonably good-looking guy.

I escorted him to the interview room where Red was waiting. We had already hooked up the video recorder and had the digital tape deck waiting on the table near his chair.

As we moved our chairs to get comfortable, Walker said, "I want to thank you for coming, Mr. Kensington. I know that this is in the middle of your workday, and I'm sorry that Saturday didn't work out for us."

"I'm sorry too." His remark was casual but not apologetic.

"First off," Walker commented, "I want you to know that we asked you here to get information. You are not a suspect, so we're not going to advise you of your rights. We're trying to solve the unfortunate death of Ginny Karsdon-Brick. I'm not sure what name you know her by, but that's the name she used."

"We know her as Miss Ginny."

"Good. Then we will call her Ginny."

Walker was trying to develop a rapport with Kensington, and he was doing a good job. Kensington seemed to respond to Red right away.

Walker asked Kensington the usual questions—his full name, address, other contact information, and his work history.

For some reason, I was looking at him, trying to figure out his ethnicity. It was more than just filling in a box on my investigative worksheet because I could not figure it out. He looked to be a mixed race, but I couldn't put my finger on what. He had some Asian features, primarily in his eyes, but his coloring looked like a fair-skinned black, and he had a strict speech pattern that reminded me of the British but without the accent. It was confusing, but soon, I guessed, it wouldn't matter.

After Walker obtained the formality information, without asking which ethnicity he was, the question was posed: "Mr. Kensington, do you have a business card?"

We did the standard exchange of cards.

"Have you ever been arrested?" Walker asked.

Kensington froze for a moment and visibly tightened his fists that were folded on the table. "No."

"Never?"

"No."

"How long have you known Ginny?"

He paused to contemplate the question and then said, "Thirteen years."

"In what capacity?"

"I was her gardener."

"Is that all? Her gardener?"

"Yes." Interestingly, Kensington didn't ask Walker what he meant by "is that all."

"How often do you do her gardening?"

"Twice a week, up until recently."

"You mean until her death?"

"No," he said, shifting in his seat. "She let me go in August."

"Why?"

"Said she wanted to do the work herself."

"Why?"

"I don't know."

"So, let me get this straight," Walker said. "She 'let you go'"— he put his fingers in quotes—"so she could do her own gardening?"

"Yes."

"Were you upset?"

I perked up at this line of questioning, as it could get into an area that might require advising Kensington of his rights. I waited for his answer, and I was glad I did.

"Oh, no. I was just disappointed."

"Disappointed?"

"Yes."

I felt like I was listening to a tennis game—the brief questions with the even briefer answers. I could not resist and jumped in as I signaled Walker that I had a question.

"Why were you disappointed?"

Kensington turned to me with undivided attention. "Because I value how her house looks and how every house looks on Kensington Road. I did not believe that she could maintain it to my standards."

"Were you afraid of losing an account?" I asked.

He looked me in the eye to make sure he was communicating his message. "Detective Hamilton, I have a waiting list for my services. There are only so many hours in the day, and I can fill every time slot with another customer. It was not about losing money."

He went on to tell us about his gardening services and how he had developed his business model. "I am expensive, have no assistants, and do everything by hand with little or no electric- or gas-operated equipment," he said, his explanation going past the scope of our investigation. Still, I found it very interesting, even if it confirmed that I couldn't afford him as our gardener.

Walker brought us back to our investigation with a new line of questioning. "How long have you known Herbert Midcrest?"

He paused, as if the question had caught him off guard. "Who?"

"Herb Midcrest, the plumber."

"About ten years."

"Do you know him well?"

"No."

"Do you socialize with him?"

The staccato responses continued.

"No."

"How often do you see him?"

"Couple times a week."

"Where?"

"On Kensington Road."

"Is that it?"

"Yes."

"How long have you known Philippe Montoya?"

"Thirteen years."

"The same amount of time that you have been doing Ginny's yard? Up until August?"

"Yes."

"How did you meet Philippe?"

"I don't remember. It's been a long time."

"I understand, but can you think back on that for a moment?"

Kensington paused, looked away, and came back with, "I can't remember."

"Okay, how did Midcrest and Montoya hook up?"

"Who?"

"I'm sorry—Herb."

"I don't know."

I signaled Red that I had a question. Walker sat back in his chair, and I asked, "Mr. Kensington, having been in that neighborhood for over thirteen years, do you know anyone who would want to harm Miss Ginny?"

"No."

"Did you ever socialize with Ginny? Had lunch with her or dinner or anything like that?"

"No."

"Have you ever been inside her residence?"

"I only do the gardening. Nothing inside. I would have no reason."

"How about the garage?"

"No."

Both Walker and I sat back. Kensington did not seem bothered and continued to look at us with his deep black eyes.

"I guess that's all for right now, Mr. Kensington," Walker said after a moment. "I really want to thank you for coming down here. I know it was an intrusion on your time, and we appreciate it."

He said nothing but smiled slightly, in a way that was almost coy or expressed a shyness.

"If you don't mind," I said, "as we sort through this situation, if we have any more questions, I would like to call on you for assistance."

"I don't mind."

Chapter 87

Got a Minute?

Kensington had been slightly cryptic with his answers. I was not sure if that was good or bad. It was time to test him as we pulled our papers together to end the interview.

"Mr. Kensington," I said, "do you have a minute to answer a personal question?"

"Okay."

"Are you married?"

"No."

"Well, then you might not understand why I am going to ask my next question." I smiled at him and said, "My wife has three pots of blue hydrangeas. She wants to plant them in our backyard. My question is, should we keep them in the pots and put them in the ground? And what kind of fertilizer is the best to use to ensure they bloom again with those blue flowers?"

Walker took his notepad and walked out of the interview room. I guessed he couldn't relate to the questioning at that point. Kensington stood in the doorway, looking at me for a moment, and responded, "Do you know the species of the hydrangeas?"

"No, Bernard, I must admit that I don't. Can you enlighten me?"

"If you leave them in the pots and place them in the ground they will have very controlled roots that will not generate sufficient size. If you want large bushes of hydrangeas, take them out of the pots and use azalea mulch to plant them. Dig the hole twice as large as the root base, and only water them when the ground is very dry." I thought he was finished imparting information, but to my surprise, he went into a staccato lecture mode and told me all about hydrangeas.

"Only use special acid fertilizer with a high concentration of ammonia and urea nitrogen. It helps reduce the soil pH that allows the iron and other elements to feed the plants. Do you have a dog?"

"Yes," I answered, taking notes as fast as I could.

"Then don't get the meal-type of fertilizer. They'll eat it and get sick. Get the water-soluble food that you mix in a watering can and sprinkle it around the plant roots. The higher the sulfur and iron, the more you are assured of the blue flowers."

Maybe this is the key to getting him to open up, I thought. *Get him to talk about his business first*, because he didn't give us much in regards to our business—the investigation of Ginny's murder.

I escorted Kensington down the stairs, took his visitor's badge, and watched him walk out of the front door of the PD. *What a very strange guy*, I thought. An aura radiated about him, but he was careful about how he chose his words, even when giving the lecture on hydrangeas.

As I was walking back upstairs, I realized I'd forgotten to check his hands or see if he had any tattoos. I wondered if he had markings on his body, like Midcrest and Montoya. I had missed a golden opportunity.

"What do you think?" I asked Walker as we sat there looking at more work on the desk.

"Strange guy, HH. Did you get the feeling he was holding back?"

"Yes."

"I thought about asking him to roll up his sleeves to look at his arms for tattoos but thought better of it. Didn't want to scare him away. *Yet*." The last word hung out there for a moment.

"I thought the same. Didn't see anything on his hands, but he was thickly dressed and that's the way I've seen him every time."

"Every time? How often have you seen him?"

"A couple of times but always from a distance. Twice on Kensington Road and once on the Hill. I was up there on a call, and he was doing some gardening. We should have asked him to show us his flute."

"His flute?"

"Yeah, according to Bauman, he plays the flute at his job sites when he finishes each yard. It's his way of reaching what he calls serenity. He plays music to celebrate the completion of the job to his exact specifications."

"When were you going to tell me that?" Walker looked at me like I was withholding secret information.

"I didn't think much of it. Do you think it's important?"

"Hell, HH, everything is important right now. It may not be important later, but right now, everything is. Make sure you note that somewhere," Walker said as he reached to answer the phone. As he listened, he mumbled, "Umm, ah, huh, how long? Okay." He replaced the phone back on the receiver and stared at it. "That was the County Lab, Serology Section. Remember the items we pulled out of the trash just before they picked it up? Strangest thing the lab has ever seen. The rag had three different stains. All three were semen, and all three different. It's going to take weeks to separate them, type them, and put them into the DNA database. They wanted to give us a heads-up."

"What does that mean?"

"I don't know yet. Let's keep an open mind, though, and let the evidence do the talking."

"I know what you're thinking, but I'm not going to say anything right now." My cell phone rang. I didn't recognize the number so I just hit the answer button. "Yeah?"

"Howard? Is this you?" asked a male voice. "Rex Holcomb here. Got a minute?"

"Sure, what's up?"

"I've been doing some snooping around regarding your case. To make a long story short, I've talked to the head of the Satanic Church, Anton LaCrioux. He's based in San Fran, like I said. He and I have developed a bit of a rapport because he doesn't like fringe groups staking claim to his church in the name of Satan and getting his church in trouble. I ran your crime by him, and right away he insisted it wasn't something his flock would consider engaging in. While I don't think that he was holding back, he did ask me a question that I couldn't answer, so I thought I would give you a call."

"What was that?"

"He'd like to know the last names of some of the players you're looking at, if you have them narrowed down. He also asked another strange question."

"And that was?"

"Whether anyone had unique facial structure or could have had plastic surgery. And also whether anyone had any unique body markings, like tattoos."

I explained that we'd interviewed many people, and the only one with markings was a plumber. We didn't know about the others.

"What was the marking?"

"He had letters—F, A, F, D, F—tattooed on his knuckles."

Rex sighed. "I was afraid of that. Those are symbols of a spin-off satanic group called a grotto or a 'magic circle' that he knows is active in Southern California. But I want to remind you that it's satanic with a small S, not the big church."

"What are the letters supposed to mean?" I asked.

"Well, it is really two things. F is the sixth letter of the alphabet, repeated three times, which translates to 666, the numbers used by Satan. It's the mark of the Beast. It represents evil. The AD is 'after death'—that signifies the recognition that there is something else coming, an afterlife, if you will."

"Holy shit." I told him about Red's call from the crime lab.

"Sounds like a typical ritual. You have to remember that your homicide took place on September 22. Not only was it your victim's birthday, but it was the height of their sexual activity and the time for preparation of blood sacrifices, which is in October and November."

I was writing everything down as fast as I could, but knew I could always call him back for more details.

"Give me just the last names of your witness list, if you will, and I'll get right back to you," Rex finished.

Chapter 88

Last Names

I gave Rex the names of our witnesses in alphabetical order: Bauman, Brick, Karsdon, Kensington, Midcrest, and Montoya. The only other thing he knew was that Midcrest had the tattoos, and Karsdon was our victim. I didn't tell him that the Karsdon on our witness list was our victim's brother, the car dealer.

We hung up, and I explained the call to Walker.

"Let's go to lunch and talk about it, HH," he said. "I'm hungry, and we have a one-thirty with the lieutenant."

I was feeling more comfortable with Detective John "Red" Walker the more I worked with him. My original opinion that he was just a gunslinger, was being framed by a more complex and serious personality assessment. If I was going to spend every waking moment with him, then I guess he owed me the benefit of who he was and what he was all about. I decided I would use lunch to do a little prying into who Walker really was. He kept his personal life very close to the vest. I just had a feeling that there was more to him than what we were seeing. I was right.

He had been in the Marine Corps prior to OHPD, having deployed in the early years of Iraq and Afghanistan. He was in communications but saw some combat, just because he was there. He came home and opted for LAPD. Like a lot of military applicants, he thought he would be an easy hire. They dragged their feet, and he decided to throw his application around to various departments in Southern California. OHPD responded quickly, and the next thing he knew, he was in the academy.

"I like hearing that," I told him. "We move quickly when we see a good one out there."

"Yeah, we do, but they may be sorry they hired me with these shootings I've had."

"They don't bother you?" I asked.

"Bother me? Shit yes, they bother me! More than the ones in Iraq. These are Americans. But with all of my shootings, the guy had guns, just like in the desert. I just seem to put myself in a position where I have no choice."

"I know; we've talked about it."

"Whose 'we'?"

"The guys." We looked at each other, and he knew I was not going to give up names.

"I lock myself in my room for days, going over and over it. I can't get it out of my system. Those department shrinks are a joke."

"I know," I agreed.

"I'm not going to end up like Johnson, HH," Walker suddenly blurted out. "I just need time to sort it out. I think this chief sees that, and that's why I am where I am."

"How do your wife and kids handle it?" I asked.

"No kids yet, and she doesn't know much more than what she reads in the papers. I don't bring it home, and she doesn't ask."

"That would never fly in my house," I told him. We were in the middle of fish and chips when my cell phone rang. This time, I recognized the number. "Hey, Rex. That was quick. Need more information?"

"Got too much already, HH."

"Like what?"

"First, let me remind you of something that we talked about. My department doesn't want me to be directly involved in any cases. Not even this one. I am an advisor only. No subpoenas and for all practical purposes, I don't exist. If my name shows up on any paperwork, I am in deep shit."

"Got it, Rex. I'd never blow your cover. Not on this case and never without your okay. Can you hold on for a minute?"

"Why?"

"I'm on my cell, and we're at Dublin's. I want Red to hear everything so we're going to walk outside and put you on speaker."

"Okay."

Walker told the waitress we would be right back and not to take our food away.

"Okay," I told Holcomb, "you're on speaker with Walker and me. We're in the parking lot at your favorite spot."

"I struck out on five of the six names you gave me."

"We thought you'd strike out on all of them," Walker chimed in.

"So did I," Holcomb quickly responded.

"I don't have much, but your guy Kensington hit a chord. Actually, just the last name hit a chord with my source. What is the first name of your Kensington?"

"Bonzo."

"Bonzo? What kind of name is that?" Rex laughed.

"Well, his real name is Bernard, but he goes by Bonzo. Does that help?"

"Not really. But here's why. Back in the mid- to late 60s, a guy named August Boucher formed a group called the Order of the Trapezoid, which later came to be the governing body of the Satanic Church, the one with a capital 'S.' You follow me so far?"

"So far," we both said in unison.

"Good. The group was pretty big, with a lot of influential people from the Bay Area, including government officials, writers, college professors, and the like. According to the historiography of the church, there were many of what they called 'associates.' In the '70s it became popular to become a member of the church with some of the more far-out people of the day." He took a deep breath and continued. "That's where a guy named Forrest Kensington pops up. He was one of those 'associates' or hangers-on in that governing board. He was married in the Satanic Church to a Judith Riley. How old is your Kensington?"

Walker ran to his car to pull out his paperwork. I walked with him, holding the phone to listen for more.

"He was born in '82," Walker responded into the phone. "That would make him thirty-two."

"That's about right," Holcomb responded. "The Kensington's got in trouble for ritualistic murders and abusing children and animals, all in the name of their religion. While they were refuting the charges, Judith got pregnant. What's your guy's birthday?"

"Why do you need to know that?" Walker asked.

"What was his birthday?" Holcomb repeated.

"December 22," Walker responded sheepishly. "December 22, 1982."

"And he was conceived on March 22," Rex stated. It was not a question.

"How in hell do you know that?" I asked. "This doesn't make any sense."

"Oh yes, it does, HH. March 22 is another peak for sexual activity and bestiality. He was conceived in an altar ceremony back in '82 that was witnessed by about one hundred people and a few animals. He was born on December 22, which is another peak date for sexual activity and bestiality. The birthday is when they dedicate themselves to Satan. His parents dedicated him to their religion."

"You said this is not a part of the Satanic Church?" I asked.

"It isn't," Holcomb responded.

"So, explain our Kensington."

"Forrest and Judith went to prison. The baby was raised by Anton LaCrioux and his wife. They had a baby girl at that time named Zeena. She's now running the church but baby Kensington ran away at twelve, and they never knew what happened to him. It was never reported to authorities, so this is the first they have heard of another Kensington. He kind of fell through the cracks. His parents died in prison, but that's another story. He sounds like he's involved with your homicide, but I'm going to let you guys figure out the how and the why. I'm over my boundaries already," Holcomb stated abruptly.

"I know," I acknowledged, "but that doesn't mean I'm not going to call you again. Thanks, Rex. See you in church. Literally."

Chapter 89

One-Thirty

We had a half hour to put this together to present to the lieutenant. I knew what Red was thinking, and he knew what I was thinking: "Who the hell is going to believe this?"

We rushed through what was now a cold lunch and quickly left the restaurant.

"Here are my thoughts," I offered as we climbed into the Crown Vic. "I think we brief the lieutenant with where we are with the case, including the pending lab issues, and we identify who we have talked to but not mention Holcomb's latest piece of info. We'll let him know we picked up a lot of evidence from the crime scene, and it's all being processed. Let him know we still don't have any suspects, but that may change in the next week. We have some leads but nothing has panned out yet."

"I don't want them to get their hopes up yet," Walker responded. "I think I agree, but what if they want more, or want us to bring in other so-called experts? Or if they want to add another member to our team? Are we becoming too possessive of our case?"

"We hold them off for one more week. When is Oakes back?"

"Next week, I think."

"Okay. We tell him we're getting search warrants and have some interviews to do. We'll be able to have the majority of the work done for Oakes to jump right in when he gets back. Is your mind racing the same as mine?"

"Faster, I think," Walker said with a grin.

We returned to the station prepared to make a detailed presentation, but the meeting lasted ten minutes. All Hospian wanted to know was who we still needed to interview and why we hadn't done it yet. We explained that Jack Brick was in Florida, and we were trying to get a number, and David Karsdon was out of town. He seemed to accept that. Then the questions got strange.

"The house is in the family trust, right?" Lieutenant Hospian asked.

"Yes," I responded.

"Who is the executor?"

"David Karsdon," Walker stated.

"When you interview him"—he paused, seeming to be choosing his words carefully—"find out what they're going to do with the house—if they're going to keep it in the family, lease it, or sell," Hospian said.

Walker and I looked at each other. We knew where this was going. But we were in for a few more surprises.

"When you find out, let me know," the lieutenant said. "Oh, and good job. Keep me posted on the progress of the case, too."

Like he gives a shit about the case, I thought. *He only cares if he can buy or sell the fucking house.*

"Oh, by the way, Walker," the lieutenant said, "Oakes is not coming back. He got a job as a football coach in a high school in Montana. He's pulling the pin. The case is yours. I'll assign you a new partner. Hamilton will have to return to Patrol."

"When does he go back?"

"At the end of next week."

"Do you think that's wise, with the current status of this case?" Walker asked.

Hospian looked at Walker with a dead stare. "That's just the way it is, Red. It's not your decision."

We walked out of the lieutenant's office with our heads handed to us. Walker said what I was thinking. "What an asshole. What a fucking asshole. I hate lieutenants!" Walker slammed the Murder Book to the desk.

"Took the words right out of my mouth, Red. But which part was worse?"

"All of it. He doesn't give a shit about this case. He doesn't care about solving it or about our being partners or even whether Oakes comes back or not." Walker pounded his fist against the wall. "He didn't ask to go through the Murder Book, or if the LAPD guy was of any help, or even how much OT we needed or anything. He only cares if he can buy or sell that fuckin' house."

I was fuming right along with him. "Well then, let's solve this case, convince the family to hold on to the house, drain the department for more OT, and go back to Patrol. Fuck them."

We walked back to the office area in complete frustration. We had been manipulated to think that clearing cases was the most important thing we could do. We had some work to do now that we knew that Oakes was not going to be in the picture. I posed the question to Walker: "What did Oakes do with the case before he left that he didn't tell either you or Hospian?"

"I'll call him tonight," Walker said firmly.

"What should we do next?" I asked Walker, like I was back to being the new kid on the block and was packing up my marbles to go home.

We started a list on the white board in the small office we now called home. We listed interviews we needed to conduct, lab work we needed to get an update on, and the search warrants we needed. All of this needed to be done within one week; otherwise, this case was not going to get solved. We were both convinced of that.

"You know what?" Walker asked. "We can do this. It's in our reach. But it's going to cost them. Can you work the weekend?"

"Can I get back to you on that?"

"Are you going to ask permission from Hospian?"

"No, I do need to run it by Clare, though."

"Oh, that boss! Got my bosses mixed up." He laughed.

"How about you? Do you need to discuss it at home?" I asked.

"Nope. Right now we're living payday to payday. I take all of the OT I can get. Too many bills right now, HH."

"Got it. Hey, what's one week?"

"You know what it is?"

"What?"

"Ka-ching! Ka-ching!" he said.

I could hear the cash register ringing in my ears.

Chapter 90

Long Days

The discussion with Clare didn't take as long as I thought it would. When I showed her how overtime would translate to the next few weeks of paychecks, she understood. I had over two-hundred hours of time on the books, and if I worked eight days straight on this case, only four of those hours would be at my regular rate. I already had built up cash overtime to the tune of over twenty-five hours. I saw her eyes gleam when we arrived at the math together. Now she got it. Still, her mantra was "But what about the kids? When will we see you as a family?"

"This is just for a little while. When it's over, I can take a month off and we can do what we want." I took the time to explain to Clare my conversation regarding how we should handle the hydrangeas. She was very impressed. "This weekend, for sure," I said. We presented it to the kids and talked about revamping our yard with a new English garden and maybe even getting the kids something nice as a reward for supporting my absence. I still had to get this case into high gear.

Walker and I agreed to divide the work. He would track all of the evidence analysis with CSI and the Crime Lab; I would interview Bauman, Brick, and Mr. Karsdon again, and we would both work on the search warrants for Midcrest, Montoya, and Kensington's body tattoos, their homes, and their cars or trucks. I'd review the financial records provided by Karsdon first before I interviewed him. Based upon what we learned, we would figure out our suspect list. Was it the neighbor, Mr. Bauman? Her brother, the car dealer? The plumber, the electrician, or the gardener? Or someone else?

We thought we knew, but we were not going to get caught in that trap. We knew, but it went unsaid.

The three-day weekend would be a blur. On Friday morning, I tracked down Jack Brick in Florida. We had a candid talk about Ginny via a Skype connection. He was dressed in business casual and seemed very at ease as we went through introductions. He didn't have much contact with her after the divorce, he said. He left California seven years ago and moved to Florida for business reasons, never to return.

"She was going weird on me," he said. "She kept looking for something that I couldn't give her. She drifted from our church and started to get into scripture readings that didn't make sense. She would travel to Berkeley and come home with phrases and literature that I had never seen or heard before."

"Like what?" I asked. "What kind of phrases?"

"She talked in terms of statements, rules, sins, and something called revisionism." He used his fingers to signify an air quote. "I felt like someone or something was bending her mind. I'm good friends, close friends, with her brother, David. I confided in him, and he totally understood my leaving. I think he knew she was losing it."

"Did she talk about Satan or anything like that?"

"No, but some of the literature she had was in that direction. It's probably all at the house. She became a packrat. Another reason I got out. I'm not a neat freak, but she was not practicing good hygiene, if you know what I mean."

I decided to probe deeper. "Did you hire workers during the last few years you were here?"

"I was gone on business a lot, Detective Hamilton. She did most of the hiring."

"Did she hire the gardener?"

"Yes, the English gardener? He's great, as I recall. She got him jobs for every house on the street, I heard."

"Who told you that?"

"Tom Bauman."

"Did she hire anybody else, to your knowledge?"

"I'm not sure. I think she just used him to get other workers. The house needed a lot of upkeep. Those old houses all do."

It was my gut feeling that he was being truthful. I could see in his eyes and body language that there was sincerity—as much as you can figure that out on Skype. He was telling the truth, but no matter what, we were never going to see him in California ever again. Not even for a visit. Or a subpoena.

"Can we talk again this way if we need to?" I asked.

"Of course. I'd like to be kept up-to-date as much as you can. At one time, we were really in love, Detective Hamilton."

The screws were tightening, but I still was not sure how it all fit. At least not yet.

Chapter 91

Statements

Before I interviewed David Karsdon, I decided to sift through the financial ledgers and statements he'd provided. Walker had gone to the Crime Lab so I had the office to myself. I originally thought that I could take the ledgers and statements home, but it was Friday, and our cleaning lady would be there, and there were other distractions. I wasn't sure that telecommuting would work for me. Clare was always my biggest distraction.

I laid out the statements in chronological order—five years of monthly ledgers, twelve per year. Each year also had a year-end summary and a summary by category and by payee. It appeared to be very straightforward accounting.

From 2010 to the present there was not much variation on an annual basis. I could tell that the totals for each year and each month stayed relatively consistent. If I needed to find any variations or deviations, I'd have to go back prior to 2010. There were the typical utilities and annual subscriptions for magazines but no mortgage payments or semiannual property tax payments on the house. I thought that strange, and made a note to ask Mr. Karsdon. There were payments for credit card purchases but no card statements itemizing the items purchased. Another note for Karsdon.

As I looked through the checks I saw listings for Midcrest Plumbing; Eclectic Electric, which I assumed was Montoya; and Kensington English Gardens. Midcrest Plumbing was a consistent monthly payment of $1,500, as was Eclectic Electric. Kensington English Gardens was a whopping $2,500 per month. Every month.

It didn't make sense. Why would there be a plumbing bill and an electric repair bill for $1,500 every month—for five years? A gardening bill would be every month but for $2,500? Even if

Kensington came twice a week, that figure was steep. I made a note to ask Bauman what he paid Kensington.

I saw a few other odd expenditures and made more notes to ask Karsdon. I wondered if he even looked at any of these statements. *Probably small potatoes for him.*

I then found the most important piece of information: the checks to Kensington English Gardens stopped in August. And so did the payments to Eclectic Electric and Midcrest Plumbing.

Fifty-five hundred dollars a month—the total for those three businesses—was $66,000 a year. For five years, that was $330,000. I didn't need to be an accountant to see this.

Our investigation had determined that Kensington had been the gardener for thirteen years. Montoya was brought in by Kensington, and Midcrest by Montoya, almost ten years ago. While I could figure that these types of payments had been going on for a long time, I really needed to see the statements for the last thirteen years. Then I would need a forensic audit to help me verify all that my nimble fingers had discovered. *Where do I get a forensic accountant?* I wondered.

I wanted to make sure that I had duplicates of all statements because if I lost them, I would be in deep shit. I spent an hour copying everything. I called Bauman and Karsdon to set up a follow-up interview. Bauman was available tomorrow, Saturday; Karsdon was not in but his assistant would call me back with a time. It was a busy time of year for car dealerships—year-end was when the majority of new cars were sold—so I figured he would be on the property this weekend.

Chapter 92

Time Again

It was Friday. Again. *Where did the week go?* Walker and I were both knocking on the door of over a thousand dollars in overtime for this week alone.

If we drained the homicide OT on this one, we would then be forced to add it to our "comp time" bank at time and a half. That wouldn't be bad either. That was why Oakes had not come back, because he was doing what we called "running time." He didn't want the big cash-out check for unused vacation and sick time until next year, so it would not all be taxed this year. I was learning too much all at once.

I called Clare to let her know I was coming home. Walker told me he was going to stay a while and try to get in touch with Oakes.

"What's for dinner?" I asked.

"Fish and chips," she said, trying not to laugh. "It's Friday." Then she did laugh. "No, I have something else you might like, so hurry home." And I did.

When I was in Patrol, it was easier to leave work at the station—hang it up with the uniform in your locker. The books are closed when the person reporting signs off on a crime report, you book a body into the jail system, or the reports get approved. It's done. It's not so easy with investigations that require extensive follow-up. While I was not a veteran detective by any stretch, it seemed like the work never got done. It stacked up like 45 rpm records. Very few are removed from your list forever.

Even if the case file or Murder Book doesn't come home with you, its memory does. Ginny's case was a puzzle with growing tentacles. Each one needed to be examined and set aside until I saw where each one of the pieces fit. Walker and I knew it was there. I could see it, and he could as well. That was the thrill of the hunt.

Homicides don't wither on the vine. They grow, they mature, and they evolve. They age well because circumstances change. Evidence comes forward, and people who know something start to dwell on it. Time nags at us. Consciences become activated.

The guilt of knowing something weighs heavily on a person's psyche. Even if that person has no remorse. The mind-bending that occurs inside the brain is comparable to the twisted perspective of people's search for a truth. Time plus guilt can do wonderful things to the thought processes that had been secreted or rationalized only in their mind.

There is no happily-ever-after if you know that evil has gone uncontested. Walker and I were counting on that notion. Mr. Bauman knew something that mattered. Even if he was the wizard of the neighborhood, he couldn't just do nothing, say nothing, or "just be." He would have to come out from under and reveal what he knew. Only then could he have the serenity that Bonzo searched for.

Like the witch in Marcia's book *Wicked*, even if she was good for the majority of her life, the direct or indirect negative acts in which she engaged were still with her. Every devil was once an angel. So it was with those who knew what was going on at Kensington Road. But who held the most guilt for the secret knowledge? Who wanted to be made whole and release the burden? Bauman? Midcrest? Montoya? Kensington? Karsdon? Or another?

That's what we had to discover. *And, we will*, I thought. *We are getting close. We need time. No one has closed a door on us. Not yet.* And I found that strange. No one denied us anything. *Do we back everyone into a corner and see who balks or defends?* Surprisingly, no one had invoked his rights. Everyone out there looked innocent— or guilty. Which was it?

As I sorted all of this out while lying beside a resting Clare, it came to me: *We have to knock louder. Much louder.*

The magnet of the case was pulling me into its field like metal filings. I woke up at five-thirty once again. It wasn't really a Saturday; it was a workday. I tried not to wake Clare, but she gave me the high sign that she knew I was leaving. "I'll be home early," I whispered.

I couldn't wait to get in. I dressed for a casual work day in my Chinos and a long-sleeved, open-collared dress shirt. I had my Glock and handcuffs, along with an extra ammo case on my belt, which would signify to anyone in the know that I was working. On a Saturday.

With our Patrol work schedules of a four-day/ten-hour shift, and a three-day/twelve-hour shift for weekenders, there were faces I had not seen in years. To no one's surprise, Walker was already in place and ready to go.

We had a nine o'clock meeting scheduled with Bauman. We discussed what approach we would take with him. We both decided that he knew things and was not being as forthright as he could be. It was time to play bad cop/bad cop.

I told Walker of my preliminary analysis of the Karsdon financial records.

"Wow, HH, that's super. What do you think that means?"

"I don't want to draw a conclusion just yet, but I think it factors in."

I'd missed my workouts over the last few days, and it felt like my muscles were atrophying. I needed to run or lift some weights. Anything to keep me more at the ready. I mentioned it to Red, and he laughed.

"I've not worked out to any degree since the police academy."

"Shame on you, Red."

"Well, maybe after this case, you can entice me to do something."

"That's a deal. I'm going to hold you to it."

We arrived at Kensington Road with five minutes to spare. Mr. Bauman was sitting on his porch with a newspaper and coffee. We exchanged greetings, and he offered us a seat once again at his table.

"Mr. Bauman, we would prefer to go inside, please." I tried to phrase it in the form of an order and not a request.

"Suit yourself. My sister is out shopping, so we have the place to ourselves."

The interior of his house had a bright and cheery décor, with white furniture and a clearly feminine touch. The Queen Anne Victorian woodwork was evident, just as it was in the Karsdon-Brick home, but without the heavy dark wood.

We moved into positions of advantage and control after Bauman chose his position on a white sectional couch. Walker started the line of questioning the way I would have. "Mr. Bauman," he said evenly, "we don't think you've been completely honest with us about what you know about Ginny's death."

Bauman blinked twice in succession but didn't speak. His body language told of his struggles to let go. No one said anything for perhaps five seconds. Bauman blinked again, shriveled in his seat and straightened up again with his hands on his knees and said, "I've been truthful on what I told you."

"Well, then you haven't told us everything you know," Walker said in a commanding voice I'd not heard before. "We're not saying you lied to us; we're saying you haven't told us everything."

"That's different."

"That's bullshit!" I blurted out from a late-nineteenth-century chair where I was sitting.

Walker held his hand up as if he were refereeing a fight. "Mr. Bauman, what *do* you know that you've not told us?"

Bauman took a deep breath, leaned back, and looked Walker in the eye. "I've been here on Kensington Road for over twenty years. I was on the homeowners' board for the first ten years but have chosen not to be involved in anything to do with the street for about five years."

"Who's been running things?" I asked, trying to get my cool back.

"Mr. Francis. Shane Francis. He lives at 497, up the street." He pointed toward the other end of Kensington Road, where the numbers grow bigger and so do the homes. "I am not sure he even knew Ginny."

"Why did you leave the board? Is that pertinent to all of this?" Walker asked calmly.

"That's a good question, Detective Walker. There's been a real division among the board and the residents of Kensington Road." He uncrossed his legs as if he wanted to unload something from his lap. "Changes in ownership of some of the houses brought a new breed of people to the neighborhood. I am not saying it's good or bad, but it's not something I could adjust to."

I asked what I thought was a simple question. "What do you mean?"

"Mr. Francis is an interior decorator, and his partner is a hair dresser. Another of our new owners is a former professional football player, with a wife and two kids. Another is a bank president who runs the Cathay Bank on Albion. It's all just new money, with people to whom I can't relate. That's why I quit the board. I was not material to the new way of doing things."

Red and I both nodded encouragingly, allowing Bauman to continue.

"For years, Ginny and I set a tone of classic Victorian maintenance and restoration. We were proud of what we'd done over the years. About five years ago, Ginny went into a different … zone, I'll call it. My wife was still alive then, but I … backed off and just let things happen. A year later, my wife passed away. About two years ago, my sister moved in with me."

"What do you mean, 'let things happen'?" I asked.

"Do you really want to know, Detective Hamilton? I'm not sure you really want to know."

Chapter 93

Changing Times

I knew what Bauman was saying. I hadn't been assertive enough to pry things out of him. I had asked him questions as I would have at the scene of a traffic collision. Bauman evidently decided that if I didn't pursue information with tenacity, then I was not going to get what he—I hoped—was going to dump on us now.

"Ginny really left us a long time ago, in my estimation." He was picking his words carefully once again. "Whoever killed her did it with her permission. She was a part of the Karsdon family, but she wasn't. She may have had the money, but she never was a Karsdon. She didn't run in David's circles or those of any of the other residents on Kensington."

A noise from the kitchen area caused me to jump in my chair, but Bauman must have sensed my apprehension.

"Sara? Is that you?" he called out.

"Yes, can you help me with the groceries?"

All three of us went to the kitchen, offering to help.

"Tom told me you were coming back, Officer," Sara said. "I didn't think you would bring a friend."

I introduced Walker to her as we walked outside.

The trunk of the car was loaded with bags of groceries—ten plastic bags and five environmental friendly bags. We each grabbed bags and brought them into the house.

"It'll take me some time to put things away, so you boys get comfortable in the living room. I'll make some coffee. And how about some cookies?"

"Thanks, Sara," I said, "we'll take you up on that, but give us some time with your brother first." We needed to get back to the business at hand.

When we were seated once again, I said to Mr. Bauman, quietly but firmly, "Tell us more about Ginny."

Bauman settled back onto the couch, and his eyes darted from me to Red and back to me again. "First, Ginny and I had a long-standing friendship. Not any hanky-panky but just friends. About five years ago, she started getting weird and hanging around with even weirder people."

I put my hand up. "Mr. Bauman, you're talking in circles here. Saying she was weird or that she was hanging around weird people is not getting us anywhere. We need information, not descriptions of people's character."

Bauman leaned forward. "Gentlemen, you do not have a clue as to what was going on here. I can tell that you are fishing around for a smoking gun. So why should I be the one to tell you what you need to know?"

Both Walker and I sat up straighter in our chairs. If I'd heard Bauman correctly, we'd just been chastised.

"We know more about this case than you think," Walker said. "But we need to know what you know. We're not here to give you information. We're here for you to give us information. Is that clear?"

"Do you know about Herb Midcrest?" he asked.

"Yes, some things," I said.

"Do you know about Philippe Montoya?"

"Yes, some things."

"Do you know about Bernard Kensington?"

"We do. Some things."

"Up until this last August, they all spent a lot of time over there, if you know what I mean."

"At Ginny's house?"

He nodded.

"Were they working on the place?" I asked. "Is that what you mean?"

Bauman smiled. "No. See, that's why I didn't tell you anything. I didn't want to be the one to say it. I thought you could figure it out."

"Figure what out?"

Bauman pursed his lips, rolled his eyes and threw his hands in the air. "Jesus, are you guys stupid or what? They were devil worshipers. All of them!" he said in exasperation.

"Yes, we know," I said. "We just needed to hear it from you."

Bauman sighed heavily in relief. "They were always getting together to do … I don't know what, but it went on at all hours."

"Any ideas as to what was going on?" Walker asked trying to bring the conversation back to a level of civility.

"Did not want to know. Did not *want* to know." He finally sat back. "Why didn't you tell me you knew?"

"Not our job to give out information. It's to get it and put the puzzle together," Walker advised.

"Have you seen their bodies? What they've done to their bodies?" Bauman asked.

"Who?"

"Herb, Bernard, and Philippe."

"No."

"You should."

"Why?"

"They've destroyed their bodies with tattoos that are symbols of the devil. I can't believe they would do that to their own bodies. It should be against the law."

While I understood what he was saying, I was after enough information to support a search warrant for those guys. We were getting there, finally.

Walker and I spent another hour getting into the details of what Bauman knew. It was not much more, but it added to the puzzle and corroborated much of our information. Every piece of information mattered now. Tying down dates, other names, and activities that were observed now became important.

It was becoming a mosaic of a case that wouldn't make sense to anyone who did not have all of the information that we had gathered. The next part should prove as interesting.

After the coffee and cookies were served and eaten to Sara's satisfaction, it was time to leave for our next interview, David Karsdon. We excused ourselves, and as we walked to our car, I looked up and down the street. I saw the Midcrest Plumbing truck off in the distance.

"Should we talk to him now?" I asked, pointing toward the truck.

"I don't think we're ready for Midcrest again," Red answered. "I don't think those guys have a clue how much we know. Do you, HH?"

"Nope."

I slid into the front seat of the Crown Vic and looked down Kensington Road. The trees were trimmed and the street had been swept. There were no noisy leaf-blowers, and there was no trash. The sun shone brightly. *Idyllic*, I thought. *Just idyllic.*

"Let's sit here for a while and listen," I said to Walker. I rolled down the windows and heard the birds tweeting and chirping in the bushes. They were looking for worms and appeared to be very successful. The dirt had been tilled well this week—on all of the homes on Kensington, even the one without a gardener.

Chapter 94

Kars

We pulled up to the Karsdon Kars dealership with a few minutes to spare. I decided to tell Red the story of Sergeant Biddle and Ginny, about the contract for black-and-whites, and the delivery of all of the new Dodge Chargers for Patrol and Detectives. He put a different spin on it that I should have thought about but hadn't.

"That could be a good thing for Orchard Hill, HH. I'm glad to hear it."

"Why? Look at the sticker price. That's a lot of money. Over a million dollars!"

"It's also over a hundred thousand dollars back to the city budget because of our one-cent sales tax. The city with the dealer of origin gets part of the sales tax that they would have had to pay anyway, if they were to buy the cars from, say, an LA dealer. Why not shop local if the price is good? And that could be why our PD has the best of everything."

"How do you know that, Red?"

"I just know it. That's all."

"You are full of shit!" I exclaimed.

"Nope."

We strolled through the new-car showroom that sparkled with cleanliness and saw Mr. Karsdon, walking the floor with an employee.

"Detective Hamilton!" bellowed Karsdon as if he was announcing a football game. His voice echoed off the highly glossed cars and marble flooring. He motioned for us to follow him to his office, which was right off the showroom floor.

"Thanks for blowing our cover, Mr. Karsdon," I said, only half joking. "This is my partner, Detective Walker."

"Good to meet you, Detective. David Karsdon," he said, as if he needed an introduction. "And I'm proud to have members of OHPD here at our dealership. I want people to know that we have a great relationship with the city and the police department. Come on in."

We were escorted to his rather stark office. Plaques all over the walls told us that Karsdon Kars was the pride of the community and the Chrysler Corporation. There was also a sepia photo of a young David Karsdon, standing next to an older man in the snow in front of a car dealership that I assumed was in Chicago. In the background was a large sign stating, "Karsdon's Kars" exactly like the sign on Albion Avenue in Orchard Hill. *Like father, like son,* I mused.

He closed the door and bid us to sit. I pulled out the file of original bank statements that he had provided and placed them on the edge of his desk.

"Have you had the opportunity to look at these, Mr. Karsdon?"

He shook his head. "No, I have not looked at those statements."

"Who does?" I asked.

"Well, my accountant gets all of the bills and decides which accounts should be paid out of the trust. We have several, as you can see. We don't muddle things up by taking money from one to the other. Ginny had her own money from our father, and I never had to supplement it from my dealership. While she had hers, it all came from my father. That's how it was set up."

"Do you realize that you paid out well over three hundred thousand dollars in the last five years for plumbing, electrical, and gardening fees on the Kensington property?"

"What?" he said rather incredulously. "Three hundred thousand dollars?"

"Yes, wouldn't you want someone to tell you that much was going out the door?"

"I would! I'll find out why those repairs were done," Karsdon said, making a note that I assumed was to remind him to call someone.

"Does the same accountant who handles your trust accounts do the books for Karsdon Kars?" I asked.

"No, thank God."

"I'd like the name of your accountant, if you don't mind. We have some questions for him. In examining the statements, over

$66,000 a year was going to Midcrest Plumbing, Eclectic Electric, and Kensington Gardens. And in looking at the property, that much work is not evident."

"I've not been there in years, Detective. I guess I should have but …" He shrugged.

"Do any of those businesses ring a bell?"

"The electrical company name looks familiar, but a lot of things go on here." He leaned forward on his desk and asked. "Do you have any suspects?"

"Just you, Mr. Karsdon," Walker blurted out.

"You're kidding! Why would I want to kill my sister? I'd stand to gain nothing. I'm not in her will, and I would get nothing from the trust. If you think her murder was a money thing, you're crazy."

"Are you involved in any religion, Mr. Karsdon?"

"I'm a fallen-away Catholic, if that's what you're after. I was a good Catholic for years, but with what's been going on with the church, I just decided to walk away for a while. Why do you ask?"

"We think your sister was associated with devil worship or Satanism," I responded.

Karsdon's mouth dropped open but no sound came out.

I was surprised by his reaction.

Then he shook his head and smirked. "Are you kidding me?" He seemed to think I was pulling his leg like Walker had done, accusing him of the murder.

I reached for the bank statements and placed them back in my briefcase. "We don't think it involves the Satanic Church," I told him, "just some spinoff group here in the community."

"Devil worship," Karsdon said, his demeanor quickly sobering. "Do you know anyone else involved with her and these activities?"

"We think so," I said.

"Would you keep me in the loop as soon as you know more or solve this?" he asked rather humbly.

He seemed genuinely taken aback by the news. Not just of the money but also the involvement in satanic activities. I would wait to see how Walker felt about it.

Karsdon reached into his desk drawer and handed me a business card with his accountant's name and phone number. "I'll tell them to expect your call, Detective Hamilton."

"Mr. Karsdon, one last question, if you would." He nodded, and I continued, "Have you been contacted by any realtors regarding the Kensington Road property?"

He hesitated just long enough to tell me what I wanted to know. "No," he said, but it was not a very powerful response. We left it at that.

"We thank you, Mr. Karsdon, and as next of kin, we'll keep you apprised of our progress. We know you're busy, so thanks for the time today," Walker said as we backed out of the office.

Neither of us paid much attention to the new and glistening showroom cars on the way out. I could feel that we were the center of attention as we left the showroom and got in the Crown Vic. Was it because we were driving a relic, compared to the new Chargers? Were my handcuffs or gun showing under my sports jacket? Or did we leave another impression that we were unaware of?

"You had Karsdon on the run with that comment, Red," I said.

"You know what, HH? We work well together and think alike."

"I've never had someone other than my wife think the same thing I was thinking at the same time. Must be some magic there, Red. That could be scary," I said half-jokingly. I mean, you're a shooter. I'm a talker."

"Maybe we can teach each other, HH. Maybe, just maybe."

He smirked. "Got to have some fun with this. What did you think of his reaction?"

"I think he had the shock of innocence that I was looking for; otherwise, he would have lawyered up. I don't think he has a clue what Ginny was up to and quite frankly, he was afraid to admit it."

Chapter 95

Check Listing

"Did you ever get hold of Oakes?" I asked Red as we drove back to the station.

"Yeah, for whatever good it did."

"What do you mean?"

"Well …" Red shuffled in his seat to find a better position to tell me what I already knew. "He had planned this for a while. He knew he wasn't coming back but didn't want to make a big thing about leaving. No retirement party of beer bust or anything. I think he's up there for good."

"Any loose ends on the case that we need to know about?" I asked, though I already knew the answer.

"Not really," Walker said dismissively. "At least nothing we can't pick up. He told me where to find the keys to his locker and his notebook for this case, and he also told me that he'd be dealing with HR to have them process his retirement. His mind was not in this one, and I think that kind of prompted him to just say screw it."

"Maybe we'll think that way some day," I said briskly, "but not right now."

"Well, we don't have our thirty in yet either, HH," Red said, laughing. "It's a long way off, so let's not even go there. Agreed?"

"Agreed," I responded as we pulled in to the station parking lot.

We walked in the back door and, by force of habit, took the stairs to the second floor. Walker took them two at a time, got winded in the process, and said, "Let's make a checklist of things to get the search warrants. There's one in the Murder Book. I think I'll call the lieutenant and run everything by him to make sure we're on the right track." He inhaled deeply to catch his breath. "Can you call the District Attorney Command Post and see if we can talk to a DA and find out who the duty judge is for this area for the weekend? By the way," Walker said, huffing and puffing, "put working out on the checklist as well. Those stairs kicked my ass!"

Walker went to the office, and I went to the squad table. Just about every phone number a detective ever needed was under every faded plastic desk blotter in the squad room. Some things are just too hard to change.

I left word for the duty DA to call me and got the name of the judge to use. There were two names: one for Saturday and one for Sunday. I picked the Sunday judge, the Honorable David Chambliss, who lived on the Hill. I jotted down the number, but I wanted to make sure we had our ducks in a row. Talking to the DA was going to be our first priority.

Walker came back from his phone call to Hospian.

"I filled in the lieutenant, HH. He likes it, but he did ask some questions."

"Like what?"

"Like, who is our suspect?"

"What did you say?"

"I said that's why we needed the search warrants, to gather more evidence. I wanted to end the sentence with the word 'asshole,' but I curbed my enthusiasm to do that."

We both smiled at that one.

"What did you tell him, then?" I asked.

"I said that it was between the plumber, the electrician, and the gardener, but we didn't know right now. I also said we'd pretty much eliminated Bauman and Brick but were not sure about Mr. Karsdon."

"You said that?" I said, smiling.

"Yeah, do you know what he said after that?" Walker posed the question like I should have figured it out by now.

"No, what did he say?"

"He asked how the interview went today with Karsdon."

"So?"

"HH, I never told him we were interviewing Karsdon today. They've already talked! I just know it."

I looked Walker in the eye and muttered, "Fuckin' Hospian and Biddle will do anything for a real estate listing! Anything!"

I briefed Walker on the information regarding the judge and the district attorney. "By the time the on-call DA gets back to us, we should have the checklist done and be ready to go to the judge. What do you think, Red? Do the search warrants tomorrow, get them signed, and serve them on Monday?"

Walker paused a moment and then said, "Let's wait until we talk with the DA. They can be skittish about all that work on a Sunday. Let me ask you this, though. Do you think we have any flight problems for our handymen?"

"I don't think so."

We went to work on our checklist for the search warrant. Walker had the template on his computer, and I had some of the details from the chronological log. I was searching through the notes and went to my notebook for some information I had misplaced. "I'll be better organized after this case. Now I have a better handle on what's needed with the Murder Book," I advised Walker.

And then I saw it.

It was the business card for David Karsdon's accountant.

"Holy shit, holy cow, holy shit!" I said, hoping Walker would look up. He did not. "Red, you won't believe this, but look at the name on the card Karsdon gave us for his accountant!"

"Yeah?"

"It's Montoya Accounting and Specialty Services. They call themselves MASS, and the key principal is Margarita Montoya."

"Yeah? So?"

"It's the same business address as Philippe Montoya, our electrician. The accounting firm is run by his wife or sister or some relative. And they write the checks!"

We looked at each other, communicating one word: *Bingo!*

Chapter 96

Flight

The phone rang, and it was the on-call Deputy DA, Carrie Wade. Walker put her on speaker phone in the office and then explained the background on the case and where we were with the interviews and physical evidence analysis. She listened intently, asking him one shotgun question after another. After about fifteen minutes of discussion, she told Walker that she needed to talk in person. She would help with the search warrants and wanted to meet us tomorrow at the station. It all made sense.

"One last thing," she said. "Do we have a flight potential with this guy Montoya or Margarita Montoya?"

Walker quickly responded, "We didn't think so until we discovered the connection. They use the same business address."

Karsdon had told us that he would let them know we would be contacting them. I got on another phone to Karsdon to see if he had placed the call. It went to voice mail. I left a message, asking him to contact me at any time, day or night, as I had an important question.

We all agreed to meet at the station at noon tomorrow. That would give me time to go to church tonight with Clare and the kids and have a nice leisurely breakfast at home.

"I had a thought," I said as we finalized our plan with Wade. "How about if Walker and I go by the address listed on the business card for Montoya Accounting on our way home? It's just outside the city in the county strip. We could swing by and see what we're dealing with and if the moving vans are lined up."

Walker gave me a thumbs-up. Wade liked the idea.

"Take some photos," she said. "Look to see who is listed on the business marquee and see if there's any activity. Let me know ASAP if there's anything going on. I'll be out tonight so get me on my cell."

We all exchanged cell numbers and agreed to touch base, even if nothing materialized. I told Wade that I would let her know if I heard anything from Karsdon.

"Bought my last car there," she offered.

"You and everybody else in town," I added. *If she only knew*, I thought. Walker could read my mind.

"Hey," Wade said, "you guys really put together a nice case. It's great to work with veterans like you. Looking forward to seeing you tomorrow."

We both had to laugh. Veterans, indeed. If she only knew.

I called Clare to let her know I'd be home after one last stop, and we could plan on going to four-thirty Mass.

Walker took his city car, and I drove my personal car to meet at the accountant's address. It was in a somewhat deserted, single-story commercial building with more vacancies than occupancies.

The parking lot was empty, except for what appeared to be a few abandoned cars. The unkempt nature of this business enterprise would not have been possible in Orchard Hill. The county area was a different story.

We spotted the uniquely designed MASS wooden sign, with a phone number and a smaller attachment reading "Eclectic Electric" below it. There was no illumination on the sign, and no lights on in the interior part of the office. I thought the use of the acronym MASS was more than a coincidence. I couldn't wait to tell Holcomb. We took the photos requested by Wade.

We looked for emergency contact information on the door but found nothing. We couldn't see inside their offices, because there were no windows in the front. I spotted the open area shed where trash bins were stored and saw they were full, but the lids were closed to keep the rain out. We walked around the rear of the building and noted the exit door and parking stalls for tenants. The "reserved for" sign advised us that these parking stalls were for MASS employees only, as if there was competition for parking with all of the vacancies.

We were satisfied that no one had been there recently. Walker returned to the Crown Vic and searched in the homicide kit for a few minutes. "Got 'em!" he exclaimed and showed me some clear plastic stickers.

"Perfect," I said, knowing what he wanted to do next.

We went to the front door and placed the stickers between the door and the jam. They were a light adhesive that would break the seal if someone used the door to get in. A person entering wouldn't see the stickers, but we would know if they had been broken. We placed them on the front and rear doors and what looked to be a bathroom window near the rear exit.

"We can come by periodically to see if anyone's entered. I'll swing by after church tonight and check it again in the morning," I offered.

"Great! I'll do the same. Just jot down the times. See you at noon tomorrow."

Chapter 97

Normalcy

The homicide was at 417 Kensington. Karsdon Kars, our police station, my home, and the accounting firm were almost right around the corner from each other.

We were all just a few miles away, but it could have been hundreds of miles. In Patrol, I would never have seen the connection. Yes, I could go home for lunch, but rarely did. I could go cruising Kensington Road to look at old Victorian homes, or go car shopping at Karsdon's lot, or go to work—all in close proximity—but never did.

I took a deep breath and welcomed the normalcy that waited inside. I would try to leave this case in my car.

"We have just enough time for you to take a quick shower, get dressed, and get to Mass, HH," Clare called out.

"Welcome home, Howard," I said to myself.

The shower was quick, the change of clothes quicker, and the drive to St. Elizabeth's rather uneventful. I joked with Geoff that he needed a haircut, and he let me know that I did too. Touché. I asked Clare if we could drive her car to church, because I was certain that my car still held the secrets of the Karsdon case.

We arrived at the church with only minutes to spare before the bells rang to announce that you were late if you were not already inside.

There was Holcomb, dressed in his white cassock, carrying his Bible at the rear of the church with Pastor Art. He saw us this time and bowed slightly in acknowledgment. He then ushered the altar servers, holding white candles, down the aisle. Holcomb carried the Bible high above his head, and the pastor followed, acknowledging those in attendance with a nod and singing a hymn to which no one knew the words other than him and Holcomb.

I had not confided in Clare what Holcomb and I had been up to. *That will happen later*, I thought, *rather than sooner*. I was deep in thought, somewhere between prayer, the readings, and work. Church was always a place to escape to. Bring your sins and worries, and they'll vanish before your very eyes. Well, not quite, but it always seemed that way. But my mind was consumed by the Karsdon case. It was a magnet that was drawing me in, more so than what the excitement of Patrol had done years ago.

As I sat listening to the readings by Holcomb and the homily by Pastor Art, I realized that my attention should be here in church with Clare, Geoff, and Marcia, but they were off in the distance. *Not good*, I thought, *not good at all*.

I tried to focus on Holcomb's words as I looked at the readings, but I couldn't concentrate. I kept reading the word "Mass" over and over.

Another week had gone by. I had not seen my old patrol buddies and not heard from Donny or McBride. There had not been a Sergeant Bennett or even a Rikelman sighting. Perhaps from a distance at Clyde's funeral I had seen them, but that was the extent. It had been me and Walker. There had been a dose of Hospian, but I could have done without that.

Mass was over before I had time to think. It was still light outside, so perhaps some discussion with Holcomb could occur outside of church. As I walked outside with the family, Holcomb was nowhere to be found. *That's best*, I figured. *No need to clutter the weekend any more than it already is.*

Clare caught me looking around and queried, "Who are you looking for, HH?"

"I was looking for Rex."

Clare pointed to him over on the side of the church—he was huddled on his cell phone—but she said, "Let it go, Howard."

"You're right." I laughed. "Hey, it's Saturday night. Let's go out for pizza, everybody!"

There were four votes for and none against. I took that to be a majority. In this family it was not always the case.

On Sunday morning, I puttered in the garden, pulling out older bushes and ground cover to make way for the more magical of plants, but I didn't know what just yet. Perhaps that would be another conversation with Bonzo.

Clare agreed to take the hydrangeas out of the pots, because she wanted overgrown bushes eventually. I let her know I would pick up the acid fertilizer on my way home, after my afternoon at the station.

"You didn't tell me you were going in again today, Howard."

"It's just for a few hours to meet with the district attorney on this case. And, I was sure I told you."

Clare sighed. "I don't think so, but I can't keep track of you lately. Is this going to continue, or are you going to get some days off? They're really working you, HH."

"I'll get my days off, Clare; don't worry." The words I wanted to say, however, I only thought: *"They" are not working me. I am working me. Or more to the point, Ginny is working me. The case is working me, even when I'm not working. The Phantom was coming for me.*

Chapter 98

Noon

I was at the station by eleven thirty. I thought I would get there before Walker and do some snooping around to find out what I had missed in Patrol. I was wrong again, as his Crown Vic was parked near the back door.

Taking the back stairs two at a time, I walked into the detective squad room a bit winded and saw him at the computer in our commandeered makeshift office.

"You won't believe this, HH. I got a call from the Crime Lab. Seems they got some OT money and caught up on some of their backlogged serology and DNA work. They processed that rag with the three different semen stains and got a hit on one."

"Only one?"

"Yeah, but a good one. Guess who?"

"Mr. Bauman?"

"Nope."

"Karsdon?"

"Nope."

"I give up. No, wait—you?"

"You're close. Midcrest!"

"Midcrest? The plumber?"

"None other. Hot damn."

"What does that mean?"

"I don't know yet, but we will, as soon as we bring him in. The only reason he was a hit was that his DNA was in the system because of his arrest record. The other two had no records, remember?"

Just then, the phone rang, announcing that the DA was here.

Deputy District Attorney Carrie Wade walked in to the office carrying a briefcase and about fifty extra pounds. She was short, with strawberry-blonde hair, well groomed, and somewhere between a drill sergeant and a fullback. The initial image was a take-no-prisoners, no-nonsense attack dog. We could not have been more pleased. Walker and I exchanged glances to that effect and got down to business.

We brought her up-to-date on yesterday's activities with the accounting firm, bank statements, and the new lab results.

"I tried one of these cases in the Valley," she said.

"You did?" we both said, almost in unison.

"We thought it was unique," I added.

"Well, they're all unique, but they have similar things in common. Have you talked with Detective Rex Holcomb of LAPD about this case?"

"As a matter of fact, we have. He's very familiar with this case and has been a big help," I responded.

She seemed impressed that we had done our homework. "Good, just don't put his name on anything."

"We already know that, too."

She went on to tell us of the things she had seen in her other case that was eerily the same—various colored candles, the literature, and symbols of Satan. "I've not seen the victim cut up like this, so that's new. Semen is common, and I think we may have multiple suspects. Other than this DNA match with Midcrest, do you have any others?"

I raised my hands up like an orchestra leader waiting to direct and said, "Hold it, hold it! I have a theory. Can I present it, so you can shoot at it?" I looked directly at Walker as I said "shoot." I felt the need to stand up to make my points and to think more clearly. I had been working on a theory, but last night in church, it had all come together. "First, I think we have three suspects—Midcrest, Montoya and Kensington." I looked to Walker for agreement and got it. I figured it was too soon for Wade, but that would come later. "Second, the murder was a satanic ritual in which all three took part." Walker and Wade both nodded. "Third, it was all about sex and money. All three were tapping Ginny as a part of the satanic thing, and they were invoicing her, with her permission, to write checks to their little church. Fourth, the payments stopped in August, when Ginny fired Kensington, although we don't know why—maybe money was going through the accounting firm to another source. When the money stopped, somebody said something that led to Ginny's being killed by one of these guys—or all three. Or even a fourth party."

Walker and Wade looked at me expectantly but said nothing.

"I think that because we have Midcrest's DNA, we should re-interview him and see where he takes us. Do we have enough to arrest?" I looked at Wade hopefully.

"Not quite. But we do have enough to detain and bring him in. We can decide all of that after we squeeze him. The semen stain may help. Where did we get it?"

"That could be a problem," Walker confided. "It was not at the crime scene. It was in the trash, on the street."

There was a brief silence in the room that signified that was another issue we needed to revisit. Wade broke the awkwardness and said, "Does Midcrest know this?"

"No," Walker and I answered in unison.

"Good."

"When do we bring him in?" I asked.

"Let's do that tomorrow," Wade said quickly. "We'll do the search warrants and get them signed tonight. Which one of you is doing the warrant?"

Walker raised his hand.

"Okay, we're *not* going to get a warrant to dig up the yard for animal parts. At least not yet. We can always do that later. Let's wait until we talk to these guys with the evidence we have."

"Okay by me," I responded. "And by the way, I've never done a warrant and need to work on my voir dire and my work history and expertise. It will not be much because I'm on loan from Patrol for this."

"You mean you're not even a detective?" Wade asked.

"No, ma'am."

After a ten-minute lecture on how to prepare my affidavit, Wade turned me loose to work with Walker on the search warrants.

She came back to see me after about thirty minutes. I had secreted myself in the squad room at an empty table and computer. I was very sensitive about even being in the squad room today. It was Sunday, and unless Patrol had a very good reason to be in Detectives' squad bay, it was hands off and stay out.

The chief had put out a notice to that effect, because detectives had complained to him that somebody from Patrol was eating pastrami sandwiches on their desks and leaving the grease to coagulate on their desk blotters, covering up valuable phone information. More important, it also covered their pictures of the wives and kids. The watch commander even had to make rounds to shoo them out if he caught anyone even close to the second floor.

I gave Wade the name of the on-call judge for search warrants. She called Judge Chambliss to let him know what she was working on and advised him that she would e-mail everything in about two hours. He would then sign it electronically, and we would be good to go for tomorrow. He'd like to meet with us before any arrest warrants were issued, he told her.

While we actually had ten days to serve the warrants, tomorrow being the first day of the workweek would be better, as our suspects would not be the wiser. We agreed to keep Wade posted regarding our activities tomorrow. She let us know what court she would be in and how to track her down.

Walker and I agreed to meet at seven in the morning to get the interview room set up with audio and video and get a fresh start on the crime scene on Kensington by eight o'clock. We would take two uniformed officers with us and hook up Midcrest wherever we found him in the morning.

Walker called Hospian and gave him an update. We were all set to go.

Chapter 99

Restless

I arrived home by four in the afternoon to a chorus of "Hey, Dad" this and "Hey, Howard" that. It was really nice to be needed. I had missed out on a few of the Sunday rituals, like taking our puppy, Bentley, to the dog park and getting him some new toys. The Sunday paper was unread. Boxes and organizing containers were stacking up in the garage.

Owning your own home means there are endless projects going, either self-imposed or spouse-imposed. Clare and I work best from lists—hers, mine, and ours. I tried to get into something that would keep my mind from what Walker and I had planned for the week. It wasn't working.

What questions should we ask Midcrest to get him to talk? Could we get him to roll over on Kensington or Montoya? My sense was that among the three, Midcrest was the weak link. He was more cooperative with us than the others and also seemed the most naïve. Perhaps we could use this to our advantage.

I tried to get into the barbecuing and dinner preparation. Sunday night dinners together were quickly becoming an expectation, now that I was on days. I took a notepad outside while I heated up the gas burners so I could jot down things that came to mind. I could tell that Clare was concerned. Or was she upset? Or was she just pissed?

After a pleasant dinner, the kids got ready for bed and stayed in their rooms. I took one of the books I had checked out from the library, as I wanted to identify some areas that would perhaps help me during the week. Clare was being very accommodating but distant. I didn't know if she was giving me the space I needed or was upset that my mind was not fully on family activities? Probably a little of both.

Later, we showered and crawled into bed with our books, propped up our pillows, and hooked up our nightlights to see who was going to fall asleep first. We hugged and kissed good night, and it took me all of five minutes before I was out like a burned bulb.

But it was a very restless sleep. I dreamed like I had never done before. I was in a fairy-tale and, almost like *Alice in Wonderland*, I was looking down a hole or a tunnel that was calling to me. The voice at the other end was familiar. It was Walker's. But there was someone with him—a faceless woman. Or a woman with a mask, like in the *Phantom of the Opera*. They were beckoning me to join them. I looked behind me, and Clare and the kids were standing in an English garden, chanting in a gentle monotone.

"Come with us, Howard. Don't go. Don't go. Be with us."

Walker and his friend were asking me to come to them. He pleaded with me, "Ginny and I need you. We both need you. You can do this, Howard. You can."

The woman with the mask called my name. "Howard, Ipsissimus needs you as an acolyte for us. Drink our wine and eat our bread. For we are the music of the calling. Come to us, come to us."

I looked back, and it was just Clare, holding out her arms.

What should I do? Jump into the tunnel? Ask Clare and the kids to come with me? Stay with Clare or go with Walker and was that Ginny? The music of the calling was playing in the background, but it was a song from *Phantom*. A voice that could have been Walker's or some other person was singing it, calling to me to embrace the music of the calling. It sounded like Michael Crawford. Walker, or someone like him, kept talking, "You can do this, Howard. If you solve Ginny's case you will be in the elite—the job and career you want. It's here for the taking. Come with us and work your magic."

I realized that Clare's poking me in the side was not part of the dream, and I woke in a start, calling out, "What should I do? What should I do?" I was sweating, tossing my head from side to side as if I was looking at Clare and then at Walker. But he wasn't there, and she was. Thank goodness.

Chapter 100

Change of Plans

When I arrived at the station on Monday morning, there was more activity than I had bargained for. Walker and Lieutenant Hospian were huddled in Hospian's office, and six uniforms were waiting outside in the squad bay. Walker called me in as soon as he saw me.

"HH, this has gotten big." He deferred to Lieutenant Hospian, who was studying a map on his desk and talking to Deputy District Attorney Wade on the telephone. He was referencing points on an area that was gridded off on the map.

Hospian hung up the phone. "We'll have a briefing in about fifteen minutes," he told everyone within hearing distance. "We need three teams of two at each location and one arrest team to take Midcrest into custody. We have search warrants for Midcrest, his vehicle, and his home. Same for Montoya and Kensington. We also have a search warrant ready for the Montoya MASS, the accounting office in the county. I think we need two more uniforms. Who is going to notify the Sheriff's that we're in their turf?"

I raised my hand to get his attention. "Can I ask a question here?"

"Sure," Hospian said.

"Why so many uniforms and search warrants?"

Walker answered before Hospian could respond. "After you left last night, I called the lieutenant one last time to give an update. We then decided that we needed to hit all locations at the same time; otherwise, evidence could be compromised or people could talk to one another. I was going to call you but figured I'd let you know this morning. Any problem, HH?"

Walker knew I was upset. It looked like this case was taken right out from under us. But it was not my case, it was Walker's, and I was just helping out. I knew I had no business being possessive about it but could not help thinking I took it too seriously. I had to keep reminding myself of that fact. Hell, I was just a Patrol guy.

"No, Red," I said, "sounds like a good plan. I think that we don't need an arrest team. We have the relationship. You and I can take Midcrest in and talk with him after we secure the locations and the vehicles."

Walker looked at Hospian for approval.

"No problem. I think that's a great idea, HH," Hospian replied.

Everything about the updated plan was right. I was just suffering from tunnel vision about what we should be doing, but Hospian had the bigger picture. We were dealing with killers here, potentially, and not plumbers or gardeners. Even though it didn't matter, I thought that the case somehow had been taken away from us. Walker knew what I was thinking but no one else did. It was my job to let that issue go.

Hospian controlled the briefing. Thankfully, I saw Sergeant Stevens in the back of the room and felt better. *With Stevens, things will go well*, I thought. It was now very straightforward, and I was along for the ride.

The plan was to send a scout team in uniform to ensure that Midcrest's plumbing truck was on Kensington. I was hopeful that Kensington and Montoya also would be servicing the area—but it was just hope. We decided to wait until nine o'clock, just in case one or more of them got a late start on their day.

I really wanted to take Midcrest into custody myself. I thought we had a decent rapport and that if he was hooked up by a stranger in uniform, he would lawyer up too soon. I wanted the chance to talk with him. Luckily, the report back was that his truck had been spotted at the far end of Kensington in front of 495. It was time to move in.

As the radio chattered that he had been spotted in a side yard, digging a ditch, I jumped on the air. "This is David 75, I'll take him. Just have some uniforms stand by."

Walker and I drove down the street a little too fast and overshot the address by one house. Midcrest was in a hole on the side of the house. He was knee-deep in mud and was not going anywhere.

"Hey, detectives, how are you doin'?"

"Good, Herb, but we need to talk with you," I said, hoping to sound official.

"I was wondering when you boys would get around to another talk."

"We need to go down to the station, Mr. Midcrest, and right now," I added.

"Okay," he said, climbing out of the hole. "I can change in my truck."

I escorted him to his truck and asked for keys. "We'll watch you change, if you don't mind. We have a warrant for your truck, so we're going to search it and, if we need to, impound it."

"You fellas seem to know what you're doin' here," he said with resignation. He sat in the back of the truck and took off his work gloves and muddy boots, as well as a second pair of pants. He then put on clean working shoes.

"New gloves, Mr. Midcrest?" I asked, remembering the gloves we'd found in the trash a few days ago. They looked very similar.

"Yeah, I've been going through them quickly. Second pair in a month," he said. "They normally last six months."

I walked Midcrest over to the Crown Vic. "it's procedure, Herb, but I have to handcuff you to put you in the car."

"Okay, if you must."

I silently searched and handcuffed him behind his back, holding his head while he climbed in the backseat. Prior to getting out of the car, Walker had activated the digital recorder we had stashed in the backseat, just to catch anything on the way to the station. I took that opportunity to read him his Miranda rights.

"This is about Miss Ginny, isn't it?" Midcrest said quietly as he tried to get comfortable in the backseat. "We can talk."

Walker was going through the truck with a fine-tooth comb, not really sure what to look for but hoping we would locate something incriminating. He was not disappointed. Uniformed officers Pat Woford and Marcus Simpson were standing by. This was the first time I had seen Woford since the encounter in the workout room with Donny, and the first time I had seen Simpson since the incident with Gabby. It was like a reunion.

"So this is where you've been," Woford said with a big smile. "I'm finally on days to finish my probation, and then I hope to get back to PMs. This day watch sucks."

And she hopes to get back to Donny, I thought.

We were parked in front of the Bauman residence, but there was no sign of him. Maybe he was staying inside and letting us just do what we do. *There'll be time to talk with him later*, I thought.

My priority was Midcrest at this point. I sat in the backseat while Walker inventoried the truck. I tried to be as low-key as I could, but Midcrest knew he was in trouble. I could read it in his face.

"David 75, David 75, come in," the radio chattered. I acknowledged. It was Hospian. "David 75, this is David 10. Can you talk?" Hospian asked.

"David 10, in one minute," I responded, climbing out of the backseat after I had just gotten comfortable. Rolling up the windows to ensure Midcrest couldn't hear, I said, "David 10, go. This is 75."

"David 75, FYI, we have Kensington in custody up the street at 417. He was working on our victim's yard. Word from the MASS office is that it's cleaned out! Empty. Didn't we have anybody on it last night?"

"Shit!" I said, after making sure my mike was not activated. I purposely pushed the mike button and trying not to sound too frustrated, said "David 10, we checked it on Saturday and at least twice yesterday."

"It's empty now! And no sign of either Montoya," Hospian said condemningly.

"Roger." I looked up to see Walker mouthing the four-letter word we all wanted to scream. I asked Hospian if he could put Kensington in interview B. "We'll put Midcrest in A and get started. Do you have Kensington's truck and trailer?"

"Roger, David 75, on the interview room, and roger on the truck and trailer, but here is what we are going to do, HH. We'll have one of our officers drive Midcrest's truck and another drive Kensington's truck to the station. We'll go over them there. As long as we have the search warrants, it would be better than impounding. We'd have to inventory everything if we impound it now. If we need to, we can make that decision later."

Even though I would have liked to impound them both, Hospian was right—again.

"Roger. David 75 out."

Chapter 101

Midcrest

Walker gave me a thumbs-up that he'd obtained some evidence from Midcrest's truck. From my vantage point, sitting in the backseat of the Crown Vic, I could see he was holding a book.

Midcrest appeared to be very relaxed. He was concerned about his truck, but I assured him we were only looking for certain items, and he would get his truck back in one piece.

"What are you looking for?" he asked.

"We'll talk about that at the station, if you don't mind," I responded.

"If I know what you're looking for, perhaps I can help."

"I appreciate that," I said, "but the truck will be at the station while we talk. I'd rather not do it out here on the street."

"Suit yourself."

We arrived at the station at the same time that Midcrest's truck was being parked in the CSI car inspection sally port. We left Midcrest in the backseat and huddled out of ear shot.

"Let's make sure we get Kensington settled into the interview room first before we escort this guy into the station," Walker advised.

I contacted the unit with Kensington and advised them to take him upstairs before we came in. We waited for about five minutes before we took Midcrest to interview room A. He was uncuffed and directed to take a seat.

The lieutenant advised me that Kensington was in B and all electronics were on. "This is your and Walker's case, HH, so take your time and let's do this right. Don't worry about Montoya right now. I'll have a team work on that. Let's deal with the suspects we have."

I was relieved. "Thanks, Lieutenant."

Walker and I huddled for a moment to get our thoughts together before entering the interview room. Midcrest was very relaxed, considering his predicament.

"How are you guys' doin'?" he asked as we came in the room.

"We're fine, Herb, just fine," I answered.

"I suppose you finally want to talk about Miss Ginny again, huh?"

We both sat down directly across from him but far enough apart that he had to look at each of us separately. Walker then began the first series of questions. "Can we get you something to drink or eat, Herb?"

"Sure. I had an early breakfast, but I could use some coffee, with a little cream."

"Comin' right up," I said, jumping up and leaving the room. I went over to the detectives' coffee table and prepared his drink as he directed. "No Peet's for this guy." I smiled to myself. "He'll have to drink this shit." I brought it back in to the interview room, along with a napkin. I also had taken a doughnut from the box sitting next to the coffeemaker. I set both items on the table in front of him.

"Thanks!" he exclaimed. "This is great!"

Walker and I looked at each other and laughed, knowing the coffee was putrid and the doughnut was a hunk of grease.

Midcrest appeared to be very forthright. "What do you guys need to know that I can help with?"

"Well, Herb," I began, "first tell us a little more about your relationship with Miss Ginny." My goal was to talk about her as if she were alive and not deal with her death just yet.

"I really liked her. And she was good to all of us—Philippe and especially Bernard."

"When you say she was good to you, what does that mean?"

He didn't speak for a long moment but then said, "Well, Bernard and I are single, ya know, and not too many ladies in our lives, if you know what I mean."

We both nodded without uttering a word of agreement.

"Well, the four of us would get together in her house and pray. Bernard would read passages to us, and we would sit around."

At this point, I felt compelled to interrupt. "By 'Bernard,' do you mean Bonzo Kensington?"

"Yeah, Bonzo. Bernard didn't like Bonzo, but he used it for business purposes. I don't know why."

"Sorry to interrupt, Herb. I just needed a clarification."

"I understand, I think," he said, looking a little confused. By then I had figured out that Midcrest was not the sharpest knife in the drawer.

"So anyway, we read from some scriptures and lit some candles. Ginny would …" He paused and took a deep breath. "Ginny would stimulate us, you know, sexually, and help us get off after the readings."

We both nodded, trying to show that we understood.

"What were the readings about, Herb?" Walker asked quietly.

"Well, they were readings from the Maharaja, the Old Testament, and the Black Mass. They would help bind us with Satan, you know. We would drink dark, heavy wine and eat some black bread and pretend it was his body and blood."

"Who led the service?" I asked gently. He seemed to have placed himself in almost a trancelike state, where he could see himself with her.

"Bernard and Ginny would read to us. They were real good at the readings. I just listened."

"Was there ever anyone else involved with your readings?" I asked.

"No. Just us four," he replied.

"Were there ever any animals involved?" I felt comfortable asking that question as he gazed off, studying the acoustical perforations on the wall. Holcomb had wanted that answer as much as we did.

"We talked about it. We talked about offering a sacrifice but felt we weren't there yet."

"I understand," I said with as much warmth as I could muster.

"I really enjoyed the readings. She was a good reader. I miss her." He seemed lost in another world right now.

"Can you tell us what happened to her?" Walker asked.

Chapter 102

The Others

"Can I have another coffee and doughnut?" Midcrest almost pleaded. "Those were real good."

Walker held up his hand as I stirred to get up. "We'll get you another coffee and doughnut, but first, could you answer my question? What happened to Ginny?"

"That's a long story. Can I at least have another coffee?"

Walker looked at me. I went back to the detectives' coffee table and acquired the goods.

Hospian saw me and asked, "How's it going?"

"Okay, I think. Got to get back."

"Have you talked to Kensington yet?"

"No, should we?"

"Well, he's been sitting for a while. Might want to check in with him."

"In a few," I said, trying to open the interview room door holding a coffee and a crumb donut.

I placed the items on the table and could tell that things had cooled down in my absence. Midcrest took a sip of coffee and a small bite of doughnut. Crumbs went all over the table.

"Umm, this is good. Sorry I made a mess here," he apologized. He brushed off his fingers on his sleeve and said, "You asked what happened to Ginny, I believe."

"Yes," Walker said encouragingly.

"Let me explain the best I can. Philippe and his wife have a small church. It's called the Church of the Living Triangle. We all supported their church, but we held our own services at Ginny's. We never went to their church. Well, about three or four years ago, Ginny and Philippe came up with a plan. Ginny said that she had a lot of money that she would never spend. She lived well but was a real packrat. You saw her house."

We smiled and nodded in agreement.

"Well …" He hesitated briefly before going on. "Ginny proposed that we support Philippe's church by invoicing her for work done on her property. She would then send the bills to her brother, who would just pay the bills and send us each our monthly check. We would then give the checks to Philippe. Bernard and me. Philippe would get one too. He would then put it in his church account. It was pretty easy."

"So let me get this clear," I said. "You billed Ginny each month for work you didn't do. She turned in your bill, and you received a check from her estate, paid by her brother. And then you gave the checks to Philippe for his church? Did I get that right?" Midcrest nodded, but I wanted a verbal response for the record, so I asked again, "Is that what you said?"

"Yes, that is exactly what we did."

"Did you endorse the checks over to the Church of the Triangle?"

"Yes, had too. That was the agreement. With Miss Ginny."

"Did Bernard do the same?"

"Well, Bernard's arrangement was a little different."

"How so?" Walker asked.

"Bernard was doing a lot of the real work on the property. She didn't need a plumber or an electrician that often, but Bernard was there every week, sometimes twice a week."

"That makes sense," I said. "So what was different about that arrangement?"

"Well, Bernard will probably tell you, but I think his check was over two thousand dollars, and he wrote Philippe a check for $1,500 every month. I'm not sure; you have to ask him."

"Okay, we will, Herb. Thanks."

"Are we done now? Can I go?"

"Not quite yet, Herb," I responded. "There are just a few more questions."

"Like what?"

"Like what happened to Ginny?" Walker said, trying to control his frustration.

"Oh, that. Well, back in August, Ginny decided that she was done with the church and also done using Bernard as her gardener. She was also done with us, as a prayer group. She wanted to do the gardening herself from then on. Didn't want to fire him and get someone else, just do it herself."

"That was back in August?" I asked.

"Yeah, I think so. Anyway, the checks stopped and so did our little reading sessions."

"Were you disappointed?" I asked.

"No, not really. I did miss the readings, but I picked up some of the books that Ginny had and just read myself."

"Then what happened?" I asked.

"Well, Philippe and Bernard were not happy. Bernard said that we had lost our serenity on Kensington Road. Her place was not being kept up to our standards, and Bernard became angry."

"How about Philippe?" Walker added.

"Yeah, him too, I guess. We had a church holiday coming up in September, and they both decided to use that day to discuss it with Ginny."

"And did they?" we both asked.

"I guess so, because that was the day she died."

"September 22?"

"Yeah. September 22. That's a day of celebration for our church and coincidently was also Ginny's birthday."

"Were you involved with the meeting or just the celebration?" I asked.

"No, I was only invited after their meeting."

"Where was the meeting?"

"At Ginny's house. They called me to come over. They said that Ginny had died, and we were going to have a service."

"Did you go?"

"Yeah. I was on the other side of town but came over."

"Where was Ginny when you arrived," I asked.

"She was on her bed, upstairs. And she was dead—I could see that."

We had developed a good rhythm of interrogation. I was praying that Midcrest wouldn't want another break. We were headed down the road now, and each step seemed vital to the case.

"How could you tell she was dead?" I queried.

"She was quiet. Not moving. Bernard and Philippe were preparing for a service—that's why they called me. They said it was important that we celebrate her life. She was very good to us."

"What kind of service?" Walker asked.

"We weren't sure what to do. At first, Philippe suggested cutting her up and offering her to Satan. I didn't want to do that. Bernard said we should just use her body as a temple or altar and do some readings. Philippe insisted on some blood, so instead of the wine, we cut her on her arms and legs and placed candles in her and read from the Black Mass book. There was enough blood of hers for each of us to drink a little."

"Did you?"

"I did. To honor her."

I had a burning question to ask but I thought it best to let some silence fill the room. "Did Bernard or Philippe kill Ginny?" I winced as I said the word "kill," but did not know another word to use.

"I don't know," Midcrest responded.

"Did you ever think to ask?" I said.

"No. It didn't seem to matter. She was dead."

At that moment, I remembered that those were the same words that Rikelman had used regarding the deaths of Johnson, Gabby, and Clyde. Exactly the same words.

Walker and I looked at each other in what was now a very small room.

Chapter 103

The Wolf

I walked out of the interview to see the smiling face of Lieutenant Hospian.

"Nice job, you guys. Very good interrogation. But I have some very bad news."

"What's that?" Walker and I said in unison.

"As you know, the MASS office was cleaned out. Sometime in the middle of the night, I guess. We checked the Montoya residence, and there's no sign of life. We checked at the airport, and they took off on a flight to Puerto Rico at 0600 hours."

"Damn it!" I said directly to the lieutenant. "I'm sorry, Lieutenant. We should have put a watch on the office."

"We still have a lot of work to do." He pointed to interview room B. "You guys need to sit with Kensington and see where he's coming from. He may not know that Montoya has slipped away."

"We'll see," Walker said.

"Can we take five first and get coffee?" I asked.

"Go ahead, if you want to drink that crap," Walker replied. "I'll go make my introductions to Kensington. Give me a few minutes with him."

I took a few minutes to settle down and enjoy some bad coffee. Woford was still in the area, sorting through potential evidence, and we acknowledged each other.

"I didn't know you went to Detectives, Howard. Donny didn't say anything."

"Well, he's had his share of issues too, Pat."

"I know," she added.

"But I'm just on loan for this case only. I come back to Patrol when we're done."

"Some people hope that's true," she said cryptically.

"What do you mean?"

"Well, I overheard some of the guys on the auto-theft table saying that one of them was supposed to get the homicide assignment. And then you showed up. They're not happy about it."

"Oh shit. I didn't think of that. They're right, you know. I just didn't think about it."

"Hope to see you back in Patrol soon, Howard," she said, smiling as she walked away.

"Thanks, Pat. I owe you one."

"Oh no you don't, Howard. No you don't. But we could be even," she said, walking away without looking back.

I knew what she meant.

I walked into interview room B and found Walker and Kensington laughing at something. I ignored it and sat in my usual position on the outside of my partner, next to the door.

"How are you doing, Mr. Kensington?" I said in greeting. "I don't know if you remember me. My name is Detective Hamilton."

"I do, Detective. Hydrangeas, right?"

"Right," I responded. He and Walker both laughed again.

Walker decided to quit playing a game and just quickly move into the conversation. "I was just reminding Mr. Kensington that my new partner had gotten some free advice from him regarding his flower dilemma. He said that he normally doesn't give out that kind of advice for free. You must feel fortunate."

"I do, and thanks for that," I said.

"Well, truthfully, you could have obtained that information online, you know."

"Mr. Kensington ... can I call you Bernard?" I asked.

"Please do," he said, sounding businesslike.

"Bernard, you hit it right on the head when you said 'truthfully,' because that's what we would like to do here. Get to the truth. Is that okay?"

"Sure."

"Good. Can I get you a cup of bad coffee or a doughnut?" I offered.

"No thanks. But some water would be nice." He was smacking his dry lips, showing he was nervous and maybe even slightly agitated. Maybe that was good. Walker left the room searching for bottled water. In less than a minute, he returned with three bottles. More than likely, Hospian was standing right outside to hand it to him.

"So, Bernard, tell us again how long you've been providing landscape services to the homes on Kensington Road," I said.

"Over ten years, as I recall. Are you going to compare it to my last statement?"

"We have advised you of your rights, have we not?" I asked because I wanted to be sure that Walker had Mirandized Kensington, but I didn't want to remind him.

Kensington was too sharp to trip up. He pointed to Walker. "He did."

"We only listen to the answers after we give you your rights anyway, Bernard, so we won't hold you to what you told us before."

"Oh, that's comforting," he said, smirking a little.

"No," Walker said, laughing, "we couldn't remember what you told us anyway."

We all laughed at that.

I had to get right to the issues. "When is the last time you saw Ginny Karsdon alive, Bernard?"

"Last time I spoke with her was in August, when she let me go."

"Are you sure?"

"I think so."

"Is it possible that you've talked with her since then, say in mid-September?"

"It's possible, but I doubt it."

"But it is possible?

"Yes."

"Up until you were let go, how many times a week did you visit her property?"

"Sometimes once and sometimes twice. It depended on the work I was doing."

"So either once or twice a week?"

"Yes." He started to look away but caught himself.

"After you were let go and before she passed away, how many times did you visit the property?"

"I didn't. I had no reason."

"Is it possible that you visited the property after you were let go?"

"It's possible, but if I did, I don't recall."

"But it is possible that you did visit the property between the time you were 'let go'"—I put my fingers in quotes—"and before her death?"

There was a long pause, and then he said, "It's possible I guess."

"Okay, Bernard, that's good. Now stay with me here. When is the last time you were in her home?"

"I'm a gardener, Detective Hamilton. I don't go into homes."

"Is it possible that you were in her home and cannot recall?"

"Anything is possible."

"When was the last time you were on her porch? Either the front or back porch?"

"I don't recall." He reached for the bottled water and after tugging on the top, finally broke the seal and took a long swig. I knew we were in dangerous territory now. I could have used water myself but that was not going to happen right now. Mine was just going to sit there and tease me.

"Don't you periodically need to go on the porch to take care of potted plants or trim the ivy or trellis?

"I guess I do, yes."

"So it is possible that you were on her porch at times? Would that be a fair statement?"

"Yes, that would be a fair statement."

"Okay, now what about the house? Is it possible that you've been in her home and just did not recall?"

"It is possible, yes."

"How many times?" Right after I asked that question, I knew I had made a mistake.

"I couldn't tell you how many times because I can't recall if I ever was inside."

He was right, and he'd caught me at my game.

Chapter 104

Coalesce

Walker chimed in to see what he could salvage of the interview with Kensington.

"Bernard, what if I were to tell you that we had witnesses who either saw you enter Ginny's home on several occasions or saw you actually inside?"

"They'd be wrong."

"But—and this is a big 'but'—is it possible that you have been inside Ginny's home but you cannot recall?"

"As I said, anything's possible. I don't recall being in there."

"What if I said we had your prints inside the home?"

"Do you?"

Walker and I looked at each other in silence as Kensington shifted his butt cheeks and took more water.

Walker stepped in. "Tell us about the church, Bernard."

"What church?"

"The Church of the Living Triangle."

"It's not mine."

"Whose is it?" Walker asked.

"I think it might be Philippe and Marguerite's."

I decided to take a chance. "They said it was yours."

"They … are … wrong." He spoke each word like it was a sentence.

"What else are they wrong about?"

"What did they say?"

"They told us that you're the head of the church and got checks from Ginny that were for phony invoices for gardening. They told us that you inflated your bill each month and pocketed over three thousand dollars a month for your church. They also said you had been doing it for almost ten years."

He sat up in his chair, straighter than ever. "That is simply not true." He looked at me and then at Walker in a more pleading manner. It was a look that seemed to say *"Call off your buddy, the bulldog."*

Walker interceded. "What part is not true, Bernard? I understand my partner dumped a lot of information on you."

"Let me tell you what *true is Detective Hamilton!*" He raised his voice, but he was on our turf and knew it. "First, it is not my church."

"It's not?" I asked incredulously. "Whose is it?"

There was another pregnant pause. "It's *theirs.*"

It was then that I saw that he knew he was in trouble. I could see it in his face.

"Who is 'theirs'?" I asked in a dumbfounded manner.

"Marguerite and Philippe. The Church of the Living Triangle is theirs."

"What part is yours?"

"None of it."

"Are you sure? Is it possible that some of it is yours?"

"Absolutely not!"

Now I could see how he differentiated what was possible and what was not.

"What about the invoices?" I asked.

"I submitted them each month for $2,500 and gave the check to the Montoyas. They wrote me a check for $1,000, and $1,500 went to the church. I did not get the full $2,500. I only took what was owed to me for gardening."

"Isn't that a little high for a month of gardening?" Walker asked, trying to seem more curious than condemning.

"Yes, but even though I'm expensive for some neighborhoods, Ginny—Miss Karsdon—told me that was the fee she wanted to pay. She had the money, so I didn't argue."

"And how long has this been going on?" Walker asked.

"About five years and not the ten they said."

"So that part was not true either, Bernard?"

"No, they're not going to pin that on me."

338

Walker sat back in his metal chair and looked directly at Kensington. "You're sure about what you just told us, Bernard?"

"I am." He said, confident that he had cleared up an injustice.

Walker stood up. "I'll be right back."

Kensington and I were alone for the first time today. I pulled out a drawer to get the digital camera. Kensington watched my every move. I turned it on and let it sit on the table.

"What is that for?" he asked.

"It's a camera."

"I know it's a camera, damn it, but what are you going to do with it?" Kensington seemed more curious than angry. I think he truly didn't know where we were going next. I wasn't going to get into the details of the homicide just yet. We had other information we needed, and the noose was tightening further.

"We gave you a copy of our search warrant, didn't we?"

"Yes."

"Did you read it?"

"No. I haven't had time."

"If you read it, you will find that we have the court's permission to take photographs of your tattoos."

"I don't have any tattoos."

"I think you do," I countered.

"I have body art, not tattoos."

"Same thing."

"No... It's... Not!" His response was once again a staccato, one word sentence.

"Why do you wear two layers of clothing? To cover your 'body art'?" I put my fingers in quotes again.

"No, Detective Hamilton," he said haughtily. "I deal with heavy brush, rose bushes, thickets, and climbing trellises all day. I don't want my arms and legs to be scratched up. It's to protect me from my beautiful but dangerous plants."

I just had been spanked by my homicide suspect. "Okay, I didn't mean to ruffle your feathers."

This guy had some principles. When I challenged him on something and he knew he was right, he was in my face. If we were on the attack, he would back off, get defensive, or even be in denial, particularly if he was being evasive. We were all claiming our own turf at this point. And he knew it.

"Bernard, I would like you to take off your two top shirts while we're in this room. I want to examine your body art, and the court has said that I can."

He sat there for more than a long moment.

"Bernard?"

"Okay."

I knew he had been searched by the uniformed officers who brought him in, but they were only looking for weapons. I was looking for evidence.

"Hand me your shirts."

He knew it was an order. He didn't have any markings on his hands like Midcrest did with the "FAFDF" tattoos. His first layer was a slightly soiled, tan khaki long-sleeved shirt with multiple pockets. The second layer was an older blue-and-gold UCLA long-sleeved sweatshirt that had also seen better days. His body art was from his waist to his neck and on each part of his arms. His well-defined torso had been marked up like the wall of a vacant building in the middle of gangland USA. There were symbols of snakes and dragons. I saw a devil's head with long horns, wearing a crown of thorns, with fire coming from the nose. The terms "Black Sabbath" and "Black MASS," in heavy script, wrapped around each bicep. There was a chalice with blood or dark wine spilling over its edge on his right side, with the droppings going into an open mouth of a corpse lying prone. The corpse had a nail in its head.

Each forearm had an inverted cross and a series of crescent moons, surrounded by a five-star pentagram that was literally crammed on to his arms. It was gross, in my estimation. To Bernard Kensington, it was body art.

As I was taking pictures of the upper torso and Kensington's arms, Red walked in with a new bottle of water for each of us. He saw what we were doing and gave an approving nod of the head.

"Can I get you a doughnut or sandwich or anything to eat, Bernard?" he asked.

"I am getting hungry. How long are we going to be here?"

"I don't think we will be here too long," I said softly. "Do you, Bernard?"

Chapter 105

Magic

I looked at Kensington as he put on just the khaki shirt. He left off the UCLA sweatshirt for now. *Perhaps for a long time*, I thought.

"I'll take a sandwich, and thanks for the water," Kensington said as he glanced at Walker.

Walker was staring at his body art.

"Now the trousers, Bernard," I said as nonchalantly as I could. He wore black heavy construction pants with light sweat pants that didn't match his sweatshirt. "Leave your underwear on. I want to see your legs. Don't just drop your trousers around your ankles. Take off your boots, and slide your pants off."

He did as instructed. I watched him reach inside his left boot and pull out a dark object. I froze and stood up, watching his hands closely. How could he have gotten a knife or gun in here?

He slowly set his wooden flute on the table, as if it were made of breakable glass. I sat back down.

My mind raced in several directions. Didn't the uniformed guys who picked him up search him? How could they not have checked his boots? What if he *had* had a knife or gun?

I moved the flute gently against the wall at the edge of the table. I wanted a clear view of his body. There was no telling what else he would pull out. He watched me with eyes that told me I might have violated some cardinal law. At this point, we were going to keep the upper hand.

On each thigh he had a list of scripture citations. "Corinthians 11:3, book of Revelations 12:17, Timothy 2:26, Matthew 25:41" was on the left, and "Corinthians 6:15, John 5:18; 8:44; and 12:31; Thessalonians 3:5" was on the right thigh. The words "I Will" were etched on each calf and a small fallen angel was imprinted on each inside ankle.

Walker and I looked at each other as Kensington dressed again, leaving off the sweat pants undergarment.

Kensington had been rather subdued during the disrobing and photography. There was no doubt his wheels were turning and churning now, though his outward demeanor didn't show it.

"I've ordered up the sandwiches," Walker said. "Did you have a preference, Bernard?"

"No," he responded, sounding sullen.

"Well, you'll have a choice when they get here. Where were we?"

Kensington surprisingly responded, "I think we clarified the fact I do not have a church, that the church belongs to the Montoya's. I did not make three grand a month off Ginny. I made one thousand, and it was for services rendered. It was not for over a ten-year period but was for five years. I hope we are clear on all of that."

Just like magic, we were back on track to what mattered.

"Thanks for clarifying that for us, Bernard," Walker commented.

"You're welcome," Kensington replied.

Is he gaining some confidence now? I wondered. *Or are we?*

I knew that the food would not arrive for at least another fifteen minutes, so we had our work cut out for us. And I knew Walker wanted Kensington to think he had just talked to the Montoya's, and Kensington would deny any new information Walker may have brought from them. And he was right. Now I was convinced that Kensington didn't know that the Montoya's had left the country.

Walker remembered exactly where we were headed, and he opened with that very message. "We have your prints inside the home, Bernard."

"Then I guess I was in there at some point in time. Can you tell how fresh they are? Ginny wasn't a great housekeeper."

We all agreed and had a brief forced laugh to get us back where we had left off. "You tell us when you think you were last inside," Walker countered.

"I couldn't tell you."

"Is it possible that it was during the month of September?"

"I don't think so."

"But is it possible?"

"Yes, it's possible."

"Is it possible that it could have been on September 22, Ginny's birthday?"

His reply was somewhat delayed. "I … I don't think so."

"Is it possible?"

"Yes, I suppose it's possible." He was speaking through parched lips now.

"Was there anyone else there with you?"

"I don't remember."

Walker straightened up and turned on the charm. "I know this is hard to remember, but it's important that you think about who may have been with you. We don't want to put names out there for you to pick out. If you remember, tell us who else was there."

I was hoping that no one would knock on the door to announce that the sandwiches were here. *Not now*, I prayed, *not right now.*

Kensington looked down and to his right. He was studying the flute. He then looked up at Walker with a face that was made of stone. "It's possible that it could have been Philippe."

Walker took a pause before asking, "Why do you say that it was him?"

"Because. Because he was angry at Ginny."

"Why?"

"The checks stopped coming."

Walker widened his eyes, hoping to seem surprised. "The checks?"

"The checks to our—I mean, his church."

Was that a slip of the tongue?

"So this was about his church?" Walker asked.

"It was always about his church." Kensington sat back in a more relaxed manner. "It's always about the church; everything we did was about the church."

"Was that day, September 22—was that all about the church too?" I asked gently.

"We were going to do something special with Ginny. To get her to start the checks again. It was her birthday, and we always did special things together on her birthday."

"What special things?" Walker left the question out in the air for a long time.

"Has Philippe told you about them?" It appeared to be an honest question.

"We want to hear it from you."

"The four of us always read scriptures and talked about our lives. Then we engaged. With her help."

"The four of you?"

"Philippe, Ginny, me, and Herb."

"Herbert Midcrest?" I asked, as if we didn't really know him.

"Yeah. He's a plumber. He had no real clue what was going on, but he was part of our little group. He's a bit slow, but Ginny really liked him. I mean she *really* liked him. Once a month, we would get together in her garage and, like I said, read and talk about Lucifer and how all of the other religions and gods were hoaxes. Ours was the true belief. Philippe was real good at that."

"Then what would happen?" Walker posed another overhead question designed to just keep the conversation going and let him talk.

"We would stimulate ourselves. You know, and Ginny would come around, light a candle near us, and get us off, one at a time, with her hand or mouth. She was real good. She would use our bodies like altars."

Let him talk, I thought, *just let him talk.*

"She would always use the same cloth. She made them herself. She embroidered our moon and star with a pentagram on it. They became our symbol."

"What happened on September 22?" Walker asked.

Chapter 106

September 22

Kensington looked down again. Then he turned and touched the flute on the table with his right hand. It was like a caress. His breath was rhythmic but controlled. The sweat clothes, his first layer, were piled behind him. He had put his boots back on and took his time with the process. I could tell that he was contemplating, thinking, and perhaps even strategizing his next round with us.

"It was Ginny's birthday," he said quietly. "We were in the garage, celebrating and doing readings. I had not done her yard in over a month, and Philippe had not received a check either. We could not communicate. We had no serenity."

"What do you mean, no serenity?" I asked.

"I … we … search for the calmness, equanimity, and tranquility. It is the repose that many search for but never find. We didn't have that, because Ginny had let me go. Her property was not being maintained, and the church was not being supported. We were out of compliance with our serenity."

I was seeing his position a bit more clearly now. Midcrest was along for the ride, and Philippe and he were vying for control. It was time for more probing questions. "Was Marguerite ever a part of your sessions?"

"Never. She ran the church but didn't take part in our services. Philippe didn't want her to, and I'm not sure she knew everything about our prayer meetings with Ginny. She just ran the church."

"Tell us more about September 22, Bernard," I said.

Kensington took a deep breath. "We argued, but it was very civil. No shouting or anything like that. You asked if I had been in the house. Only once. On that day. Most of our time was in the garage. Philippe was angry—angrier than I was. He zapped Ginny with a 220-volt portable gun he carried. It's like a Taser on steroids and sends out a shock wave. I thought it killed her. She was still

346

moving around, and he was going to zap her again." Kensington seemed in pain now, mental anguish showing in his entire body. "I asked him if she would die from the shock, and he said, 'Hell, yes, but not right away.' I told him that I would put her out of her misery rather than watch her suffer. So I did."

"How?" Walker and I asked at the same time.

"I gently wrenched her neck. Broke it, I think. I mean, I did not want to break it. I only wanted for her not to suffer. I did not want her to suffer. I used to be a wrestler, and I knew how to do it, painlessly. I wanted her to go quickly. No more pain."

"How did she get to the upstairs bedroom?" I asked.

"Philippe and Herb carried her. I was too emotional."

"Did you follow them?"

"Yes, I didn't know where we were going because I had never been inside. They carried her up and took off the rest of her clothes and put her on the bed."

Walker held up a hand to stop Kensington. "Bernard, what if I were to tell you that Montoya said he did nothing to cause her death. That it was all you. You just broke her neck in a fit of rage."

Kensington looked at Walker as strongly as he had looked at either of us on this fateful day. "I would tell you that you and Philippe are wrong. I loved Ginny, cared for her deeply. I didn't want to see her suffer. She was suffering."

"How can we prove that?" I asked.

"Look in his truck. You'll find his handy tool. It shoots 220 volts. It's white and black and may be on one of his tool belts. Or you can ask Herb. Have you talked to Herb?"

"Not yet," I lied.

Walker continued his questions. "Why did you place candles in her as you did?"

"During our many conversations over the years, we talked about what we would want if we died in the company of any of us or someone from the church. Ginny had mentioned she wanted to go out as an altar sacrifice to the moon goddess Diana and to Lucifer." He paused for another deep breath and then continued. "Cain had offered a sacrifice without blood when he killed Abel. That was in the book of Genesis 4:8. She wanted the blood and asked if we would drink her blood in honor of the Antichrist. We all agreed."

All three of us sat back in our chairs, exhausted from the ordeal. There was a tap on the door. Were the sandwiches here? I don't suppose there ever is a good time to take a break in an interrogation of this magnitude. We could not have done it before the last go around. Now seemed like a good time.

"More water, Bernard?"

"Yes."

Interrogation room doors are a fire trap waiting to happen. They're soundproof and can only be opened from the outside, unless you have the secret 888 key. We knew it was safe for us to step outside into the squad bay, leaving Kensington alone, to think.

"We'll bring back the sandwich and water for you in a minute," I told him.

I still didn't think that Kensington knew Montoya and his wife had flown the country, or we had Midcrest in the next room. We had to get some corroboration from Midcrest regarding some of the details that Bernard had described. Was there a shock gun, or did Kensington kill Ginny by himself? We also needed other details, but we did have enough to go after the Montoya's.

Hospian was waiting for us with a smile on his face. "The good thing about the Montoya's fleeing to Puerto Rico is that it's a United States territory. For extradition purposes, it's almost like dealing with another state—I would bet dimes to doughnuts they don't know that. What a revelation you guys witnessed in there," Hospian said.

Walker smiled as he responded, "Well, sir, it was more than a revelation; it was a damn good interrogation. He never lawyered up."

Hospian knew it but was not going to give us anything. At least not right now.

"What's that sound?" someone in the squad bay asked.

I listened. Everybody listened. It was a flute. *The* flute. The message was being sent to the entire second floor of OHPD headquarters. Kensington had a revelation and had reached serenity, finally.

We walked back to the interview room with his sandwich and water, placed it on the table, and walked out. He never wavered from the music of his own making.

It was time to talk briefly with Midcrest again.

Chapter 107

Midcrest Two

Walker and I stepped into Interview room A where Midcrest was eating his sandwich.

"You guys were gone a long time," he said. "Thanks for the sandwich. Did you go out to lunch?"

"No, Herb," I said easily. "We were working on another case."

"Busy around here," he observed.

I nodded, but I wanted to compare what he'd told us with Kensington's story. "Can we go over some things, just to get some clarification?" I asked.

"Sure. Can I finish my lunch while we chat?"

"Okay. First, when you attended the religious services with Ginny, Philippe, and Bernard, were they in the house or elsewhere?"

"Well, I was thinking about that. I might have said the house, but we were actually in the garage. I kind of view that as a part of the house."

He started to explain the differences and similarities, but I held up my hand. "I think we get the idea, Herb."

"Who killed Ginny?" Walker blurted out.

Herb thought for a moment, staring off at something that only he could see. "That's a tough one, boys."

"Why?" we both asked.

"Because I feel a little funny telling you. It could have been both of them."

"Both of whom?" I asked.

"You know."

"We need to hear it from you, Herb. We don't want to put words in your mouth."

"Oh, I get it. Well, Philippe and Bernard were arguing with her over the money. Maybe not arguing the way you think, but discussing, talking. I think Bernard was also upset that she'd fired him. More because the property was starting to get rundown than that he needed the job. Those places need a lot of work, ya know."

"We know," I said, "so what happened in there?"

"Philippe hit her with something. Not sure what it was. They had an argument, Ginny and them, and he hit her with something. Then Bernard pulled him aside, and they talked. Then Bernard kind of wrenched her neck. I don't know if she was already gone, but I think she was then."

"Did you help her in any way?" I asked him.

"Sure. I helped Philippe carry her to the house. So yeah, I helped."

"Did you take part in the altar service in her bedroom?"

"I did."

We knew what that meant, as we had the evidence on the rag that led us to his DNA.

Chapter 108

Wrap Up

What a day! What a week! What a case!

There is still a lot of work to do, I thought. We had evidence to pore over, trucks to search that were still in the parking lot, and statements to get transcribed. Kensington and Midcrest needed to be fingerprinted and booked at the county jail. And it was only Monday.

The next part of this case included issuing warrants for the Montoya's, extradition proceedings, and lab results. We also should go to each of their homes, as the search warrant called for. We only had ten days to get all of that done.

My head was spinning with what else was to be accomplished when I caught a glimpse of Sergeant Stevens in the hallway.

"Hey, Sarge, can I get the names of the officers that transported Kensington to the station?" I had not forgotten about the flute.

"It was Morrison and Laidlaw. Why?"

"Just wanted to thank them and put it in my report," I lied, turning away so he could not read my face.

I needed to find the officers before end of watch. I walked quickly down the stairs to the parking lot, thinking they might still be around. I saw Kensington's truck and trailer on the side of the building where CSI was housed. No one was around. I looked at the side of the truck with the sign and advertising information. There, in the middle of the English garden mural, was a black candle, complete with a flame, surrounded by a multicolored arrangement of flowers. *Right out of a Monet,* I thought. Kensington probably would have corrected me, as Monet was French, but the candle wasn't.

I opened the slider door and looked inside the van. It was well organized and meticulous. On the side was a rack with tools and sprinkler parts. On the top shelf was a box of black candles. Some had been used, but most were unburned.

I pulled the box from the shelf and, to my surprise, saw printing on the side that read: "*These candles are to be used for all rituals. Do not mix with red. Use on enemies, for protection from negative forces and to reverse negative thought forms. Our black candles absorb, conceal, and create confusion and chaos. They can also be used to celebrate new beginnings. Satan rules in black and can influence self-control, endurance, patience, and serenity. Use during a waning moon, but do not use to celebrate a birthday or any other day of celebration. Use with root chakra for additional power.*"

I heard someone call my name and turned to see two uniformed officers.

"Heard you were looking for us," one said.

They introduced themselves, and I laughed out loud at the fact I've been on OHPD for almost seven years, the majority on PMs, and we've never met.

"Can you believe I have never worked with either of you in all my years here?" I quipped.

"Yeah, with these crazy shifts, I guess it is possible," Laidlaw said, as I read his name tag to distinguish between the two.

"Great to meet both of you," I said. "Do you have a minute?"

"Sure."

I explained that they had missed the flute in Kensington's boot and that we discovered it in the interview room.

"Jesus," Morrison said, his face going ashen, "are we in trouble?"

"Well, not with me. I knew it was there because we've been watching these guys, but—and it's a big but—you've got to be careful. Work on your searches and make sure you double-check. That could have been a gun."

They both looked at me with fear on their faces.

"This is just between you and me. And my partner, Detective Walker. We haven't told Stevens or anybody else. Oh, there is one other person who knows." I let that hang out there for an extra second.

"Who?"

"Our suspect, Kensington."

We all had a good laugh at that.

Morrison stopped me as I was going back into the station. "Detective Hamilton?"

"HH to you guys, please."

"HH, why didn't you turn us in?"

"Because after this week, it will not be 'Detective Hamilton' any longer. When I'm through, I go back to Patrol. I'm just on loan for this case. You could be my partner in a few weeks. That's why. I need you watching my back, not stabbing it."

I went back into the station to meet with Walker. As I was taking the stairs up two at a time, the chief was coming down them.

"Already heard, HH. Nice job on the homicide."

"Thanks," I said rather sheepishly, "but how did you find out so quickly?"

"What department do you think this is, HH?"

We laughed and parted ways.

No one had said anything about my use of force on the suspect who shot AJ. What was going to happen to Bresani? Were there going to be any more deaths in the department? What about Donny and Wolf? What was Joanie going to do with the baby? The Phantom was reaching out to me.

Just then, my cell rang. I didn't look at the number; I just said, "Yeah?"

"HH?"

"Yeah."

"Mel here. Guess what?"

"You passed your oral board and background, and you are starting the academy next week."

"How did you know?"

"What department do you think this is?"

I walked back into the squad bay, laughing to myself over the conversation with Mel. Hospian called me into his office. I was anticipating another "atta boy" or "great job" accolade.

"HH, Patrol needs you ASAP. You have some days off still coming, and I would ask you to turn in your OT hours as soon as you can. Plan on being back to Patrol on Friday. Walker can take care of things."

"Okay," I said, rather stunned at the sudden turn of events.

"Becoming a detective here is definitely in your future, but nobody really goes from Patrol to Homicide. I think you know that."

I nodded in agreement. I really knew that I was just a good cop and did what I was told.

"Put in your app, and when we have a vacancy, we'll consider you. Maybe a long-term loan in the future, when we get some recruits off their probation and get some bodies out of the academy. In the meantime, stay in touch."

"What should I do tomorrow?" I asked.

Hospian paused a moment and then said, "Tell you what; come in to Detectives tomorrow and help Walker get things organized. I'll work it out with Patrol. I may assign someone else to help him. Not sure yet. There are guys waiting to get Oakes's position, so I've a lot to sort out."

"Okay," I said with some finality.

I was trying to place everything in perspective. Now I was swimming in it. Who was going to help Walker with all that was left to be done? This case was far from being wrapped up. Hell, even in the movies the detectives got to bring everything together. *This is still a cluster fuck!* I caught myself. *You are caring way too much here, Hamilton. Do not let the Phantom get to you!*

I was ready to go back to Patrol but not that rapidly. Leaving the case half-completed was not what I wanted to do. It was all a bit of a shock. I walked out into the squad room, saw Walker, and gave him the news.

"I already heard."

"How did you hear so quickly?" I asked.

"What department do you think this is, HH? Just remember that I'm a trainee too. My days are numbered." We laughed again.

I pulled my hand out of my right front pocket, shaped it like a pistol with my index finger, and simulated pulling the trigger and blowing on the barrel.

"Okay, Shooter," I said.

Walker came back. "Okay, Talker."

I laughed all the way home.

Printed in the United States
By Bookmasters